SOUL BONDS

Book 1 of "Circles of Light"

_____

E M Sinclair

Soul Bonds – Book 1 of *Circles of Light*
First published 2007

Typeset by John Owen Smith

Published by Murrell Press

© E M Sinclair 2006

E M Sinclair can be contacted via the **Circles of Light** Facebook page.

ISBN 978-09554135-0-6

Printed by CreateSpace

Chapter One

What had woken her? She checked the safety of her five eggs then extended her senses to test a wider area. There, above her head, through several feet of rock, came a sound. She rose, her wings folded close to her great body. Her nesting cave was hidden from the main entrance by an almost right-angled curve giving her maximum protection, and towards this curve the She-Dragon moved.

Her graceful neck lifted her head cautiously to the edge of the corner. White sunlight filled the cave mouth but nothing moved. More clearly now a clatter of rocks spattered across the opening, accompanied by a grunt. A creature fell onto the narrow ledge and rolled into the cave.

The She-Dragon's golden eyes expanded as she probed the creature's life-pattern. Mainly blue, pale, fuzzy, of a subtly different shading than the Dragon patterns she was most familiar with, but clear enough. Young. A female. The creature began to rise, it was briefly silhouetted against the white light before it came unsteadily deeper into the cave and dropped in a heap.

The Dragon's nostrils flared. So, a member of the two-leg tribe – but why here? She probed the creature again and was dismayed to find the colour had paled, the life pattern blurred. A howl of despair streaked through the haziness making the Dragon blink with sudden pain.

She advanced now, the only sound the faint slither of her tail, and drooped her head over this small creature. She lifted it delicately in her jaws and turned back into the nesting cave.

Kija, the She Dragon, had never had contact with the two-leg tribe. From her earliest solo hunts, she had always sought food from flocks and herds well away from the places where the two-legs gathered in their strange dwellings. Most of the female Dragons did the same, although the males, hunting more often in groups, frequently descended on the fatter herds guarded by the two-leg creatures.

Kija gently put the limp form beside her eggs and settled again on the sandy floor. Faint light came from the cave entrance – sufficient for the large golden eyes of the Dragon to examine her trophy. It was very small indeed, smaller than a newhatched Dragon. Her long, delicate face bent closer and she realised with some surprise the creature had two hides. The green hide was baggy on its arms and legs, but the fore and hind feet and the face were pale, sand-coloured, and tight fitting. Its head was covered with thick black hair and black hairs lined each eyelid.

A click sounded again but this time Kija recognised it. She turned her attention to her eggs and probed lightly over the five. To a Dragon using special sight they all seemed to throb with a deep yellow pulse, but one was showing a clearer golden pattern. Kija hummed deep in her throat and the life pattern quivered in response. 'Soon now.' Kija projected the thought gently. She returned her attention to the strange creature. Its pattern was steady now but faint. Its body smelled hot and dry. Kija was unsure whether it was just sleeping or in the sleep before death. Did the small one need liquid, Kija wondered? She had brought many mouthfuls of water from the lake a mile below her nesting cave during the last few days, to form a small pool in a rock basin beyond her eggs.

She dipped her muzzle in the pool then touched the small one's face with the wetness. Kija drew back a little to watch. As nothing happened, she repeated the face wetting once more, then settled herself comfortably again. She would not leave the cave now until her children were safely out of their shells, so this small creature would have to wait too – if it lived. Kija slept lightly, her Dragon sight aware of any change in the five eggs or the still unmoving small one.

The sunlight had dimmed a little in the cave entrance when Kija opened her eyes. She checked her eggs immediately to find two more had intensified in colour and had stronger life patterns. But something else had roused her. She gave her attention to the strange one and found its colour too had intensified and its life pattern pulsed far more strongly. The hairs on its eyelids flickered and its mouth opened slightly as Kija watched. She dipped her muzzle in the water once more and dampened the sleeping face. She made no attempt to probe its mind, just projected calmness and strength. The eyelids flickered again and Kija saw unfocused green eyes gaze in her direction.

The small body stirred. The eyes blinked and then gradually focused in the dim light. The creature levered itself suddenly backwards with a strange high squeak. Kija's mind was nearly swamped by the flood of distress and fear that poured towards her from the small one's body. She began the deep soothing hum, which she had used to encourage one of her eggs, at the same time sending pulses of friendliness to the small one.

The green creature took a breath, which shuddered right through its body. 'You're a real Dragon aren't you?'

Kija stopped humming. It had made odd noises, was it a form of communication? She probed gently into the coloured haze of its mind and had a clear picture of herself reflected back. Very carefully Kija formed a picture of the small one to replace the Dragon in its mind. 'Tika – small one.'

Clicks distracted Kija again. One egg was vibrating now and Kija concentrated entirely upon the imminent appearance of her child. Tika, her uninvited guest, watched as the huge Dragon lowered her face to the egg. Even to human eyes, one of the eggs was about to hatch. The chills of apprehension still rippled through her despite the Dragon's calming thought projections, but curiosity proved stronger than apprehension.

The Dragon's eyes, many-faceted prisms, were flashing in rapidly changing colours, a topaz gold predominating, as a crack splintered through the centre of the egg. Tika watched, almost forgetting to breathe, as the crack widened and a thin delicate snout emerged. She laughed out loud as a small Dragon climbed shakily from the debris of shell. The adult Dragon hissed in dismay as her child's head turned to the sound of laughter and his eyes began the rainbow whirling of prismatic colours.

The human child stilled as the Dragon child's eyes met hers. Kija sent a mind cry to her sister Dragons nesting nearby – what to do, what to do? A Dragon child always looked first into the eyes of one of its own kind and through that first long look imbibed a firm foundation of Dragon ways. This child of hers was eye locked with a small two-leg creature – what knowledge could he drink from her eyes when she saw Dragons as fearsome beings?

A surge of conflicting advice poured into Kija: 'Leave them.' 'Break the lock – there is time to lock with him yourself.' 'Kill them both at once.' That last was Nula, her thought patterns harsh and cruel as always.

But Kija's child was moving, his eyes glowing orange, moving towards Tika – the stranger. He was projecting strongly – thirst – terrible thirst – then hunger. And Tika stretched out her two upper limbs and embraced the newhatched Dragon, which was nearly the same size as herself. She guided him carefully to the pool of water Kija had made for just this purpose and let him drink. As he drank, Tika's hand rested lightly on his back between his wings and then she half turned to look at Kija.

Kija received impressions, of awe, of confused disbelief, and of a strange warmth. But Kija had no time to spend on this worry now, two more eggs were cracking and she sent a sharp warning to Tika to stay by the pool while she locked eyes with another son and then a daughter.

When Kija had nudged the two new children to drink at the pool, she studied the remaining two eggs. One would hatch within a few hours but the other one would take another night perhaps.

Kija looked at her first hatched son. He was resting against Tika, his eyes partly closed, still projecting hunger but it was not such an urgent need as the thirst had been. There was a call outside the cave and a flurry of heavy wings. Kija transmitted her thanks for the fresh meat that one of her neighbours had brought for the children's first meal.

Then the She Dragon turned her gaze back to her first son. His name would be Farn, but what was to happen to him? Dragon-born bonded with a two-legged one. Would the rest of the Treasury allow the pair to live? Kija could recall no precedent for such an event and her heart was heavy as she looked at two so-different children lying sleepily against each other on the sand of the nesting cave.

Over the next few days, until the last of Kija's eggs had hatched, Kija paid little attention to Tika. She had offered the small two-legs some of the fresh wapeesh meat brought by other females but the two-leg child would not eat it. Kija's clan sister, Krea, dropped a branch with fruits still attached to it on the cave's ledge and these Tika ate.

Tika slept nearly as much as the Dragon children during these first days. She had run away from the town far, far down the mountain, and after the first shocked terror of realising where she found herself now, she relaxed and accepted the situation as inevitable.

Whenever Farn woke, so did Tika, and while his siblings huddled against their mother, Farn leaned heavily on Tika. As Kija fed her children from the freshly killed wapeesh she placed small sized pieces of the meat beside Tika who then fed them to Farn.

Tika woke more frequently than the new Dragons and at these times she sat watching Kija. The great Dragon's eyes whirred constantly but Tika felt only a buzzing sensation, couldn't understand any of the communication Kija was obviously having with other Dragons. Tika was aware of other Dragons being close by; at least one who was bringing food to the cave, but how many others she couldn't guess.

When she locked eyes with Farn she had felt herself being turned inside out – all her thoughts, feeling, memories gushing from her into his eyes. She had also felt Kija then, putting other things in her head, which in their turn emptied into Farn.

Six days after Tika's arrival in the cave, Kija led her children to the outer entrance. Tika walked beside Farn who seemed bigger each day. The sound of heavy wings warned Tika and she shrank back against Farn as a huge green shape surged towards the cave's ledge. She felt Farn protesting and Kija's sudden burst of anger. Then the green shape was gone. Eyes blinking in the light of sunset after the cave's shadows, Tika gasped. Dragons! So many of them! Draped on crags, lounging at ease on tumbled boulders.

This was the other side of the mountain Tika had somehow scaled on her escape from the town – a plateau of gigantic rocks strewn over a shallow bowl between towering peaks. As she looked more closely, she realised all the Dragons were looking towards herself and Kija's five children.

She shivered as she focused on a very large green Dragon whose eyes were fixed whirring red prisms – Nula. The name was in her head and for the first time since Kija had spoken to her when she had first woken in the nesting cave, she heard Kija again: 'Beware small one, this one intends you harm, and you too my son.'

A smaller honey-coloured Dragon glided from a high perch and landed neatly on the ledge. Tika felt warmth and affection enveloping them all. This Dragon was Krea, clan sister of Kija, the one who had first brought wapeesh meat to the cave.

'So handsome a brood!' Tika understood clearly. Then 'And a two-legs! Does it really communicate?' Tika heard Kija laugh.

'Yes, but even less well than new children! If the Treasury accepts these six children, would you care for Farn and the two legs, Krea?'

There was a pause, Tika had the sensation of being turned inside out again, and then she heard the amber-scaled Dragon agree.

'Of course I will – you know I like a challenge.'

There was laughter felt from several different directions and Tika was aware of Kija relaxing slightly from the tenseness she had held since their emergence from the inner cave.

'They should die. Now.'

The voice was loud and harsh in Tika's head. She looked immediately at the green Dragon, Nula. She was slightly smaller than Kija, her scales a shifting darkness of greens. There were several dark scars along her back and one on her face, pulling the left eye crooked.

Several voices called 'No!' and one added they should wait for the full Gathering of the Treasury to decide the issue. What was a "Treasury?" Tika wondered, with vague thoughts of the men in the Lord's house in the town. Krea's mind voice murmured that a Treasury was a full Gathering of Dragons, males and females both. At the moment, the females were gathered here whilst Kija hatched her eggs, the males were far off, hunting and playing.

Nula and two rust-scaled Dragons lifted above the rocks and wheeled out of sight. Tension fled from the remaining Dragons. Kija sighed. 'I see no harm in this two-leg child. She bonded with my son Farn and I have the notion it was intended to be thus.

10

I have called her "Tika"'

Several voices called 'Welcome!' and Tika felt herself blushing. She pressed closer to Farn, uncomfortable at being the focus of attention. She sensed amusement gradually fading as these Dragons rose against the fiery sky and departed the plateau.

Kija turned to her second son and three daughters. Her eyes blazed, then she turned and drifted in a gentle glide from the ledge across the width of the rock strewn bowl. The four young ones watched closely then rustled their wings rather self-consciously. One daughter gulped audibly and launched herself towards the great golden figure of her mother. She dropped perilously, but a few undignified flaps restored her equilibrium. The three remaining children followed in her wake.

Krea gazed at Tika. 'I think we may remain here a few days,' she said thoughtfully.

Farn cried that he too must do his first flight – he was first born, he MUST fly now.

'Very well,' Krea agreed. 'Watch closely.' She glided slowly away from the ledge as Kija had done. Farn took a deep breath, and followed.

As Tika watched Farn flying after Krea, she realised Kija and her other children had vanished beyond the high rocks. She felt appallingly alone suddenly, exposed on the open ledge. She followed Farn's attempts to copy Krea's movements precisely, and only as both Dragons returned to the cave did she realise how close to panic she had come. She could see no way down from here – the ledge jutted out over a sheer drop of several hundred arms she guessed. There was no way around the sides of the cave and certainly no footholds down from there even should she get round the overhang.

Krea instructed Farn on adjustments he should make in his practice flights and sent him back and forth across the rocks. When he landed panting slightly and stumbled towards Tika's outstretched arms, Krea called a halt. 'Both of you go back further into the cave,' she instructed. 'I will fetch food quickly, before darkness comes.'

'Flying is wonderful Tika,' Farn murmured. 'Why can you not fly?'

'Because I have no wings,' she retorted snappishly.

His eyes flickered, the prisms glinting blue and silver in the deepening darkness. 'You can, you can! You can ride on my back!' He purred his strange chuckling laugh at her. 'On my back,' he repeated. He yawned mightily. 'And I am so hungry.'

'Krea will bring food soon,' Tika soothed him while her mind blazed with the idea of herself, Chena, slave pet of the Lord of Return, seated on the back of a great Dragon in flight across a vast sky.

Chapter Two

Krea kept Farn and Tika at the cave for four more days. Farn practised his flying powers until he was trembling with exhaustion. Then he curled against Tika and slept deeply. Krea spent some time away from the cave, returning with meat for Farn – usually two or three hoppers rather than the large wapeesh. Krea discovered, after some considerable probing, that Tika could eat meat only if it was burnt. This mystified the honey-coloured Dragon, but she obligingly belched fire over one of the hoppers. When she turned to give the scorched meat to Tika, she was bemused by the way the two legs had shrunk against the cave wall. Fear emanated from her in great waves.

Krea left the meat and removed herself from the cave. She soared high into the evening sky, coiling higher and higher as she pondered the small one's reaction. She called on a short distance range for Kija, but clearly she and her children had already travelled far.

When Krea returned, she found most of the burnt meat had been eaten and Farn sniffing at the remains with a disgusted curl to his lip. Tika seemed calmer although Krea felt a continuing hint of nervousness from the two legs.

'Why were you so afraid Tika?' Krea asked gently. Before Tika could reply Farn interrupted:

'Because two-legs don't make fire.'

'We do. We do make fire. Just – not quite the way Krea did it.'

'Aah. So how do you make fire?' Krea asked.

'It takes a while. We use stones – flints – which make a spark when you bang them together. Usually, if a fire goes out, we borrow a little piece of fire from someone else's.'

'That sounds complicated,' Farn said, and he sat up and belched. Krea moved surprisingly fast for her size as a few flames flickered from Farn's mouth and nostrils. He belched

13

again, and choked. It sounded to Tika as if Krea was as near to anger as she had so far witnessed. Farn closed his mouth, and hiccoughed as tears and smoke streamed down his long snout. Tika hugged him, mopping his face and murmuring sympathetically to him.

Krea settled herself and remarked, mildly enough, but leaving no doubt that she meant each word: 'You will not attempt any tricks such as fire-making Farn, until I have instructed you thoroughly.' Her eyes glowed softly as she waited for his agreement.

'No Krea, I'll only do things when you have shown me the proper way.' He gave a mighty sniff. 'But when can I fly with Tika on my back?' His eyes began to sparkle blue lights again although a little moist still.

'Not for a while,' Krea replied. 'You must wait until your growth is sufficient and you can carry her safely.'

'Will we have to stay here until then?'

'No. I had thought that tomorrow we would leave and start our journey into the Ancient Mountains. If we wait too long we will be late for the Gathering. I will carry Tika to begin with. Now rest, both of you. I will teach you many things as we travel.'

In the first paleness of dawn the two Dragons and the human child stood at the edge of the high cave. Tika shivered and immediately Krea enquired: 'Are you cold?'

'A little,' said Tika, 'but I'm nervous too,' she added honestly.

'I have wondered how you heat yourself. We of the Treasury can regulate our body temperature to a certain extent.'

Tika plucked at the fabric of her green shirt. 'We wear clothes. Thicker ones and as many as we can in the winter.'

Krea registered surprise. 'I thought that was a deformity of your own hide,' she exclaimed. 'Where can we find you more of these "clothes"?'

'I suppose only in a town, but I have no money to buy anything.'

'Money? No, do not try to tell me now,' Krea said hastily. 'A town is your name for your strange caves on top of the ground?'

'You mean houses. Lots of houses together make a town.'

Farn had been listening intently but he now interrupted to point out he was most eager to begin their journey, and the sky was light already, and were they going to stay here talking till noon? Krea stared hard at Farn and he stared equally firmly at the sky.

'Come Tika, lie on my back and hold fast where my wings grow from my body. That's right – not so tight – I will not let you fall.'

'Come *on*!' Farn urged, and lifted from the ledge.

Tika had her eyes tight shut for the first minutes but was aware of barely any motion. Perhaps Krea had only moved forward, perhaps they were still inside the cave. She opened her eyes and could only stare.

They were flying! *She* was flying, on the back of a Dragon! She looked back to see the cave but already they were over the circling peaks rimming the plateau and the cave was gone from sight.

They flew directly towards the rising sun and Krea did not call a rest until nearly midday, by which time Farn was very tired. They flew above more bare and wind-twisted rocks, plateaux and occasional deep gullies. They kept fairly low, seeming to skim the very highest crags and Tika understood this was for both her benefit and also for Farn's.

After several hours of flying over this barren landscape, one or two gnarled tapisi trees appeared, clinging to rocks and bent as low as bushes by the wind. Obviously, this whole area knew seasons of fierce weather, Tika realised, and she guessed they were lucky at the relative gentleness of the present wind.

Gradually the number of tapisi increased and the surface of the ground was faintly furred with sparse green. Krea kept them in flight until a thin silvery ribbon indicated a watercourse. She slowed and turned into an easy glide, landing smoothly at the side of the stream. Farn landed beside her, his exhausted muscles making his whole body shiver.

Tika slid from Krea's back and helped Farn to the water where he drank deep and long. Tika was herself drinking the icy water when she heard Krea: 'You have done well hatchling. I am most pleased with your endurance. We have covered a better distance already than I had hoped for so we will remain here till next dawn. Rest while I seek food.'

Farn sank onto the short grass beside a tapis and began

rubbing his forefeet under his armpits. Tika watched, gradually understanding he was getting oil from glands there, which he then worked over his wings. 'My wings must stay supple,' explained Farn. 'The hide can crack if it becomes dry, then I might not be able to fly.'

Tika helped, stretching out the wings as Farn kneaded and smoothed in the oil. She rubbed some of the oil down Farn's neck and spine and the upper length of his tail, amazed as ever by the way the scales grew in such an orderly way. Each one overlapped the next like a Lord's armoured coat, yet so pliant and warm. Except for his wings and what Tika thought of as "hands" and "feet", his whole body was turquoise scaled. His feet, with four toes bare of scales, were covered in smooth, darker blue hide, as were his hands and wings.

Dragon hands had three "fingers" and an opposable thumb from which the tips of retractable talons could be seen. Farn's head was drooping onto his chest with weariness when Krea landed with meat. She had a volu for Farn and an already scorched hopper for Tika. The volu disappeared inside Farn in less than the time it took Tika to eat the much smaller, but very hot, hopper. Farn groaned with satisfaction and stretched out on the grass, his head on Tika's leg. Within seconds he was sound asleep.

'I think we have travelled enough for Farn today,' Krea said softly. 'He has done well but he is still too small yet for prolonged journeying.'

The pale honey-coloured Dragon also stretched herself on the grass, her eyes half closed.

'Tell me of yourself Tika,' she said gently.

What was there to tell, Tika wondered? The Dragons had rummaged through her memories several times she thought so what more did Krea need her to tell?

'I would know how two legs live. Do you have Clans as we do? Why do you live in one place all the time? Tell me of your Clan, Tika.'

'I am – or I was – slave born. My mother was a slave captured in a raid by the Lord and his Fighters, from a tribe far north. I think my mother was damaged when she was caught, at least, I remember her as being weak all the time. She died when I was

16

nearing my third Cold Season.'

Krea hissed quietly. 'What is a "slave", child?'

'A slave is someone taken by force from their home and who must then obey their owner in all things.'

'You own each other?' Krea's eyes whirred as she concentrated on understanding Tika's strange words. 'We of the Treasury own only ourselves. I cannot understand this at all.'

Tika sighed. 'Well, I was born a slave because Mother was a slave. But I look like her – she had dark hair and green eyes and most of the Lord's people are fair, with blue or brown eyes. So the other children always picked on me or blamed me for any trouble.' She felt Krea struggling to feel the exact meaning of her words.

'I had work to do, cleaning houses, clearing stones from the gardens, and sometimes when the Lord was home, I was summoned to be his play pet.' Tika paused. 'I have had my fourteenth Cold Season and the women said I would soon have to be his pretty. I'm not quite sure what I'd have had to do but I had an idea. I didn't like it. So I decided to run away.' She looked straight into Krea's glowing eyes and finished: 'I would rather have died on the mountain than live as a slave-pretty to the Lord, and be passed on to his Fighters when he tired of me.'

Tika fell silent and Krea also was silent, thinking of what Tika had told her and trying to comprehend. 'You say you have been fourteen Cold Seasons in this world, and I understand you to mean this Lord would mate you soon? Is this the usual age for two legs? How long do you live? We of the Treasury are barely adult by the time fifty Cold Seasons have passed. None speak at a Gathering until they are of that age – indeed even then it is considered rash. Usually we say nothing there until a hundred Seasons have matured us to a little wisdom.'

Tika gaped. 'I think the Lord is near forty, and he is considered getting old. Erm, may I ask how old you are Krea?'

'Why, I have seen more than seven times a hundred Cold Seasons small one; I am well into my middle years now.'

Tika's mind could scarcely grasp what she was hearing. Quietness settled over them as both considered what they'd learned of each other.

The afternoon passed in this quietude until Farn awoke. 'I'm hungry,' he announced.

'There are hoppers nearby, see if you are able to catch some for yourself. I will seek elsewhere and will be maybe a longer time away. I will return as soon as I can.' Before Farn or Tika could ask questions, Krea was rising and moving fast towards the nearest peaks.

'Do you know how to hunt?' asked Tika.

'Of course. Hunting methods are one of the things we learn in the locking bond when we hatch,' Farn replied.

'But you locked with me,' Tika pointed out, 'and I know absolutely nothing about hunting.'

Farn's eyes flickered green fire, then he said with some relief, 'Well I do know how, the memories are there.' He looked at Tika. 'You stay here and I will fetch us some hoppers.' He marched importantly across the grass towards the more numerous tapisi, then slowed to a stealthy tiptoe. Tika suspected she could well have a long wait for Farn's return with food.

The sky had indeed darkened enough to allow a few stars to shine when Farn reappeared. With some difficulty he carried four hoppers. Tika ran to him as he emerged from the tapisi.

'How clever!' she exclaimed. 'How did you catch them so quickly?' She took two hoppers from one of his forelimbs and two from his mouth. He spat out clumps of fur then raised his head to its full height.

'Quite simple really. I ate the first one I caught. Shall I scorch one for you Tika?'

'Go on then, but do be careful, Krea hasn't taught you the proper way.'

Prudently, Tika moved slightly behind Farn as he pushed one of the hoppers away from the others. He inhaled deeply, and belched. A gout of fire shooshed from his mouth, searing the fur from the hopper. He turned the hopper over, belched once more and another jet of flame shot forth. He looked proudly at Tika, his eyes rather watery, as smoke wreathed from his nostrils.

'Oh very good,' applauded Tika. 'You really can do it!'

'Of course,' Farn replied rather smugly, although he had to clear his throat for a while.

After they'd eaten, they settled again by a tapis, and Tika asked Farn if he knew why they had to go to this Gathering.

Eventually he said, 'The memories tell me there is a Gathering around the time of the beginning of the Cold. It is when all give an accounting; new children are shown and accepted into the Treasury. If any have died, the song of their life will be told.' He yawned. 'They were very good hoppers didn't you think Tika?'

'Oh yes,' she laughed, wrapping her arms round his slender neck. 'They were wonderful and mine was so well done!'

Tika woke before dawn. She could just make out the large bulk of Krea's body lying beyond Farn. She hadn't heard her return last night and she had stayed awake until the stars had moved quite noticeably in their paths across the sky. She had so many things to think over, so much had happened in so few days, she hardly dared believe it was all real.

Now she was awake again after what felt like only a brief sleep and Krea was back. Krea stretched and turned to Tika. 'I found some more hides for you,' she said, sounding pleased with herself. Tika wriggled free of Farn's wing and went to Krea's side. Beside the Dragon was a heap of material. Tika lifted it, untangling it to discover two blankets, a pair of trousers and an enormous pair of frilly underbeneaths.

'Where did you get these things?'

'I went to some caves above ground. These hides were hanging on a vine nearby, so I brought them for you.'

'Did anyone see you?'

'Of course not. We can move very quietly if we so wish.' Krea sounded a little put out at being questioned rather than thanked.

'I do thank you Krea,' Tika said quickly. 'I'm sure I can make something, a tunic or a cape with these two blankets, and the trousers should be fine if I roll up the legs and tie something round my middle.' She picked up the frilly underbeneaths. 'I'm not sure what I can do with these.' Krea rumbled. 'But I'll think of something Krea. Thank you so much.'

Mollified, Krea stretched again.

Farn had woken and was investigating the pile of material. 'Are we leaving soon?' he asked. 'Or would you like me to get you some food first?' Tika felt Krea clamp down on laughter as she too struggled to keep serious.

19

'Perhaps a hopper each before we go. Never eat too much immediately before a long flight Farn.'

Farn headed for the now more visible tapisi.

'How many did he catch last evening?' Krea enquired.

'Five, and, er, he scorched one for me.'

Krea chuckled. 'And he didn't choke himself?'

'No he didn't.'

'It isn't really difficult to make fire,' Krea confided, 'but it can cause distressing effects the first few times!'

Farn was not very long at all before returning with three hoppers. When they'd eaten, Tika spread out one blanket, piled the other things into the middle and then knotted the corners. Krea and Farn watched with interest as she slung the sack over her shoulder, leaving her hands free to hold on to Krea during their flight.

The days passed and still they flew deeper into this seemingly endless mountain range. Krea decreed when and where they would rest. Tika had lost count of days but she noticed the moon was nearly full again when Krea announced that Farn was to carry her.

The first take off was nerve-wracking to Tika as Farn wobbled precariously until he adjusted his flight to accommodate her extra weight. He and Krea took turns carrying her for a few days until Krea judged him able to carry the two legs all the time.

When they landed, Krea took Farn on hunting forays while Tika tried to fashion a cloak for herself with one of the blankets. She used a huge thorn from a cloud bush to fasten the cloak at her throat. The tapisi appeared more like real trees the further they travelled and cloud bushes grew around the bottom of the trunks. After they'd eaten in the evenings, Krea told the two many things, of Dragon ways, of old times, of her youth, and of her clan.

'Is a clan sister a real sister?' Tika asked one evening.

'It is one hatched of the same line – Kija is my clan sister but she was hatched long before I was. As a clan sister she locked eyes with me on the day of my hatching. I was one of ten eggs, and my mother invited four of her clan to bond each with one or two of her eggs. She could not have raised all ten alone.'

Of such things Krea spoke, many of which Farn seemed to have rudimentary knowledge of in the memories he had received at his hatching. Krea spoke of patterns, of bloodlines among the Clans and of distant Treasuries who were connected together in the vast web that was the Dragon world.

As they prepared once more for another day's travel, Krea remarked that they were close to the Gathering Place. 'Three more days and we will be within the Treasury.'

'Where is it, Krea?' asked Farn. 'Can we see the Place yet?'

'When we are in the sky, I will show you where.'

Once aloft, Krea indicated directly ahead to the just risen sun. 'You see the line of tallest peaks there? The one that seems to have lost its topmost part? That is our destination children – the Gathering Place of the Broken Mountain Treasury.'

It happened with no warning at all. One moment they were flying at a steady wingbeat and the next, flames surrounded them.

Tika heard Krea scream to Farn to 'Go down!' He obeyed her instantly, sliding through the suddenly smoky air until he touched the ground. He stood full upright, his wings extended, the talon at each wingtip holding him utterly steady. Tika remained clinging on his back and they both stared upwards in horror.

Two rust-scaled Dragons were attacking Krea. They were fractionally smaller than the honey-coloured Dragon but still they were two against one.

Farn and Tika both received a piercingly clear command from a twisting and turning Krea: 'Hide yourselves! Find a rocky place, a cave, not among the tapisi! Hide yourselves my fosterlings! Keep safe and go to the Gathering! Hide!'

Farn lifted from the grass and flew fast and low into the tapisi then he doubled back and hovered at the edge of the woodland. His prismed eyes blazed as he sought a cave or a niche in the rock face a distance beyond. Tika's gaze was still on the Dragons above them. Flame bursts roiled as the two rust Dragons dived again and again at Krea.

Farn at last saw what he needed, a narrow shadowed crack in the rocks opposite. 'Hold tight,' he ordered Tika, and shot forward at a tremendous speed. He twisted suddenly so he was flying almost sideways on to the ground, then they were in a slit of a cave and tumbled together on the floor. Untangling themselves, they looked out at the continuing horror.

21

Krea screamed in their minds: 'Guard yourselves! Close your thoughts! Pray for my safety beyond!'

The smoke cleared briefly letting Farn and Tika see Krea, and they saw the honey-coloured Dragon falling. Falling out of the sky, great wounds gaping along her belly and flank. The rust scaled pair spiralled down after Krea, blasting fire into her body as she crashed to the ground.

Tika felt Farn's grief boiling towards rage and she forced him back to the furthest recess of their hiding place. She grasped his head, forced his eyes to lock with hers. 'Quiet! Don't make Krea's death pointless! She has died to save us! Hush, blank your mind and stay still!' He moaned once then clung to Tika, both of their minds blanketed to the outside world – one of the first things Krea had taught them.

Vocal screaming cries came to them, then an eerie silence. Tika knew somehow the two attackers were still out there, searching for Farn and herself. She held tight to Farn, willing him to stillness and silence. Then a crackling roar accompanied by a dense resinous-smelling smoke told Tika that the tapisi had been fired in the hope of flushing out the two of them.

She waited. And waited. Farn seemed to be asleep as she cautiously sent her mind out, searching for any life pattern nearby. Nothing. She realised she was stiff with cramp from holding Farn for so long and tried to ease the protesting muscles.

Farn stirred and she murmured him back to unconsciousness. Let him sleep, the smoke was clearing enough to show a darkening sky. Dawn would come soon enough for whatever she and Farn would have to face.

Chapter Three

At the Gathering Place of the Broken Mountain Treasury, many Dragons had already arrived and settled into the numerous caves encircling the Place. In one such cave, no more favoured than any other, rested Fenj. He was the most aged of this Treasury, deeply respected – and deeply tired.

For more Cold Seasons than he liked to recall, he had begged the Golden Lady Emla to release him from this weary body. She had sympathised with his longing to be reunited with his beloved mate, Skay, but refused to permit him to die. She told him he must wait an event. An event the importance of which he alone would instantly recognise. There were ominous movements in the world, even among the Treasuries, Emla told Fenj. He found the idea of trouble in the Treasuries very difficult to believe in, but quite likely among many of the other tribes of the world.

A shadow darkened the clear sky before him and Kadi landed. She was a dark blue Dragon, nearly as aged as Fenj and gifted with the power of long speaking.

'Fenj, I heard Krea call. She seemed maybe two or three days easy flight west of here. It was a great cry I heard – not really a call. I have been unable to long speak her since that call.' Kadi allowed Fenj free access to her memory and feeling of what had occurred.

'Whom should we send to seek her?' he asked thoughtfully.

'I myself will go,' Kadi replied. 'Krea is of my clan. Her mother is my daughter.'

Fenj pondered a moment longer, the gleaming black body appearing relaxed and at ease while his mind raced through identities, possibilities, likely results.

'It would be proper for you to seek out Krea. Long speak me at regular intervals so that I may know what you discover.' He inclined his long beautiful face towards Kadi, who bent forward until their brows touched lightly. 'Go safely old friend.' And then Kadi was lifting, rising above the Gathering Place and speeding to the west.

Tika had eased free of Farn who still slept, and crept to the slender crack in the rock face. It was hard to believe that yesterday, somehow, Farn had flown through such a narrow place. She peered cautiously out, looking first back the way they'd travelled, then towards their destination.

It was a still-smouldering desolation below. The tapisi were burnt to mere stumps and the grass burnt from the thin soil down to the edge of the narrow trickle of a stream. As she looked to her left, the sun rose above the cluster of peaks that Krea had pointed out as being their goal. She also saw the large Dragon body, black and charred, lying where she had fallen.

Then Tika felt tears burning down her face and she clamped her hands over her mouth to keep the wailing grief trapped inside lest she rouse Farn. But he was suddenly beside her, looking where she looked, great tears rolling down his narrow face.

'What do we do Tika?' Farn sounded so forlorn Tika realised with a jolt he was but two moons hatched. He had grown so fast and, with the help of the memories, he seemed to know so many things, it was easy to forget just what a baby he really was still. He sniffed. 'I think I will have to go quite far to find food and I think we should stay together.'

Tika tried to stem her tears and urge her brain to think clearly. 'There is water here Farn. Must you have food now, or can you manage without for a while? Is there anything in your memories about what we should do with Krea's – body?'

'It is a foggy memory – it is not something a young Dragon should need to know. It will become clearer as I grow older. There IS something we should do, but I can't tell what.' His mind heaved with shock and distress again and Tika hummed and murmured to him soothingly. After a while, he added, 'I feel hungry but I do not have to have food for two or three days I think. As long as I drink water, I will manage well enough. What about you?'

'I was often not fed in the town. I can go without food for quite a long time I believe, but, like you, I must have water.'

'Are they gone?' Farn's voice trembled. 'Can we go down to

the water do you think?'

'Open your mind Farn, listen as far as you can. If we do it together it makes us stronger.'

Farn let out a gusty breath. 'I hear nothing except a far distant mutter. Nothing nearby, not even a single hopper.'

'I heard nothing either. Come on, I'm sure it is safe to go down. They believe we perished in the tapisi fire.'

After they'd drunk at the stream and Tika had splashed water over her tear-hot face, they turned reluctantly upstream. Towards Krea's body.

'I think we have to stay near her, I can't tell for how long. But we have to pray for her safety beyond.'

'That is what Krea said – the last thing. Do you know what it means Farn?'

'No Tika, but I do know it is important.' And Farn wept again.

They approached Krea's ruined body and Tika was relieved to see that the Dragon's face was hidden from sight, pressed into the ground with a shattered wing concealing it.

Farn slumped to the ground in misery while Tika began to clear a narrow space all around the body. She had no idea why she felt it was necessary to move the charred tapis branches and singed turf away from Krea, she just did. Finally bare rock encircled Krea and Tika sat leaning against Farn. 'Do we just hope Krea is safe or is there a Dragon god we should pray to Farn?'

He stirred. 'There is only the Golden Lady Emla, and she would surely help Krea on her journey beyond.'

Somehow, that day drew to its close. Farn again flew Tika to the narrow cave above and they settled quietly at the opening. Tika suddenly stiffened. 'Farn! What is that? From the peaks of the Broken Mountain? Is it one of them returning for us? Oh Farn!'

His eyes flared and whirred into deepening splinters of blue. 'It is a Dragon, but not one of yesterday's attackers. We should stay hidden Tika, and close our minds in case this one also means us harm.' They crouched together at the rear of their hiding place and waited.

A great shriek made them clutch desperately at each other.

Then searing through their minds, came an eerily beautiful song, repeating a falling cadence which tore at their very hearts.

Holding Tika between his body and his wing, Farn moved as though summoned to the cave opening. From deep inside him the same chanting song came surging forth, and a fraction behind, Tika's voice soared to join the other two. On and on went the music until at last, as the full moon shone brilliantly down on Krea's body, the song whispered to silence.

Tika and Farn stood looking down at a great midnight blue Dragon. She stood, her wings spread anchoring herself fully erect beside Krea's dead bulk.

Kadi, for it was she, raised her eyes to the two figures high on the rock face.

'Come down children. Tell me what foulness befell you at this place.'

Kadi took most of the information from Tika, Farn was far too deeply shocked and grieved by the murder of Krea by Dragon Kin. He soon sank into a deep sleep and Tika looked at him in concern.

'Do not worry Tika. I have caused him to sleep thus. Later I will help heal this wound in him. But continue this telling.'

Tika told all, from her accidental arrival in Kija's nesting cave to the moment she and Farn had tried to hide from this blue Dragon, Kadi.

'Can you open your mind to mine child? It will help me to fully see what you have spoken of.'

'Krea was teaching us – she said I was better at mind speaking clearly than Farn. But of course, I cannot fly or make fire,' she added with a small sad smile as she stroked Farn's wing. She felt Kadi in her mind as the softest touch and relaxed, letting the Dragon find what she would.

'So. It would seem Kija fed memories through you to Farn when you locked with him at his hatching. Some of those memories are also now with you, but this very action has woken something within your mind. You have abilities I have never encountered in Dragon patterns. We will have much to learn from each other in the days to come.'

'Can you tell me what we should have done for Krea? Both of us felt there was something but we didn't know what it was.'

Kadi's eyes had a tiny golden flame in them as she gazed at Krea's body. 'You cleared the circle around her, which was correct. You sat with her, which was correct. Neither of you knew enough to sing her Life Song until I came to begin it for you.'

Tika felt an enormous sorrow filling this Dragon who seemed as comfortable to be with as Krea had become. The gleaming faceted eyes turned to Tika. 'Krea's mother was my first born…'

Without thought, Tika went swiftly to Kadi, wrapping her arms as far round the Dragon as she could reach. 'And is she "safely beyond" now? She asked us to pray her there, but we did not understand what she meant.'

'Yes small two-legs. She is safe but close by. One more day we must sit with her, then we go to the Gathering. Go now. Sleep beside Farn. I must far speak Fenj of the Treasury to tell him of these dreadful events. Then I shall seek food. I will listen back to you – if you have any need of me, call to me. I will come.'

Tika curled close to Farn and she too fell asleep, but not in as deep a sleep as the young Dragon. She was aware of the soft sighings of the wind, the sifting of the tapisi ashes blowing together and of Farn's faint snores and whimpers. She knew when Kadi returned and it was only then that she too sank into the depths of a healing slumber.

As the next night fell, Kadi told Tika and a still very shaken Farn that they would begin the last stage of the journey to the Gathering Place. 'Flying at night is little different from day, particularly when the moon is full and the sky clear as now,' she told them. 'We will also be travelling fast so I will carry you Tika.'

Farn objected. He had clung to Tika since Krea's death and he wanted to carry her to ensure her nearness. Kadi understood what was uppermost in his fears.

'No other attack will come Farn. Fenj knows what happened here and he has already begun his flight to meet us. No Dragon would dare attack Fenj and we should be with him before this night is done. Keep close to my wing and you will have Tika within reach of you.'

They had fed well earlier, on meat Kadi brought. Farn had not even suggested he help to find food, staying near Tika and Krea's body. Tika hugged Farn and then climbed onto Kadi's back. The Dragons rose and circled the place where Krea had fallen. Kadi slowed and bade Tika and Farn to look down.

From the blackened corpse a pale golden mist drifted. Gradually, the outline of a great Dragon took form. The Dragon rose clear of the body and then lifted higher. The face turned towards the watchers.

'Krea!' Tika and Farn's minds cried out in unison. The spectral Dragon drifted upwards until it seemed to disappear in the brilliance of the moonlight.

'Now,' said Kadi, 'we fly hard.'

Farn was obviously tiring badly after many hours of fast non-stop flight. Tika was concerned enough to question Kadi about the possibility of their stopping to rest. Kadi replied that they had nearly reached the prearranged place where Fenj would await them. Farn could rest then until the following evening.

Very soon thereafter, Kadi began to slow the pace. She began to glide lower, scanning the tapisi-fringed lake below. A black form became clearer as their height decreased, resolving itself into a massive Dragon. 'Be calm, it is Fenj.'

Tika was aware that Farn was just too exhausted to think of anything except forcing his wings to continue beating. She would have to deal with this meeting alone.

Farn crumpled as soon as his feet touched ground and Tika scrambled from Kadi's back to rush to his aid. She urged him the few paces to the water's edge, encouraged him to drink deep, and then settled him on the springy turf. While she was caring for Farn, Kadi had revealed all the recent events to Fenj.

'Tika,' Kadi called quietly, 'there is food if Farn is able to eat?'

'He's asleep already,' Tika replied. 'Will he be safe here?' She felt, but didn't hear, a quick communication pass between Kadi and Fenj.

The huge black Dragon answered her: 'He is safe small one. Join us here so he will not be disturbed. There is fruit here and scorched meat also.'

Tika walked slowly to where the two enormous creatures reclined. Fenj really was the biggest living being Tika had ever imagined, let alone seen. Kadi had seemed big, but she was in truth much slighter than this Fenj. Tika felt herself pulled towards him nonetheless, and found she was sitting with her back against Kadi's side, facing Fenj. And then the questioning began. Kadi said little, leaving Tika to answer Fenj.

He was obviously disturbed by Krea's death and he asked permission to view Tika's memory of the attack. She relaxed against Kadi and opened her mind to Fenj.

A silence grew until Tika said, 'I recognised those two Dragons, and if I did, I'm sure you know they seemed to be followers of Nula. She tried to attack Farn and me the first time we came out of the nesting cave. She told Kija to kill us both just after Farn hatched. Why does she want us dead? How could she let Krea be killed just for being with us?'

'These things must be answered at the Gathering small one. I have told Kija of an attack – I told her you and her son had survived, not revealing to her that Krea gave her life for you. Kija told me Nula and her followers seem in high mood – again, I did not reveal why I asked after Nula. So you see child, the four of us here know of the attack which destroyed Krea, but – only we four and Kija, know that you still live.'

Fenj paused, glancing skyward. 'We will move into the shelter of the tapisi for the day hours. Kadi will find food later and when night comes again, we will take the pair of you within the Gathering Place, secretly. Even Kija must not know you are there. She would want to see you, and you and Farn would be unable to withhold the news of these dark deeds.'

His eyes, a slatey grey like shadowed snow, glowed at Tika. She felt his great age and the wisdom he had gathered during that long lifetime. And she knew she could trust him implicitly.

Fenj rose, his great body shimmering in the growing light of day. 'Come, we will shelter deeper within the tapisi. Many of the Treasury overfly this place, and some will land here during the day. I have already discovered a place well hidden but where we can see clearly over this area.'

Kadi roused Farn who stumbled along behind Tika. He was very unsteady on his feet and Tika's concern for his condition was increasing. Very quickly the ground rose sharply and Tika had to grab hold of cloud bushes to pull herself up behind Fenj.

'Hold my tail small one, it will make the climb easy.' Tika hesitated at the idea of hanging onto Fenj's tail but after again nearly losing her footing completely, she did as he bade. Within seconds, she found herself whisked up beside the black Dragon onto a patch of grass. They were under an overhang of grey rock half buried under cloud bushes. Farn was pushed up by Kadi and herded towards the back of the natural shelter.

Tika watched as the midnight blue Dragon gently touched brows with the black Dragon. Then Kadi went swiftly back down the slope they'd just climbed.

'Rest Tika. Hold close to Farn. I will watch here. We will speak more when you are rested. Kadi will remove all trace of our passage. Do not worry,' he added, 'I have shielded all three of us from any other Dragons' sight.'

Tika woke with the sun just declining from midday and immediately checked Farn. He still slept but he seemed easier, less tense and fretful. The black Dragon was lying before them, his gaze on the lake.

'Leave Farn to sleep on. I have begun the healing his mind needs. He will be better when he next wakens.'

Tika rose but could see no way out of the shelter without actually climbing on Fenj. He laughed. 'Lean on my back small one and look at the lake.'

Tika looked, then looked harder. She shook her head in disbelief. There were Dragons in the water, quite clearly playing. They raced in circles, vanished under the surface, popping up unexpectedly close to others. They were obviously having tremendous fun. Several leaped from the water, scattering droplets from their bodies in brilliant showers. She couldn't decide what colour they were – they seemed like rainbows now taking the blue of the sky, now the green of the lake and again the silver of the water drops.

'They are of the Water Clans,' Fenj said. 'Only happy when they are in or near water in their family groups. They attend the Gatherings but are not really interested in anything unconnected to water.'

Tika felt his fondness for these sparkling Dragons in his voice as he spoke of them. As they watched, other Dragons passed overhead, some singly, some in tumbling groups.

'There is one more day before the Gathering begins,' said Fenj. 'And you and Farn will then appear before the whole Treasury. When Kadi returns, she and I will carry you to my cave. You will be unnoticed if you stay low between my wings.'

'How will you get Farn in there? Surely he will be noticed flying with you or Kadi, however late you wait?'

'Kadi will carry him as though he was a food animal she has hunted and killed. We can seal his mind so he will not be fearful or struggle. It is the only way for us to get you within the Gathering Place. You must be present for the Naming of Nula and her cohorts as Krea's slayer.'

'What will happen to them?' Tika asked. 'Will you kill them?'

Fenj turned his head to look at her.

'By the stars, no!' he exclaimed. 'We do not kill our own. Or we should not,' he amended sadly. 'She will be Forsaken by the Families, by the Clans and by the Treasury and cast out of the Dragon world.'

Their conversation was interrupted by splashings and shrieks from the lake – the Water Dragons were lifting, rising higher, sunset light flickering over their bodies.

'They're magic!' whispered Tika.

'No, they are Dragons,' corrected Fenj. 'Magic is a very different thing.'

Chapter Four

It went exactly as Fenj had planned. When Kadi returned, she woke Farn and explained how she would carry him into the Gathering Place. Tika was relieved to see that Farn appeared much calmer. He obediently lay as Kadi instructed him, and the dark blue Dragon lifted him with her feet. Her upper limbs also took some of his weight and his tail was curled between their two bodies. Kadi rose with her burden and Tika admitted it certainly didn't look as though she was carrying a young Dragon.

As Kadi began her flight, Tika climbed onto mighty Fenj and tucked herself into the hollow between his wings. He rumbled. 'Do try not to wriggle small one, it tickles.'

Tika kept as still as she could while ridiculous visions of herself falling just because a great Dragon was ticklish flicked through her mind. She was aware the instant they passed the protecting ring of crags and flew over the Gathering Place. Although Fenj was shielding her thought patterns she felt a great thrumming, like bees in a hive, pulse through her. She realised it was many Dragons communing with one another. Fenj drifted along the edge of the mountain wall until he was directly above the cave he occupied and then dropped quickly, straight to its entrance.

He lowered himself to the usual elegant reclining position and checked carefully for any unwelcome watchers. Kadi had already deposited Farn well back in the cave. He greeted Tika with a huge yawn and yet again slid into sleep.

'You may get off now,' Fenj said. 'But stay well away from the entrance. You will see all tomorrow, but for now, stay hidden. Rest if you can for the Gather will be difficult for you I fear, but know that Kadi and I are your shields.'

Tika found sleep impossible as the night crept slowly by, but at last it was near dawn. Fenj allowed Tika to move forward well shadowed between his shoulder and the rock wall. She bit her lip to keep herself silent. She had thought there were a great many Dragons outside Kija's nesting cave, but here the number was amazing.

Dragons of all shades and all sizes flying from cave to cave, some on the bare central floor of this hidden arena. Dragons were calling and crying vocally as well as communicating through their mind speech. Farn joined her, squirming low along Fenj's side.

'As the sun rises, so we will sing to the Golden Lady and beg her to bear witness to our Gathering,' Fenj told them. 'The time is near.' He reared himself onto his haunches, Tika and Farn slipping lower until they could only just peep out at the scene below.

A brilliant shaft of sunlight flared over the peak of Broken Mountain, its light shining directly onto a circle of smooth black rock on the inner wall of the Gathering Place. The black circle seemed to absorb the light rather than to reflect it at first. Then pieces of quartz round the circle's edge began to sparkle with, to Tika, a painful brilliance. At that moment hundreds of Dragon voices burst into Tika's mind, singing a song of Greeting – to each other but also to the Golden Lady, Emla.

As the song continued, the sun was suddenly reflected from the black circle, making a yellow puddle of light on the central space below. Tika's skin was prickling as the voices sank to a hushing ripple.

Fenj spread his wings wide and welcomed the Dragons to the Gathering. 'I look forward to greeting new hatchlings and to blessing new pairs. There is much to discuss first, though it grieves me immensely to tell of trouble.'

As he paused, Tika and Farn felt an instant tension spring up among the Gathered Dragons. They had already glimpsed Nula, with one of her rust coloured followers, in a cave opposite to Fenj's, and Kadi perched to one side. Tika could feel Farn becoming agitated again and she reached to hold his arm tightly.

Fenj turned his head slowly, grey eyes flashing as he looked at each Dragon in the huge circle. 'I tell you with despair in my heart that Krea is dead.' There was a tremendous upheaval at his words. Farn and Tika clearly recognised Kija's agonised cry. Tika held ever tighter to Farn. 'She died foully, slain by Dragon Kin, but also nobly, in defence of her fosterlings. And she did not die in vain, for those two survived.'

Tika's eyes had been glued to Nula and she watched now as the dark green Dragon hissed viciously at her companion. The second rust coloured Dragon was moving nervously on a ledge just below Nula.

Several Dragons floated down to the space below Fenj. Tika noticed they were all large Dragons and all of different colours. She guessed they were the leaders of various groups or families. One red Dragon demanded Fenj tell more details of Krea's death, and a Dragon darker gold than Kija also insisted Fenj tell all that he knew. When the telling was done, Kadi's voice called: 'Fenj must Name the evil doer, for the killers are from this very Treasury.'

A stunned silence met this announcement. The Dragons were already appalled at the idea of Dragon killing Dragon, but the idea that a death had been brought about by one of their own Treasury was nearly beyond their belief. Nearly, but not quite. Kija suddenly screamed into the silence: 'Who was it Fenj? You said my first born and the bonded two legs survived this terror, but where are they? Name the killer of Krea and let us ask why she was killed.' A rumble of agreement came from the whole Gathering.

'The two young ones who follow Nula destroyed Krea.' Fenj spoke quietly but oh so clearly.

Silence fell again as every prismed eye turned to where Nula perched. The two rust scaled Dragons cringed back against the rock under the glare of those eyes but Nula drew herself upright. Suddenly she launched herself down in the midst of the leaders.

'All of you are unworthy to name yourselves Dragons,' she snarled. 'Brood after brood of hatchlings are raised soft hearted and mild mannered instead of fierce and proud as we were meant to be. Then this final degradation – a pitiful two legs allowed to lock eyes with a first born son. Such abomination should be wiped out! Fenj teaches you to take only what you need; he says killing for sport is a wrongness. Hah! Dragons are hunters, fighters. We could empty the world of all the tribes of two legs – those of the plains whence came the creature I would see dead – those of the hills and of the deep woodlands. They are useless – even as food.'

Hisses sounded all around at this last. Fenj's eyes blazed as he looked down on Nula. 'You say so – dare you tell us you have eaten of the two-legs' flesh?'

'Of course. I am a Dragon, Fenj, not a puling feathered sky singer. I eat what I want, as I want.' Nula's eyes were a green darkening to black, as were her scales and hide. Her tail thrashed incessantly and smoke wisped from her nostrils. The scars on her face and body seemed more marked in her great rage.

'Nula, the Gathering of this ancient Treasury Names you Forsaken by all here. You and your apprentices will leave us. Never approach any of this Treasury. None will answer your call from this day forth. But still I ask that you can go safely beyond when your time comes.' Fenj bent his head, averting his eyes from Nula and every other Dragon followed his example.

Nula gave a scream of fury and rose, her two followers hastily flying in her wake. She circled once, screamed again, then was gone.

Fenj raised his head. 'I must know now who among you shares the Forsaken One's views. It is true, a young two legged one locked eyes with Kija's first born. I admit I was greatly surprised that it could happen at all, but I have witnessed the two together. I tell you the bond is true. However strange or difficult it may be for you to believe, as I confess it was for me, these two are of a great importance. So says the Golden Lady. There is much to do. They must learn together and faster than is usual for hatchlings. I will therefore ask any who are willing to help in this task. Do any dissent?'

A crimson Dragon called: 'May we have a little time to consider these things Fenj?'

Fenj pondered. 'You will all Gather again at moonrise to give me your true thoughts. Now, let us try to put these things aside for a short time whilst we give honest welcome to new hatchlings.'

Several Dragons flew into the space, with two or three youngsters close beside them. The adult Dragon called the names of each hatchling and each was warmly welcomed by the whole Treasury.

Last to descend was golden Kija with her four children. She called their names then she stood erect and called loudly: 'Farn, my first born!'

The Dragons rustled their wings and looked about, until Fenj said quietly, 'Here is Farn and his soul bond, Tika.' He drew to one side and indicated that the pair should stand and go forward. Farn's eyes were sparkling as he looked down at his mother. Tika stood with her hand lightly resting at the base of his neck and looked at Kija also. She felt Kija's enormous relief as the Dragon saw that neither of them had been physically damaged at least. This time, the inspection by so many pairs of faceted eyes did not cause Tika to cower back. Rather she stood relaxed beside Farn.

The Dragons below began to move. Small groups formed, joined others, split off again. Clearly there was a great deal of discussion going on. But Farn was telling her to climb on his back, quickly. Tika did so and before she was really settled, he was in the air, gliding down to Kija. He wilted slightly under Kija's intense stare but finally Kija spoke to both of them: 'You seem to have dealt with these terrible events quite well.'

Tika interrupted to say Fenj and Kadi had both helped Farn. Kija's eyes burned into Tika's. 'Farn, go with your brother and sisters while I speak privately with Tika.'

The five hatchlings, all shades of blue but for one creamy little female, flew from rock to rock in a game of chase. 'I would see what happened Tika if you please.'

Tika opened her mind and showed Kija just what had happened. Kija wept and Tika hugged her as she had Kadi. 'She said you were her clan sister. Fenj said Farn and I did the correct things when she died.'

Kija shuddered.

'We all knew that Nula was embittered, verging on madness some of us feared, but that she would do this... Enough. We must speak quickly of other things. What did Fenj mean about the Golden Lady?'

'I don't know. He hadn't mentioned her to us. Who is she Kija?'

'She is the One who speaks to all who listen. No doubt Fenj will tell us more at tonight's Gathering. Now, what of Farn? There is a fragile place within him still, despite the healing he has received.'

'Well,' Tika frowned. 'We were both upset and frightened,

but he seemed worse than I did. I know Krea was his family, but
I'm not sure – I thought perhaps he took it all so badly because he
is still so very young.'

Kija was watching Farn and his siblings as they came back
across the open space.

'I felt it was intended, that you should bond with Farn and it
now seems Fenj knows more of this matter.'

By now, Farn had left the other hatchlings and returned to
Tika's side. His sapphire eyes flashed as he asked: 'Has Tika told
you what an excellent hunter I am Mother? And I'm just as good
at making fire!'

Tika grinned at Kija's rather startled expression. 'I'm sure my
son. But modesty is also a useful skill to learn.' She turned,
calling her other four children, and they rose up and over the
circling ramparts.

Many of the Dragons approached Tika and Farn throughout
the day, asking gentle questions, most of them tactfully avoiding
the death of Krea. In the middle of the afternoon, Fenj called
them to his cave. Neither of them noticed how many Dragons
watched Tika slide easily across Farn's back before he lifted them
gracefully to Fenj's cave.

Settled comfortably beside the black Dragon, they found meat
had been put ready for them. As they ate Fenj told them: 'The
Golden Lady has spoken to me. She told me many things, which
are hard for me to believe, but some I must tell the Gathering and
a little more I must tell you two alone.

'The balance of the world has – broken. The Lady Emla and
the Grey Guardian between them maintain this world. Emla says
a Balance Weight has been lost, or stolen, and thus are things
slipping awry. The Seasons are muddled already – I'm sure even
the two legs have noticed that much.

'Worse to me are the changes amongst we of the Treasuries.
Barely a few Seasons ago, those such as the Forsaken would not
have contemplated killing another of the Kin. We would have
worked with them, seeking the mending of their spirits. I have
news that such things are happening elsewhere in the world.'
Fenj paused. 'The Golden Lady tells me that you Tika, are not
the only one from outside the Dragon Kin to lock eyes with a
hatchling and thus become bonded.'

Tika sat up abruptly. 'Another child? Like me?'

'No. Not like you. From what the Lady allowed me to see, I think it is a male Nagum, a two legs but not of your kind. He bonded with a female first born in a Treasury many leagues from here.'

As the moon cleared the high rim of the Gathering Place, it was again filled with Dragons. Fenj stayed on his ledge where all could see him. The leaders of the Families announced that after much discussion and thought, they were no nearer understanding what had happened than before. They all agreed, however, that they would accept Fenj's decisions, as had been their way for many generations past.

Fenj lowered his head for a moment then straightened and repeated parts of what he had already told Tika and Farn. 'The Lady decrees that these two must be readied for a journey, as quickly as they are able. They must seek for something which has been lost, and on their success depends the continuity of our world.'

There was silence from the Gathered Dragons, then a great sigh came from them. One voice began softly to sing and gradually others joined in until a great pattern of song wove over them and on up to the night sky. It was a song of goodwill: praying the Golden Lady would grant courage and fortitude on two young travellers. Tika recognised her name and Farn's in the repeating lines of song.

She glanced at Farn and saw with a shock that Fenj was limned with a nebulous golden glow sparkling back from his black body. The song changed to one of affection for the Golden Lady and the wish that she would continue her care of her Dragon children.

Tika did not remember anything more until she woke halfway through the next morning. She was alarmed to find herself alone, no Farn or Fenj. She hurried to look down from the cave to the Gathering Place. Very few Dragons were in sight. She called to Farn, afraid he had vanished with Kija and she was abandoned here.

A flurry of wings and a blue Dragon descended before her nose. Farn purred his odd laugh. 'I thought you would never wake. I've been busy for ages.'

'You had lots of sleep before we got here,' retorted Tika, then instantly regretted her sharp words as Farn looked so dejected. 'I'm sorry. I know it was a healing really – you couldn't help but sleep.'

Farn cheered up. 'I've been doing different kinds of flying Tika. It is strange flying over water you know. Kadi said tomorrow we will go high.' He tilted his head back, blue silver eyes whirring as he gazed skywards. 'What do you suppose clouds feel like?' he wondered.

Dragons left the Gathering Place in their Families and Clans during the next few days. The Treasury lands spread for many hundreds of leagues around its central Place at Broken Mountain. This Treasury lived mainly amongst the high peaks and deep valleys within the vast range of the Ancient Mountains.

Farn worked hard under the tutelage of Kadi and of his father, the blue Dragon Jorab. He learnt quickly and Jorab told Fenj there was little more to teach the hatchling – stamina and endurance would improve as Farn grew. They must all remember he was still barely half-grown.

Kija and a crimson Dragon, Seti, worked with Tika. Two of Farn's sisters, the cream-coloured Jeela and the blue Shar, shared Tika's instruction. It was quickly clear to Kija and Seti that Tika's abilities were strong. She could soon mind speak over increasing distances and could hear just as well from afar. Usually, the Dragons told her, one could far speak well but the listening would be a weaker talent, or the other way about. Rarely were both equal in strength as with Tika. And Jeela was nearly as apt as Tika. Shar could far speak but could only hear from much shorter distances.

Seti taught them mind healing as well as taking them outside the Gathering Place to find plants and roots that could be used as medicines. Shar was the one who always found the required plant quickest.

In the ever earlier nightfalls, Fenj spent time with Farn and Tika, telling them all he could of the Golden Lady and, reluctantly, of the Grey Guardian. He explained that between the two of them, harmony reigned in the world, each holding the other and so it must always be. Tika asked why the Lady had not suggested the Dragons destroy the Guardian so she could be solely in command of these Balancing Scales?

Fenj sighed. 'No, no. Always the two there must be. Think Tika, all must have its opposite to balance it – daytime must have night-time to follow, Hot Season follows Cold. Think small one, how could you know you are joyful if you have never known sorrow?

'This Balance between the Lady and the Grey One is already failing. One of the weights in her care has been lost and so the scales dip in the Grey One's favour and we see already the consequences beginning.'

'You mean Nula?'

Fenj hissed. 'Her name is unspeakable, she is Forsaken.' He calmed himself. 'The Forsaken could have been healed but the sourness within her grew until it outbalanced the goodness in her spirit.

'There was a time when she was the kindest of Dragons. She lost her first brood in a terrible ice storm. The storm came from nowhere while she was hunting and when she was able to reach her cave again, her three hatchlings were frozen in death. She sorrowed, but then appeared to be recovered. Her second brood died in their eggs – it sometimes happens so.

'All the Treasury grieved for her in her losses but she had fosterlings and seemed content. Four Cold Seasons past, she did not arrive here at the Gather – Dragon Kin do not *have* to Gather but most of us enjoy this time. It is when we renew old friendships and exchange news – a social time.

'When the Forsaken came to the next Gathering, all remarked her changed. She told no one of her doings, kept aloof. And all noticed her manner of sneering criticism. Many Dragons avoided her company from that time – they told me she made them feel unsettled – and hatchlings were kept out of her way.'

Fenj fell silent and Tika and Farn waited patiently. Finally he shivered his wings and concluded: 'Perhaps I should have challenged her, forced her to take healing. Perhaps Krea would live still but for my negligence.'

'No,' said Tika slowly. 'I think she must have found or been found by the Grey Guardian. Does he speak to you as the Lady Emla does Fenj?'

Fenj was startled. 'He has never bespoken me, but now you

suggest it, it would seem plain that he *could* do so. You think he spoke to the Forsaken and encouraged her feelings of ill will?'

Tika shrugged trying to explain her idea. 'It just came to me when you spoke of the Guardian. The Lady speaks to you and you listen and tell the Treasury of her words and – the Forsaken is so very different to all the other Dragons I've encountered, I just thought … if she hears the Guardian tell her opposite things to the Lady, as you say everything has an opposite, which could account for her cruelty?'

Farn yawned then looked guiltily apologetic. Fenj chuckled. 'Indeed Farn, you have worked hard these few days. Take Tika and rest. The time approaches all too soon when you must leave here.'

Chapter Five

Next morning, despite Fenj's warning last night, Tika and Farn were dismayed to find Kija and Seti waiting to bid them farewell. Kija's eyes were a buttery gold blaze as she told Farn not to be boastful or rash but to consider his actions always as reflections of his Treasury birth. She asked Tika to take care of Farn, to beware of letting him overtax his immature strength. Finally, as both Farn and Tika felt engulfed by her affection and concern, she was lifting, rising to the peaks with her other four children close beside her.

Jeela flew last, turning again and again to see them, her mind calling farewell.

Shar too called, 'Safe travelling!'

Farn's father Jorab had gone in the night, to rejoin a group of males heading north towards the desert lands edging the Ancient Mountains. Seti merely told them to remember their lessons and they would do well, then she too was gone. And so, suddenly, the central Gathering Place was empty, seeming bigger than ever with just the four of them, Fenj, Kadi, Farn and Tika.

'These are the last things,' said Fenj. 'The Lady has told me you must take two things particularly from our collection.'

He looked at Kadi then both huge Dragons turned towards the gleaming black circle set high in the rock face. Tika was aware of Fenj and Kadi's minds working together. She concentrated hard to see exactly what they were doing. It felt as though they were unravelling a piece of woven cloth, threads being slid free of other threads. As Tika strove to follow the pattern of what they did, the black circle split down the centre and folded silently back, revealing a cave behind. 'Come.' Fenj rose and flew smoothly to the cave with Kadi a second behind him.

'Come on,' said Farn excitedly, urging Tika to climb on his back and lifting rapidly to follow his elders.

This cave, like Kija's nesting cave, had a kind of entrance

place then a short tunnel twisted away concealing another cave from first glance.

Tika heard Farn's squeak of gleeful astonishment as she entered the second cave behind the others. She stared, amazed, at the great jumbled heap in front of them. Farn immediately started nosing amongst the glittering pile while Kadi watched. Fenj told Tika: 'Dragons love sparkling things – drops of water, snowflakes, stars in the sky, shining stones. And a thousand Seasons past, we would collect any such things we found. The best we brought here for all to enjoy at the Gathering times. Most of us have small collections of our own hidden away.'

'A real Dragon's hoard of treasure,' Tika whispered, watching jewelled coronets and scabbards, necklaces and brooches slipping down the pile as Farn poked through it all.

'What?' Fenj asked in some surprise.

'There are stories about Dragons having these great hoards of treasure,' Tika explained.

'Stories? Two-legs tell stories of us?' Fenj sounded dubious as well as faintly shocked. 'What are these stories?'

'Usually of Dragons capturing beautiful princesses and bearing them off to hidden places where they live on top of heaps of jewels.' Tika paused, belatedly remembering how most of such stories ended.

Fenj asked, 'Whatever does the Dragon do with a two-legs princess?'

Tika gulped. 'Well, sometimes he eats her, but more often a handsome prince turns up, battles and kills the Dragon and takes the princess home to marry.'

Grey eyes and blue whirred rapidly and Tika suddenly had that turned inside out sensation again.

'I do wish you wouldn't do that,' she complained. 'It makes me feel really sick.' She felt Kadi and Fenj withdraw from her mind extremely rapidly. 'That's better,' she said graciously.

Kadi apologised first. 'Please forgive us Tika. We are unused to communicating with your kind. The few two legs we have attempted contact with do not seem to be at all aware of our attempts.'

Fenj rumbled in agreement.

'Look!' cried Farn. He had a golden coronet afire with

43

sapphires and bloodstones. He twirled it on one extended talon. 'Sparkles!'

'Yes, yes,' said Fenj, 'but there are two things the Lady said you must take with you Tika. Look in my mind and you will be able to recognise them.'

Tika slid into Fenj's thoughts and saw a piece of amber embedded in gold, hanging from a thin golden chain. Beside this was a dull leather scabbard with the silver hilt of a sword protruding from its top. She looked at the great heap Farn was happily prodding through and groaned. 'The scabbard should be easy enough, it looked like old, worn leather and there isn't much leather in this lot, but the necklet…'

Farn was persuaded to see the items in Tika's mind and the four began searching through the hoard. It took a long time, mainly because all of them were often distracted by the beautifully crafted objects they sorted through. The three Dragons admired the brilliant flashing of the stones, Tika was dumbfounded by the wealth the stones represented.

It was Kadi who found the leather scabbard and pulled it free of a rope of great milky egg-stones of the sea. Much later, Farn began scrabbling excitedly: 'It's here! I saw its edge! Tika come and help!'

Sure enough, the rim of a gold encased piece of amber showed beneath a heavily encrusted shield. Tika's fingers worked the amber free with its knotted golden chain.

'I have it,' she announced but only Kadi glanced up momentarily. Tika looked at the Dragons more closely. They were dreamily bemused by the glittering collection. Fenj started a miniature landslide with an extended talon. Farn was half covered with goblets and necklets, crooning happily.

'Come,' Tika ordered as commandingly as she could. 'To Fenj's cave.' Slowly, reluctantly, Kadi was first to back away then leave the cave. Fenj and Farn seemed not to have heard a word. Tika went to Farn, pushed the heap of sparkles off his legs and belly and hauled at his arm. 'Out. Now Farn. Do as I tell you.' Farn at last turned to look at her and his eyes regained their focus as Tika clasped his face in her hands. 'Now Farn. Go to Fenj's cave.'

That left Fenj. Tika eyed the enormous black Dragon and

seriously wondered if she would be able to tear him from his dreamy contemplation of this treasure hoard. She cautiously probed into his mind and then suddenly felt Kadi's mind there too.

'Fenj, come away. You are behaving like a hatchling.' Fenj reared onto his haunches and rumbled. He looked at Tika and gradually his eyes recognised her and lost the vagueness of the hoard's enchantment.

She stood aside, indicating he should leave the cave before her and he obediently moved past, his tail catching an edge of the sparkling pile. Tika moved right behind him as he hesitated, forcing him on through the passage to the outer cave. She glanced back at the treasure, shook her head in disbelief and hurried after Fenj. She was carried to his cave in silence. It was only as she climbed off his back that he spoke: 'I am sorry Tika. It has been long since we opened the circle to look at our collection. We found, many, many Gathers past, that we forget Time when we gaze on so many shining things. The Gather decided we should seal it away after we were nearly trapped here by snow and ice storms – so many days had passed and we were too dazzled to realise it.'

Kadi and Farn were rubbing the worn scabbard with their own body oil, Tika saw, and already it was beginning to soften and shine again as leather should. Farn had moved up to begin working on the loops to which the scabbard was fastened.

Tika sat at the cave entrance trying to pick free the tight knots in the gold chain. The pendant it supported was the size and shape of a sky singer's egg, with the back half shelled in gold and filled with smooth amber to the front. Within the amber was a tiny black speck. Fenj lay watching her mutter over the knots. 'Why not use your mind, small one?' He suggested. Tika stared at him, then at the chain. She saw where the links needed loosening and threading through twisted loops like so – and the chain lay untangled on her knee. She dropped the chain over her head, the amber and gold egg hanging low on her chest. She lifted it and peered at the black speck within the amber.

'What is this mark?' she asked curiously.

'Again, use your mind.'

Annoyed with herself at having to be reminded of her new

abilities a second time, and so soon, Tika was too tense at first. She looked out over the Gathering Place, breathed deeply and looked again at the pendant. It was a tiny curled frond she thought, and then she looked even closer. It was no plant, it was a Dragon. But so small! Scarce as big as her smallest fingernail, yet utterly perfect. She closed her hand around it, looking at Fenj as her mind threatened to explode with more questions.

'No, no,' he said. 'I have never seen a living Dragon so small. Once I saw new-laid eggs broken by a rock fall and inside were Dragons tiny beyond belief, but even they were not so small as what you hold there. The Lady told me nothing of these things she said you must have. Maybe it is to be revealed to you alone as you travel.'

Next morning Tika awoke first to see bright light within the cave. She stood up from beside Farn's still sleeping body, her blanket cape crumpling to her feet. A layer of snow, two finger-widths deep, lay on the outside world. Picking up the cape and wrapping it around herself she went to look out over the Gathering Place. The sky was a brittle blue, the rising sun a feverish red.

'You must leave today,' Fenj told her. 'It is early for the snow to come, but you cannot delay here any longer.'

'But you haven't told us where we must go. You say we must find one of the Lady's Balance Weights, yet you haven't said even what it looks like. Surely you, or Kadi, or – anyone – would be a better choice than Farn and me?' There was an edge of panic in Tika's voice.

'The Weight is a small disc of gold with a hole in its centre. That is all I know. Whether there are patterns upon it I cannot tell you. You travel to mountains first, north of here. They are not part of this Treasury's lands, but are the lands of the Sun Treasury. Kadi has bespoken the Eldest of that Treasury – Seela – and she replied that the Lady has spoken with her also. She will tell you more than I have been able to do perhaps. She awaits your arrival and she has been told of the Forsaken One. Her Dragons too will shun the Nameless and word will be passed thus to all the Dragon Kin.'

'And how far is it to reach Seela?'

'Eight or nine days travel. Half of that time you will be over this Treasury's lands and will perhaps see some of those whom you met here. Then there is a distance over barren land where food is scarce, and you should then see the Sun Mountains ahead of you. It is not a difficult journey thus far.'

'Do you know where Kija went? It seems strange to me that she should leave Farn, her first born after all, to have to do this by himself.'

'She has four other hatchlings to raise. Three is the most we usually have in a brood. She will be kept very busy training them to become independent of her. And I know she will work them hard, as she is anxious for Farn and you. If your journey takes much time, I think Kija will try to find you, to be of assistance in your task.'

Farn and Tika ate the food Kadi brought them and then they knew it was time to leave, both the safety of the Gathering Place and the reassuring company of the two elder Dragons. Tika awkwardly strapped on the scabbard belt and sword, and she was surprised at how familiar it immediately felt at her hip. She had occasionally seen the Fighters teaching the Lord's boys the art of swordsmanship, but she had considerable doubts as to whether she would draw this sword without seriously damaging herself let alone any opponent. She had decided she would practice privately – when Farn left her to hunt for their supper perhaps.

With her cape wrapped around her and the other blanket, trousers and frilly underbeneaths held between her body and Farn's, she looked at the two Great Dragons. Her mind, and Farn's, was engulfed in affection and goodwill; she caught the faintest underlay of sadness and apprehension but she knew Farn did not feel it in his excitement.

Kadi and Fenj reared upright, towering over Tika and Farn. Their wings were outstretched, holding them tall and steady. Grey eyes and blue blazed in kaleidoscopic colours:

'Go safely hatchlings. You have the protection of the Golden Emla and our thoughts will be with you as long as possible. Call to us if you have need.'

It was Kadi's voice in their minds as Farn began to rise out of the Gathering Place, but it was Fenj's voice at the last, repeating: 'Go safely hatchlings!'

47

Chapter Six

For three days Farn and Tika journeyed north from Broken Mountain. The weather stayed clear but frost spiked each blade of grass when they woke just before dawn now. There had been no snow yet in the valleys, but white shawls covered the higher slopes. They had met no other Dragons, only sky singers and hoppers, feeding on the cloud bushes and starberries. Once Tika saw a solitary high drifter, floating effortlessly, his eyes on hoppers far below him. There were a few bell trees now, among the taller and more slender tapisi.

Farn's strength had greatly increased since the flight to the Gathering Place with Kadi. They landed at midday but not because Farn needed to rest. Tika found she had to walk for a while, stretch her legs and arms after sitting still for too long on Farn's back.

It was the fourth evening and they had stopped earlier than previously. Tika was cramped, and trying to think of a way of exercising her limbs whilst on Farn's back, which would not interfere with his flying or unseat herself. Farn was tired of a diet of hoppers and said he would try to find a volu, for supper.

Tika jumped, and stretched, and ran up and down between a tapis and a rocky outcrop. As she turned from the rock for the third sprint, she felt hands, human hands, grab her. One hand was over her mouth and the other viciously tight on her upper arm, holding her hard against a leather overtunic.

Her heart seemed to stop, then leaped into high-speed pulse as she twisted and struggled. Whoever held her, spoke roughly to her but she could not understand his words. Why oh why had she put her sword with her cape and bundle by the tapis while she did her stupid exercises?

She reached up and back with her free hand and caught an ear. She held on as tightly as she could, digging in to the flesh with her nails and tugging downwards. Her mind was quite clear after

48

its first instant of panic, and she called quickly to Farn, telling him what was happening to her. She was also thinking furiously – who had hold of her, was he one man or one of a group of hunters? Or one of a band of Fighters?

The question was answered for her as she was spun around and pushed violently towards a group of men. They were dressed as Fighters, but none she recognised. They all had stripes of colour across one cheek, indicating they were of a Lord's band. Hoarse voices called out as they encircled Tika. She half understood a word here and there, but could not make any real sense of their speech.

'Use your mind,' Fenj's words whispered in her memory, and she probed carefully into the mind of a Fighter who kept aloof from the taunting roughness of the rest of the men. She was immediately submerged in a confused jumble of feelings and thoughts: jealousy, irritation, boredom, petulance. She realised she could understand his mind where she could not understand the vocal speech of these men.

This one was the supposed leader of the Fighters. They fought for a Lord Jal-Sidar, who ruled a town, many leagues west. They had been raiding into another Lord's territory but had little to show for many days hard riding on the speedy fengars most Fighters preferred. Now the leader watched as these boorish fools played with a peasant brat. They were not reliably obedient to all his orders so he unwillingly left them to have their fun now.

As he glanced at the men, pushing Tika to and fro in their midst, Tika felt his sudden, stupendous shock even as she saw his widening eyes and gaping mouth. She laughed aloud, disconcerting her tormentors. Those facing the same way as their leader showed similar dismay, one even dropping flat to the earth and covering his head with his arms. She laughed again as she turned, knowing what she would see. Farn was marching steadily from the tapisi towards them, his wings raised, his prismed eyes flashing sapphires. He came to a halt a short distance from the Fighters.

Tika walked past men now rigid with terrified disbelief, and stood against Farn's belly as he reared upright. Then he belched. Fire flared from his nostrils, singeing the turf at the Fighters' feet. They were rooted to where they stood it seemed. Farn belched once more and as one, the gang turned and fled, wailing, beyond the outcrop of rock.

'They did not harm you Tika?' Farn asked with concern.

'No, just scared me at first. Can you hear their mind speech?'

'No,' said Farn after a while. 'I hear a babble but I can make nothing of it that could be called speech.'

'They have just reached the place they left their fengars. I think they were looking for hoppers for their supper and found me instead. Their minds are a shrieking muddle.' Tika laughed, rubbing Farn's long neck affectionately. 'Thank you. You were extremely good at sending them on their way!'

Smoke was still trailing delicately from Farn's nostrils. 'Of course.' He said it automatically, adding: 'Why did they hold you? Did they want to harm you? Do you know these two-legs?'

Tika hesitated. 'They caught me because I was here. For their sport I suppose. No,' she concluded, 'I did not know them but it is how Fighters behave towards many people like me.'

Farn turned back to the tapisi. 'I'd caught a volu, and a hopper when you bespoke me. I dropped them a little way through the tapisi. Will those two-legs return?'

'No. They are leagues away already. When they reach a farm or a town, they will tell of Dragons here. They will be laughed at.' She thought for a moment. 'Or if they are believed, many more Fighters will come here for the fame they would win by killing a Dragon.' Farn looked alarmed. Tika said quickly, 'We will tell this to Seela, and she will warn her Treasury. You go and fetch our supper – I will bespeak Kadi so that she can tell Broken Mountain Dragons to watch for two legs in the mountains now.'

As they travelled, over hills now rather than mountains, they watched for any signs of two legs below them. Farn's vision was acute, while Tika searched with her mind. Time passed quickly as she tried to untangle the melange of the different "voices" she heard – the odd, scolding, repetitive comments of a bushy tail as it reminded itself where it had already stored nuts for the coming Cold Season. She heard the quiet thoughts of a shaggy honey finder as she sought a snug place to outsleep the Cold.

Tika was amazed to find so many of the small feathered ones communicated with each other although it was a fairly simple enough form of speech. She was even more taken aback when a great eyes realised a stranger was in his mind and spoke directly to her, enquiring what she was doing. She apologised for her rudeness and explained she was a two legs and had only just discovered mind speech. The great eyes hurrumphed testily and went back to sleep, his mind firmly closed.

'Farn, do you communicate with all creatures except two-legs?'

'I think we can. There is not a great deal to talk about with many of them, but we can if we choose.'

They were gliding down to land beside a stream that was nearly a river for their evening halt. Farn drank and then went off to find food for their supper. He was gone only briefly, returning with a volu and three hoppers. He sprawled on the grass eating the volu and watching Tika. She still walked up and down, bringing her knees high to loosen calf and thigh muscles.

'Farn,' she asked, 'can you talk to trees, or rocks, or stars?'

Farn was silent for so long Tika knew he was searching through the memories given to him at his hatching. She continued flexing her legs and arms as she waited.

At last he said, 'I'm not sure. There's something to do with trees from a very long time past. It isn't relevant now anyway. It seems trees do, or did, talk, but very, very slowly, so mostly we gave up trying to speak with them.'

Tika came to a standstill in front of him. 'So all things can talk? So all things must be able to think.' She sat down and hungrily reached for a scorched hopper. She had eaten half of it when another thought struck her. 'Does a hopper know you are about to kill it?'

'Dragons kill because our bodies need meat. We kill very quickly, usually before the volu or whatever, is even aware of our presence. We send calmness to their minds as we kill them to help them safely beyond.'

As they continued to the Sun Mountains, Tika thought hard of this ability to mind speak. Of how her life had changed so dramatically. A life which she had believed ended when she ran away from the town of Return. She had truly thought she would die of hunger, of falling among those high crags, or of being eaten by some hungry beast. And now she found herself on a silver blue Dragon's back, treated with respect by others of the Dragon Kin, setting forth on an important search.

She hoped Seela would have far more information to give her than Fenj had done about that last. It was difficult to believe that the Chena who, for fourteen Cold Seasons, had been a slave, held in contempt and abused by most of the Lord's household, was now this Tika, soul bonded to a Dragon.

On the fifth day of travelling, the Sun Mountains appeared as a bump on the horizon, looming ever higher the closer Tika and Farn approached. As they rested on the sixth evening, Seela mind spoke them both.

'Welcome to the Sun Treasury! You have made a swift journey Farn. With so much strength in your wings already, surely you will be one of the mightiest when you are full-grown!'

Tika laughed as Farn stretched fully upright, looking extremely pleased with himself. She felt Seela's amusement as Farn had the grace to look a little ashamed of his pride.

'Tomorrow,' Seela told them, 'fly the length of the valley beyond the pass where you are now resting. I will await you at the end of that valley. Sleep well!'

They flew next day, through the valley as Seela had directed. To begin with it was narrow, set deeply between soaring rock walls. Gradually it began to widen until the rock faces were many leagues apart. They passed over a long lake, its waters a strange blue tinged with brownish red, then continued up the valley over the river which fed the lake. At last the terrain narrowed again and began to rise.

Soon after midday, Farn said: 'She is there – on a ledge of that peak.'

Tika looked where Farn indicated but could see only a purple speck, her vision being far inferior to Farn's.

'Seela!' called Farn. 'We are come. May we land at your cave?'

'Be welcome, bonded ones. Food and friendship await you.'

As Farn spiralled lower to approach Seela's ledge in a gentle glide, Tika had the opportunity to study this new Dragon. Seela was as massive as Fenj, but she was a deep purple rather than black, with dark blue tints shimmering over her scales. Her eyes flashed, pale mauve sparking with a deep gold within them.

Farn landed and as Tika slipped from his back, he stood erect and greeted Seela formally. Unsure of how she should act towards such a Dragon, Tika let fall her bundle and stood straight beside Farn. Her left hand on her sword hilt and her right flat over her heart, she bowed to Seela and repeated Farn's words: 'The Golden Lady keep you safe through all the Seasons.'

By the time Seela had heard all they had to tell, stars were pricking the sky. Farn was unable to conceal his yawns and Seela sent him deeper into the cave to sleep. A comfortable silence grew between her and Tika, eventually broken by the two-legs.

'Fenj said you knew more than he of the Lady's wishes for us?'

'You are to meet the other two-legs who is bonded,' Seela told her. 'It is a male Nagum, bonded to the first born daughter of Hani. Hani is unusual in that she is shy, she keeps to herself. She mind speaks to some of us in this Treasury but is overwhelmed by social Gathering times. She stays mostly at the farthest edge of our range. We knew she was brooding three eggs and she bespoke me when the hatchings began. She has spent one moon cycle teaching her first born and the bonded one all she can and has left them now to take her other hatchlings to her usual Cold Season place further towards the dying sun.'

'A Nagum?' Tika's mind was churning. Nagums were characters from tales such as the ones she had heard involving Dragons. A picture formed of a two-legged creature, hunched and deformed, with a snouted face, wild eyes, fangs and talons.

'No, no, no,' said Seela testily. 'That is a Linvak. Nagums are a shy and gentle tribe concerned with plants and flowers.'

Tika tried to grasp these new ideas. How many tribes were there of whom she knew nothing? Were there stone men and giants too?

'Try to concentrate please,' Seela moved restlessly. 'There are many tribes in this world indeed, of whom you seem totally unaware. Some may appear strange to your eyes, as many do to ours.' (Tika had a feeling Seela was being a touch personal with that remark.) 'However, as we have learnt, so must you – not to judge others, especially just on their appearance.'

Tika had by now controlled her thoughts and Seela calmed herself.

'The Nagum, Mimnan and the bonded first-born, Ashta are on their way here. I have bespoken both of them, so they are prepared. I believed Nagums to be shy creatures, and a daughter of Hani's could also be as timid as her mother. I trust the Lady her reasons for choosing this pair for her task. I see you wear a sword – I cannot imagine a Nagum knowing how to use one.'

Tika kept her mind blank lest Seela see that she also had little idea on the correct use of a sword.

'Join Farn now and sleep easily while you may. I will stay here.'

'Do you not need to sleep Seela? I noticed Kadi and Fenj were always awake whenever I roused in the night?'

'We need very little sleep as we age, small one. Indeed, as we draw closer to the beyond, why waste the time we have left in sleep? But you and Farn are extremely young, and still growing, so – to sleep with you!'

When Farn and Tika woke they found fresh meat waiting and Seela in the same place as when they'd slept. She told them Ashta and Mimnan would arrive during this day. Her pale mauve eyes shone softly. 'The Lady would meet you soon.' The prismed eyes began to whirr as she continued, 'No one has met the Lady in the flesh for a great many cycles. She speaks only in our minds now. There was a time, long since past, when some of the Kin were regularly admitted to her presence.' Seela was clearly becoming concerned. 'There have been changes, alterations, in the pattern of the world, but I now fear we may have deliberately ignored some of the warnings. If the Lady is to meet you, things must be further awry than we believed.' She rustled her wings in agitation. 'Last night, Fenj told me other Elders have been warned by the Lady. A bad time is at hand and she says we must instruct the Treasuries to keep close to their Gathering Places. We must seek back through the memories, for such a time we have witnessed before says Emla.'

Farn flew Tika from the ledge to a swift flowing stream that poured from the heights. Seela had said the Sun Mountains were rarely as cold as the Ancient Mountains. The snow-caps on their peaks never came far down their slopes. But already, at the close of this Gathering Season, the white lace was drifting lower, as they could see.

Farn was eager to meet another young Dragon bonded as he was outside the Dragon Kin. He had felt a slight oddity in his position with others at the Gathering Place. Tika was more apprehensive. Despite Seela's words, she still retained the images of Nagums from tales told in long dark evenings.

The two wandered along, up the streamside, till they reached the place where it gushed from high in the mountain wall, frothing white as it fell. The force of its fall had gouged a basin where the water swirled then made its escape to tumble on down through the rocks. There was little vegetation, a coarse grass scattered thinly, lichens and mosses clinging to the water splashed sides of boulders and a very few starberry bushes.

Farn found a hopper colony, which provided him with a snack. Dabbling his hands in the snow cold stream, he asked over-casually, 'It hasn't been difficult to find Seela. Do you think this journey the Lady wants us to make will be much more difficult? Or dangerous?'

Tika draped her arm round his neck. 'I think it's all going to get very difficult. Fenj and Seela both feel worried to me. If *they* are worried, I think we will be scared stiff.'

Farn reluctantly agreed that that was what he had begun to suspect, but before more could be said, Seela spoke in their minds.

'Come to greet your companions! Ashta and Mimnan are here.'

Chapter Seven

Many, many leagues to the north, in the Realm of Ice, the Grey Guardian Rhaki was comfortably ensconced in his library. While far above him icy gales blasted the already heavily snow-covered mountains, here in his Stronghold he was warm and secure. He sat in a huge carved chair well padded with many fat cushions. His feet were stretched towards a glowing fire, the heap of ashes beneath the embers testifying to the fact it had been burning many hours.

Rhaki had been studying his books but now sat, his eyes fixed on the fire before him. He had spoken to Nula and realised she was of no further use to him. It had been only a minor experiment anyway. He had found it amusing that Emla seemed to place such faith in her oversized lizards. He had thought to try contacting one himself and tempting it away from Emla's influence.

When he last bespoke Nula, he had been amazed at the raging anger and dark insanity that answered him. She had killed the two incompetents who had failed her. She refused to speak to him when once she realised it was indeed Rhaki bespeaking her. Through the confused miasma of her mind he divined her plan to descend to the plains and destroy any two legs she could find.

He'd withdrawn his thoughts and laughed at how easily Emla's Dragons could be turned from her path to his. This was all trivial anyway; his main purpose was to obtain at least two of Emla's six remaining Weights. With one lost and, with luck, two more in his possession as soon as he could manage, the Balance would swing to him irrevocably.

Rhaki left his chair and paced to the long oak table heaped with books and parchments. He paced back to the fire, deep in thought, his great height and almost skeletally thin body casting a monstrous shadow in the dim light. He turned again, this time moving to a deep, curtained embrasure. He held back one of the heavy curtains and peered through the thick glass.

Snowflakes flattened where they hit and a sharp rattle could be heard from the grains of ice beating at the window. Not a night to be out, thought Rhaki. At least it would make Jal less likely to dawdle at any farm or tavern. The storm must be a blizzard down on the plains but Jal knew better than to plead bad weather to his master for too long a delay.

For a moon and a half, minds had been closed to Rhaki. He had been unable to sneak into any thoughts where Emla laid claim. He let the curtain drop back, shutting out the wild whiteness and returning to his worktable. He gazed unseeing at a map, held unwound by a book on one end and a lump of rock on the other.

Rhaki tried to imagine how the minds of a human or a Nagum would choose a route towards him. They had Dragons with them, but how or why they had made pets of a pair of young Dragons, Rhaki dismissed as of no importance. He was hoping Jal would at least have discovered their names. Once Rhaki had a name, he had something to work with. He had heard they had been seen in the foothills of the Spine Mountains. He mused again on the idea of pet Dragons. By the stars! A pair of fengars would have been less noticeable and more useful companions surely?

There came a gentle rap on his door. 'Come,' said Rhaki, moving back to his fireside chair.

Obviously Jal was intent on proving his devotion to duty; his hat was hung with rapidly melting icicles and his greatcoat was heavy with snow water. He started to squelch towards his master. 'Stay,' Rhaki ordered sharply, just before the man set a soaking boot to a rather valuable carpet.

'The two you sent me to seek after are within the maze of the upper Spine Mountains, Master. They would seem to be heading for the Highlands rather than directly here.'

'Seem? Do you not know more surely? What reports from the herders on the Middle Plains?'

'Master, some herders saw two Dragons with riders on their backs. There is turmoil at such tales. Even those who saw the Dragons try to believe they imagined such a sight. Those who did not see the Dragons pour scorn on the idea.'

'There has been no contact, no approach, made by the two I

seek to any others?'

'No Master, the opposite rather. They avoid humans and go far around towns and cities.'

'And their names?'

'I regret, no names were spoken Master.'

'Hmm,' Rhaki's long fingers drummed on the broad arms of his chair. Jal did not move, a puddle spreading from his boots and steam rising from his coat. Rhaki abandoned his thoughts, 'Go then Jal. Standing around in wet clothes will do you no good.' He waved dismissively and Jal bowed soggily and left his Master's presence.

So the Dragons were being used as transport, not just as pet companions as he had supposed. Rhaki decided that that proved how simple minded and docile they must be despite their great size. He felt Emla had made a sad misjudgement here; fengars were naturally aggressive and fought fang and hoof with their riders whereas a slow and ponderous Dragon would be of no significance. Misjudgement by Emla was advantage to himself.

They were in the Spine Mountains were they? He would appear to the Shardi later and tell them they could earn much of his pleasure by capturing these two servants of Emla's. And he would have to remember to be very clear that he meant he wanted them captured alive.

Rhaki pulled a tasselled cord beside the fireplace. At once, two knocks sounded on his door. 'Come, Bark.' Rhaki did not bother to turn as his body servant entered. 'I have work to do but I will need food later. Roast meat, cheese, fruit and hot wine outside the door in two hours. See to it Bark.'

'Yes Master.' Bark bowed his shadow-like form at Rhaki's back and silently departed.

Rhaki lifted a lantern from the mantelshelf and lit it with a taper from the fire. He took a heavy cloak from a hook and wrapped it around his tall body. Going to the wall opposite the fireplace, just beyond the long run of bookshelves, he laid his hand on the smooth rock. He moved his fingertips lightly, feeling for the slight indentations, then he pressed harder in a particular sequence. The apparently seamless rock opened smoothly into a dark space.

Stepping into the opening, Rhaki paused to touch points on the inner wall and silently the rock resealed itself. He had no real need of the lantern as he stepped quickly along the passageway. He knew this downward sloping path by heart. It amused him to use a light, as most humans would have to do. He had long ago accustomed himself to all things to do with darkness. Twenty minutes later, he was before an apparent dead end, but once again he pressed his fingertips to certain spots upon the cold rock. Once more, a doorway swung open and he left it open as he entered the chamber within.

Taking a taper from a jar on a shelf beside the entrance, he took flame from the lantern and touched it to candles set around the room. It was perhaps five man lengths across, and perfectly circular. The wall of living rock curved gently up to make a high domed roof. As each candle was lit, Rhaki kept his gaze firmly on the flame, never glancing to the centre of the room. When the last candle shone perfectly straight, he pinched out the taper, returning it to the jar.

Rhaki stood just inside the open door, his eyes on the rock before his feet. Slowly, he lifted his gaze to look on the Sacred Balance. Seven black disks gleaming dully in the steady candlelight, floated chest high from the floor. One of Emla's Weights WAS lost he thought exultantly, although he strained to keep his mind as calm as he could lest anyone or anything be observing him, unlikely as that might be.

The Weights had hung in their impossible suspension above an inlaid circle of crystal and gold set into the floor, always level with his eyes. At the end of the last Cold Season, he had come to this chamber and had been stunned to see they had begun to drop lower. It could only mean that Emla had lost one of her counter-weights. Rhaki had fled the chamber then, unable to control or conceal his excitement, but he had returned several times since to verify this unbelievable fact.

He dropped his gaze again and lifting the lantern, he turned to leave the chamber. Unable to resist the melodramatic gesture, he waggled his fingers as he closed the rock door, causing the candle flames to be instantly extinguished. He retraced his steps only a short way and halted by another door. This more conventional in that it was clearly outlined on the wall and opened towards him.

He entered a cupboard that in turn gave into a large room, faintly lit by glow lamps. A door on the opposite side of the room gave access to the household staff who worked in here. They had no knowledge of this rock doorway at the back of the cupboard, from where Rhaki could peep out to ensure he was alone.

This was where Rhaki kept various beasts. There were hoppers, squeakers, feathered singers and a few, very poisonous, writhers. After checking there were no servants cleaning or feeding the collection of animals, Rhaki swiftly left the cupboard and went to a caged run full of hoppers. They became tame very easily and now rushed to the side of their cage in the hope that this two legs had food for them.

Unlatching a small door, Rhaki thrust his hand inside, grasped a large black hopper and pulled it from the cage. It screamed eerily with the shock of being so suddenly removed from its brethren, but Rhaki held it firmly and took it with him, back through the cupboard.

Further yet up the rock passage went Rhaki and the now silently shivering hopper under his arm. Another hidden doorway, and Rhaki was in a room he used for certain rituals, magics, experiments. Putting the lantern he still carried on the tabletop, he then lifted the hopper so that it was face to face with him.

Rhaki began to chant softly, monotonously, staring into the hopper's large brown eyes, which quickly became glazed and fixed, its body relaxed and limp. He laid the hopper gently on the table, its ears drooping and its pink nose twitching with each breath. Still chanting, Rhaki pushed his cloak back, freeing his arms, and placed a large goblet upon the table beside the hopper.

From the hundreds of jars, and pots, and bottles, lining shelves on each wall, he chose certain pinches of needful ingredients. There was a great importance in adding these ingredients in the correct order, disaster could result from the slightest error – a sorely beset stomach being the very mildest of these.

Rhaki added a small quantity of wine – the very best from the distant South Land vineyards, and stirred the potion with a long sliver of bone. Laying aside the bone, he lifted a thin curved blade in his right hand while he turned the hopper with his left. The blade sliced down through the hopper's breast and Rhaki's fingers were seeking through the chest bones for the beating heart. He held the heart above the goblet, squeezing every drop of blood from it. Tilting his head, he swallowed the heart and raised the goblet to his lips. He drained the potion then turned to a smaller table where he sat gazing steadily into a bowl of glassy black stone. He put his bloody hands on either side of the bowl and stared into its emptiness with total concentration.

'Shardisi! Your Master is ready to speak to you!'

Inside the bowl, the blackness swirled as if a finger stirred paint. Colours flickered through the black, whirling dizzily. Gradually a scene began to clarify, becoming the interior of a cave of ice. Several white shapes appeared in the scene, slowly taking more solid form. A shaggy faced, hulking beast glared at Rhaki, whose body sat empty and rigid at the table in his stronghold. His spirit form was in the presence of these Shardisi, looking, he knew, completely solid. The terror plain in the yellow eyes made a mockery of the bared fangs and clenched claws of these slow-witted creatures.

Rhaki stood before them, calm and relaxed. One by one, the Shardisi fell to their knees, whimpers of fear replacing the snarls.

'Two will try to pass through your lands – small creatures of two-leg tribes. They may have Dragons with them.' Fear boiled off the hairy bodies at his feet. 'There is nothing to fear from Dragons, my fearless ones! The two-legs I would speak with, so you are to capture them for me. I repeat, they are to be brought to me alive or you will feel your Master's anger.' Moans came from the now prostrate Shardisi. 'Look at me Shardisi, look at your Master!'

Slowly and fearfully, yellow eyes lifted to look at Rhaki. He spread his open hands towards them. 'Please me, and I will give pleasure to you.' His form wavered, and winked out, the Shardisi now groaning and sighing as ecstatic pleasure pulsed through their ungainly bodies.

Rhaki stirred. He was slumped at the table, his outstretched hands empty, dropped beside the bowl. His heart raced and his head ached. Forcing himself to his feet, he poured a little wine into the goblet, swirling it around before drinking it. He took a soft cloth and wiped the goblet clean and dry before placing it beside the amplifying bowl. Such an expenditure of power always drained him utterly. But creatures such as the Shardisi had to be approached thus, they took notice of nothing more subtle.

The hopper's corpse Rhaki wrapped in another rag and took with him as he wearily left the room. It was a great effort to climb the passage back to his library and he sighed with relief as the rock door slid silently shut behind him. He doused the flame in the lantern and removed the cover from a glow lamp over the fireplace. He tossed a couple of logs, and the hopper, onto the embers of the fire and removed his cloak.

Outside the other door he found a large tray with covered dishes from which arose the inviting aroma of roast meat. He stooped, biting back a groan and making a mental note to have a higher bench put beside his door, and returned to his fireside with the tray. Despite his fatigue, he made himself eat the hot meat, and drink some of the spiced wine, to restore a little of the energy he had lost in contacting the Shardisi.

He ate some cheese and found himself going over recent events yet again: the death of Jerak, whose power all believed to be the strongest of all, yet he, Rhaki, had destroyed Jerak with his cunning and his superior craft. Then the first intimation that Emla had been so careless, so foolish, as to lose one of the Weights entrusted to her keeping.

Yet again, Rhaki started to go over his intricate plans to find that lost weight and to steal more from her, making his position finally unassailable. He leaned his head back on his chair and closed the dark eyes so deeply set in his gaunt face. No, no, he was far too exhausted for serious thought he told himself. He contemplated instead his dream of the future – a future in which he alone held the power of this world. The future in which Emla would have to beg him to spare the lives of her various creatures. He chuckled happily at the thought of a future in which all would tremble at the name of Rhaki and abase themselves before their Master.

Chapter Eight

As Rhaki slept his exhaustion away, so Emla was wide-awake. She sat on a simple stone bench in her moonlit Garden. Tomorrow the young ones would be in her presence and she must study them and make the decision that could so easily mean their destruction.

Emla was the One who spoke to all who would listen, and when the Linvaks from the Swamp Lands had made their approaches to her, she had been glad for the opportunity to help them from their darkness. She had ignored all those signs – the fact that her involuntary revulsion had not diminished the more she spoke with the Linvaks, rather the reverse. The fact that their servility never lessened; always they grovelled before her and agreed too quickly with all she said.

Emla had told herself this was all because they had been neglected, had had no true guidance since their creation and subsequent escape into the world. She was forced to admit that that escape should have been seen as suspicious even then. But despite Jerak's occasional discourses on the need for care, caution, and awareness of the dark side of the Balance, Emla had been engrossed in her work to the exclusion of all such warnings. And thus the Linvaks had been given the freedom of her House and Garden and had learned where the Sacred Balance was kept.

A morning came when Emla's maids told her the Linvaks had gone, vanished in the night. Emla had puzzled for a while as to both their unexpected arrival and now this equally unexpected departure. It was another day before she had cause to go to the Pavilion of the Sacred Balance. As soon as she entered and realised she had to tilt her head rather than be able to see the top weight at eye level, she knew. Six golden disks floated, a handspan apart, above the brilliant mosaic circle set into the floor. But the smallest, the seventh, was gone from the top of this floating column.

Anger and despair had alternated in her during the first days following her discovery. Of course, she had sent guards in the direction of the Swamp Land immediately. They returned saying they had found no trace of Linvak on the paths and trails at all. And she could make no contact through mind speech. None had seen Linvaks pass, humans, sky singers – no one at all.

For the first time, Emla directed men to stand watch day and night around the Pavilion and herself set certain other wards that would warn of any creature approaching her House. 'A bit late,' she imagined Jerak grumbling, 'but better late than never I suppose.'

She had examined every book she possessed that made any mention of the Scales of Balance. She had concluded that the loss of the smallest Weight, although serious enough, could be held in check with careful effort on her part. If her vigilance were to slip now though, she would face a hard struggle to maintain the equilibrium.

Emla had found among the books, and in some parchments written in Jerak's own hand, obscure references to Dragons. She had at first believed her tired brain was reading things not really there but as she worried at the phrases, gradually some clues seemed to emerge. She admitted to herself that she could be clutching at clouds, but determined to follow the clues and see whence they led her.

Emla had neglected the Dragon Kin over the cycles. She bespoke the elders of the Treasuries on occasion, but so many newer things had taken her attention that it was very long since she had thought closely of them. They had been one of the first creatures she had changed. Jerak had trained her, had shown her the possibilities lying dormant in so many of the creatures of this world.

She had begun working on her own, slipping into minds concerned only with daily survival. She saw how, by widening a pathway here and nudging a vague concept there, it was possible to expand these creatures' perceptions. Her first subjects had been feathered sky singers, as they were easy to keep caged and quickly lost their fears. She discovered they were very limited though, they showed no interest in other forms of life unless it was for crawlers, which they ate.

Then a hunter had brought her a great eyes with a damaged wing, and to Emla's astonishment he seemed to "overhear" her work with the sky-singers. She concentrated on working with the great eyes and within days had proved that he had an individual mind, which could respond to hers.

She widened her research to include squeakers and hoppers. Her results indicated that they saw themselves as integral parts of a group, not individuals – like the sky singers did, in fact. They were separate beings, but only really complete within their groups. Emla moved on then, to the creatures of the Plains – wapeesh, lumen, fengars.

To her surprise, she found little difference in these animals either. She realised that those who dwelt in close groups had enclosed minds: more solitary animals proved to have some interest in things outside of their immediate group needs. Many Seasons passed as Emla strove to understand the ways of so many varied minds. She had just discovered the Dragons, who in that long ago age lived only in the Spine Mountains, and with mounting excitement she was becoming aware of by far the greatest intelligence she had yet encountered.

While Emla was thus engrossed, her brother Rhaki was studying the Craft of Power with the Seniors in the ancient city of Gaharn at the foot of the High Lands. They had never been close, Rhaki taking pleasure from early childhood in teasing Emla, a teasing which grew gradually into a subtle but sadistic bullying. She learnt quickly to avoid both his company and his attempts to get into her mind. His ability to use the mind speech never progressed beyond the most elementary level while she found it as natural to use as vocal speech.

It was at this time, when Emla had made her first journeys to meet Dragons in their original Treasuries, that the Grey Guardian, Kovas, began to weaken. He had summoned Jerak and told him a successor must be appointed, as he would soon go beyond. Rhaki was Named Grey Guardian despite there being older and more experienced members of the Craft who may have hoped for the honour. But Rhaki was the closest in the blood lineage and thus was raised to the Guardianship.

He gloated openly to Emla while remaining modest before all others. She had been Named successor to the Golden Lady whilst still a small child and it had rankled bitterly that Rhaki, the elder of the two, had not also been Named. But now, he was already come into his Power while she was still playing games with her pets! With a great fuss and magnificent ceremony, Rhaki left Gaharn for the Realm of Ice.

Twelve cycles after Rhaki had departed, Emla came to this House to spend the last Seasons with Caris before she went beyond and Emla took her place as the Golden Lady. Tales of Rhaki's increasing power spread through the lands, although he never returned to Gaharn. At the time of Emla's raising to the Ladyship, Jerak spoke to her of his growing fear for Rhaki. The Power had begun to control Rhaki rather than he control the Power. He refused to respond to mind speech or to letters sent by Jerak and the Seniors. Rumours spread of great, hair covered, killing beasts Rhaki had brought into being to protect his Realm. Tales of two-leg tribes whom Rhaki had altered to something far less than human, which he had been dissatisfied with so had set loose into the world. Thus such as Linvaks came to be.

And Jerak. His fears finally decided him to journey to the Realm of Ice personally, to face Rhaki to discover what he planned and to remonstrate at his misuse of the Power. Not one soul knew exactly what transpired, except that there was dispute between Rhaki and the ancient one Jerak. Jerak would argue with words, but Rhaki would argue with the Power, forcing Jerak to use a Craft he had not called upon since time out of mind.

For many days, lights blazed luridly in the northern skies, by day and by night. The ground trembled and all things went creeping in terror. All the people of Gaharn knew when Jerak fell. They all cried out in pain as a great heat screamed through each and every one of them. The heat was followed by a numbing cold and utter silence. The Seniors and Emla tried again and again to reach Jerak's mind but met only silent cold. Rhaki appeared before them as they sat Gathered, his spirit form showing by its solidity just how full of Power he was, and told them arrogantly that Jerak was no more, and he, Rhaki, wished no further intrusions in his Realm.

Season followed Season, and life went on in its balanced way. Seniors continued their work, students studied the many disciplines under the Seniors' watchful eyes, and the human

66

citizens of the Realm of Gaharn lived their peaceful lives.

But now the Linvaks had stolen a Weight of Balance. Emla consulted the Seniors and Iska, Yash and Kemti moved up from the city to the Lady's House in the High Lands. These four pored through the books and documents to learn how they might locate and retrieve the gold weight. Another Senior, Yar, spent his days far seeking the Linvak until finally he glimpsed a place deep below ground, where the weight shone in darkness. Yar was of very great age and this concentrated task exhausted him. He was able to indicate a southerly direction as being where the Linvaks hiding place was but then the Senior healers insisted he must work no more at such intensity.

In gratitude, Emla sent him to a House of Rest a few leagues distant and begged him to remain there as long as he wished or needed. Perhaps the beauty of the place would soothe him and inspire him to compose some of the music for which he was famed.

Yash had concluded that the reference to Dragons that Emla had uncovered in Jerak's writings was of vital importance now. He questioned Emla closely on all she could tell of the Dragon Treasuries. He was surprised by the great intelligence, morality and sense of kinship Emla described to him. Everyone knew of Emla's fascination with the workings of the minds of all living things, but most assumed the interest was of a purely basic and academic nature.

As the Season of Soft Rain followed the Cold Season when the weight was lost, Iska and Yash withdrew to another Pavilion within Emla's Gardens. They remained in seclusion, working with the Power, as day followed day. The Hot Season was beginning when the two Seniors emerged. Emla and Kemti were shocked by their frailness. They had worked nearly two moon cycles and were spent and exhausted, but they could report success.

'We found two young ones whose minds differ from all others but have similarities with each other. These two we contrived to be in place in time for the hatching of Dragon broods.' Iska sipped the hot tea and moaned with pleasure. 'It was luck that two of the best Dragon females had eggs at this particular juncture.' She put her head on one side thoughtfully. 'Then again, perhaps luck had nothing to do with it.'

'Who can tell?' agreed Kemti. 'We never imagined any would steal one of the Weights of Balance and who, even among us, would have guessed what Emla has disclosed to us of the Dragon minds? All this great length of time, none else thought to delve deeper into all creatures as she has done. Perhaps if we had the right books, or understood some of the seeming riddles in the ones we do have, we would find that all this is foretold.'

Yash nodded. 'I feel strongly that these events are part of the Pattern. When we first touched the mind of the human child, both Iska and I were aware of something falling into place. The same when we found the Nagum child. It is meant, I am sure, Lady.'

'So now we must wait, more than one moon cycle, and hope we have chosen correctly and the bonded pairs will seek us willingly.'

Thus had it happened, and now Emla sat alone waiting for the stars to fade. With the new day would come also the bonded ones, and she must judge whether they were strong enough to face what they must. Kemti was still at work on the piles of books he had gathered from Emla's library; Iska and Yash slept already, still easily fatigued despite the help of senior healers and cosseting by Emla's household.

It had been agreed that Emla would greet these four young ones alone, in the quiet and calm of her Garden. Only when she felt the four had no fears of her would she call the Seniors to join them. This plan had displeased only Gan Jar-Sarl, the Chief of her Guard. He was also a Senior, strong in the Power, but he had chosen the freer life in the Lady's Guards rather than the confinement of study or classroom.

Eventually Emla agreed that Gan could stay by the long veranda encircling the main House so that he could witness this meeting. No one else was to dare even to peep from behind a curtain. Emla wanted nothing to upset or frighten her guests.

A shawl was wrapped gently across her shoulders and she turned to smile at Shan. Her personal maid tugged Emla's hand gently. 'Please my Lady, come to your rooms for a little while. It will be dawn soon enough. Rest while I prepare a bath for you.'

Emla glanced at the sky. Yes, it was indeed nearing dawn. 'Very well, I shall bathe and take some tea and perhaps some honeybread.' She stood, slipped her arm round her maid's waist and laughed softly. 'And then you can help me dress and make me look wonderful for our guests!'

Chapter Nine

Emla stood, midmorning sunlight making her robes shimmer around her tall figure in ever-changing colours, and waited calmly. Two specks in the southern sky grew bigger until they could be seen to be pale blue and pale green Dragons. They drew closer and now two figures were visible, sitting behind the Dragons' wings.

The Seniors, hidden within the House, stared at each other in amazement as their minds were filled with a glorious song of praise and greeting to the Lady. Four very different voices, but harmonising perfectly in their song.

The Dragons were circling now, finally gliding to land before the Lady. She looked at them for a moment, too overcome suddenly to speak. The young Dragons shining with life and newness, their two riders unkempt and ill clothed, but standing tall as the Dragons stood erect to make a formal greeting.

Suddenly Farn and Ashta looked worried, prismed eyes whirred rapidly. The human and the Nagum turned to the Dragons in concern. It was Farn who finally addressed Emla. 'Lady, we do not know the proper greeting for you. We are ashamed to dishonour you.'

Emla laughed, knowing suddenly all was well. She moved closer to the four, her hands outstretched. 'It matters not, my dear ones, you are here and that is what matters. I am Emla and I bid you warm welcome.'

Human and Nagum found Emla's arms around their shoulders. 'I had thought we would talk,' said the Lady, 'but I should have known you would be weary and hungry.' She laughed at the surge of agreement from four young minds. 'Come then, and take no notice of Gan and his sword – he will do you no harm!' They were near enough to the House now for Gan to hear the last remark and he glared at the Lady in outrage.

'Shan! Bara!' The maids came running to the door and

stopped to stare. 'Close your mouths girls! These are my guests. Fetch tea and juices and all the foods you can think of! We will sit here in the sun.' The maids rushed to obey and Emla bespoke the Dragons regarding food for them. 'We ate well this morning, but Mim and Tika tire of meat and there has been little fruit for them where we have journeyed,' Ashta answered her.

Farn and Ashta reclined on the soft lawn edging the verandah and Tika and Mimnan automatically sat leaning against the Dragons. Emla was about to suggest they join her beside a low table but thought better of it on seeing how at ease they looked where they were.

Ashta's eyes whirred as the Seniors came out of the House.

Iska spoke first, looking straight into Ashta's eyes. 'I had not realised how beautiful you are.'

Kemti and Yash murmured their agreement. Farn's head stretched a little higher and Tika laughed. Farn glanced down at her and drooped a little. 'Sorry.' The Seniors were not sure they had heard correctly and looked a little puzzled.

At that moment though, the maids returned with trays laden with all kinds of different pies and tarts and breads. 'Come, help yourselves,' Emla invited. She gave a warning look to the Seniors whose minds were quivering with questions. 'Eat your fill, Tika and Mimnan,' she said. 'Perhaps you may feel like telling us your stories when you have eaten enough.'

Mimnan, having reseated himself beside Ashta with a heaped plate of delicacies, rose to his feet again. He bowed carefully to Emla and said aloud in a gently fluting voice, 'If it please your Ladyship, you must call this one Mim. We do not use our whole names until we are considered responsibly grown.' He blushed, the red of his cheeks clashing with his russet curls, and sat down again.

'Aah. Mim,' repeated Emla thoughtfully. 'Tika is the correct name for you?'

'Well.' Tika rose as Mim had done to speak to the Lady. 'I was called Chena when I was a slave, but Kija – that's Farn's mother you know – she called me Tika. It means "small one" in the Dragon tongue.' She thought for a moment. 'I will always be called Tika now I think my Lady.'

When Tika and Mim had eaten, both of them relishing the

71

change from meat only for nearly every meal, it was decided that Tika and Farn should tell their tale first. Emla asked, 'Mim, Ashta, would you like to stay or is there anything you wish to see or do that I can provide?'

'Mim would see your Garden, Lady.' Ashta said as Mim leaned against her, blushing again.

'Of course! Gan,' she called. 'Ask someone to find Lorak and have him come to us please.'

Very shortly, an elderly battered looking human male appeared before Emla. He gave a creaky bow. 'Lorak, my guest would see the Garden. He is called Mim and knows much of plants I believe.' She smiled at Mim. 'And Ashta?'

'I would see these plants also my Lady,' replied Ashta. 'I know a little of medicine plants, but I would learn more.'

Lorak glanced at both Ashta and Farn, showing not a flicker of surprise at the sight of Dragons. 'You won't see the Garden at its best of course,' he said. 'Already the frosts have finished many of the flowers.'

'Lorak, you know full well, the Garden is always perfect for each Season. Take Ashta and Mim then and let them share some of your growing magic.'

Lorak and Mim bowed and, with Ashta, set off along the side of the great House.

'I wonder, do all gardeners always complain?' Emla asked thoughtfully. 'Too much sun, too much rain, too little rain, too cold, even though the Garden looks quite beautiful even as they complain.'

'Lady,' Iska reminded Emla firmly, 'we would hear the story these two can tell us.'

While Tika and Farn were beginning their tale, Mim was gazing ecstatically at a cluster of shining white cup blossoms. His three fingered hands reached to not quite touch each perfect trumpet bloom. 'These have ever been this one's favourite of all,' he told Lorak.

'Hmmph. Awkward things to grow I find. They sulk if you try to move them.'

'If you tell them why you have to move them,' Mim explained earnestly, 'and take a great deal of the earth they are already

72

rooted in, they will move happily.'

'Really?' Lorak studied Mim more closely. Mim's very broad upper face, with the large eyes tilted sharply upwards at the outer corners, narrowed quickly to a pointed chin. Lorak realised the blue eyes had vertical pupils, that was what seemed "different". 'What are you boy, you are not human nor are you one of the Lady's folk?'

'This one is Nagum. We spend our lives caring for growing things, in a land far from here.' The fluting voice held tones of wistfulness.

Lorak's gaze rested on Ashta, whose long face was buried in a low spreading green bush. She spoke in Lorak's mind. 'These are good to eat slowly when the body feels too hot.'

'We call it fever break.' Lorak took a leaf in his twisted fingers, a bitter scent rising as he bent the leaf in half. Time passed swiftly as Mim and Lorak exchanged tips for successful gardening. Lorak was highly gratified by Mim's rapture when shown the vegetable section. Ashta listened, occasionally asking a question, but mainly glad that Mim was so happy.

Then Yash bespoke them to ask if they would speak with the Seniors now, and both Lorak and Mim were startled to see how low the sun had already sunk. They made their way back to the verandah to find Tika and Farn gone, apparently with Gan Jal-Sarl. Lorak surprised Emla and the Seniors, and probably himself, by bowing deeply to Mim as he left. 'An honour to show you the Garden, Mim. I would be pleased should you care to visit again. You know where to find my workshop.' He winked, bowed to Ashta and stumped back across the velvet lawns.

'Well,' said Emla. 'I've never known him so polite.' She looked at Mim with interest.

'He was most kind to this person my Lady. This one's heart is much gladdened to have seen your wonderful blossoms.'

'We have heard how Tika and Farn became bonded and of their troubled beginning. Which of you will tell us your tale?'

Ashta's faceted eyes flashed rapidly. Mim leant back against her as she said, 'Mim will tell how he came to my mother's nesting cave in time to bond with me. Then I will tell the rest.'

One of Mim's hands clasped a pendant hanging from a chain round his neck, while the other hand continually caressed Ashta's wing. He took a deep breath. 'This person was in the woodland beyond the village, seeking seeds of a plant that his mother deeply desired. He was alone, even the small brother this one usually had with him was left at home. You see, they were very special seeds, most hard to find, and this one was seeking them to give as a gift. He was far from the village when smoke was in the air. The trees were nervous, they always are when untame fire is loose. It took this one much time to return.'

Mim stopped, his huge slanted eyes brimming with tears. Ashta rumbled in agitation and Emla said quietly, 'You do not have to tell any more Mim. If you would open your mind and allow us to see, it will be less sore for you my dear.' Mim nodded once, closed his eyes and relaxed against Ashta.

The Seniors and the Lady saw devastation. Smouldering ruins where only a brief time before small dwellings had stood. Amidst the smoking heaps of tumbled walls were other heaps they saw, as Mim had done, the charred bodies of his parents, his baby brother, cousins, neighbours and friends.

It was Linvak work. When Mim's wits gathered themselves a little, when the first appalling shock was ebbing, he realised the whole place stank of Linvaks. Mim did not remember how many days it took him to bury all the members of his small community. He planted the seeds he had gathered around his family, and then he left. He wandered aimlessly back into the woodlands, finally collapsing under a bell tree and sleeping for he knew not how long.

He woke to a bright morning sky and to the woodland softly murmuring around him. He had only the clothes he was wearing, every other article in the village had been destroyed. He looked in each direction, then, weeping again, he gently plucked a bell flower from the tree above him and tossed it in the air. Whichever direction it landed in, that was the way he would go. It was of little importance to him now. The bell flower settled softly and Mim began walking.

In four days he was clear of the dense woodlands he was accustomed to and climbing ever steeper slopes. He ate berries and shoots that he gathered as he walked, and drank water from the busy streams. But as the trees became fewer and the land more mountainous, food was in short supply. Finally the icy stream he had been climbing beside, disappeared under rocks. Mim sat for a while by the birthplace of the little stream and gazed back the way he'd come. The woodlands were in truth already leagues behind him. He looked up at the way he seemed to have chosen. Sheer cliffs confronted him, cracked with gullies and scarred by rock falls.

He got to his feet and began to climb. He had nearly gained the top of a crag when small stones began to patter down, prelude perhaps to a more serious fall of rock. Looking to each side, he saw the barest ledge to his left. His four bare toes clung to this tiny lip and he pressed himself as tight to the crag as he could. His outstretched hand suddenly discovered space, not stone. Mim realised he didn't really care much as to what happened, he just hoped death didn't hurt too badly. As the ledge beneath his toes began to disintegrate he launched himself round and into the emptiness.

He slid a short distance, was jolted to a stop and spun sideways. He raised his head to see he was at the mouth of a shadowed cave. He imagined a pair of eyes glittering with colours was staring at him. Then he lost consciousness.

The silvery green She Dragon, Hani lived apart from others of her Treasury. She liked solitude and found Gatherings exhausting. Hani dreamed of the music the winds made as they chased through and over her mountains. She dreamed of the flowers she had spied far down in the woodlands, that they suddenly bloomed, all their riotous colours covering these grey and barren rocks.

Hani had been dreaming as she waited for her three eggs to hatch when a noise had disturbed her. She investigated the entrance area of her nesting cave and found Mim. His curly hair was the exact shade of the flowers Hani had thought most enchanting in the woodlands. That fact, combined with the pain and distress filling his small body, made her carry him gently back to lie by her eggs.

When he woke, he showed no surprise or fear, being so lost in his unhappiness. Until, that is, Hani's first born daughter wobbled out of her shell. Then Mim gasped and held his hands out to the beautiful hatchling, crying, 'This one is honoured to greet you!'

Emla watched, sitting as still as stone, as Ashta lowered her graceful head to press her brow to Mim's. His eyelashes were damp with tears but he smiled sweetly at Ashta. She raised her head to look at the Seniors seated beside Emla. 'And so I was bonded with Mim. Mother placed some memories with Mim when she saw what had happened. She far spoke Fenj and Kadi, and they told her it was meant to be so.

'When I was able to fly strongly enough, Mother sent us to the Sun Treasury, to Seela. That is where we met Tika and Farn. At the Gathering Place of the Sun Treasury there is a hidden cave that Seela showed to us. Tika came, but she refused to allow Farn to enter with us.' Ashta's eyes paled and had a slightly unfocused look.

Mim shook her arm and explained to Emla: 'There was a great pile of sparkling things. This person had to find an ornament and a short knife amongst these treasures.' He held up a white gold and amber pendant, the twin to Tika's yellow gold one, and the knife he had at his belt. 'Tika said she found the Dragons become fascinated with sparkling things, which they collect. They even forget time so days go past while they look at their collection. Seela did not come in with us, but it was difficult to make Ashta stop gazing at all the bright stones.'

Mim sat back against Ashta again as she continued their story. 'And the next day we began our journey here. Seela warned us to be wary and to keep from towns or two leg tribes. We were surprised one dawn by some herders on the Middle Plains. They made a great noise and threw things at us, but we flew swiftly from that place and took no hurts.'

Ashta's eyes flared dark red suddenly. 'Twice, Lady, there was a great coldness, a darkness, that tried to creep into all our minds. Tika found it went away if we sang; while our minds were busy with song, there was no space for the darkness to slip in. But we do not understand what it could be.' She waited a moment but as Emla remained silent, Ashta concluded, 'And so we came to you, Lady, to do whatever you bid us do.'

Silence reigned as Ashta's telling ended. No one moved for several minutes, then Iska shivered. 'It is nearly dark!' she exclaimed. 'Where are Tika and Farn?'

'Farn has hunted and brought meat for me to the border of

your Garden, Lady.' Ashta moved away from Mim and lifted gracefully into the evening sky, and as she did so, Tika and Gan returned to the company.

'I had rooms prepared for you within the House, but I think you will prefer to stay in one of the guest pavilions. Shan!' Emla's maid appeared at her side. 'Have you readied the place for my guests? Hot water, night gowns, glow lamps?'

Shan grinned. 'And hot soup on its way Lady and a few other titbits.'

'Good.' Emla returned her maid's smile. 'Then I will wish you good night, dear ones. Farn and Ashta will know where you are, of course?'

As Mim and Tika nodded, Emla rose. 'Go with Shan then and tell her of anything you need. We will meet at breakfast. Sleep well!'

As Shan led the human and Nagum away, all heard her whisper, 'What's it like, flying through the air?'

'We'd better question Shan later, she will probably have found out far more important things than we have done!' Yash said ruefully.

'Come,' Emla entered the House. 'And you Gan. I told the girls to prepare a meal for us in the library and then to leave us till the morning. We have much to consider.'

They ate in silence for a while. Emla's tall figure folded onto a stool at one side of the bright fire while equally tall Iska lay back on one of several couches grouped around the hearth. Gan remained standing with Yash, one each side of Kemti's chair.

'We learned much, but nothing relevant to the retrieving of the Balance Weight,' Yash broke the silence.

'They – the human and Nagum – have no idea of the perils they face.' That was Gan. 'The human has no notion how to use a sword and, from what she told me, the Nagum will refuse to use a weapon anyway. Tika seems quick witted, more so than many humans I've encountered. I have yet to assess the Nagum, but my feeling is there is a deepness in him. The question is, what does that deepness contain?'

'Emla, what did you tell the Dragons of us when you first contacted them?' Kemti leant forward for her reply.

Emla sipped her spiced tea and continued to study the fire flames. 'I told them we were an ancient people. That our minds used the Power and no other two-legs seemed to do so. That some other creatures did have a small knowledge of the Power. And that,' she turned to face Kemti, 'is absolutely all I told them.'

'And yet,' said Iska softly.

'Yes,' agreed Emla. 'I too was shocked at the repetition of that phrase – "go safely beyond". I have never heard it spoken to or by any other creatures than ourselves.'

'So why do the Dragons use it, and what does it mean to them? Would these young Dragons know?'

'I do not think so Yash, they do not have the full memories they would have received if they had bonded within the Dragon Kin. And,' Emla added, 'what did you think of those two?'

'They are so beautiful,' sighed Iska. 'Such colours, such delicacy in their faces, such eyes!'

Emla laughed and Yash groaned. 'Obviously Iska is now their devoted champion!' said Kemti, and even Gan's stern face twitched with amusement. 'Seriously, I felt great steadiness and strength in their minds. Their bodies are clearly magnificent. I would suggest that Ashta is the stronger character – she seemed older than Farn at times although they are almost exactly the same age. Also the death of Krea has left a scar in his mind, despite the healing he was given. It is apparent in a certain insecurity he displays, an unsureness.' Kemti looked to the others for any disagreement so far.

'Their talk of darkness worries me,' said Gan. 'My first instinct says it was the Guardian trying to bespeak or coerce them.'

'My feeling too,' Emla agreed.

'But Tika worked out a way to block him, and very quickly too. That gives me some hope for them.'

'Yash and I have narrowed the area to search for the Balance Weight, which the Linvaks have hidden. It is still far inside Linvak territory, which, as you are all aware, is a damp, treacherous ground with a jungle type of woodland over much of it. I wonder though if it is a false trail Yar was allowed to glimpse?' They were all listening intently to Iska now. 'You said he saw the Weight underground. The Linvak dwell in the Swamp

78

Lands – hardly suitable ground to go digging tunnels in I would suggest.'

Gan began to pace. 'You are right Iska. It must be a false clue poor Yar was given. But then we are back at the beginning again. You sent me straight in the direction of the Linvaks homeland, quite understandably at the time, Lady.' He bowed in half apology to Emla. 'Perhaps that was what whoever planned this theft intended and the Linvaks went – elsewhere. It may not be too late to stir a memory among some of the farmers close by the city or this House, Lady. Linvaks travelling through their fields would not be soon forgotten.'

'See to it, Gan, at first light.' Emla's eyes had a spark of hope in them as she gave the order. 'One more thing.' Emla stopped them as they began to move to the door. 'We have to discuss Jerak.'

Yash raised an eyebrow. 'Jerak is dead Emla. What is there to discuss?'

'No,' said Iska. 'Jerak is not beyond – surely that is an obvious fact? We would know if he had gone beyond.'

'Then where is he?' Yash asked in exasperation born of weariness.

'Is the Guardian really strong enough to hold such a one as Jerak?' Kemti sounded doubtful.

'Wherever Jerak is, he is not beyond. I agree with Iska completely on that point. But he is also not here.' Emla placed her teacup carefully on a side table. 'So should we name a new Justice, and if so, who?'

Chapter Ten

Shan tapped the door lightly and entered Emla's bedchamber. She put a tray bearing herb tea and hot bread rolls beside the bed and stood back. 'Good morning my Lady. Which robe will you wear today?'

'Good morning Shan. I think the darker green, with the embroidered sky singers.' Emla sat against her pillows drinking her tea as her maid went to select the robe from the connecting dressing room. As Shan returned, smoothing the soft fabric as she laid it on a couch, she glanced at Emla through her lashes.

'What is it Shan?' Emla smiled. 'Tell me.' She patted the side of the bed invitingly.

Shan plumped herself down beside the Lady. 'Well. Those two guests of yours, not the Dragons.'

'Go on.'

'I thought the one called Tika was but a child, maybe nine or ten Cold Seasons old. I could scarce believe it when she said this will be her fifteenth Cold Season!' Shan drew her legs up on the bed and went on. 'She is so small Lady, and I do not think she will grow more than another three or four fingers at most. Then she said she was human.' Shan's eyes were round with the pleasure of gossip. 'Truly, Lady, I had thought she was a child of your people – she looks so like you, especially. But if she is so small, she cannot be. But I have never met a human like her.'

Emla coughed as tea went down the wrong way.

'Why, Lady, I was younger than this Tika when you first chose me as your special maid, and I was bigger than her even then. And look how I have grown since.' Shan leaped from the bed to twirl in front of Emla to underline her point. Her blonde braid swung heavily at her back. It reached to her narrow waist above which swelled a very generous bosom balancing equally generous hips below. Emla knew very well that over the last four or five Cold Seasons, Shan had been happily fending off the attentions of most of the male members of the household staff, probably including old Lorak she thought grimly.

'Yes indeed Shan, you have certainly grown.' Emla pushed aside the bedcovers. 'I will bathe and dress now. Send someone to Lord Kemti please, telling him I will be in the library before breakfast and wish to speak with him there.'

Shortly thereafter, Emla entered the library to find Kemti standing by one of the long windows. He came towards her, asking, 'What is it Emla? Have you discovered something new?'

'I do not know,' she replied. 'Listen closely.' Quickly she related Shan's words. 'Could it be possible a human has our blood? But it has been forbidden since the beginning. Human females were so damaged if they were bred with us. If they did conceive, most miscarried the offspring and then died themselves, or they bore a weakly child which did not long survive. I have to know if this is a possibility Kemti.'

'The idea was abandoned so long ago. Who would have considered attempting such crossbreeding again now?' He frowned, the Guardian uppermost in both his and Emla's thoughts.

'I will study the patterns of both young ones. But I will discuss this with no one Emla. I think it best we keep this idea to ourselves until we can be sure, one way or the other.'

Over breakfast, it was agreed that Farn, Ashta and Mim would spend the morning with Gan, as he tried to evaluate their physical strengths and weaknesses. Tika was to go with Iska and Yash, and they would try to discover the extent of her mental differences from humans they had previously examined.

Tika and Mim had slept soundly in the pavilion to which Shan had led them the previous evening. A fire burned cheerfully in a large hearth and glow lamps made the main room bright. There were four sleeping chambers and two washing chambers, with great tubs already filled with hot water, curving behind the main room.

Two very young maids were to attend Tika and two young boys attended Mim, all under Shan's expert eye. The baths had been a revelation to Tika and Mim. After an initial reluctance to immerse themselves, they had wallowed luxuriously until the water grew cool. They found their clothes had vanished when they emerged from their tubs but were each wrapped in thick woollen robes and taken to the fireside. There they ate a warming supper and then found their heads nodding and their eyes closing. Farn and Ashta already slept on the open sided veranda encircling the pavilion as Mim and Tika sank into comfortable beds. New clothes awaited them when they woke, obviously copied from their old travel worn ones, by someone during the night. Now, breakfast finished, the two Dragons and Mim left with Gan, and Tika looked a little nervous.

'Why do we not walk a little, so you too can admire Lorak's work?' Iska smiled.

'I know little of plants, Lady Iska,' replied Tika. 'I would like to walk though.'

'You do not have to call us Lord or Lady,' Yash told her, as he and Iska walked one each side of her. 'It is a formality but not always necessary.'

They were some distance from the main House by now and Tika suddenly exclaimed at the path they walked on. 'How are these patterns made? It must have taken a great time to find so many pebbles just the same colour and size.' Iska and Yash watched as Tika stepped along a line of grey blue stones. She turned with the design and came back to where she had started. Then she followed a line of black stones. 'It's a spiral, isn't it?' she asked. 'It looks so simple, but how hard it must have been to make it just so.'

The three strolled on, Tika delighting to find various stone patterns set into the broad paths everywhere two or more paths joined each other. They spoke easily of many things, Iska and Yash changing topics seemingly at random. They reached a meeting place of five paths, in the centre of which was set a low walled, star shaped pool. Tika admired the glazed tiles picking out yet another spiral pattern around the walls before she glanced at the pool itself.

'Whatever are those?' She was looking at several very large golden swimmers, lazily finning through the clear water. Iska sat on the wall and dabbled her fingers in the water. The swimmers drifted towards her, gently nibbling her fingers.

'We call them sunfish. They just seem to float about, eat, and look beautiful. Quite a good life I suppose, but a little boring after a while I would imagine!'

Tika laughed as the sunfish came hopefully to her fingers. Yash joined them on the wall. 'I was just thinking how nice a cup of tea and a little something to nibble would be, myself.' He looked questioningly at Tika.

'Sounds a good thought to me,' she agreed.

Retracing their steps, Tika stopped suddenly on the middle of one of the stone patterns. 'That's what it was,' she exclaimed. Iska and Yash awaited enlightenment. 'As we flew in towards the House, it all made a pattern. From higher, you can see the House, and the pavilions set around, and lines of tapisi, and curves of lawn, and clumps of small fruit trees, then single bell trees marking points in the pattern.'

Tika looked at the two Seniors. 'Of course, you would know all that, knowing this House as you must.'

'I think I read something about it.' Yash answered, adding casually, 'Can you read Tika? Did you have books in the town you lived in – Return, I think you called it?'

Tika seemed uncomfortable with the question. 'A few people could read. It was said to be a strong magic, too strong for most of us, especially for slaves and women of any class.'

'But,' Yash prompted her gently.

'There was one old woman I had to do certain tasks for quite often. She was a relation of the Lord's so she was of some rank. She was always reading when I was in her rooms. Sometimes she talked to me, quite kindly, sometimes she read little pieces out loud from her book. She made me stand by her and she would point to the marks as she said the words. One day, I had been cleaning her rooms, and she pointed at some marks and asked if I knew what they meant – and I did! There were several clumps of marks that I had got to recognise.

'The old woman was very sick though, and the last time I saw her she lay in her bed. She told me to fetch her a book and then to find some of the marks I knew. When I did she took the book away again.'

They had reached the veranda now and Yash and Iska sat on the first step while they waited for Tika to finish. Her voice was low and she looked out over the gardens rather than at the Seniors as she said: 'The old one said I would be killed as a magic maker if any discovered I could read the marks. I must never let anyone know of it. Then she sent me from her and the overseer came to me later and said she had ordered that I be beaten.' She drew a shaky breath. 'When I woke after the beating, I heard someone say the old one had died. I have tried to forget the marks in the books since that time.'

Yash rose to his feet, holding a hand out to pull Iska up. He put his other hand lightly on Tika's shoulder. 'Let us find some tea, child, and something to eat.'

Farn and Ashta were demonstrating the strength of their fire to Gan, trying to focus the gout of flame that emerged when they belched. Mim met Tika and the two Seniors as they crossed the entrance hall of the House.

'The Lord Kemti asks will you go to the library for a few minutes Tika. This one has just come from there now.' In a tight beam of mind speech directed to Tika alone, he added, 'He stared at this one for a while and made marks on some parchment. Then he stared some more, then he said this one could go.'

When Tika rejoined the others, the conversation dwelled only on mundane matters – the weather, the gathered crops, the standard of wool from the Lady's herds of lumen, and the sudden departure of travelling sky singers

'Do as you will for a while, young ones. We have tasks we must busy ourselves with. If you need anything at all, do not hesitate to ask any of the house people.' Iska was following Yash to the door as she spoke.

A great crack, then a crash, shook the room at that moment, and the Seniors were not far behind Tika and Mim as they raced out of the building. 'Farn!' screamed Tika's mind as Mim's was calling for Ashta.

They found a fair crowd with the two Dragons in an area behind the House – obviously a stable yard. Fengars were shrieking, eyes rolling as they put their heads over half doors. Their fangs were bared and the doors shook as hooves thrashed in frenzied attempts to get out and do battle.

Gan was sitting on the ground before Farn and Ashta and looked dazed. Mim felt Ashta's guilt at perhaps hurting this two-legs, while Tika was swamped by Farn's embarrassment. 'I did not wish to damage anything Tika, really!' Farn said in a rush, eyes whirring frantically. 'This Gan asked if we could burn stone such as the piece on top of the roof. I said "of course" and I thought he intended me to do so! So I did, and I could, and it fell just beside him. I meant no hurt Tika!'

Tika stroked Farn's face soothingly. 'No harm was done – I don't think.' She looked at Gan. Several people were assisting him to his feet. He looked at the sculptured figure shattered beside him for a few moments, various expressions chasing across his face. Then he looked at Farn. All shades of blue were whirring in the Dragon's eyes and he moaned sadly in Tika's mind. As she continued to calm him, she realised Gan was now staring at her. Eyes as sapphire as Farn's glared at her furiously.

Tika appealed urgently to Mim and he helped her to repress a terrible urge to shriek with laughter. Then Iska's head blocked Gan's stare as she patted dust from the Chief of Guards and asked if he was injured. Voices calling explanations to new arrivals on the scene and the fengars' continuing cacophony deafened and pained Mim's sensitive ears badly. He turned away with Ashta's head at his shoulder and moved towards the gardens. Tika and Farn followed them closely. Tika then led them to the star shaped pool beyond the sight of the House.

She and Mim sat on the wall, mutually agreeing it might be best, given the circumstances, to give Gan adequate time to calm himself somewhat. Farn recovered quickly from his agitation, finally remarking, 'Of course I knew I was able to knock down stone,' with his usual innocent self-confidence. Then he went to see what was fascinating Ashta in the pool. He lounged beside her, their chins resting on the wall, as they stared enchanted at the sparkling sunfish.

'Do humans always talk so loudly?' Mim asked Tika. 'This person has only seen a few human hunters passing through the Nagum woodlands, and they were not loud.' His ears had folded over themselves tightly to protect his highly sensitive hearing. Tika averted her gaze as Mim's ears slowly and cautiously uncurled and moved, quivering, in different directions. She had seen his strange ears in action before but still found it rather disconcerting.

Tika showed Mim the patterns in the stone paths. Mim was

interested, his three long delicate fingers tracing along the patterns. 'This person thinks they must mean something quite special, so much work to make them. But it is too hard for this one to understand the meanings.' Tika agreed but then suggested they get the Dragons away from the pool. She had the definite feeling that the sunfish were fascinating them as thoroughly as the sparkling jewels had done in the Treasury collections.

She was right. Neither she nor Mim could distract them through mind speech, resorting eventually to physically pulling and pushing them to get their eyes turned from the swimmers. Some time had passed since the mishap in the stable yard by the time Farn and Ashta were persuaded to move back along the path to the House. Once they were on the lawns, Mim advised the pair to hunt together and then to return quietly to the pavilion where they had spent the night.

Blue and green eyes flashed questioningly. Mim and Tika exchanged glances, then Mim sighed as he explained, 'When there has been trouble, it is sensible to keep out of the way for a while. If you are seen, it seems to remind the annoyed one to immediately recall the trouble, and to start the scolding all over again.' Tika nodded in firm agreement. Both Dragons pressed their brows against their riders' brows, then lifted gracefully from the grass.

'Should we keep out of the way a bit longer do you think?' Tika asked Mim.

'Perhaps we should go to the pavilion,' he replied. 'These new clothes seem to have become rather dirty. The Lady and her people appear to set much store on the cleanness of everything. This one's mother was much the same.'

Tika slipped her arm around Mim's waist, her dark head reaching his shoulder, nearly. Although he had shown Emla and the Seniors what events had catapulted him out of his woodlands and into this so different world, only Ashta, Tika, and Farn were aware of the terrible, constant pain Mim felt. The deep, abiding pain of such total loss, and also guilt, at not being there to share that horror. He struggled to come to terms with the fact that he alone had survived.

Having tidied their appearance, Tika and Mim sat quietly at the doorway of the pavilion, watching the sky flush with sunset colours. 'Someone comes,' Mim warned. Seconds later, Tika heard footsteps pattering along the stone path. Shan burst round the corner and skidded to a halt in front of them.

'There you are! They are all in a tizz, thinking you had flown away!' She looked at their slightly worried expressions and laughed merrily. 'You are in no trouble,' she said and reached to catch a hand of each. 'Come quickly, they all wait your presence at the supper table.' She pulled them along with her at a fast trot until they neared the House. She dragged them to a standstill and straightened their clothes and hair, as if they were mere babies, as Tika vigorously complained. When they apparently met with Shan's approval, she moved ahead of them to conduct them, as honoured guests, into the dining chamber.

Emla and the Seniors welcomed the two with some relief, and urged them to be seated as servants began bringing in steaming dishes of food. Tika noticed Gan seemed a little remote, his silence a little forbidding. She eventually managed to ignore his coldness and chatted freely with Yash and Kemti.

It was full dark when Emla decided it was time Tika and Mim should retire to bed. They had both been stifling yawns for some time. In the safety of Emla's House, the fact that they had been living on a great deal of nervous energy in the last moons was apparent in their need to sleep. Emla wished them good night, and again Shan escorted them to the guest pavilion. And again hot tubs awaited them, but this night they made no attempt to sit up by the fire afterwards. From bath to bed and dreamless sleep, unaware of the wards of Power Emla had woven around the whole estate, but particularly around their pavilion.

On the veranda, Ashta waited, checking her precious Mim slept peacefully, then that Tika also lay quietly. Satisfied all was well here, and lulled by Farn's gentle snores, Ashta too closed her eyes. She wondered fleetingly what the Golden Lady and the Seniors had to discuss of such great importance. She had sensed tenseness, excitement, strong in one of the Seniors, when she had peeped in the windows of the dining chamber earlier. She yawned, rested her head on Farn's back and she too soon slept.

Gan spoke immediately the library door closed behind the man-servant. 'Several saw Linvaks, Lady, the night they went from

Soul Bonds

here. Travelling fast, so the people told my men – with some relief. But travelling beyond Gaharn, along the feet of the Spine Mountains. No one thought to follow of course, so that is all I have discovered. It does seem clear that Yar was deceived. I have sent a small group of my best scouts to see what is to be found, although too much time has been lost for us to be too hopeful.'

'That is good news though, Gan. We can know for certain the Linvaks were under someone else's orders. If the taking of the Weight had been their idea, they would have fled to their homeland as was falsely revealed to Yar.' Emla sank onto her usual fireside stool. 'I believe Kemti has news for us?'

Iska, Yash and Gan were seated now while Kemti stood before them. He spread his long thin hands almost helplessly. 'I scarce know how to begin,' he said. They waited. 'Emla suggested I examine the patterns of Tika and Mim.' Yash and Gan looked surprised. 'I did only a visual testing. If they are agreeable, and you so wish, I can do organic tests tomorrow, but I am convinced personally by the visuals.' He took a steadying breath, his black eyes shining in the light from the glow lamps.

'Mim's pattern shows some Nagum characteristics. It also shows Dragon characteristics.' All were listening intently now. 'And Tika – she has human patterns, but also she has markers clearly indicating she shares our blood.'

Gan's reaction was stunned amazement, Yash looked totally intrigued. Iska nodded. 'You have not surprised me with this news of Tika. I felt something of this nature would be revealed. But Mim – are you saying Dragon bred with Nagum? Surely neither race would contemplate such a thing?'

Kemti strode back and forth across the library, from pool of glow lamp light through shadow into light again, and back. 'I have wrestled with this all day. I went over and over the scenes in Mim's memory when he showed us how he reached the She Dragon Hani's nesting cave, and I think I have the only explanation.'

'Well by the stars Kemti, tell us!' Yash nearly shouted at him.

'Mim was injured. He had cuts and bruises from his climb and his fall. I believe Hani licked him with her tongue to clean and mend his hurts. It is the only way I can find as being the cause of his having Dragon patterning. Maybe Nagums, or this particular Nagum, was somehow receptive to this sort of implantation. And instead of his body rejecting these new patterns, they were accepted and grew rapidly to the extent I can see so plainly.'

'Are either of them aware of this?' asked Emla.

Kemti considered for a moment. 'No, I believe not.'

'And what if Mim mates with a Nagum in the future? What offspring will be brought forth?' Iska sounded disturbed.

'Seeing what perils lie before them, it hardly seems necessary to consider the distant future he may well not survive to see,' Gan retorted.

Iska winced at his bluntness but kept silent.

'We must all think on this,' said Emla. 'Consider what it can possibly mean – to Tika, to Mim, to the Dragons, and to ourselves. I will hear your views tomorrow. I think we will discuss it no more tonight – it will only blur the issue. Kemti has given us the facts, and it is these facts I would have you think on.' Emla stood up, drawing the gold threaded shawl she wore close around her narrow shoulders. 'I had intended to speak with Mim and Tika tomorrow. I will delay until I have your thoughts on Kemti's discovery, and on exactly how much you feel these children should be told.'

Chapter Eleven

Farn awoke to a soft humming sound. He opened his eyes and discovered a small fur-covered beast with sharp pointed ears, crouched inches from his nose. Its eyes were tight shut and its body shook with the buzzing noise it seemed to be producing. Farn stared at this orange coloured creature in fascination. What was it, he wondered? He had never seen its like.

'I am of the Kephi,' a voice murmured in his mind.

Farn's prismed eyes glowed with interest. 'Do you live here Kephi? Why have I not seen you these two days?'

The eyes of the Kephi opened slowly, revealing eyes as blue as Farn's own. 'Kephi is the name of my tribe, my own name is Khosa, Farn of the Dragon Kin. I am Queen of the Kephi on the Lady's estate. We watched your arrival and thought it prudent to see what habits you might have before introducing ourselves.' Khosa's mouth opened, long whiskers bristling forward as she yawned. 'You seem harmless, so I came to greet you.'

Now she moved, her hindquarters sticking up high, a long tail rising above and her front half stretching low towards Farn. Ashta had woken and was gazing at this small thing with considerable interest. Farn said politely, 'Perhaps we will see you again later Khosa. Ashta and I go to hunt our breakfast now.'

'I wondered,' Khosa sat neatly upright before the Dragons, her tail wrapped over her front feet. 'We Kephi are great hunters. We eat only meat, like you. I thought I might join your hunt.'

'But do you fly?' Farn asked. 'We travel beyond the Lady's grounds.'

'I know.' Khosa fixed an unblinking stare on Farn's whirring eyes. 'You could carry me.'

After some thought Ashta said, a little doubtfully, 'You could ride on us I suppose, but you are so small, could you stay safely on our backs? We could carry you in our mouths perhaps, or our hands?'

The superior stare transferred to Ashta. 'I think not in your mouth, nor in your hands. I can hold on, like thus.' Khosa's front paw lifted and needle-like claws appeared from the dainty pad.

'Hmm. I think Farn is best suited to carry you,' said Ashta hastily.

Before Farn could think of anything to say, Khosa sprang lightly up between his wings. Ashta was already rising upwards. Farn also rose, slowly and very carefully, hoping fervently that the claws Khosa had displayed were not as dreadfully sharp as they had looked.

Mim and Tika found themselves breakfasting alone. They had expected to spend the morning with the Golden Lady, but Shan informed them she would see them later in the day. 'She has a great deal of business to attend to you know. There are often visitors from Gaharn asking her advice on all manner of things. And her other work too.' Shan helped herself to a handful of berries as she spoke. 'Well, to speak truly, I do not understand what she calls her "work", but it keeps her very busy, often till late at night. She is a lovely lady to work for though. I consider myself most fortunate that she chose me for her maid. And don't you think she is the most beautiful of ladies?' Shan never seemed to expect an answer when she was in full spate. 'I expect she will send me to fetch you when she is free of duties later, so don't you go hiding anywhere, like yesterday. I must go and ready my Lady's heavier robes – it was quite chilly this morning didn't you think? Oh,' she popped her head back round the door. 'She said you should go to Lord Gan when you have eaten. It almost went out of my head!' And she was gone, her laughter floating behind her.

Mim and Tika looked at each other. 'Why must we go to him?' Mim asked. 'Do you think he will punish us for yesterday's mishap?'

'Well I will not let him punish you,' said Tika. 'It was Farn who knocked that thing off the roof – Ashta had nothing to do with it.'

Reluctantly, they left the House and were halfway to the stable yard when Gan came out of a side door in front of them. 'There

91

you are,' he said briskly. 'We will start teaching you some of the fighters' craft. You both have been given weapons, now you must learn to use them. Where are the Dragons?'

After a pause, Tika replied, 'They were hunting, but they are talking to – I'm not sure who, or what. They say they will be occupied for a while, unless we have need of them. I have told them we do not.' She felt it was still a trifle soon to bring Farn into Gan's vicinity.

'Right. Come in here then.' He led the way back through the door he'd emerged from and they found themselves in a large barn-like building. Strange figures swung on poles in one corner and racks of assorted weaponry lined one whole wall. 'We will not need your real weapons, you will begin with these wooden ones. Less chance of serious injury.' Gan strode to the rack and chose two swords as Tika pondered on his use of the word "serious" in conjunction with "injury".

Gan handed one sword to Tika. It was weighted similarly to the real sword she now owned, but the blade was merely a blunt ended pole with no edges to it. She looked up from the weapon to see Mim, his eyes huge in his pale face, and both hands firmly behind his back. Gan was holding the practice sword towards Mim, expecting him to take it as had Tika.

Finally, Mim said, 'This one's people do not use these things. We harm no one.'

Gan continued to stare at Mim, his face impassive. Then he said quietly, 'And where did that get your village, Mim?'

Tika gasped, and Mim's face paled even further.

Mim turned from Gan to look earnestly at Tika. 'You understand, advise this person if you will, to help him know the rightness.'

Tika was dismayed. How could she help Mim make a decision like this? Thinking hard as she spoke, she said slowly: 'My ways are different Mim. You have been scolded, but I have been beaten. You lived in peace, in a loving family. I was a slave pet. I will fight any who ever try to harm me again. Thus I will learn from this Gan as best I can.

'We have some sort of task ahead of us. Farn and I both believe there will be difficulties and dangers. We have already agreed we will accept any task the Lady Emla sets us. You must

92

choose your own path Mim, the one that is meant for you. It is not a matter of rightness or wrongness.'

For a few moments it was as if the three of them were in an isolated bubble. Absolute quiet, where before they had heard voices from the stables and screams from bad tempered fengars. Tika felt a strangeness in her mind and realised it was Gan. He was about to try to force Mim's decision. Tika hurled a mental barrier against him without even thinking what she was doing.

Gan rocked back on his heels and turned his eyes to her. Surprise grew in his expression as he discovered he was confined. Somehow, Tika had encircled his mind, there was no tiny space through which he could even summon another Senior to his aid. 'Do not touch Mim,' Tika said coldly in Gan's head, as she continued to look steadily at Mim.

A pale green head appeared round the door, followed by the rest of Ashta's already large body. Mim went straight to her, his arms going round her neck. Gan felt a tingle, and realised Tika had undone whatever it was she had done to his mind. He opened his mouth but this small female forestalled him. 'Why do you not tell me what these things are that swing in the air?' And he found himself walking across the barn with her.

Gan explained that anyone should, (he slanted his gaze at her as he emphasised "should"), be able to hit a stationary target. Hitting a target which moved unpredictably was considerably more difficult. He was demonstrating the correct grip she should have on the sword hilt when Mim said, 'This one will learn to use the short knife he has been given, but he will not use a sword.'

Gan turned. Mim had crossed the barn and was close by Tika and Gan. Ashta had sat down by the doorway, her eyes flickering as she watched them. Gan nodded. 'I am glad Mim. If you are going into places unknown, I would prefer you to go knowing some tricks to defend yourself at least. Would you consider learning to use a staff?' He lifted a pole, slightly longer than Mim's height, and grasped it, a hand at each end. He made a few moves, indicating how a sword blow could be deflected with this simple pole.

'Yes,' Mim agreed, 'this person would learn the staff.'

Gan opened a smaller side door and yelled beyond, 'Sket! Motass! Riff!' Three human males hurried into the barn immediately. 'I want you to show us, very slowly, a few moves of defence with the staff and sword. You Sket, use a sword, Motass, take the staff. Riff, find two other practice weapons for our visitors.'

Tika and Mim watched, as Sket and Morass seemed to dance gently round each other. It looked simple enough. As though Gan had read their thoughts, which Tika knew he had not, he ordered: 'Normal practise speed!' The gentle dance turned into a blur of spinning men and weapons. Mim and Tika had a strong suspicion this was going to be far from simple.

Emla was with the Seniors in her study, a room at the highest point of the House. They had agreed that the alterations in Mim's body had implications which they were unable, at this moment, to fathom. The news that Tika shared their blood had more obvious overtones. The Lord of Return, as Tika had explained, had captured her mother, in a raid. All Tika knew further was that she had come "from the north", that she had been "damaged", and that Tika resembled her physically. But all the humans that the Seniors had knowledge of in these lands conformed to the fair-haired, blue or brown eyed type.

Kemti proposed, hesitantly, that Rhaki had bred with a human female and the resulting child had, amazingly, survived. 'Because of the predominance of markers indicating Tika is one of our race, over the human markers,' he said, 'it would seem clear that Tika cannot be first generation cross breed.'

'Are we to assume then that Rhaki has done this deliberately, that he knows of this child? Could there be more of them?' The Seniors were aghast at Emla's cool suggestion.

'I have the sense Rhaki does not know, or, if he has a suspicion that he may have impregnated a human female successfully, he would be amused. Forgive me Emla, he is your brother, I know,' Iska shook her head, 'but he always pursued the Power so blindly. I saw him when he was but a student remember, and several of his teachers noted this tendency in him. He saw a goal and charged headlong, never pausing to consider the meanings of any particular stages on the way to that goal.'

'You mean,' queried Yash, 'he may have used a human female for his amusement and ignored what any chance offspring might become should it survive?'

'Yes.' said Iska. 'And I suspect Tika may have strength beyond ours. The She Dragon Krea said she saw abilities in Tika's mind such as she had never seen, and that they would learn from each other. Alas, Krea went beyond too soon, and learnt no more.'

'I found the humans I studied to have latent Powers, but they had convinced themselves completely that all or any uses of the Power were evil magics,' said Emla. 'It would be interesting to learn what event of such obvious magnitude frightened them from ever using the Power.'

'Yes,' said Kemti, 'but not now Emla. Can we concentrate on this particular human in this particular time please?'

'I think we will have to tell Tika some of our findings at least. Perhaps, with our help, she may find she has more knowledge than we on this whole matter, still buried within her.'

'It is possible Iska,' Yash nodded. 'Will you explain to her Emla, or should we all be present? And what of Mim?'

'I will speak with them both, after their midday meal. Mim I believe, is closer to her than anyone has ever been, except for Farn.' Emla fell silent. 'Should the Dragons be present also?' she asked.

'Yes.' Yash and Iska nodded their agreement with Kemti. 'All together will be best I feel. But I would ask that we three, and Gan, are allowed to be close by, and are able to hear all that passes. If there is anger from any, we should be at hand to assist you Lady.'

Emla looked surprised, the thought of any danger from her four guests clearly had not occurred to her. 'Very well.' Before she could say more, there was a knock at the door and Gan entered at her call. Kemti explained quickly what had been decided as the other Seniors began to leave.

'But wait,' Gan said urgently. 'Tika is using the Power, whether she is aware of what she is doing fully or not.' He related the events in the armoury and how he had been held completely helpless.

'That confirms it,' said Iska. 'We must tell her all we know now. She must be given guidance on how to use her Power, but she must know how to control it also.'

Emla did not attend the midday meal. She remained in her study, a maid bringing her tea and fruit there. The Lady needed some time to prepare herself for this difficult meeting. Difficult inasmuch as she feared to hurt any of these four. They were so young! Her mind repeated those four words yet again. The human and the Nagum – of similar age – a scant fifteen Cold Seasons!

She tried to recall how she had been at that age, but it was far too long ago. The Dragons had not yet completed one full cycle of Seasons. By the stars, they would be in danger from their very youth and their lack of experience of this world. Emla stood by the window, breathing deeply, and forcing herself to a calmness she was very far from feeling.

Both sides of the great double doors of the entrance hall had been opened so that Farn and Ashta could come inside. They reclined at the foot of the broad staircase, allowing maids to come in and out without being in their way. The maids were round eyed with excitement at being so near to the beautiful creatures. Tika and Mim were standing by the fireplace as the Lady descended the stairs. Emla paused beside the Dragons, their heads all at the same level. She stroked their faces gently, then walked towards Tika and Mim.

Emla moved a stool so that she could sit facing the Dragons, and then suggested that Mim and Tika made themselves comfortable near her.

'There are things to say, dear ones. And they are hard things. I will say them to you straightly, and then you may question me. I swear by the stars that I will answer all I can as truly as I know.'

Tika and Mim waited, tension plain in both of them.

'Tika, I would speak of you first. We know now that you are of our race more than you are human.' Tika stared, her face white with shock. 'I can tell you in more detail later if you wish, but for now I will say only that your mother, or maybe her mother, or maybe even further back, brought forth a child fathered by one of my race. Remember Krea spoke of abilities in your mind? We have also glimpsed such in your brief time here. We need to test you, ascertain your strengths and teach you how to live with them. I tell you truly child, we may not understand all your Powers, but unless you learn how to control them, you could do

96

great harm both to others and to yourself.'

She raised her hand as Tika opened her mouth. 'No dear one, wait until I have spoken to Mim.' She turned her great green eyes to Mim's odd, triangular face.

'A Nagum you were born Mim, but you are no longer wholly Nagum. We believe Ashta's mother, in healing your hurts when you arrived in her nesting cave, transmitted Dragon life into your body. Now, you are both Nagum and Dragon, dear one. I hope you will come to see this as not a lessening thing but as an enlarging one.'

Emla looked at the two young ones before her, then at the Dragons behind them. Ashta's eyes were glowing softly and the Lady was aware that she was speaking privately to Mim's mind. Farn's eyes held excited sparkles. Emla knew he had not understood how deeply the information she had just imparted had hit Tika and Mim.

'The Seniors whom you have met here, are the very best of the many brilliant minds we have in Gaharn. They are within call now and if you wish, they will join us and help me to answer your questions?'

Receiving no answer, Emla bespoke the Seniors to come to her anyway. Quietly, the four tall slender figures came down the stairs, Iska last. The three males ranged themselves behind Emla while Iska sat on the lower stairs, a hand resting lightly on each Dragon.

The silence lasted a long time but no one stirred. It was clear that Mim and Tika were speaking with the Dragons. It was Mim who spoke first, his fluting voice soft as he said, 'This one finds your news beyond his understanding Lady. If this one is of the Dragon Kin, will he begin to look like a Dragon?'

'Mim, this has never happened before,' Yash replied. 'Or if it has, we have no knowledge of it. I do not think your body will change, but I cannot say this for sure.'

The silence fell again, and again, it was Mim who broke it. 'This one thinks it is perhaps best. His family is gone. Now he has true family again if he and Ashta share blood as well as the soul bond.'

At last, Tika seemed to rouse herself. She stood and walked to Gan. Her head reached scarcely to half his height. Standing beside him, she looked at the Golden Lady. 'You say I am of your race – will I suddenly grow to be as tall as all of you?'

'It seems unlikely,' Kemti answered her. 'I would surmise the female who first bore a child to a male of our race, came from a line of small humans.'

'And this male, he bred with one female, then with the daughter he got on her? That is, if I understood the Lady rightly?'

The Seniors were taken aback at just how thoroughly Tika's mind had grasped the full facts from Emla's brief outline. 'It would seem to be so, Tika,' Kemti agreed. 'We do not know if it was done knowingly or not, or if the male is aware of the existence of offspring. We believe not, but,' he emphasised again, 'we do not know.'

'You keep saying "this male". Are you sure there is only this one who has done this, to my mother's mother, or maybe further back?' Tika quoted Emla's words back to her.

'Tika, you must be aware how long-lived are the Dragons. Our race is to the Dragons, in longevity, what they are to humans.'

'This one male,' Tika continued doggedly. 'You know who he is?'

Emla bowed her head for a moment then looked up directly at Tika. 'We believe he is Rhaki. My brother. The Grey Guardian.'

The afternoon hours passed slowly, with silences broken by a question from Tika, a reply, then silence again. Farn had gradually realised Tika was not excited but enormously confused. He projected comfort, reassurance and love to her, as did Ashta and Mim, of which she was aware and deeply grateful.

At last, Iska slipped forward onto her knees beside Tika and held her shoulders lightly. 'Enough child,' she murmured. 'No more for now. Tomorrow you can ask more, but enough for today.' She glanced at Emla who nodded and said:

'You will do better I think, to return to the pavilion now, just the four of you. I will have food brought to you later, and if you have need of us, you only have to call with your minds.'

Iska and Emla rose, both gently pulling Tika to her feet. She looked dazed, dark marks of exhaustion round her eyes. Gan watched as she turned to the doorway, admiration for her courage filling him suddenly. She stopped, half turned to look back at Emla and said, 'If my sort-of father is your brother, then we are truly blood kin Lady?'

'Indeed we are,' the Lady smiled compassionately. 'I am your "sort-of" aunt.'

Chapter Twelve

The sky had been clouding from the south, heavy, grey, rain filled clouds, and as the servants left after bringing food to the guest pavilion, the rain began to fall. Mim and Tika sat by the fire, waiting for Ashta and Farn to return from their hunting.

'This one does not know what to say to you, Tika.' Mim said. 'Does the Lady's talk change a great deal for you?'

Tika sighed. 'At least I know more of who I am I suppose. But there are so many pieces missing. This Rhaki is the Grey Guardian and he is the one who is trying to unbalance the world. Yet he is also my father in some way, and the Lady's brother.' She looked across at Mim, his high tilted eyes with their vertical pupils gazing back at her in deep concern. 'And you Mim, how do you truly feel to know you have Dragon blood?'

He smiled his sweet smile. 'This one was shocked at first hearing. Now, he is truly glad. Ashta is his blood sister, so this person has family again. Do you yet know of the Powers the Lords and Ladies spoke of Tika?'

She frowned. 'There is something. It is like a tickling inside my head. Each time I think I have nearly got hold of it, it is gone again, or moved somewhere else. Oh.'

A small furry creature was stalking from one of the bedchambers. Mim and Tika watched. Tail aloft, it marched to the hearth and sat, its back to the warmth, and stared, first at Mim then at Tika.

'I am Khosa,' came the thought to their minds. 'Queen of the Kephi of the Lady's estate.' Her blue eyes regarded them with interest.

'Greetings,' Mim and Tika managed to reply.

'I hunted with the Dragons this morning.'

'It was you they were talking to,' exclaimed Tika.

Khosa inclined her head slightly. 'Farn carried me. It was most interesting.'

'The Lady has not spoken of Kephi to us, and this one has not seen you before. Are you usually hidden from people?' asked Mim.

Khosa lifted a dainty paw, orange furred as was the rest of her, licked it thoroughly and swiped it round an ear several times. 'Two-legs like the Kephi,' she replied. 'We stop squeakers overrunning the food stores, we are pleasing to look at, and we are quite friendly.' She continued to wash herself fastidiously.

Tika and Mim watched, mesmerised by the rhythmic motions of the slim paw. Khosa now crouched lower, tucking her front paws neatly under her chest, and making a soft humming noise. 'You see,' she remarked smugly in their minds, 'you are much calmer than when I first joined you.'

She was right. Mim and Tika looked at each other and Tika smiled for the first time for hours.

'We Kephi do not speak with two-legs, as I am now speaking to you. The Lady has tried to get into our thoughts but it is a simple thing to bar her entry and pretend we are nearly as simple as hoppers. Thus we go anywhere we wish, in the House or the estate, and we know all that goes on.' There was no mistaking the smugness in Khosa's tone now.

'So why are you speaking to us?' Tika asked.

The eyes, which had closed, slitted half open again. 'You and your Dragons interest me. I would journey with you when you leave here,' she said calmly.

As she made this announcement, the clatter of wings at the door told of the Dragons return. Mim went to push back both of the double doors to let them inside. Ashta entered first, a few raindrops still sparkling on her face and head, but most of the wetness already gone from her scaled body.

'Greetings Khosa,' said Ashta politely. Farn was just behind her and he stopped abruptly. As Ashta moved to recline by the sidewall, Farn peered worriedly at the tiny orange shape before the fire.

'Greetings Khosa. You were not wanting to hunt again were you, we've just come back,' he asked.

Khosa did her hind-end-up, lower-end-down stretch, then resumed her crouch as she replied. 'It is too wet for the Kephi to enjoy the hunt at this moment.'

Tika felt Farn's rush of relief and resolved to find out later just why such an insignificant creature made him so nervous.

'No one notices Kephi, unless we wish to be noticed,' Khosa continued. 'I heard the talk earlier, of your changed life patterns. I have heard much of the Seniors' discussions. They take no heed of a small Kephi apparently fast asleep on a sunny window seat.' The smugness was back in her tone. 'We have to be close to listen to minds,' she admitted. 'We cannot hear from far. I can be of great use to you I think, which is part of why I desire to join your party.'

Farn sat up, his eyes whirring blue, green and gold colours. 'Join our party? Tika, did she say she would come with us?' He sounded horrified at the idea.

Khosa fixed him with the uncompromising stare he remembered from this morning. 'Kephi can slip into tiny places, and listen to any talk we wish. Could something your size do the same? If we are seen, most of the two-legs make strange noises that they believe we find attractive, then they feed us, or caress us.'

'But,' Farn went on weakly, 'you are Queen of the Kephi here. Do you mean to bring all your tribe too?'

Tika and Mim looked alarmed now. Khosa's eyes closed. 'No,' she said shortly. 'I tire of being Queen. I tire of the demands of my own, too numerous Kephlings, and of deciding silly disputes. I wish to see more of the world than this estate and I wish to be without clamorous Kephi bothering me.'

Next morning, Tika awoke to find Khosa sitting on her chest. 'I would prefer you not to mention our talk last night, to any other two-legs. If any remark on my presence with you now, you have only to say that you are greatly taken with my beauty and sweet nature. I go to hunt now with the Dragons.' And she was gone.

Despite the demands she knew the day would bring, Tika smiled. Farn would not be greatly pleased at Khosa's decision to hunt this morning. The claws had dug into his shoulders once only, due to Khosa's excitement apparently. But once had been enough for poor Farn.

Gan was the only Senior at the breakfast table. He looked up as Mim and Tika arrived. 'We thought we would continue your instruction with weapons this morning. Lady Emla and the other Seniors are busy, but I am to tell you they will come to speak with you now, if you would prefer?'

'No Lord Gan,' Mim answered. 'This person would not wish to interrupt the Lady's work.'

Tika agreed. 'The news I was given yesterday was a great shock Gan,' she told him, 'but it seems more manageable this morning. I am willing to do whatever has been arranged.'

It was a strenuous morning, at the end of which, Tika and Mim found themselves sore and bruised. Gan pronounced himself moderately satisfied with their progress and suggested they have one last bout with Sket and Motass called in as their opponents. Riff leaned against the wall to watch. Until now, Gan had worked with them separately. Now they must each try to defend themselves against men with a new approach.

Sket and Motass both took up practice swords, as did Tika, while Mim used a staff. They found this practice bout very different, realising too late that Gan had indeed been dealing fairly gently with them. Gan stood aside watching closely, calling a sharp word now and then.

Unfortunately, Tika and Mim were far too occupied to notice Farn's arrival. He stared aghast as two males attacked Tika, and Lord Gan stood by and permitted it! He belched.

A jet of flame hit Sket's sword, which he dropped with a yell. Tika spun round, using rapid mind speech to explain to Farn what was happening here. Sket held his hands clamped in his armpits as Motass jumped up and down on the burning sword.

As Farn understood he had witnessed a sort of game, he drooped. The sapphire eyes whirred miserably. 'This Gan will be angry with me again!' he moaned. Tika hugged him soothingly, glancing back towards the others. Her eye caught Mim's and she saw he was losing a battle against laughter. He bowed to Gan then left the barn hastily, a huge grin spreading over his face as he passed Tika and Farn.

Tika looked at Gan. He was speaking to the men, telling Motass to put some salve on Sket's burned palms, and then dismissing them. As they turned to leave, Tika called: 'Farn is sorry he hurt you Sket. Truly, he thought you were really attacking me and meant me real harm.'

Sket managed a grin. 'You need a lot more practice with a sword, lady, but with a Dragon on your side, I can't see as you'd need the sword. Come in right handy in a true battle, they would Lord Gan!'

'You had better get cleaned up before you join the Lady, Tika. And tell Mim he controlled himself well.' Tika looked at Gan's face more closely. By the stars, he thought it had been funny too. Perhaps there was a sense of humour under that grim exterior, after all.

The rain beat down harder than ever and the heavy clouds made it necessary to uncover the glow lamps in the central hall of the Lady's House. Emla smiled at Mim and Tika, saying, 'I am relieved you seem to accept what has happened to you. I know that what we had to tell you yesterday must have affected you both deeply. We have tried to arrange how best we may help your Powers develop Tika, and yours also Mim.'

He looked startled. 'This person has no Powers Lady, except for the mind speech.'

'Oh yes you have, dear one. You have the Power to help plants grow, do you not? And there is more in you that we will help you learn how to use.'

'This one has no wish to learn magics, Lady. Nagums believe there is a great wrongness in magic.'

'Mim, I will tell you the first lesson: all magic is the same. Do you understand? Do you Tika?'

Tika was studying the tiny Dragon set in the depths of the pendant she wore. She thought for a few moments longer, then met Emla's gaze. 'I think you are telling us that magic is magic, like – water is water? It is what a person does with it that matters. If you use magic for a bad purpose, it is not the magic itself that is bad but the will behind it. Is that it?'

'Exactly so, Tika,' agreed the Lady. 'Do you understand Mim? The magic, or the Power, is simply something there to be used if you know how to. It is not available to all. But someone such as you, Mim, could not do harm with the Power.'

'But I could.' Tika spoke softly.

'Yes Tika, you could do great harm, as you could do great good. This is why you must let us try to teach you how to manage the Power you are capable of drawing to yourself.

'Now, if it is agreeable, Yash and Gan and I will work here with Mim for a while. You go with Iska and Kemti to the library. Tomorrow, perhaps, we will change around.'

Iska and Kemti were rising from their couches when Tika asked: 'Lady there is one thing.' Emla waited for her to continue. 'What is the meaning of these ornaments both Mim and I had to find in the Treasury collections? I understand the need of swords perhaps, but what is the use of these?'

'We are still trying to find out ourselves, dear one. We have been through so many old books and papers. They are described clearly in many writings, but the purpose of them is hidden in riddles. Iska and Kemti will read some to you – maybe you yourself will understand where it is all confusion to us.'

Iska and Kemti were gentle as they tried to show Tika how to go into her own mind. 'The tiny part that is "you", that you send into another mind, send it deep into your own.'

Frustration grew as Tika found herself just unable to catch the tickle she had described to Mim. When a rather pretty teapot, full of hot spiced tea brought by a maid, crumpled into a mess of pottery shards and dark liquid, Iska called a halt.

'I did that,' Tika exclaimed in horror. 'I didn't mean to!'

'No, we know,' said Kemti, as Iska removed the tray and went to arrange for more tea to be brought, 'but perhaps it is good that it did. You can see what can happen without control, and this was a very small thing – it could so easily be far worse. Try once more Tika, focus your mind as narrow as the moonlight's path on water.'

Iska had returned and sat beside Kemti, watching as Tika concentrated. 'She's there,' murmured Kemti.

'I believe she is,' agreed Iska.

Tika's voice sounded distant as she said, 'I can see it! It is wound round and through my mind – but wrongly!'

'No!' both Iska and Kemti cried, and then both slid into Tika's mind, and stopped, stunned by what they saw. Tika was right, there was something wrong. The golden threads of the Power were tangled in places, not forming the filigree patterned net the Seniors knew from each other's minds. But as they watched, the tangles unsnarled here, were rippled into a smooth curve there. Tika's concentration was absolute, and by the time the threads of

105

Power glittered in a delicate tangle-free net, she was beginning to shake.

At last it was done, and Kemti caught her as she began to topple forward from her chair. He looked at Iska over Tika's unconscious body. Her face reflected the awed amazement he himself was feeling, then the two Seniors busied themselves laying Tika gently on a couch and tucking Iska's woollen shawl around her. A maid tapped the door and Kemti went to take a tray of fresh tea from her.

'Well,' he said.

'Well indeed,' echoed Iska.

'Could you make out how she did that?' Kemti asked, as Iska handed him some tea. 'It was a form of healing, but faster, and more complex than I have ever seen.'

'Yes. And when you realise that she has not been able to see the Power in our minds, to be able to do what she has, to herself … Kemti, the Power she has is far greater than I have heard of, let alone ever seen.'

Iska tried to reach into Tika's mind, and was not entirely surprised to find her way blocked. She nodded. 'She is guarding herself. I believe with the net of Power correctly in place, much knowledge has already been absorbed by her mind.'

'I told Bara to ask Emla to come, when she could leave Mim.'

'I think she will sleep now. She is drained of strength, but even as she sleeps, the Power will be working within her.'

The door opened and Emla was there. Kemti and Iska explained what had taken place and Iska opened her mind to let the Lady see what they had seen.

'Events seem to be moving faster than we imagined,' Emla said. 'We must pray to the stars she wakes safe – and sane – but I think we must not try to waken her.'

Again the door opened. Gan said, 'Mim said the Dragons were becoming upset, Farn especially. He tried to climb the stairs to reach Tika. Mim calmed them and has come to verify Tika's safety.'

Emla gestured to Tika's sleeping form. 'As you see Mim, she sleeps. We think she will sleep long. Somehow she has – rearranged – her mind. It was as great a shock as was the news of her relationship to us was yesterday.'

'She should be in their pavilion, where Farn can be with her,' said Gan surprisingly, and he stooped, lifting Tika easily. Mim hurried down the stairs after him. Gan stopped as Farn's body surged onto the lower stairs. He held Tika slightly away from himself, towards Farn. The Dragon bent his long face close over Tika's, many colours whirring in the prismed eyes. A long moment passed, then Farn backed away to allow Gan to continue. As Gan reached the outer door, he slowed, waiting for Farn to keep pace with him. The blue head was slightly higher than Gan's as Farn kept as close as he could.

Mim ran ahead, opening the doors wide, and Gan carried Tika through to the bedchamber that Mim indicated. It was a tight fit, but Farn forced his large body through the smaller door. The attendants had already uncovered glow lamps, but now Gan recovered most of the ones in Tika's room, leaving only a single lamp softly lighting the chamber. He pulled up the quilts, tucking them loosely around her. Farn had already reclined close to the bed, resting his head on the covers, close to Tika's face. Gan found himself placing his hand lightly on the Dragon's head in understanding of his concern.

'I will wait with you, if you permit it Farn.' He spoke to the Dragon's mind. 'I will sit with Mim and Ashta until she awakens.'

'Thank you Lord Gan,' Farn replied, his distress blurring the words.

Supper was brought, but no one had any appetite, and eventually Mim curled up against Ashta and slept. Ashta remained awake, her senses alert to Farn. Gan also stayed awake, rising several times from his chair to look in where Tika lay still sleeping. He hadn't noticed the Kephi slip in at some point during that long evening and endless night. It was just there when he looked in, curled between Farn's head and Tika's arm. It did not seem to be bothering Farn so Gan left it there.

Just before dawn, Tika began to swim up to consciousness. She was immediately aware of a change in herself. She felt as though her mind was stretching, widening. A buzzing sound roused her further and as she recognised it as Khosa's odd music, her eyes struggled open.

Two pairs of blue eyes stared at her from very close range.

One pair was quite calm, the other pair was whirring madly. She smiled at them both, reaching one hand to scratch Khosa's ears (a caress the Kephi was inordinately fond of) and gently touching Farn's face with the other. Her mind was flooded with Farn's relief, his explanations, his worry.

In the main room, Ashta bespoke Gan and Mim: 'Tika has woken, and she is well.'

Chapter Thirteen

Rhaki had received reports that Emla's scouts had tracked the Linvaks to the Spine Mountains. He hoped they would carry on and find what remained of the Linvaks themselves. He would like to see Emla's face when she received that tale! They had served their purpose – to a certain extent. Rhaki had not known of the Linvaks approach to Emla or of their theft of a Balance Weight.

How had they even conceived of the idea, and what had they planned to do with it? Rhaki was still annoyed with the Shardi. They had dismembered, and eaten, most of the Linvak band, totally failing to learn the whereabouts of the Weight. He scowled as he thought of the Shardi. Their stupidity was rapidly outgrowing their usefulness, he was beginning to think. He had not the faintest clue as to how the Linvaks might have forced a Weight free from its place in the time-suspended column of Power.

They had not a trace of Power in them. He should know, he had made them after all. From a simple human stock, he had bred in other lines, including Shardi. His plan had been to make a race of docile slave beasts, capable of understanding and responding to basic commands, and then carrying them out satisfactorily. They were far from attractive to most who had seen them, but Rhaki found their grossness gave him a sense of mild pleasure. Their bodies were of human form and stature, but they had extremely short necks supporting large heads, which were entirely bestial.

Rhaki was amused when snouted faces had first appeared in his breeding experiment. Too late, he found their vocal chords affected, so that sounds other than grunts and snarls were physically beyond Linvak capabilities. Too late also, he discovered how ill tempered and intractable were their natures. So he released them into the world, to live as they could.

There were reports of terror among some of the herders and

small towns, but then the Linvaks reached the Swamp Lands far to the south. It seemed they thought it an ideal environment and settled there. Occasionally, they raided a few leagues beyond their lands, bringing fear to the scattered farmsteads. Mostly, Rhaki forgot their existence for generations at a time.

His trusty Jal had gone to the Shardi himself, with a large band of heavily armed men. Finding no living Linvak, no Balance Weight, and no information regarding its whereabouts, Jal had expressed Rhaki's deep displeasure to the Shardisi. Their leader was killed, slowly and very painfully, as the lesser Shardi were invited, at sword point, to watch.

Now Rhaki was leaning over his worktable, studying a map. If the Linvaks had travelled directly from Emla's House, detouring the city of Gaharn, to the place where they had died, then the Weight must be somewhere on that route. He had tried, unsuccessfully, to penetrate the Pavilion where Emla's weights hung, in an attempt to get a mental 'taste' of the Weights. If he could do that, he would then recognise that 'taste' again, and thus find where the Linvaks' hiding place was.

He had ordered Jal to return to the scene of the Linvaks' slaughter with a larger force of men. They were to watch for scouts from Emla's Guards, and they were only to watch. Rhaki knew that Emla, and that arrogant Gan, would have also deduced that the Linvaks had hidden the Balance Weight. If it were already in Rhaki's possession, the shift of Power in his favour would be only too obvious to them.

Rhaki straightened his tall body, and the map he had been holding open curled itself closed. 'Come, Bark,' he called before there was any tap at the door. He found his staff were always unsettled by such small instances of his powers, although never Bark. His body servant brought his usual meal of meat, cheese and fruit. When he had placed the tray on the smaller table beside Rhaki's fireside chair, he turned to his Master. Bowing low, he whispered, 'Master, a letter comes from Gaharn.' He held out a rolled parchment.

'You may go,' Rhaki said, taking the scroll. As the door closed behind Bark, Rhaki tapped the roll lightly against his palm. This was the first direct communication from the Golden Lady and her Seniors since Jerak's unfortunate visit here. Unfortunate for Jerak, that is.

Rhaki tossed the unopened parchment into the blazing fire as he sat down. He did not wish to enter in to any discussions or debates with Emla and her advisors. He wished to do away with the lot of them. His spies reported that the human child, the Nagum and their two Dragons were now at Emla's residence, but so far he had been unable to infiltrate a single spy into her House. Or indeed into the city of Gaharn. Nor had he found a suitable creature to corrupt, coerce, blackmail or bribe into passing on information.

He had destroyed Jerak, but he had not been able to take any of Jerak's knowledge to himself in the process, as he had hoped. The ancient one had fought harder than Rhaki had been prepared for and he had been nearly at the limit of his own strength when Jerak fell.

He would wait now, to see if Emla's scouts would backtrack the Linvaks trail or continue through the Spine Mountains. It was vital he obtain the Balance Weight, and oh, if he could only discover how a mere Linvak had removed that Weight from its place! As he stretched his slippered feet to the warmth of the fire, a jolt of pain seared through his mind.

Rhaki clutched the arms of his chair and jerked upright, his eyes wide and unseeing. He flung up every mental barrier he could think of as the pain roared through him again. What was it? By the stars, *who* was it? Someone was taking Power, but where – who? The seconds grew to minutes and there were no further hammer blows to his mind. Rhaki's eyes regained their focus, his brows frowning as he concentrated. There had been a familiarity somewhere, amidst that pain. A familiarity, and a strangeness. How could that be? Was it Emla perhaps, acting in concert with some of the Seniors, combining their minds against his? As a student he had learnt this could be done, indeed had been done, but far back, beyond any living memory.

Rhaki strode to the door, wrenching it open. He made his way rapidly through chambers and passageways until he neared the great gateway to his stronghold. Most believed this entrance, set in the side of the mountain, the mountain itself deep in the Realm of Ice, was the only means of access. A very few knew of the long tunnels, taking many days to travel through, which led to several different exit points.

But now Rhaki had need of guards. In a barrack room alongside the great gateway, he stopped. 'Four of you, attend me,' he ordered. From the crowd of human males who had fallen silent at Rhaki's appearance, four came quickly forward, buckling sword belts as they came. Rhaki's finger pointed to one man among a smaller group, clearly of higher rank than the majority.

The five men marched behind Rhaki down a sharply sloping passage running against the outer mountain wall. As they went ever lower, so a stench and a clamour rose upwards. Finally they came to a door of metal bars, through which could be seen Rhaki's more recent experiment. Two door guards sprang to attention as Rhaki arrived and he gestured for the door to be unbarred. Two of his soldiers exchanged glances. This was their first sight of the Cansharsi, as Rhaki had named them. 'Draw your weapons and be prepared. They are occasionally unpredictable.' Rhaki smiled coldly and entered the long cavern. There were many creatures there. They seemed at first glance to be four legged beasts, but as those nearest to the door became aware of visitors, they reared onto their hind legs so that they stood taller even than Rhaki.

There was a predominance of human features to the faces now turning towards Rhaki. Except for the tusks protruding a handspan from their upper jaws. All four limbs ended in three clawed hooves, and their bodies were covered in thick coarse hair. As the furthest Cansharsi became aware of Rhaki's presence, the shrieks and trampling slowly ceased, and they pushed closer to see what was taking place.

Rhaki spoke quietly. 'Soon, my children, I will have work for you. You must organise yourselves now, as you have learnt, into groups who will work well together. There will be no squabbling between you once you begin my work. Is this understood?' There were barely intelligible calls of agreement in distorted human voices.

'You will form your groups calmly and I will return to you tomorrow. I will come alone then, without guards, showing my belief in your trustworthiness and willingness to obey your Master.'

Rhaki waited until the chorus of Cansharsi voices faded to

silence again. 'You will also decide, calmly, which of you will remain here, for reasons your group leaders know. When I return I do not expect to find any injuries, or deaths, to have occurred among you during the night.'

The deep-set dark eyes gazed over the crowded Cansharsi, then Rhaki moved to the door. The door guards slid the heavy bars into place again as soon as the last soldier was outside. Rhaki paused as they neared the upper level and the barrack rooms. 'You two.' He looked at the two younger men whose first visit to the Cansharsi this had been. They stood to attention, their faces pale and sweaty. 'You handled your fear well there. You were afraid, were you not?' Unaccustomed to conversing with their Master, they hesitated. Finally one licked his lips and muttered.

'Uncomfortable Master, rather than really fearful. The smell and the look of them things.'

'Quite so,' said Rhaki kindly. 'Return to your work. You, Verim, stay.' The officer stood stiffly beside Rhaki as the four soldiers hurried on up the passageway.

'You were with the patrol led by Jal seeking the Linvaks?'

'Yes Master.'

'He said you were efficient. Work with him from now on, Verim.'

'Yes Master.' Verim's face flushed with gratification. Rhaki could read this one's mind easily enough: work well with Jal and his future was assured. Rhaki smiled, not wholly pleasantly, and dismissing Verim, he continued back to his study.

Once there, he summoned Bark. As he waited, he stared into the fire, his thin fingers absently rubbing his temples where the pain had been. 'Bark,' he said, 'sit.' The shadowy figure sat on a straight-backed chair near the worktable. Rhaki turned to him, noting Bark seemed even thinner and more faded than ever. 'Bark, do you remember when you were a student?'

'With you, Master? Yes,' whispered the hoarse voice.

'Do you recall the lectures on combining minds for the purpose of multiplying the effect of the Power?'

Bark sat silent for a while, eventually replying, 'I do, Master.'

'Well,' said Rhaki impatiently, 'what do you recall?'

'That none had seen it attempted, or knew of any who had.

They said it was perilous to try to draw so much Power to focus on one thing.' Bark paused, then added: 'My mind is damaged, as who should know better than you Master? I would be of no use to you in such an experiment.'

'I am aware of that Bark. But could it be done, do you think? I admit I have never thought of it since those distant days of learning.' Rhaki turned his eyes away from Bark, back to the fire. 'Earlier this evening there was – a disturbance – in my head.'

'Yes, Master.'

'What do you mean – "yes master"? Are you just agreeing with me, or did you already know this somehow?' Rhaki was plainly exasperated.

'I too, Master, had a "disturbance of the mind" as you put it.'

'You did? But your mind is damaged. You hear thoughts imperfectly, and only of those very close by.'

Bark was silent once more, then, his voice even fainter due to this increasingly rare use of it, he said: 'I can only say, Master, that there were two daggers of pain in my mind. It was like a brilliant light, revealing all the dusty corners.' He lapsed into silence yet again. 'It was a great drawing of Power, Master, but only a single mind.'

'Are you sure? I thought there were two at least, one of whom I nearly recognised '

'No, Master, I regret to disagree with your Lordship, but somehow I know there was but the one.'

'And was this one familiar to you also?'

'Yes, Master. It was the ancient one.'

'Jerak?' Rhaki spun round to face Bark. 'I destroyed him!'

'No, Master. You caused him to flee for his survival, but survive he did.'

Rhaki found himself in his armchair, gaping at this cadaverous wreck. 'How long have you believed Jerak has – survived?'

'Master, he did survive. I knew he had not gone beyond, while I was caring for you in your prostration after the great struggle between you both.'

'By the stars, Bark! Why did you not tell me this sooner?'

'You did not ask me, Master,' Bark whispered huskily.

'If Jerak is not beyond, where is he Bark? Have you any information you would care to share with me on that matter?'

114

'He is far, yet not, Master. I do not know the place where Jerak is.'

'Leave me.'

Bark rose, bowed to Rhaki and left.

Rhaki stayed sitting by the fire, his brain racing through possibilities as to where Jerak could be. Was the ancient one surviving physically, or just mentally? Was he hidden somewhere like an animal, licking his wounds and regaining his strength? Could Rhaki perhaps glimpse him in the bowl of seeing?

Pausing only to wrap his cloak around him, he opened the hidden door, and almost ran down the dark passage. He had no need of the special drink this time, he would not be sending forth any of his own Power. He seated himself, calmed his too rapid breathing, then placed his hands either side of the black bowl. He made his mind concentrate on an image of the old one until it seemed Jerak was actually present.

'Show me where this one is.'

The bowl's inner blackness shifted, swirled, and slowly cleared. Rhaki stared into its depths. Jerak was there, looking as he always looked, but enclosed in a nebulous sort of bubble of some kind. All was darkness around the bubble, giving Rhaki no hint as to the precise location of it. As the scene faded, Rhaki sat back. He had no idea what this meant other than that Jerak, somehow, still existed. He would search through some of the oldest books he had, maybe he could find a clue there. It was late. Rhaki stood, his hands supporting his lower back for a moment. Then pulling his cloak closer round himself he made his way back to his study.

He planned to move the Cansharsi, with great secrecy, to positions far apart. The first groups had been moved ten nights ago – they were destined for the southern lands. In heavy merchant wagons, some were on their way to the Lower Plains beyond the Ancient Mountains. Others were being similarly carried far to the south of the Middle Plains, close to the borders of the Swamp Lands of the Linvak.

The horde of Cansharsi still in his stronghold, were destined for the High Lands, the place where they met with the Spine Mountains. So widely scattered, on his signal they would be loosed to wreak what havoc they wished. The population of the entire countryside would swamp the high council in Gaharn City with requests for assistance. The Guards had not had real battle experience for five human generations. Then, they had put down a rising of overly aggressive humans, west of the Ancient Mountains.

Rhaki seriously doubted that the Guards would have enough men to field even three medium sized bands, let alone a modest army. He had cultivated the men of the western areas over many Cycles of Seasons, teaching them to enjoy the subtle thrill of cruelty. Several Lords, as these strutters and braggarts liked to call themselves, had achieved high standards of unpleasantness. Two in particular pleased the Grey Guardian – the Lord of Far, and the Lord of Return.

He had made the arduous journey to their lands on several occasions, twice in this Cycle of Seasons in fact. They knew only that he was one of the People of Gaharn and thus a true Lord. It amused Rhaki to watch them pick up his occasional hints and add quite interesting embellishments of their own to them, in forms of torture for instance.

Their minds were extremely inventive and quick, except when it came to the subject of the Power. Then, they made their silly gestures to ward against evils. As if a wave of their fingers could halt the true Power if it was sent against them! But Rhaki was almost fond of these humans. They had even surprised him once or twice, with the agility of their minds.

Now, some of his Cansharsi would stir them up a little. That should be an entertaining squabble to witness. Rhaki expected the humans to beat the Cansharsi there. But he would wager the exhilaration of battle would inspire the humans to ideas of invading northwards, into Gaharn territory.

Oh yes, Rhaki had planned for a very busy Cold Season, allowing him to risk a personal visit to his beloved sister. He hoped to find her at home, with a greatly depleted household Guard in attendance. So he would put thoughts of Jerak slightly to one side for now, and exert his not inconsiderable talents to availing himself of Emla's Balance Weights.

Chapter Fourteen

Tika knew another mind had helped her to reshape the distorted web of Power in her own. She did not know whose it was, but she felt it was benign. Therefore it could not have been the Grey Guardian. She also knew that Emla and the Seniors present at this House, had not assisted her, nor had they any awareness that someone had.

Tika was stunned by her enhanced perceptions. Her slave birth and upbringing, where to show any emotion was to invite rebuke at the least, would keep her silent on this matter, for the time being at least.

The Seniors were aware, to a certain degree, of how she was feeling. Among them, children of twenty full Cycles began to experience the growth of the Power within them. But they were taught to expect this transformation, and were helped through each slow stage by those who had experienced it themselves. Tika was young, she had had no teaching, no warning of how this would feel. With her, it had been forced so suddenly, within hours, instead of over many Seasons.

When she first woke under Farn and Khosa's blue stares, she wished she could stay safely where she was for a while longer, to try to accustom herself to the newness in her mind. But she was aware of Ashta, Mim and Gan in the outer chamber, already on their way to see her.

Tika pushed herself up against the pillows, dislodging Khosa from her chest. The Kephi stalked to the foot of the bed and sat straight, every hair bristling with indignation. Ashta's head appeared round the door, green eyes pale with concern and affection. Then Gan stood beneath Ashta's jaw staring at Tika, Mim beside him.

The mental barriers he held firmly in place made no difference. While Gan remained totally unaware of the fact, Tika's mind slid easily past the shielding. She saw his concern and fear for her safety, and – something else. She did not recognise it, but it made her pull rapidly back and out of his thoughts.

Gan bowed slightly. 'I am glad to see you well Tika.'

'It feels as though I've slept for ages.'

'You have,' said Farn. 'I have been here all the time.'

Khosa's cool tone commented in Tika's mind: 'So have we all, dear Farn.'

'Oh. Oh yes,' Farn amended. 'Ashta and Mim and Gan. And Khosa.' His eyes whirred as he glanced quickly at the Kephi's back, and away again.

Tika swung her legs over the side of the bed, hugging Farn. 'I must have missed dozens of meals,' she said. 'It feels as if I have, anyway.' She grinned. 'I am so hungry, I could eat a Dragon!'

Farn's eyes blazed in horror, until Ashta murmured, 'She jokes, Farn.'

'Oh.' Farn was temporarily abashed, then he suggested eagerly: 'Fly with me when we go to hunt, Tika. I have missed carrying you these past days.'

Tika looked at him. Innocence radiated from the silver blue Dragon. He obviously assumed that Khosa could not accompany him if he carried Tika. Tika heard the Kephi laugh, and she replied: 'Yes, I will Farn. And I think I will see how this funny little Kephi thing would like to fly.'

Farn wilted as Khosa spluttered: 'Funny little Kephi thing?'

Mim reappeared, having momentarily vanished back to the main chamber. He held out a slice of fruit tart to Tika, taking a mouthful himself from a second slice. 'We ate little last night – it is all still on the table. Come, join this person for food, then we will both go with the Dragons.'

Farn squeezed himself back through the bedchamber door and watched as Tika helped herself to a motley selection of foods.

'You feel fit enough to fly with Farn this morning?' Gan asked casually.

'Oh yes. I think it is a very good idea.'

'I will tell the Lady Emla what you are doing. I am sure she will wish to speak with you as soon as possible.'

'I'm sure she will,' Tika thought, but said aloud: 'Mim and I will come for breakfast when we return – we are sure to be hungry again by then!'

Mim laughed, following her out of the pavilion. Khosa followed, and as Tika climbed onto Farn's back, she sprang lightly into Tika's arms. Farn shuddered, but then gathered himself and lifted easily upwards, Ashta and Mim beside him. Tika glanced back and saw Gan standing unmoving at the door of the pavilion, watching them draw swiftly away.

When they had disappeared beyond the trees, Gan remained a moment longer, then went slowly towards the House. The Seniors were already at breakfast and Emla arrived as Gan sat down.

'I saw them leave,' Emla said. 'Tika woke safely?'

'Yes,' replied Gan. 'She and Mim decided to go with the Dragons – Farn suggested it. They will not be long I think.'

'Have you noticed any change in her?' Kemti asked.

Gan did not reply for so long that Kemti was about to repeat his question, but finally he said simply: 'I believe she is stronger now than any I have ever heard of.'

'Why?' asked Emla as Iska asked simultaneously: 'How do you know?'

Gan's long hands raked through his black hair. 'Her shielding is beyond my ability to breach. I suspect she could see into any of us and we would be none the wiser of it. Somehow, she is now fully – aware. I can tell you no more, except that both the Dragons, and Mim, were desperately fearful for her last night. Mim slept eventually, but Ashta and Farn were helping her in some way I was unable to understand through the entire night.'

As Emla awaited the return of her four guests, eager yet apprehensive to see what changes were apparent in Tika, Kija was searching for Fenj.

Kija had asked Kadi to foster her second son and two of her daughters. Then, with her youngest daughter, Jeela, she had begun hunting Fenj. He had gone to his secret place, a small valley, hidden deep among great peaks, where he had spent the last few Cold Seasons. Increasingly, as he aged, he sought solitude to prepare himself for his journey beyond.

As the soaring mountains shielded this little valley from the

119

worst storms, so Fenj shielded his mind whilst he stayed here. The Golden Lady had bespoken him as he flew to his secret place, telling him the young ones had reached her safely. She had looked gravely at Fenj as she said: 'Fenj, my dear one, you have waited so patiently. Begin your journey to Skay when you will.' She smiled at him. 'I remember you newly hatched, and how much time have we passed through since then? If you must now go beyond Fenj, know you have helped set things in motion for a changed future. The outcome of these changes, be they good or bad, even we cannot foresee yet. But go knowing how hard we will strive to make a good future.' She lifted a slender hand in farewell and blessing. 'May the stars see you safely beyond, old one, if that is to be your decision.'

Fenj lay now on the ledge of his cave. So many Cycles to ponder on, and now he was unsure whether he was being selfish in wanting to go beyond. They were so very young, Farn and Tika. Could they find the strength and the wisdom to do whatever lay before them? Fenj knew instinctively that trouble was not far off, for the world, not just these two, but they would certainly be in the midst of it.

At last, Fenj relaxed the mental shields he had established and bespoke Kadi. She sounded irritable.

'We have all been trying to find you Fenj. How can you advise or help if you block yourself off from your Treasury when they might have urgent need of you?' She was surprised, and then worried by Fenj's humble reply.

'Apologies Kadi. I have concluded I am indeed selfish. Is something amiss then? I was about to ask you if there was more news of the young ones.'

'Well. Kija is trying to find you, with that young daughter of hers, Jeela. If you are no longer keeping aloof from us all, you can bespeak her yourself. She will tell you of a mad idea she has got into her head. And I always thought she had sense. Really Fenj,' Kadi sounded more irritated than ever, 'I have her other three hatchlings in my care, and if there is a whole mind between them, I will be very surprised. I had no idea what mischief was until now. Call Kija, old friend, and do not hide yourself away as you have been doing. There are still things we must do.'

So Fenj stirred himself. He drifted down to the pool below his cave and drank deep of the icy water. Then he bespoke Kija.

'Where are you Fenj?' Kija demanded. 'I must speak with you face to face.' After seeing from her mind where she and Jeela were now flying, he gave her a picture of the route to his valley. 'We will bring food with us Fenj. We will be with you soon.'

Fenj returned to his ledge and rattled his wings vigorously. If you can help in any way, you must, you foolish old Dragon, he adjured himself. He must shake himself free of this lethargy that he had allowed to develop. As the sky darkened and he watched for Kija and her daughter, he constantly lectured himself on his laxity. What would Skay think of his attitude lately? She would be ashamed, and angry with him.

He heard a high call from beyond the northernmost peak and responded with a resonating bass note. The golden She Dragon wheeled overhead, her pale ivory daughter at her wingtip. Kija carried a wapeesh, and Jeela a volu.

'When did you find this little valley, Fenj? The mountains crowd so close about, I have flown over here many times and yet never even noticed it.'

'Long in the past Kija, with Skay.' His eyes glowed the shadows on snow colour. 'What is it you must speak to me of so urgently?'

'Eat, Fenj.' Kija studied him critically. 'You have not eaten for a while, have you?'

'Now I come to think of it, perhaps not. But I've had much to ponder on.' Fenj defended himself, sounding almost like Farn. Jeela choked on a piece of volu and apologised hastily as her mother's eyes turned knowingly in her direction. When they had eaten their fill, Kija sent Jeela to rest. The young Dragon had been trying to hide her yawns for some time, but reluctantly she moved into the cave and was almost instantly asleep.

'You have flown hard, Kija, and Jeela is small still. What is so urgent? Tell me now.'

Kija reclined opposite Fenj on the ledge and looked up at the night. Starlight flashed in the golden facets of her eyes. 'It is Farn and his soul bond, Tika.'

'But Kadi, and the Golden Lady, both say they are safe and well.'

'They are – at the moment.' Kija sighed, settling more

comfortably. 'I told you, at the Gather, how strong was my feeling that Farn's bonding with a two legs was meant to be. That feeling grows in me, but so does a feeling of great peril. Farn was sorely wounded when he witnessed Krea's death. I fear the scar will not mend easily or soon, and it weakens his courage and strength.'

Kija turned her head, her star filled eyes glittering. 'I must go, with Jeela, to join my son and Tika. Jeela will never grow as large as you or I, but her courage is large. In the brief time in the nesting cave and again at the Gather, she felt a strong affinity to both her brother and to the two legs. If I had left her with Kadi, she would simply have tried to follow me anyway.'

'And what is it you wish of me?'

'Fenj, I do not know where the Golden Lady dwells, nor how to get there. You must tell me this.'

Fenj rustled his wings, then he said: 'She lives in the High Lands beyond the Spine Mountains towards the rising sun. But until Farn and Tika went to her, none of the Dragon Kin have ventured that way since the days of my mother's mother.' His eyes whirred in distress. 'The Spine Mountains were originally our territories, you know that. And you know why we left, putting them many leagues behind us.'

'Do you mean the Shardi?' Kija asked.

Fenj hissed, his head moving from side to side. 'The Shardi. They suddenly appeared in our mountains. They killed some of the Kin, destroyed many broods.' He closed his eyes. 'They ate those they killed. The Lady told us to seek the further places, saying the Shardi would only live along the range of the Spine Mountains, right to the Realm of Ice. They would not cross the flat lands, nor do they like warm places. That is why the Lady, and, I believe, some of her People, helped shield Farn and the other bonded Dragon, on their journey to her.'

'I will think on all this Fenj, and decide what I must do, in the morning.'

The two great Dragons remained quietly on the cave ledge, watching the sky fill with stars, while both their minds filled with plans and schemes.

The last few days had been busy at the Golden Lady's House.

Emla and the Seniors had worked with both Tika and Mim. Mim's reluctance eventually responded to Iska's gentle reasoning. He found himself doing small things, such as moving a chair with the Power, something he would have regard fearfully as a wicked magic, only a short time before.

The work with Tika was different. Emla and Yash were instructing her in control. It was now so easy for Tika to draw Power to herself, but she was told that too frequent or trivial usage of the Power would diminish her control. She would find herself needing to use the Power more and more until she was controlled by it, rather than the other way about.

At the same time Tika was hiding. Yash and Emla were fully aware that Tika's strength was beyond any they had experienced. They also knew that she was allowing them to see only a tiny fraction of her altered mind. They agreed to accept the situation; if they tried to force her, the damage she could now inflict on their minds, chilled them to think of.

They were fascinated by how Tika actually manipulated the Power. They would lift an item in the room, and send it here or there; Tika would do the same, but she held the Power differently. She wove many, scarcely visible threads, to form one greatly strengthened line, whereas the People rarely used more than the one line of Power.

Mim and Tika spent their mornings with Gan, becoming slightly more adept with weaponry. Mim had asked why they had to continue these lessons after he discovered he could use the Power to freeze his opponent in his tracks. He was persuaded it was a necessary skill and he agreed not to use the Power against the long-suffering Sket and Motass again.

Several times Gan noticed a strange look in Tika's eyes – they seemed to become unfocused, as if she was day dreaming. He eventually told Emla and Kemti, telling them he believed she was far speaking someone. Kemti was for confronting Tika, asking her outright if she was far speaking, and if so, to whom. Gan and Emla disagreed. They felt they could trust her judgement. They saw no reason to suspect the Guardian was trying to influence her. It did not occur to any of them that Tika could be far speaking Dragons.

After days of rain, at last they woke to a clear bright day, albeit frosty cold. Mim was entranced with the white hoar coating each smallest piece of plant. IIe went off in search of Lorak, even before breakfast, wanting to know how the plants dealt with this weather, the Nagum woodlands rarely enduring such cold. Ashta said she would accompany him.

Tika decided that she and Farn would have a morning off from weapon practise, too. She sent one of the pavilion maids with a message to the Lady, saying she would be flying with Farn this morning. Farn was not thrilled to hear Khosa agree that a flight seemed a splendid idea.

In the House, Gan said: 'They cannot delay much more. The snows will close the mountain ways soon now. Have you decided if they are to seek the Balance Weight or will you send them straight to face the Guardian, Lady?'

'We know the Weight is hidden. We know Rhaki has not gained possession of it. Jerak's writings say that two pure souls can confront the Guardian, with a higher chance of living to tell the tale than either you or I.'

Yash said: 'If he refuses to reply to our messages, why should we assume he would agree to meet Tika and Mim? He has no idea of their Powers as yet. If he did, he may see all the more reason not to let them near him.'

'We have to try,' said Emla quietly. 'Discussion has always been our way, and even now, with the Guardian setting himself so apart from the People, we must continue to try.'

'We are aware he is your brother, Lady, but…' Kemti began.

'No,' said Emla sternly. 'He is my brother by blood, never has he been a brother of my heart or my soul. I do not delay dealing with him for any reason other than that it is the way our People have always been. Are we not trained from birth "to listen, to learn, to discuss, to decide"? We must still give the Guardian time to explain himself before we contemplate –' she hesitated, 'before we contemplate force,' she finished firmly.

It was midmorning when Mim cried to their minds: 'Come Ladies and Lords! There are visitors! Come quickly!'

The Seniors looked at each other, they could sense no new life patterns within the grounds. They rose and hurried out to stand grouped on the veranda, five immensely tall, graceful figures framed by the equally tall doorway.

124

Mim was running towards them, Ashta and Lorak following behind. Lorak still clutched a plant in one hand and a gardening implement in the other as he stumped along, a trifle breathlessly, beside Ashta. Mim stopped at the foot of the shallow steps leading to the door, his face beaming with delight as he looked up at the Golden Lady.

'Look!' He turned, pointing to the sky to the southwest. They looked. Four specks grew larger as they drew nearer the House until they could be seen clearly. Four Dragons, coming to the Golden Lady.

Ashta's eyes were blazing with excitement. Farn was the only Dragon she had met, other than her siblings, her mother, and Seela of the Sun Treasury. Farn landed first, gently gliding to the lawn near the steps. Tika slid from his back, Khosa in her arms, and walked to join Mim. As the other three Dragons landed beside Farn, Tika looked up at the Seniors.

'Fenj comes to join us Lady, as do Kija and Jeela.'

She could feel the awed amazement in the Seniors as they looked at the enormous black Fenj now rearing erect to make formal greeting. Kija's golden bulk also towered up, wings stretched to steady herself, and the much smaller, creamy scaled Jeela copied her elders. Kaleidoscopic colours whirred in prismed eyes as Fenj said: 'We of the Dragon Kin greet you again at last, Golden Lady.'

For a brief moment, no one moved. Then, to the Seniors' astonishment, the dignified Lady Emla was running down the steps. As she reached Fenj, he lowered himself and her outstretched hands held his beautiful old head between them. 'To see you thus, Fenj, after all this time! And I so sorrowed, thinking you would choose to go beyond!'

Fenj muttered something about selfish old Dragons, quite clearly overcome by this welcome from the Lady. She turned to Kija, touching the gleaming face as she said: 'Of you I have heard much, Kija. I am proud to greet you as my guest, and bid you truly welcome.' She moved towards Jeela. 'And you! You are so dainty, yet I see such strength within you!' Her smile embraced them all. 'Come, let us talk. Will you enter my House, my dear ones?'

Jeela moved forward then stopped guiltily, looking at her

mother. Emla laughed, 'Come Jeela,' she said, putting her arm around Jeela's shoulders. 'You shall lead the way with me!' Kija followed, then Fenj, the Seniors standing aside, speechless at the sheer size of these two magnificent Dragons.

Chapter Fifteen

The great hall of Emla's House did not seem quite so great once Fenj and Kija had entered and settled themselves. They were as interested as Jeela to see inside one of the strange dwellings two-legs used. When all were comfortable, Emla looked around at them.

'The time for any concealment is past,' she said. 'One of the Weights entrusted to my care has been stolen. Linvaks took it, how I do not know. In all our time of having charge of the Balance, we have never enquired into how the Weights remain in their suspension.' She spread her hands. 'We know it is a complex use of the Power, but complex in a way we have long forgotten – if we ever knew it. Some of our Seniors are experimenting, in Gaharn, to try to replicate the means of suspension. But that is beside the point. We do know that the Linvaks went towards Death Pass in the Spine Mountains, at the juncture where those mountains turn north, to the Realm of Ice.

'Gan's scouts report a great killing took place near there. There were remains to account for all the Linvaks who guested here. Therefore, none escaped that slaughter. If the Guardian had got hold of the Weight from the Linvaks, his Power would already be too great for us to contain. I believe he would not hesitate to demonstrate that Power to us. That he has not done so, leads me to conclude it is not yet in his possession.

'Thus, for whatever reason the stars alone know, the Linvaks have either hidden the weight, or passed it to someone, or something, else.'

She paused. Fenj had been rumbling for a while and he now asked: 'How did these Linvaks die Lady?'

'Shardi.'

Fenj hissed. 'I did not know they came so far south Lady.'

'There have been reports over recent generations that they venture further south from the Realm of Ice with each Cold

Season.'

Emla continued: 'The Shardi, and the Linvaks are creatures of the Grey Guardian. We believe there are others but we do not know for sure. Jerak, our ancient one, went to the Realm of Ice last Growing Season, to try to reason with the Guardian. He did not return. We know only that there was a great use of Power, but we have not heard from Jerak since then. I believe he is still with us, but wounded, trapped, imprisoned – I cannot guess.

'We have to decide whether Tika and Mim should try to reach the Guardian's stronghold and the place where his Balance Weights lie, or search for the one that is hidden somewhere in the Spine Mountains.'

'It would seem neither option will be a pleasant or easy task,' Kija remarked. 'With Shardi helping us look for the Weight no doubt.'

Emla gave her a quick smile, 'Truly said, Kija. There is one more thing.' She looked now at Tika and Mim. 'These two have been altered.' Kija and Fenj both rumbled, their eyes beginning to glow. 'No, not intentionally, and not by us,' Emla said quickly. 'You, Fenj, are far more than the intelligent little hatchling you were when first we met. Maybe you can understand better than I, if you study their life patterns.'

Fenj and Kija both stared hard at Tika and Mim. They gave no indication of surprise at first, then suddenly both Dragons half rose, their eyes flashing. Tika and Mim also rose, standing close beside Farn and Ashta. Jeela stared in fascination from the two legs to the elder Dragons and back. The Seniors realised with growing alarm that they were quite unable to penetrate the Dragon minds, or Tika's and Mim's.

Tika broke the spell. 'You see,' she spoke so all could hear her, but specifically to Fenj and Kija. 'I will do what I must and what I can.' She looked at Emla. 'You have neglected the Dragon Kin too long, Lady. Though their minds follow different pathways, they have grown over the generations. They are as strong as you are.' She moved forward a few paces, facing Emla and the Seniors directly. 'See then, what they have just seen.' And she laid open her mind, and the Seniors saw, with considerable shock, what the Dragons had seen.

The web Tika had reshaped had grown. It was now a

128

glittering complexity, far beyond their understanding. It was beautiful, symmetrical, intricate. And it evidenced an enormous increase in Power.

'Even so,' said Tika, 'I do not know if I can overcome the Guardian. I know much but, as before, there seem to be pieces missing, gaps across which I cannot guess how to bridge.'

'Will this happen with all humans cross-breeding with the People, I wonder?' Kemti was enthralled.

'I do not think so. I do not know why it happened to me.' Tika paused. 'Jerak did not tell me that, when his mind spoke to me.'

'Jerak?' Iska queried softly. She looked at Emla. Emla's hands were over her mouth, her green eyes huge as they returned Tika's equally green gaze.

'Jerak helped you,' she whispered. 'Jerak fathered the Guardian and me, Tika, but he has been long lost to us.'

Tika closed her mind to them, retreating to sit leaning against Farn. 'He gave me some knowledge,' she said. 'It felt a bit like it did when Kija put memories into me when I bonded with Farn.' She was studying the gold and amber pendant she always wore as she spoke. She looked up at Emla again. 'I knew his name somehow. I could not see where he was, but it looked like this.' She lifted the oval drop on its thin chain. 'He was in a dark place, but inside something. He said, "go to the Guardian," so I suppose we must.'

Suddenly, she looked an undersized human child, confused at finding herself in these strange circumstances. Mim stretched his hand to her, stroking her arm lightly. Farn and Ashta were pouring affection and support to her.

Tika looked again at Emla. 'I would see your Balance Weights now. You have not allowed Mim or me to see them yet – have you feared we also might take one from you?'

Emla looked aghast. She rose, moving swiftly to kneel before Tika. Her long fingered hands caught Tika's small ones. 'Oh my dear one, no! I have had no doubts of you since we met!'

She was interrupted as a maid bobbed into the hall. 'Excuse me, my Lady, but there's someone as says they must speak with Lord Gan if you please.'

At Emla's nod, Gan left the hall. He was back almost at once.

'There is trouble, Lady, on the Middle Plain. Some creatures, never seen before, are attacking the farms near the foothills of the Spine Mountains. I must organise assistance at once.'

As he turned to leave again, Emla called, 'Gan, you must send men of course. But you will not go yourself.'

'But –' Gan scowled, then bit his lip, bowed abruptly to Emla and left.

Emla stood for a while deep in thought, then turning to Tika again, she held out her hand. 'Come, we will go to the Pavilion of the Sacred Balance.'

It was an odd group that arrived at the guarded Pavilion: five Dragons, four of the tall slender People, a small human female and a male Nagum. And an aged human gardener who busied himself unobtrusively among the nearest shrubs. Two of the guards whom Gan had set around the Pavilion opened the doors for the Lady. 'I am not sure Fenj and Kija will be able to enter,' Emla looked at the doorway then dubiously at Kija's golden bulk and Fenj's black hugeness.

'We will see well enough from the door, Lady.' Fenj said.

The Seniors entered, moving round the sides of the Pavilion, leaving the doorway clear. Ashta, Farn and Jeela peered in, Fenj and Kija's heads above theirs. Tika and Mim stood one each side of Emla, staring at the golden Weights.

It was quiet. The Weights hung, apparently unsupported, in the centre of the Pavilion above a crystal and gold mosaic circle. Six disks of gold, a hole in the centre of each, as though a chain, or a rope, should have threaded through them. The lowest disk was a man's fist in thickness and a man's arm length across, the one above was slightly smaller, and the next smaller still.

'So the one that has gone would be the smallest?' Mim asked.

'Yes,' agreed Emla. 'About a handspan across and one finger thick. They are all immensely heavy we believe, heavier than they might appear. Kemti can show you later how the one that is lost might look and feel. We can only estimate their heaviness though. We do not know who made them or whence they came. They were here when we first came. The Seniors of those days were more knowledgeable then in certain matters. This land did not really need their skills it was decided, once our city was built and functioning.'

130

Kemti shook his head. 'In those long past days, it was decided the People would live simply, without many things that were once thought essential to our lives.' He sighed. 'Knowledge should never be forgotten though; set aside perhaps for use in a future time unknown, but never discarded.'

Mim and Tika were not listening to this exchange. They were studying the suspended Weights. 'This person sees, Tika,' said Mim, his words bringing the Seniors closer.

'Yes,' agreed Tika. 'It is quite a simple knotting of threads really except…'

'Except for the way Time is woven into it as well,' finished Mim. 'It is Time, isn't it? That silver line this one sees?'

'I think so. We will stay here a while Lady, just to look at the working.' They sat on the floor staring at the Weights.

Iska asked, 'Can you both truly see how the Weights are hung?' Mim looked faintly surprised.

'Yes of course. Can you not see it Lady?'

'None of us can,' replied Yash, and added to Emla: 'Can Mim see it too, or is he sharing Tika's sight?'

'He sees it too,' Tika said rather shortly. Yash bowed apologyetically. 'We will join you later,' she added pointedly.

'We will wait in the House then.' Emla moved to the door just as a small orange Kephi marched in, tail aloft, settling itself comfortably on Tika's lap. 'If that Kephi bothers you, just push it out.'

'Push it out indeed,' Khosa slitted her eyes at Emla. Tika scratched Khosa's ears and the Kephi collapsed, crooning in bliss. 'It's not bothering us, thank you.' Tika returned her concentration to the Weights.

Outside, Emla looked a trifle nonplussed as to how to entertain five Dragons but Kija solved the problem. 'We travelled here with few stops to eat Lady. We would find food if you permit?'

'Of course,' said Emla. 'As we told Mim and Tika, we will be in the House when you return.'

Farn, Jeela and Ashta looked at Kija. 'There is a place, quite near, where live many volu,' Farn told her helpfully.

'Very well. Show us where then. Fenj?'

'I do not really hunger,' said Fenj. 'I will look at this place where my Lady lives.'

'You are not going to stop eating again, Fenj, you will need all your strength if you insist on coming with us.'

'I will bring you hoppers,' Farn offered.

Fenj pondered. 'Are they plump hoppers here?'

'Of course!' said Farn, eyes whirring in delight. Kija gave him a rather long look, then she began to lift into the air. Fenj watched them go, Farn looping between Ashta and Kija, his small sister following each move. As they disappeared, Fenj looked about him. Guards stood around the Pavilion but the Seniors had vanished into the Lady's dwelling. A grunt came from some shrubbery.

Fenj moved, extremely quietly for one of his immense size, and extended his neck over the bushes, coming face to face with Lorak. This old human's face registered alarm as he said, 'I am a friend of young Mim, that is, I mean Lord Mim, your Lordship.' Fenj's eyes shone like grey pearl at this flustered two-legs.

'I am quite sure you are a very good friend to Mim. I am Fenj of the Broken Mountain Treasury.' His words rang deep in the old man's mind. 'And you are?'

'Well now, I am Lorak of, of – her Ladyship's Garden.' Lorak bowed. Fenj sensed a great obstinacy in this old human, who he reflected, was but a mere child compared to one of his own great age.

'I would know what you do, Lorak of the Garden.'

'Oh. Well now. If you would come this way, your Lordship, I can show you some of my work.'

Emla was a little puzzled to see Fenj wandering across her lawns, with Lorak trotting beside him gesticulating vigorously, but she was distracted by Gan's abrupt arrival.

'My Lady, I should go with my men. They await my order to depart, but really, I protest that I should lead them.'

'I know how you feel Gan but no.' She raised her hand as he began to argue further. 'The first thought that occurred to me at the news of trouble on the Middle Plain was – is this another false clue? I grant there is probably something unpleasant happening there, and maybe in different times I would send many men, led by you, there immediately.'

Gan's expression changed as he realised what she was saying. 'The Guardian?' he asked. 'Pulling our attention, and your

Guards, one way, while he moves in another?'

Emla nodded. 'I will listen to everyone else's opinion on this, and that includes the Dragons, Gan. Then I will decide. I tell you now I am strongly persuaded that the lost Weight should be abandoned in favour of reaching the Guardian.' She moved back to the window as Gan went to the door. 'Gan, have you any idea what Lorak could be doing with Fenj?'

Mim and Tika had studied the pattern of Power holding the Weights suspended. They agreed it was a fairly straightforward holding weave, except that time was involved. At last Tika got to her feet, gently passing Khosa to Mim. 'It comes back to the same thing every way I try to see how it is worked, Mim. What do you think?'

'Yes.' He climbed to his feet, Khosa draped bonelessly over his shoulder. 'This person sees only one result, should it be undone.'

'The Dragons should be back. Let's go to the hall.'

Kija and the young Dragons had indeed returned some time earlier, and were already in the great hall. The Seniors had found a great difference conversing with Kija, and realised fully for the first time just how very young Farn and Ashta were. Because of their size, the Seniors had mistakenly assumed they were far more adult than in fact they were.

As Tika and Mim walked back to the House, enjoying the fresh crispness of the late afternoon, Tika paused. 'There is Fenj,' she nodded across the wide lawn. 'He's with Lorak. I did not know Fenj had an interest in plants.'

Mim watched the great black shape advancing, Lorak at his side. He smiled, his eyes sparkling, but he merely said, 'Lorak knows many things.'

They entered the hall to find the fire blazing and the smell of spiced tea and hot pies welcoming them. 'Fenj is just coming.' Tika took a cup of tea and wrapped her hands round its warmth as she sat beside Farn. It was chillier outside than it had at first seemed.

Fenj filled the doorway. 'Apologies if I am late, Lady.'

'Not at all Fenj.'

'Your hoppers are safe,' Farn told him.

'Thank you Farn.' Fenj reclined opposite Kija.

'May I ask what you found of interest with Lorak?' Emla's curiosity got the better of her.

Fenj's eyes whirred softly. 'A splendid creature.'

The Seniors exchanged glances: Lorak – "a splendid creature"?

'I saw many beautiful growing things, flowers, and I think he called them "vegetables"? Then he showed me his workshop.' He sighed. 'I tasted what he called a "beverage" – extraordinary! And very pleasing.'

Emla sat upright. That would bear checking on – Lorak was brewing again was he? But Fenj repeated: 'A splendid creature!'

Tika intervened. 'Lady, Mim and I have studied the Weights in every way we can.' Everyone's attention was on her now. 'It would be easy to just reach out and take one. They are not tightly held in their places. We believe the Linvak may have simply taken it on impulse. Do Linvaks know of the Balance, or of its purpose? We think they did not, that one of them saw the gold, and took it. But,' she glanced at Mim as if to confirm what she was saying, 'we do not believe the Weight can be replaced, even were it found.'

'If it is so easy to remove,' Yash queried, 'why may it not be just – slipped back into position?'

Mim answered him. 'Because Time is woven into the holding pattern. This one also tried many different ways to see how to untangle Time from the suspension. There is no way to do so.'

Kija asked: 'By taking a Weight entrapped with a thread of Time, what would happen – either to the Weight, or to the one who stole it?'

The Seniors were impressed by Kija's quick assessment of Mim and Tika's words.

Tika replied: 'We believe the Weight is gone, completely – we cannot begin to guess where. The Linvak, by tearing Time from its place, would have torn Time in himself.' She shrugged. 'He may suddenly have grown old, or shrunk back to infancy. Either way, he would have been destroyed.'

'So perhaps the Linvaks were not involved in any "plan"?' Iska thought aloud. 'Maybe they were as crude and simple minded as we thought them?'

'They had wit enough to know they had stolen something of

great value, and then to hurry in the opposite direction to the one we would assume they'd take,' retorted Kemti.

'We believe they did not know what it was they had taken,' Tika repeated. 'They may be servants of the Guardian, but this was not planned or done on his orders. We are convinced of that.'

Emla had been watching Tika closely. Now she said: 'There is more, is there not Tika?'

'Yes Lady. I understand now why Jerak said "go to the Guardian"'. Her audience waited tensely as she paused. 'I believe that Jerak meant we were to remove the smallest Weight from the seven in the Guardian's keeping. Thus it will restore an equality again.'

Fenj rumbled, as did Kija. The younger Dragons, especially Farn, were becoming greatly agitated. Tika slid her arms round Farn's neck, her voice slightly muffled against his scales. 'Already the balance of the world is changing, therefore action must be taken swiftly. But the one to take the Weight from the Guardian will suffer the same fate as the Linvak must have done. Time will destroy them.'

Chapter Sixteen

There followed a day of bustle and planning. The Dragons were stunned when Emla suggested they would remain at her House. Fengars would carry Mim and Tika, and a full band of Guards would accompany them. Kija became irate enough for smoke to begin wisping from her nostrils. Iska pointed out that the Dragons would only be able to go so far, because of the rapidly approaching Cold Season. Further north, in the Realm of Ice, the Cold Season lasted for nearly the whole Cycle anyway. Food would be scarce the further north they travelled and the icy temperature and increasing snow would speedily weaken the Dragons.

Kija lifted furiously into the sky to calm herself, and Fenj followed after her. Emla was extremely concerned to have so upset Kija, but Mim consoled her in his gentle way. 'This one knows you are but concerned for the Dragons well being,' he said in his soft fluting voice. 'But they worry for us. They will come with us, whatever you decide Lady.'

'You have to have Guards with you Mim. The two of you will never reach the Guardian alone.' He smiled sweetly, but did not reply.

Tika was trying to soothe Farn. He was distraught to think she may travel without him. He could not imagine not having her presence beside him. Ashta was similarly distressed, but her feelings were not so obvious as were Farn's. Jeela tried desperately to offer comfort to both her brother and to the pale green Ashta, to whom she had quickly become attached.

The peace and tranquillity the House had become accustomed to for generations, vanished. Gan was busily organising men and supplies, the Seniors were consulting maps and arguing over routes, the household staff were scampering everywhere with messages, and Lorak had retired to his workshop.

When Kija and Fenj returned, Kija went immediately to

remove the young Dragons from the great hall, and took them to the quiet of the guest pavilion. She told them what she and Fenj had decided. She calmed them enough that Farn's appetite returned, to the point where he suggested they hunt.

Fenj went to the great hall and faced Emla. 'We will go on this journey Lady.'

'But Fenj…' Emla began to protest.

'No, Lady. You do not understand the harm you would cause the four bonded ones should you part them. Mim and Tika are not as aware as we are of how they too would suffer.'

'Fenj,' said Emla firmly. 'You cannot survive in prolonged cold or snowy conditions. Your Treasuries move to lower slopes once the great storms begin, do they not? And Tika and Mim will surely need help from trained Guards, sooner or later.'

'Lady.' Fenj reclined more comfortably along the fireside wall, and Emla sat on her usual stool. 'Kija and I have thought hard. We suggest your Lord Gan has a band of men begin travelling to the Realm of Ice. They will not travel as fast as we, but they should not be too far behind us.

'Kija and I will consent to carry Lord Gan and three other Guards. She and I should easily be able to carry two each. The young Farn and Ashta can bear only their bonded ones yet, and Jeela is too frail to carry any such burden.'

Emla looked at Fenj, speechless at his suggestion. Never had he offered to carry her when she had first known him. Never had she heard of any Dragon bearing a rider, until Tika and Mim. And now he was freely offering to carry two Guards. The thought crossed her mind that it might prove difficult to persuade three Guards to the idea of riding on Dragon backs.

'I do not understand these maps you have spoken of, but Tika and Mim seem to,' Fenj continued. 'If they know the directions and arrange a place where we may meet the band of Guards, there should be no problem.'

When all were collected together in the great hall that evening, all were exhausted. Maids were still busy sewing thick cloaks for Mim and Tika to wear over fleece-lined shirts and trousers. Boots had been stitched of the softest but most durable leather, and also lined with soft fleeces. Neither Mim nor Tika had ever

137

worn anything on their feet before and found the boots very strange.

Gan was reporting that his full band of Guards would leave at first light. They had plentiful supplies and a string of extra fengars. He looked a little uncomfortable but finally came out with: 'I think there will be only myself and two Guards to travel with the Dragons.' Emla raised a questioning eyebrow.

'The men say they are willing to face ice, snow, Shardi and Linvak, but fear they will fall to their deaths as soon as the Dragons fly above tree height.' He shrugged helplessly. 'Sket and Motass feel the same, but they say as they have been working with Mim and Tika, and they know how inept they are with weapons, they think it is their duty to accompany them.'

Fenj rustled his wings softly. 'So there will be this Sket? And Motass? And yourself, Lord Gan? Why do we not ask Lorak to join us? Splendid creature! He is by the door I believe, so why do we not ask him now?'

Mim hurried to the door and pulled inside a defensively embarrassed Lorak. Tika was laughing openly, and Emla was struggling not to.

'Now Lorak of the Garden,' said Fenj. 'Will you accompany us to the Guardian's stronghold?'

'Well now, your Lordship, I don't see as why I shouldn't. A bit of travelling before I die. New places, new plants. Yes indeed, your Lordship.'

Fenj said: 'Wonderful! I shall carry Lord Gan, and yourself, Lorak of the Garden!'

Emla glanced at Gan's face, caught Tika's eye, and bit her lips very hard.

Emla went to speak privately with Kija and then suggested everyone go to rest to prepare for the start of their journey. They had agreed on a later departure, giving the band of Guards time to get a fair distance along their route.

As the Seniors moved to the staircase and the Dragons and Mim left through the main door, Tika held back. When the great hall was empty but for herself and Emla, she said: 'Jerak told me these were real.' She lifted the amber and gold pendant. 'He said –"they will serve a purpose". I do not think he knew what that could be. But somehow I knew they were real, from the beginning.'

Emla reached to take the pendant in her hand, looking closely at the tiny dark speck. 'Is it a plant, or a tiny crawler?' she asked Tika.

Tika grinned. 'Fenj told me to "use my mind" to see. Shall I dare tell you, Lady, to use your mind?'

Emla smiled back, then focused on the egg shaped drop. Her smile faded as she saw what the speck was that was set deep in the amber. She loosed her hold of it and looked at Tika. 'You say it was real?'

'Yes,' Tika nodded. 'I can not quite reach the memory, but yes, it was real. Or perhaps it still is.'

Emla pulled Tika gently towards her, held her for a moment, then released her. 'Go to bed, dear one. Remember in all the days to come, we will be thinking of you constantly.'

Tika was surprised to find Mim, Ashta and Jeela fast asleep already when she reached the guest pavilion. Farn was yawning hugely and struggling to keep his eyes open. He managed to say: 'There you are at last!' And then he was asleep. Khosa was sitting on Fenj's neck, glaring at Kija. 'She even tried to make me sleep!' she spluttered indignantly at Tika. Tika looked at Kija.

'I only helped them rest, small one. The Lady herself suggested the idea. Like a healing. A long easy, restful sleep, which you also need.'

'I know. I am going to bed right now. Come on Khosa.' Khosa strutted under Kija's nose, then bounced into Tika's bedchamber. She watched as Tika looked at the newly made shirts and moved them from the bed where they had been laid out.

'What is that?' she enquired, as Tika examined a leather sack, fleece lined, with a drawstring top.

'The maids think it is for carrying underbeneaths. It is really for you.'

'You think a Kephi is going to be carried in a sack? A Kephi Queen?' Khosa's eyes blazed and her tail thrashed wrathfully.

'It will be cold where we journey. See how snug this will be.' Tika coaxed, as she held the sack open. 'Look at it before you refuse to use it.' Khosa turned her back. Tika sighed, left the sack on the bed and climbed into the bed herself. 'Goodnight

Khosa.'

As Tika and Mim arrived for breakfast next morning, they found Gan explaining that his Guards would already be many leagues from Gaharn. They had gone through the Lower Pass of Gaharn and would thus keep to the southern side of the Far High Lands. This meant that the mountains would give them some protection from the storms that were battering down from the Realm of Ice. Gan estimated it would take the band at least ten days to reach the Waste.

As Mim and Tika helped themselves to food, Gan continued. 'I know the Dragons could do that distance in half the time, maybe even less. But I want them to become entirely accustomed to carrying riders and baggage. I would also like to find out how swiftly they respond to any command. Do you think they will find the panniers cumbersome?'

'This one thinks they should be comfortable enough. Fenj and Ashta seemed not to notice them particularly when we tried them yesterday. As long as they are evenly loaded and are not in the way of their wings, there should be no difficulty.'

'How are Sket and Motass?' Tika asked innocently.

Gan smiled reluctantly. 'Extremely apprehensive,' he said. 'Has anyone seen Lorak this morning, and can anyone enlighten me as to why he is coming with us?'

'Fenj seems to like him, very much.' Mim shrugged, his face straight but his eyes gleaming. 'Will Lorak bring some of his beverage, Lord Gan?'

Gan's smile vanished. 'I trust not.'

Mim and Tika returned to their pavilion to find Shan checking, yet again, that their new clothes were packed properly in leather carriers. She gazed at the two, her round cheeks flushed with excitement. 'Won't you have tales to tell when you come back!' she exclaimed. 'Flying off, stars know where, on the backs of great Dragons!'

'Would you like to come with us Shan?'

'Stars, no!' Shan cried. 'I like to sit by a nice warm fire and sleep in a comfortable bed. But I like to hear stories of wild adventures.' She hesitated, then threw her arms around them both, pressing them to her ample bosom. She gave a resounding kiss to each of them, then whirled away to the door. 'You make sure you look after yourselves and come back and tell me all about it!'

Tika said: 'It is strange that Shan seems quite bothered about us. I do not remember anyone being bothered about me before.'

'This one does,' said Mim quietly.

Before the Golden Lady's House, the five Dragons waited. They all bore double pouches, linked with a broad strap of soft leather and loosely tied underneath their chests. The company's clothes and some foods, such as dried fruits, traveller's bread, herbs and spices were evenly distributed among the Dragons. Kija had at first refused to allow Jeela to carry anything, but the ivory Dragon had thrown such a tantrum as to earn her brother's deepest admiration. She was now proudly waiting, with a smaller pair of pouches across her shoulders, containing some food, and maps – "things of importance," Tika had told her tactfully.

Gan came round the side of the House wearing a thick blue cloak, the Lady's insignia of a golden blossom embroidered at the left shoulder. He had on a close fitting leather helmet, fastened under his jaw. At his belt, hung a long sword, and the hilts of two daggers were visible at his right side. Behind him marched Sket and Motass, their expressions those of condemned men facing immediate death. Kija regarded them impassively as Gan led them towards her.

He persuaded Sket and Motass onto Kija's back, where they perched, pale faced but resigned. Then he walked across to Fenj. As Gan approached, Lorak appeared. He had a strange hat jammed on his head, a thick but shabby cloak, and various bags at which Gan cast a deeply suspicious glare. He said nothing though, as Lorak clambered onto Fenj's back.

Emla and the Seniors moved from Dragon to Dragon, bidding them and their riders farewell and safe journeying. Emla took each long beautiful face between her hands and pressed her forehead to each brow. She spoke softly to Mim, her hands on his shoulders, then stooped to kiss his cheek. He turned, blushing and climbed onto Ashta's back.

The group of Seniors had reached Fenj now and Gan bowed deeply to the Lady. 'We will spare nothing in this task my Lady,' he said.

'I know Gan. And you know, we will not stop searching for

any information that is yet hidden here in books or parchments. Our hearts go with you.'

Gan bowed again and climbed up in front of old Lorak. And so Emla came to say farewell to Farn and Tika. As Emla began to speak, a furry orange face poked out over the neck of Tika's cloak. 'Are you taking the Kephi?' she asked in surprise. 'Surely it will be but a nuisance?'

Khosa slitted her eyes as Tika laughed. 'No Lady, she will help keep me warm!'

'Well, if you think so.' Emla did not sound entirely convinced. 'Now you go into dangers we cannot guess. Remember, you must control the Power in you, and also remember, the nearer you come to the Guardian, the more the urge to use it may grow in you. But if you do use it, he will be made aware.' The Lady looked at Tika, conscious that there was nothing more to say. She hugged her tightly for a moment, then pushed her gently to Farn.

As the Seniors stood before the House, Emla slightly before them, the Dragons began to lift skywards. Sket and Motass saw nothing, their eyes were firmly closed, but the other riders looked back. The four tall People below waved to them as they circled once. As they began their flight north towards the Realm of Ice, they heard Emla in their minds: 'Farewell dear ones! May the stars keep you safe!'

Chapter Seventeen

Rhaki was humming to himself as he walked through the main passageways of his stronghold. He had spent the morning checking the progress of several human females. They were quite newly captured, from the Sun Mountain area, and had not settled too happily where they now found themselves.

Rhaki had spoken to them on many occasions, explaining his experiments in breeding, and how marvellous their participation would be. One female had tried to physically attack him. Of course, he had been shielded by the Power, he never took pointless risks on these sorts of occasions, but he had been a little surprised. And hurt, that she had displayed such smallness of mind. He had her removed of course.

Most of them were pregnant now. One he had bred directly with a Shardi, had recovered from her injuries, but she seemed overly lethargic. The others he had had impregnated variously, under his supervision. He felt a slight regret that there was no one who could appreciate his work. He had considered writing a report and sending it to the Seniors in Gaharn, but he knew their reaction would be one of horror rather than the fascinated interest in his efforts that he craved. One day, he consoled himself, the world would know of his triumphs in the field of cross-breeding.

Rhaki sat at his table, comparing his notes on the present human females with ones he had experimented on a generation or so ago. Yes, the human stock seemed more willing to accept different genomes now. Previously, there had been early rejection of the foetuses whereas now, all seemed to be developing well.

'Come,' he called before the rap on his door. Jal entered, bowing as Rhaki turned to him.

'Master, the Cansharsi are causing panic in the lower Middle Plain, but are now in the Swamp Land. I do not think many Nagum will be affected – their communities have drawn together and moved deep into their woodlands. The Cansharsi became bored with nothing to chase, and they refused to go far into the woods. The Linvaks distracted them and they are now destroying Linvak settlements rather than moving out towards the farms and towns of the Plain.'

'Are the Linvaks able to withstand the Cansharsi force?'

Jal looked uncomfortable. 'Master, the Linvaks do not appear able to plan very well, or consider different options. The Cansharsi can. But the Linvaks fight well, and to the death.' He was only too aware that Rhaki had created both creatures, but was unsure if he should take the liberty of criticising the apparent feeble mindedness of the Linvaks.

'Move some of the Cansharsi still waiting this side of the Ancient Mountains out on to the Plain, Jal. Send Verim to take charge in that area,' he added thoughtfully. 'What is your opinion of him, anyway?'

Jal pursed his lips. 'He is trustworthy Master – so far.'

'So far?'

'I believe his goal is personal fortune. He would like to become a Lord such as those of the southwest, Master. I hope I may be proved wrong, but I feel he could be tempted by anyone offering him a step towards that ambition.'

'Very good, Jal,' said the Guardian. 'The conclusion I also had reached. Send one of your own men to be his servant. He is unlikely to find a better – employer – out there, but just in case.'

'Yes Master.' Jal cleared his throat. 'A large band of Guards has left Gaharn, Master.'

'Really! How interesting!' Rhaki smiled complacently. 'Heading for the Middle Plain.'

'No Master. Heading north.'

'What!' Rhaki's smile became a scowl. 'North you say? Why would they choose the Cold Season to advance to this Realm?'

'Master, five Dragons have been seen flying a similar route. I think there is a connection.'

'Keep me informed. See to this personally Jal.' As Jal bowed himself from the Guardian's presence, Rhaki began to pace, thinking furiously.

It must be coincidence. The news of the Cansharsi attacks

could obviously not have reached Gaharn. Emla would have despatched Guards to assist any who called on her for help. What was she planning? If only he had a pair of eyes or ears within her House!

He calmed himself with an effort. The Guards would find little help along the route they had chosen – a few isolated farms where human renegades eked out their livings, the scavengers in the Waste Land. None of those would welcome a large body of armed Guards from the distant city of Gaharn. And the weather would increasingly hamper their travelling.

Rhaki completely discounted mention of Dragons. They fled from heavy snow and extreme cold: these five Jal reported must have lost their way. They could have no reason, other than suicide, to fly north at any time, let alone in the Cold. Rhaki decided he must have more information. Jal must try to place someone in this band of Guards – a menial more or less would surely pass unnoticed, and he must redouble his efforts to get a spy into Gaharn.

Emla's Guards had made good time so far. The weather was still only chilly rather than cold. The fengars had been as well behaved as could be expected of them in the excitement of leaving their stable prisons. The band was led by Soran, a human whose military capabilities Gan held in high esteem. They had covered twenty-five leagues on this first day's march, and had made camp for the night just north of the entrance to Death Pass.

Soran set a double watch around the camp, to be changed every two hours. There were no grumbles as all the men were aware of the recent Shardi slaughter of the Linvaks. His chief officer, Trem, one of the few humans with some ability to far mind speak, told Soran that the Dragons were halting for the night also, higher in the hills before Death Pass.

Gan had told his officers of his intention not to press the Dragons hard at first, and that he wanted to see how they might be used in battle. Soran and the other officers were very grateful to be on the ground; they had grave doubts as to the wisdom of humans attempting to fly.

The Dragons had made their landing in a ravine whose topmost edges were sprinkled with snow. Several fissures in a rock face formed shallow caves near which the humans made a fire. Kija, Fenj and Farn hunted, returning with meat for Ashta and Jeela as well as for the two legs. Sket and Motass had finally opened their eyes on the journey and looked at the land spread below them with fascination. They agreed that flight was not quite as alarming as they had feared, but they were glad to be standing on solid ground once more. Lorak busied himself brewing a spicy tea, which Gan sniffed suspiciously before sipping.

Gan moved to where Kija and Fenj reclined after they had all eaten. The others stayed around the fire, listening to Sket and Motass tell tales of their battles. In truth, these "battles" were fairly minor affairs, the land watched over by Gaharn being a peaceable place for many generations.

'How did you become Guards?' asked Tika.

'I lived on a farm outside Gaharn city and I always said as I would join them if they'd have me,' Sket replied.

'What about you?' she asked Motass. Lorak chuckled and Motass glared at him.

'I come from beyond the Ancient Mountains.' He fidgeted with his dagger hilt. 'There are rich merchant routes there, coming from the distant south. I, erm, was with a Gang.'

Puzzlement came from the young Dragons and Mim, but Tika stared in surprise.

'You were a Ganger, Motass?'

'Yes Lady, but long ago. See, I don't remember no family, excepting two brothers. They was older than me, took care of me and that. They joined the Gangers, and so I went too.'

"What is this – "gang"?' Farn demanded.

'Gangs are like groups of Fighters – remember those you scared away? They attack travellers, and steal their goods. They kill the travellers, or take some as slaves.'

'And you did these things?' Farn asked Motass in astonishment.

'Well not for long,' Motass said defensively. 'Lord Gan came along and fought several Gangs. One of them was the one I belonged to, see, and I was only a little thing – about your size Lady. I only went on two raids and Lord Gan nabbed me on the second one. Anyways, Lord Gan, he says to me, he says, "If you want to come and take training boy, you are free to do so." Well, I asked him what if I said no? He said he'd have to kill me then.' Motass shrugged. 'So I joined the Guards.'

'Your brothers?' enquired Mim.

'One was killed in the first raid I was taken on, the other one escaped before Lord Gan's men could catch him.'

'Is your brother like you?' Jeela asked curiously.

'Well, we was said to look alike, if that's what you mean.'

Sket laughed. 'But Motass has much nicer manners these days!'

'All this fighting you seem to do,' Farn puzzled. 'Do you like to kill other two-legs so much? Are you not afraid they will kill you, or wound you dreadfully?'

Before either man could reply, Gan said: 'The Guards are unspeakably brave, are they not, men?'

Sket choked on his tea, Lorak laughed aloud and Motass struggled to attention. 'No, no,' Gan continued. 'I only tease them Farn.' He sat with them beside the embers of the fire. 'All who fight know fear very well, Farn. Perhaps it is necessary to a certain extent – if you fear, you may be more cautious, but that caution could well keep you alive.'

As he spoke, Khosa stalked between Farn and Ashta. Farn watched her nervously as she sat neatly and began her endless washing. Tika ran a finger down Khosa's spine as Gan remarked: 'I do not understand why you brought a Kephi, Tika. She is bound to get lost or left behind somewhere.'

Slowly, Khosa turned her head to stare at him. 'Kephi are not as stupid as we have led you to believe. I suggest you get used to that idea, Gan. And my name is Khosa. I am Queen of the Kephi of the Lady's estate.'

Gan realised his mouth was open. He shut it with a snap that rattled his teeth. Khosa kept her unblinking stare fixed on him, and Farn shivered in sympathy. 'We Kephi choose not to speak with two-legs, but I have decided to speak with all in this company. Just so that there is no misunderstanding about leaving a "stupid Kephi" behind, at any stage.'

Her gaze moved steadily from Gan to Sket, and on to Motass. Lorak was grinning. Gan said weakly: 'You have obviously spoken to Tika and Mim before. And Lorak?'

'We approve of Lorak.' Khosa said regally, and went back to cleaning her whiskers.

Jeela had bespoken her mother privately after Gan joined them by the fire. Now the golden Dragon's head loomed from the darkness into the fireglow. 'Jeela says she hears someone calling from far.' Kija spoke to them all. 'It is too far, even gifted as she is, for her to know who calls. She is sure it is one of the Kin. Can you hear, Tika?'

Tika concentrated along the line of direction Jeela showed her. 'I hear nothing,' she admitted after a few minutes. 'But if Jeela says she heard a call, then know that she did.'

Fenj had moved closer to the company. 'Who then, Kija? Surely Seela is not close enough, nor Kadi? So one of the Kin must follow us.' Farn and Tika looked at each other.

'No,' said Jeela. 'I would know Nula, no matter from how far.' She shivered her delicate wings. 'Her voice I would know,' she repeated.

'There is little moon,' said Gan, 'therefore I would guess whoever follows will also be awaiting sunrise, as are we. We will not hurry to leave in the morning, so Tika and Jeela may listen again.'

At dawn the Dragons went to hunt their breakfast, leaving Jeela to listen, with Tika. The men rekindled a small fire and made tea, chewing on the cold roast meat left from supper. They all watched the pale Dragon and small, dark haired Tika concentrating. Tika leaned against Jeela, both appearing quite relaxed, both pairs of eyes closed. A silence seemed to expand around them as they focused intently to hear the faintest mind call.

Jeela's eyes opened, the prisms glittering with honey and silver lights. Tika said aloud to Gan and the men: 'It is a male, known to Fenj. He comes fast.' She opened her eyes. 'He will reach this place where we are now, by midday.'

'Why is he following us?' Gan asked urgently.

Tika was clearly transmitting Gan's question to the distant Dragon. A puzzled expression crossed her face, then a quizzical smile. She looked at Gan and shrugged. 'He says he likes adventures.'

Khosa remarked from her perch on Lorak's knee: 'My feelings

exactly.'

'You may well change your opinion before this journey is done – your majesty.' Gan retorted.

Khosa gave him her unwinking glare at his sarcastic tone, but did not deign to reply.

'Will we wait for this Dragon?' asked Mim.

Gan considered. 'The weather looks as though it will hold fair for a few days more. I think we should wait. I want all of us alert though, just in case he is corrupted as Nula was. I would rather face him now than have him on our tail indefinitely.' He looked around their camp. 'I think we should move into the caves, so our backs are protected at least. Just in case,' he repeated.

He, Sket and Motass went to inspect the defensive possibilities of the caves as Fenj returned with the other three Dragons. As Mim told them of the change of plan, Farn's eyes whirred excitedly. 'We found a place where there were so many of the plumpest hoppers Jeela! If we are waiting here a while, I can show you the place.'

Jeela looked at the two hoppers her mother had brought back for her, then at Farn. Her eyes sparkled with the same excitement. Kija sighed. 'Very well. But only to fetch hoppers Farn. Return swiftly.' The two youngsters were already lifting before she had finished speaking.

Mim laughed and pushed Ashta gently. 'Go on! This one knows you want to go too!' Ashta needed no more encouragement – she was rapidly up and after Farn and Jeela.

'Can you hear him yet, Mim?' Tika asked quietly.

'No, but you know this person only clearly hears Ashta well.' He looked at her. 'Have you any idea who it could be?'

'I really don't. He said Fenj knew him that was all.'

'We will soon know. Why do we not climb up there and watch for him?' He pointed to the ridge above the caves.

'Race you,' she grinned suddenly, starting to scramble over the boulders. It was higher than it looked but they reached the ridge easily enough. They brushed the thin snow off a rock and sat watching the southern sky. The wind was strong and cold now they were on the exposed ridge. Its icy fingers probed round their ears, down their necks and tried to push through their shirts.

Gan suddenly realised Tika and Mim were missing.

'Up there.' Khosa remarked, flicking a glance up the rock face. Gan was aware of Kija's sympathy for his having to deal with difficult children as he glared upwards.

'Will you please get down here. Now. We cannot be sure this Dragon is not following to do harm to you.' As Tika and Mim continued to sit, staring down at him, he folded his arms. 'I said, "down here", and "now".' They looked at each other then began to slide down from the ridge.

'His voice is quiet, but this person thinks Gan is angry perhaps.'

'I don't see why he should be. We would see a Dragon long before it got here, and we can use the Power, and Kija and Fenj are right there. I do wish he could stop treating us like infants.'

As they arrived in front of Gan, the three young Dragons returned. Tika felt the laughter building in Mim as he watched Farn approach. She risked a quick glance from beneath her lashes at Gan's thunderous face, then slipped her arm round Farn's neck. His sapphire eyes whirred with concern. 'There is trouble Tika?'

'No Farn,' she managed to say. 'Everything is fine.'

'Is this Gan angered?'

Gan made a great effort to change his scowl to a near smile; the result was a grimace of pain. 'No,' he said at last, 'I am not angered Farn. A trifle edgy – shall we say?'

At that moment, perhaps fortuitously, Jeela said: 'He is near!'

Gan ordered everyone to move closer to the caves, where they stood scanning the sky to the south.

'There!' cried Farn.

'You see him?' asked Kija.

'Of course.'

Slowly, minute by minute, the tiny dot grew larger, until even old Lorak could see the Dragon shape speeding towards them. Tika and Mim both felt shock ripple through Fenj's mind. Mim caught Tika's hand as Fenj suddenly moved forward, away from the sheltering rock wall. He reared upright, his wings outstretched as his great bass call roared towards the approaching Dragon. As an equally deep call was returned, Kija said to the company, amazement plain in her tone: 'It is Brin! First born of Fenj and Skay's first brood!'

As Fenj's son circled to land in a swooping glide, Soran's scouts
were informing him of signs of Shardi not far ahead. He ordered
the Guards to be even more alert and to keep a tight formation.
To his left, the land sloped away fairly gently and about three
leagues ahead, sunlight flashed on the river Skar. To his right, the
ground rose steeply, littered with great boulders, for a league or
more, to the feet of the towering escarpments of the northern
High Lands.

The Shardi were probably watching, waiting for nightfall,
when the Guards would make camp. In the late afternoon, Soran
rode ahead with Trem and one of the scouts. 'There, Sir.' Soran
looked where the scout was pointing. He wheeled the fengar to
the right. There was a clear area for several man lengths, then an
uneven line of boulders half-circling towards the sheer rock
behind. The cliff angled outwards far enough to give some
protection to Soran's force from attack from above. At Soran's
nod, Trem rode back to signal the men to follow.

Well-trained as they were, the Guards unsaddled the fengars,
rubbed them down, and then replaced the saddles to be ready for
action. The spare fengars were securely tied, well apart, at the
back of the overhang. Should there be a Shardi attack tonight, the
fengars would fight each other if they could not reach an enemy.
Soran ordered fires to be lit, both to allow the cooks to prepare
hot food for the men and to use to light torches should the need
arise. About the only thing known of the Shardi, apart from their
fcrocity, was the fact that fire terrified them.

Shardi were usually seen in groups of ten or twelve. Their
size, speed, and blood chilling screams made them appear far
more numerous to the few who survived an attack. Gan and
Soran had worked the Guards on various tactics to try to deal with
the Shardi but had had no opportunity to put these tactics to the
test. It had been difficult getting the Guards to understand the
fear and panic they would likely feel during a Shardi onslaught.

Eventually, Gan had enlisted the aid of some of the Seniors of
Gaharn who had used Power to suddenly fill the Guards' minds
with terror. Only when the men had been regrouped and calmed,
had they fully realised what they might be called upon to face.
Again and again, Gan and his officers made the Guards learn to
control at least some of their panic, and maintain their positions,

151

rather than flee in all directions. Gan hoped this unorthodox training might prove of some value, but, as yet, the Guards were untried.

Soran instructed his officers to keep moving amongst the groups of Guards tonight. By the unusually subdued atmosphere in the camp, Soran knew they were apprehensive about what the rapidly descending darkness might hide. As Gan had told Farn, fear made men cautious. But too much fear led too easily to panic, and that Soran had to keep at bay at all costs.

Chapter Eighteen

Fenj had been overwhelmed by the arrival of his first-born son. Brin was a wanderer since soon after his hatching. Always curious to know what lay beyond those peaks, where that river might lead. Cycle after Cycle of Seasons passed, and still Brin never seemed to develop the steadiness expected in a mature Dragon of the Treasury.

His wanderings took him further, he was gone for longer at a time. Fenj had not heard word of him for several human generations and had resigned himself to never setting eyes on this son again. And yet, here he was. As massive as Fenj, his crimson scales shimmering in the sun, his eyes blazing still with dreams of adventure. Kija looked at him, then at Farn, and she sighed. A watch would need to be kept on the pair of them, despite the great difference in their ages.

Brin explained he had been "far away south", but as he journeyed back towards the Ancient Mountains, he had begun to hear rumours of strange events. 'I heard that hatchlings had bonded with two-legs.' He looked at Farn and Ashta with great interest. 'Then I heard of Nula.' Fenj and Kija hissed, and Brin amended quickly: 'I heard the Forsaken was attacking farms and herders' camps. I was near enough to her at one time to hear her thoughts.' He looked around at his audience. 'She is mad. She killed and ate the two of the Kin who served her. She mutters to herself, over and over, most makes no sense. She is mad,' he repeated.

'None of this explains why you decided to come after us,' Kija snapped. 'And we would prefer a sensible answer, Brin – no non-sense about adventures.' She glared at him, her eyes frosted gold. 'I could always fly faster than you when we were hatchlings together, and I daresay I could still deal with your silliness.'

Brin's laughter rumbled through their minds. 'Oh I remember Kija! I'll behave myself!' He grew serious. 'I have journeyed

153

far through all these many Cycles. I have seen many things I had never heard tell of, and I think you have not either. I have even travelled far to the north.' He let that information sink into their minds. 'Yes,' he continued, looking to his father, 'Dragon Kin live still in the north.'

Fenj became greatly agitated. 'They cannot.' His eyes were slate grey now. 'The cold and the Shardi make it impossible for us.' He explained to the two-legs: 'Long, long in the past, it was less cold, so the Kin did dwell further north. But since my mother's mother's time, none have done so.' He raised himself above Brin. 'The Kin can *not* live there.'

'But they do,' Brin replied calmly. 'They have changed themselves a little to help them master the cold, and they share their lives with a race of two-legs.'

Kija, Fenj and Gan were listening closely now. None of them knew of any race of two legs in the north, only the Guardian's servants and a few renegades and runaways. Except Shardi. As that idea dawned, Brin rattled his wings. 'No, no. Small, very small. They live inside the mountains mostly.'

'And you have met these northern Dragons and the two-leg race?'

'Yes.' Brin swung his head from side to side. 'I, erm, went a little further north than I had intended and had to shelter in an ice cave from a great storm. I was greatly weary and I slept. When I woke, the cave was blocked to an extent I could not break through, even using fire.' The company was leaning closer so as not to miss a single word. 'The back of the cave suddenly grew a hole, and there was a two legs and a Snow Dragon.'

'So there are tunnels in the northern-most ranges?' Gan asked. 'Which would perhaps allow us to approach closer to the Guardian's Realm without exposure to the cold and storms?'

'Well, it was quite a while ago,' Brin explained, 'and I was not with them very long. I had no reason to ask where their tunnels led.'

'You have given us much to think of, Brin.' Gan looked skyward, somewhat surprised by how much time had been spent listening to Fenj's son. 'I think we may as well stay here, and make an early start tomorrow.' He turned suddenly, staring at Tika and Jeela. 'You hear that?'

154

'Yes!' Tika was pale. 'Shardi are attacking your Guards!'

'We cannot reach them in time to help, we have allowed them to get too far ahead,' Jeela added. Both she and Tika, and then Farn, gasped.

'Trem is injured, he –' and Tika crumpled at Gan's feet.

The Shardi did not merely seem more numerous as they attacked the Guards, they were. Soran guessed, in the first charge the Shardi made from the sides of the overhanging cliff, that there were at least fifty. The sentries yelled, in the same instant the Shardi rose, screaming from the rock cover. The men and officers, including Soran, froze for seconds that felt eternal.

Then the mounted Guards swung into their saddles, fengars already shrieking defiance back at the Shardi. The foot Guards formed into their groups, between which the scarcely controllable fengars charged. Men ran to light torches and distributed them through the company. Swords were already in action, it was too late to use crossbows. The rank smell of the Shardi was a weapon in itself; men gagged as the stench rolled over them in advance of the hairy bodies.

The Shardi were a quarter as tall again as the humans, some even taller. Their stooped shoulders and ungainliness belied the extreme speed with which they could move. Soran had no time to see how his groups held, as a Shardi burst from the crowd, rushing straight towards him. Its hands, with their long curved claws, reached for him. He choked as the foetid breath from its screaming mouth engulfed him and he fell back a pace, panic boiling through him. He caught desperately at that panic, even as he raised his sword to force away one of the outstretched arms.

Yellow eyes glared at him as he thrust forward sharply and then danced back out of reach. The Shardi looked down at itself. Blood was soaking through the white hair of its belly. It snarled, baring discoloured but by no means blunt, fangs at Soran, and surged forward again. Claws ripped along Soran's forearm but he scarcely noticed. His sword was deep in the Shardi's chest, too deep. He drew his dagger with his left hand, still gripping the sword hilt despite being unable to pull it free of the Shardi's body.

The Shardi's eyes were glazing but it still pressed towards

him. Soran backed, the Shardi staggering after, in a macabre dance, until they were in a melee of fighting men and Shardisi. Human shouts and yells mingled with the fengars' shrieks and the Shardisi screams – a deafening, mind numbing cacophony.

At last, the Shardi Soran had impaled stumbled to its knees and he was able to wrench free his sword, his foot on the Shardi's face to gain leverage. For a moment, Soran looked at the blank eyes, the realisation that he had actually destroyed one of them filling him with elation. As he looked around to see how the Guards were faring, he saw the Shardi were withdrawing. Guards began to chase the shaggy retreating backs until Soran roared for them to halt. He ordered them to regroup, tally the dead and injured, check their weapons and stand ready.

He was amazed to see fifteen dirty white shapes sprawled motionless, several of them charred where burning torches had been thrust at them. Fifteen Shardi dead! But as his eyes encountered the growing line of Guards' bodies being laid gently together, he saw what fifteen dead Shardi had cost his band of Guards. Four of his ten officers were among the dead, three more were injured, one of those severely. Trem was one of the injured, unconscious but with no obvious mortal wound.

No fengars were dead, although a dozen were crippled, the muscles of their backs and rear legs torn by swiping Shardi claws. They were all still at a high pitch of battle rage and their handlers and riders needed all their strength to calm them. Soran felt as if his legs were suddenly made of water in the reaction to this first taste of murderous battle, but he forced them to obey him, moving from group to group of Guards.

He praised them all on standing firm, one man raising a slight laugh when he told Soran: 'Warn't so awful as what them Seniors put in our 'eads, Sir!' Soran joined the laughter, resting a hand lightly on the man's shoulder. 'I think I am inclined to agree with you, Kran!' As Soran took the proffered mug of steaming tea from his officer, Baras, the screaming began again from beyond the boulders. Soran dropped the mug and hurried to the front groups.

Four more times in that long night, the Guards faced Shardi attacks. As the Shardi fled for the fifth time, Soran saw that the sky was faintly streaking with dawn. Most of his surviving

Guards sank exhausted to the ground wherever they stood; a very few men still on their feet offered assistance to fallen comrades. Soran lent on his sword, his head bowed for a moment. 'By the stars, no more,' he prayed fervently.

As he raised his head and straightened his aching back, a hand touched his sleeve. 'You must get your wounds attended to, Sir.' He glanced round, seeing with relief, Trem, standing beside him. Trem was very pale, a purpling lump showing under the hair on his forehead, but he was alive, thank the stars.

'Have the Healers see to the men first Trem, I only have scratches.'

'No Sir, this sleeve says there are more than scratches here.' Trem pulled gently at Soran's sleeve and he saw with considerable surprise, the sleeve was quite sodden with blood. Stunned with weariness, he found himself being led back into the overhanging shelter of the cliff.

'And you Trem?' he asked. 'When did you awake? Are you all right?'

Trem managed a smile. 'I have a headache worse than any hangover, Sir,' he said, 'but I was able to use my sword in the last two Shardi attacks.'

Soran gestured at the sky. 'Day is coming and Shardi prefer the darkness.' He sank onto a cloth stool where the Healers were working on wounded Guardsmen. Trem squatted beside him.

'I thought they only attacked in small numbers – but there werc fifty, if not more, in that first charge Sir. Maybe these Shardi will not keep to their preference for only fighting at night, either?'

Soran stared at him, appalled. 'I pray you are wrong Trem.' He groaned. 'But get the fittest men prepared and on watch immediately.'

The dawn gradually lightened the sky, making the scene of the fighting clearer, but much worse. There was a total of twenty-three Shardi bodies, but more than a hundred dead Guards, and twice that number of injured. The Healers had given Soran a bitter drink that numbed his whole body as they dug deep into the great gouges on his arm. He had not realised he had been similarly clawed across his back, until the Healers began cleaning and stitching there as well.

157

Now he went to each of his injured men, speaking to those who were conscious, murmuring a prayer for those the Healers shook their heads over. Then he went to the silent, still rows of his dead. Salak, his most junior officer, was listing the names of these dead as Soran approached. He looked up at his commander, tears gleaming on his cheeks in the fingertips of sunrise light. 'Sorry, Sir,' he stammered, coming to attention and rubbing his sleeve across his eyes.

'No, Salak, you do well to grieve for these brave men.' Soran looked squarely at his junior officer. 'Even I, your commander, have never seen so many dead from one night's fighting. There is no shame, Salak, in weeping for these comrades, no shame.' Soran swayed as he finished speaking, and as Salak reached out to him in alarm, Trem appeared at his side.

Trem helped Soran back to where the Healers worked. There, he sat him down on a stool again. A moment later, Trem had Soran's bed roll spread for him and eased him on to it. 'No.' Soran's voice was the faintest whisper. 'I must speak to the men, praise them. I will rest later.' He made a feeble attempt to rise.

'No, Sir, I will speak to the men. You must sleep.'

'Maybe an hour Trem. Just an hour, then waken me.' Trem did not bother to answer. Soran was asleep already.

There were no more attacks as the daylight grew. Trem assembled the uninjured Guards and praised their valour. He ordered that they should ready their weapons, then get hot food inside them. And double watches were to be maintained around the camp. He detailed a rota for all the men to take a turn preparing burial places for the dead.

A Healer stopped him as he passed, handing him a drink. 'Your head pains you badly still Trem. This will help.' Trem looked at the dark thick liquid dubiously.

'I would gladly take a potion to ease this headache, but I will take nothing that makes me drowsy.'

'This will not, I swear by the stars.' Trem drank it, grimacing at its unpleasant taste, and returned the cup to the Healer.

'Is Lord Soran still sleeping?' he asked.

The Healer nodded. 'He has some fever but we will give him a herbal tea when he wakes. Sleep is the best medicine for most of the wounded, him included. Did you see him Trem? The

whole night through, whenever we looked out at the fighting,
Lord Soran seemed everywhere at once.' The Healer's voice
dropped further. 'He killed a Shardi alone, you know.'

'How could I know.' Trem retorted. 'The flat of someone's
sword hit my head in the first minutes of the first attack!'

'Thank the stars Trem, it was the flat of the sword!' The
Healer smiled. 'Why do you not sit beside Lord Soran? If you
too sleep, it will do you no harm.'

Trem had opened his mouth to reply when his eyes went
blank. The Healer was at first alarmed then quickly realised
someone was far speaking the officer.

Trem did not recognise the female voice calling his name.
When she knew she had his attention, she told him she was called
Jeela, sister to Farn. His mind wobbled slightly as he realised a
Dragon was bespeaking him. He had thought that only the People
could mind speak widely, with only an occasional human, such as
himself, being able to communicate with the People. It had never
occurred to him that other races had the ability. Jeela was asking
him urgently what had befallen the Guards, and was he badly
hurt?

How did she know he had been knocked unconscious, he
wondered in amazement. He tried to marshal his thoughts.
Briefly he told of the five attacks they had withstood, the many
Guards dead and injured. As he sent that thought, the actuality of
the events he was describing crashed upon him. But Jeela said:
'We are nearly to your camp, Trem. We will talk then. You
seem to be still hurt – Tika is still sick. Soon we will be there.'
And her voice was gone from his mind.

Trem blinked, seeing the Healer standing before him. 'Was
Lord Gan able to speak to you from so far?' asked the Healer.

'No,' Trem replied. 'It was Jeela, one of the Dragons.'

The Healer's eyes widened, then he took Trem's arm, leading
him to where Soran lay. Trem hardly noticed as he was gently
pushed down on to a stool, all he could puzzle over was what, by
the stars, had his being hurt to do with the Lady Tika being sick?

It was nearing midday. Trem had sat quietly for an hour
beside the still sleeping Soran, then roused himself. His savage
headache had dulled to a manageable throb – as long as he did not
turn his head too fast. Looking at the injured, Trem realised they

would be forced to stay here at least another night. He found Baras and Salak and the three officers organised the Guards to drag some of the rocks closer to the overhang. He wanted a fairly solid wall of stone, half circling the camp. Three narrow gaps were left: Trem thought the Shardi might be stupid enough to try to enter the camp through these spaces rather than climb the rock wall. If they did, it would enable the Guards to deal with them singly as they attempted to enter.

Now, as the protective stones rose head high, a watchman called to Baras: 'In the sky Sir, the Dragons!' All stopped their labour, watching as the Dragons neared. Six Dragons rather than the five they had seen at the Lady's House only two days ago.

Black Fenj landed within the rock walls first, Gan instantly slipping from the massive shoulders and hurrying towards Trem and Baras. Kija and Brin landed next, with the three young ones close behind them. Gan had seen from above the rows of fresh turned plots of ground marking so many burials and his eyes were still drawn to the place, but he said: 'You have done well indeed – we will hear everything soon but Healers are needed for the Lady Tika and Farn.'

Now the Guards all saw the pale green Ashta was half supporting Farn. The silver blue Dragon's eyes were dull, his head lowered. As they watched, Mim slid carefully from the back of the great crimson Dragon, holding Tika's body in his arms. Healers were hurrying from the overhang as all the men drew closer.

'Trem.' Gan spoke urgently. 'What happened to you? You were telling us of the Shardi attack and broke off suddenly. Tika said you were hurt and that is when she collapsed. We have been unable to awaken her since.'

Trem frowned, then winced as the skin on his brow pulled tight. 'It was the Lady Tika I called Sir. The Golden Lady told me to call her in an emergency, as she was the most powerful far speaker or listener. It felt as if she was standing right beside me Sir. Then I was hit on the head.' He indicated the dark lump on his forehead. 'I was unconscious for several hours Sir. I know no more than that.'

Gan turned to the Healers. 'We believe Tika expended too much Power in sending her mind here. She saw with Trem's eyes

– something we rarely achieve, as you are aware. The Shardisi attack was shock enough, but combined with Trem's sudden loss of awareness, we fear her mind has lost its way back to her.'

The Healers looked grave as they examined Tika. 'We need one with more Power than we possess Lord Gan. Is there such a one, among the Dragons perhaps, who could work with us?'

Kija said at once: 'Fenj is known for his gifts of Healing.' She looked towards the black Dragon.

His eyes were whirring the shadows-on-snow colour. He said: 'I have been afraid to try – I have no knowledge of the ways of the minds of two-legs. I would gladly offer my strength to use through your Healers now though.'

As Fenj moved closer to the group around Tika, Motass went to Farn. He stroked the long drooping face, offering what comfort he could to the stricken blue Dragon. Sket and Lorak, the latter clutching several leather sacks, stayed beside Brin. Fenj reclined beside the Healers.

'Will your Healers mind if I enter their thoughts Gan?'

'Please Lord Dragon,' one of the Healers bespoke Fenj. 'We hear you now. We will be grateful for any assistance you are able to give.'

'Bring Farn close before we begin,' Fenj directed. It seemed a huge effort for Farn to move even the few paces forward. 'Lie beside her Farn,' Fenj said gently. Farn fell rather than lay at Tika's side, his head with the prismed eyes now so very colourless, near hers.

The Healers knelt on Tika's other side, clearly about to begin, when a small orange Kephi stalked between men's legs, up Tika's body and crouched upon her chest. One of the Healers seemed about to say something but changed his mind after a glare from the Kephi.

'Gan, you also must help,' said Fenj. 'You have more of the Power. These Healers are strong but they are human, not of the People.' Gan squatted at Tika's head.

Then began a strange time. The Healers were astonished at the web of Power within Tika's mind. But it was as dull as were Farn's eyes, where both should be sparkling. Fenj poured his strength steadily through the Healers, as Gan tried to focus on where to repair Tika's mind. The Dragons and Mim followed it all, but the human Guards saw only the Healers kneeling rigidly, perspiration rolling like great tears down their faces.

Suddenly the Kephi did her hind-end-up, front-end down stretch, and the stillness was broken. Tika moved, groaned, faint colour tingeing her cheeks as her eyelids fluttered open. Farn's eyes began to show gleams of sapphire as Gan gently raised Tika, letting her rest back against his shoulder. Fenj spoke rapidly in direct speech to her, explaining what had been done. She looked at Farn, putting an arm round his neck to bring the beautiful face close to hers.

'Well,' she replied to Fenj, 'at least I will know to be more cautious another time!'

'Indeed you will!' Kija snapped. 'And kindly remember that my son is your soul bond and thus he suffers with you!'

Chapter Nineteen

The last daylight was fading rapidly. Khosa's fur suddenly stood on end, making her seem twice her usual size. Tika caught Mim's arm, pulling herself to her feet. 'The Shardi are near,' she said aloud. Khosa deflated herself and prudently retired, with Lorak, behind the Healers under the overhanging cliff.

'Remember,' said Gan quickly. 'You two must remain out of range of the Shardi. You must not be trapped or, stars forefend, killed. You have a task to accomplish beyond here, no matter what happens. I need your word that you will not involve yourselves in this fighting.'

Ashta, Farn and Jeela were all beneath the cliff with Mim and Tika. Ashta and Jeela were both nervous while Farn, who had swiftly recovered as Tika was revived, showed definite signs of excitement. Gan glared at him. 'Your word as well, Farn. You must remain here.' Suddenly inspired, he added craftily: 'You are needed to protect these four.' Farn stretched his neck high, eyes flashing blue ice.

'Of course. I will guard them marvellously well Gan.'

'Hmm. See that you do.' And Gan left them to join a still shaky Soran at the front of the Guards.

Shardisi screams began beyond the rock wall, answered by furious shrieks from the fengars within. Mim clutched his ears and even Farn was shaken by the sudden fearsome uproar.

As Trem had hoped, three Shardi appeared where gaps had been left in the wall, but unfortunately others also appeared over the top. A blast of fire hit three Shardi on the wall top. Their shaggy hair-covered bodies bursting into flame, they fell back, shrieking. Brin had been standing at the left side of the camp and now Mim and Tika saw that Kija was standing parallel to him. As they looked, Kija spat fire at another Shardi rising on the wall.

Despite apparently killing nearly half the Shardi numbers last night, there seemed the same number, if not more, this night.

Also, something of greater intelligence than the Shardisi possessed must be guiding their attack in some way: after a couple of blasts of fire from Kija and Brin, the Shardi stormed through the gaps faster, hurling themselves into the groups of Guardsmen. Obviously, the Dragons could not project their fire then, for fear of injuring the Guards.

Mim nudged Tika, and pointed to Fenj. The massive Dragon was lifting, up and over the rock wall. Fire poured from his long jaws followed by screams of pain from the Shardi gathered outside. The few Shardi inside tried to escape, ignoring the swords slashing at them in their panic to get away. Fenj moved out of sight, Brin and Kija lifting to follow him. Gan ordered the Guards to remain at the ready. Baras, six men and two scouts slipped quickly through the left-hand gap in the rocks and followed the Dragons. The mounted Guards were still outside, their fengars shrieking as they raced after the fleeing Shardi.

Gan said to Soran: 'They could be being lured into a trap.'

'I do not think so Sir. The Shardi have not shown intelligence enough for me to believe they could think ahead to that degree.'

'Soran, those Shardi knew enough to get among the Guards once the Dragons began to use fire. They are being directed by a higher mind somehow, I think.'

As he spoke, the adult Dragons reappeared, landing within the camp. Smoke trailed from their jaws as Fenj reported: 'They continue to flee, Gan. They head for the deeper mountains northwards. There were many on their way here, but as those fleeing came up with them, they all turned and fled.'

Brin's eyes were flashing gold and red with exhilaration. Kija said: 'You will calm yourself please Brin, before you speak with Farn. We had to hurt those creatures to protect our friends here, but it is not a practice we should encourage in the young. Or enjoy,' she added crossly.

Fenj rumbled in agreement and Brin made an obvious effort to calm himself. Gan and Soran exchanged glances, then Gan said: 'Keep men posted to watch, but I suspect there will be no further attack tonight. Let the men eat and rest, Soran, but then bring your officers to join us.'

As they collected around one of the campfires, Jeela spoke to all of them. 'Tika follows the Shardi.'

Gan said quickly, 'Is she safe? Surely it is too soon for her to do such a thing.'

'Farn is with her, sharing strength, and she is not attempting to communicate with them.' Jeela shivered at the thought.

Farn was reclining beside Ashta, Tika leaning against him. Both were relaxed, eyes closed as though sleeping peacefully.

'You are sure they are safe, Jeela?' Gan repeated.

'We are sure,' Kija replied. 'They are within our mind range, and we can force them back should the need arise.'

They settled themselves by the fire and listened as Soran recounted the events of the previous night. He gave rough estimates of the numbers of the dead, the seriously injured and the walking wounded. Just as he finished his account, Tika and Farn stirred. Gan looked enquiringly as Tika.

'They are already about eight leagues from here, and still running.' She shuddered. 'They are truly foul beasts.'

Farn rattled his wings. 'They turn on each other. The wounded among them have been killed and –' he faltered, 'eaten by the stronger.'

Gan stared into the fire as he considered. Finally he looked round at them all. 'I think the seriously wounded should be taken back to Gaharn where they can have the best chances of healing. The Healers here can make the fengars calm enough to pull the wagons slowly for that distance. I am truly not sure to what extent fengars will be of help to us in this mountainous region. What say you Nomis, they are under your command?'

Nomis tugged his long moustache as he thought. 'I would suggest we could perhaps take a dozen of the most tractable beasts,' he said finally. 'They could carry some of our provisions, or men if need be. I agree, they are not suited to this mountain travel. Shall I go and choose out twelve to continue with us Sir?'

'Yes Nomis, and ask a Healer to come to me here when it is convenient for him. How many Guards are still fully fit Soran?'

Soran looked at Baras as that officer had been checking the surviving men.

'Less than one hundred fully fit Sir,' Baras replied. 'Forty-seven with wounds that should heal in a few days. Eighty-four seriously wounded. One hundred and two dead, including four officers.' He looked up from the parchment he had consulted as he spoke. A voice behind him said: 'I am sorry to tell you that Officer Kerim has just died.' Baras glanced at the Healer. 'He did not regain awareness – he died peacefully.' The Healer's hand rested briefly on Baras's helmeted head.

Gan stood abruptly. 'Soran, pick twenty of the Guards whom you consider best to continue this journey. The rest will return to Gaharn. Such a large band was perhaps an ill-conceived idea on my part to start with. The smaller our numbers, more chance maybe of being less noticed. Baras and Salak, you will return with them.' Both men looked as though they would protest but Gan raised his hand. 'You both remain unharmed. You both experienced the Shardi attacks last night and remained alive and unhurt. You will tell the Guards in barracks of what happened and work on tactics and strategies to combat any future encounters with Shardi. Trem and Drak are but slightly injured.' He raised an eyebrow questioningly at the Healer.

The Healer nodded. 'They will be restored in days, Lord Gan.'

'Nomis must come, as he knows the handling of fengars.'

'Will fengars be more help or hindrance Sir?' asked Drak.

Soran replied: 'They will serve as food if they have to, so yes Drak, some must come.'

Gan nodded. 'My thought also, Soran.'

'We will be coming, won't we Sir?' Gan turned, seeing Sket and Motass standing in Fenj's shadow. 'We really feel as we should,' Sket added.

'Seeing as how we be the Lady Tika and Lord Mim's personal Guards, so to speak,' Motass added hopefully.

'Oh yes,' Mim agreed. 'This one thinks they must continue with us.' As Tika nodded, Gan made no comment. Motass and Sket were good men – if Tika and Mim found their presence reassuring, well and good. His eye fell on Lorak sitting against Brin's side.

'Lorak should return to Gaharn I think,' he said firmly.

'Oh no,' Fenj and Mim spoke in unison. 'Splendid creature!' Gan heard Fenj murmur, and he groaned inwardly. He had a feeling Lorak was going to be a thorn in his foot for some time.

'Gan,' Tika said, 'we are too far to mind speak the Lady Emla without great effort, yet she must know how things go with us. The way these Shardi attacked is different you say from previous times. Clearly the balance is sinking lower in the Guardian's favour. Time and strength must be used to go forward therefore, not used to report back to Gaharn.'

'Merigs,' said Brin.

Kija repeated thoughtfully: 'Merigs.'

'Merigs,' agreed Fenj.

'Merigs?' asked Gan helplessly.

'Those dark feathered ones,' Ashta explained. 'They do not sing, they croak as though they have hurt their voices. They are messengers anyway – perhaps they would agree to take messages to two-legs, as this is a time of such trouble.'

'Are there Merigs here?' Gan asked.

'I have seen several,' Khosa announced. 'They are not very well mannered.'

Tika laughed. She would wager that Khosa had tried hunting one of these Merigs, and had been unsuccessful. Khosa slitted her turquoise eyes at Tika and climbed onto Mim's legs.

'Perhaps you could ask them, Kija?' Gan felt Kija was probably the most diplomatic choice.

'I will seek them at sunrise.' She settled more comfortably. 'They sleep now.'

'I will do the rounds of the men. You get some rest.' Gan smiled at his officers. 'You have done well, but you all need rest.' He moved away from the fire with the Healer. They heard him asking which two Healers would be best suited to travel on with him and his company.

'Tika, this person was most afraid when you collapsed. Will it happen again do you think?' Mim was curled against Ashta, his cloak pulled around him. Tika, lying similarly against Farn, replied slowly: 'I do not know Mim. It was frightening. I was more in Trem's mind than I have ever been in any others'. When he lost awareness, it was as if I too had received a blow.' She lifted her cloak slightly to allow a persistent Khosa to creep closer to her warmth. 'But I was awake. I knew I was lost – disconnected – I cannot describe it. I could not judge time – it seemed days may have passed, or only minutes. But then I heard voices calling.

'I made myself move towards the voices – it was like trying to walk through deep mud. I nearly gave up, it was so hard.' Mim lay watching her, listening closely to every word.

Farn said suddenly: 'The two-legs helped us.'

Tika reached a hand up to stroke his face. 'Yes. Jerak was there. He said we had to get back – who else could do what was needed, he said.' She met Mim's eyes. 'We tried once more to get to the voices calling us – and we did.'

'This one thinks you and Farn have something very hard to do,' Mim said slowly. 'And Ashta and this one must help you as best we can. But it is you two who are of the greatest importance.'

Farn shivered his wings, eyes flashing briefly. 'We will sleep,' he ordered. Mim smiled.

'Yes Farn. We will sleep.'

They had travelled some five or six leagues by the next noon. The sky was a dull grey with yellowish streaks of cloud and the increasing wind was icy cold. The Dragons had flown ahead, checking there were no Shardi, seeking out the easier routes and hunting for their own food. Gan had decided they must travel closer to the mountains as they afforded some protection from the weather, which was clearly deteriorating. He had flown on Fenj's back for the first part of the day then rejoined the rest of the company on the ground.

When his teeth finally stopped chattering, he asked Mim and Tika if they had any idea how much cold the Dragons could endure. 'This one does not know, Gan,' Mim replied. He was shivering in spite of his new fleece lined clothes and cloak. 'This person has never been this cold. Nagum woodlands have occasional chilly days and nights – but nothing like this.' Gan looked at Mim with some concern, but Tika spoke directly to his mind: 'Mim will manage all right.' Gan looked at her but made no reply.

Lorak marched with Sket and Motass among the Guards. Judging by the occasional bursts of laughter, they were all quite happy despite the cold. Nomis had the fengars well under control at the rear of the company. The Healers walked behind Tika and Mim, and Gan dropped back to speak to them. Tika said softly: 'Use a little of the Power Mim, enough to bar the wind from chilling you. Try, it will only need a tiny effort. Look in my mind and see.'

'This one is still not happy with the Power Tika.'

'Mim, if you suffer too much already – and this is still only a tiny taste of the real northern cold – you will slow us all in our journeying.'

Mim winced at the firmness in her tone, but he slid into her thoughts, watching carefully as she showed him the simple weave of threads of Power to protect him physically from the cold wind. 'Now you do it,' she ordered. He did so, and almost at once, there was relief from the aching of his face and ears. Tika grinned at him. 'Not such a bad idea, was it?'

Gan ordered no halt until the dull daylight was darkening toward evening. A scout had just returned to report that the Dragons were settled a league or so ahead, but half a league higher on the mountain slope. The company could soon see Brin's crimson body perched on a high ledge beneath which were the other five Dragons.

Tika grabbed Mim's hand and began to run. There was an urgency in her sudden movement which worried Gan but he quashed the urge to race after the pair. There were no Shardi near, that he was sure of, so whatever was wrong he would find out soon enough.

And he did. As they arrived at the sheltered plateau where the Dragons had chosen to land, he signalled Soran to begin the routine setting up of an orderly camp. Then he turned to the Dragons. It was Jeela. Tika and Mim were pressed each side of her, Kija half curled around her small daughter. Ashta and Farn were deeply distressed, green eyes and blue whirring rapidly.

Gan called over his shoulder to the two Healers and hurried to the Dragons. Fenj said: 'The little one is too cold Gan. She has tried to hide her suffering but she nearly fell from the sky. Farn flew beneath her and tried to take her body on his own until Brin took her. She is hurting Gan.'

The Healers moved forward with no hesitation. Never had they been called upon to heal a Dragon, but their training sent them instantly to offer what help they could to a creature in pain. They laid their hands on the little ivory Dragon and she tried to raise her head. Her eyes were half closed, and to Gan's horror, he saw great tears sliding down her long face. Then he realised Tika and Mim were weeping, and he turned away. He barked orders to the nearest Guards who rushed to find kindling, adding tight pressed faggots they carried in the supply packs.

Lorak pushed through the Guards, dropping various bags and sacks as he passed Gan. Gan watched as the old man unfastened his worn, patched cloak and swung it over the small Jeela, tucking it with infinite gentleness over her delicate wings. Gan bespoke Fenj, asking if Jeela would recover. 'This time, yes Gan. She can not go further I think. But,' he added, 'there will be much upset and argument. She is smaller than any hatchling I have known, yet she is strong in her spirit.'

'Is she aware that she will have to give in?' Gan asked.

Fenj gave a mental shrug. 'She knows, but she will ignore that knowledge. Let us wait until she is restored now.'

The fire the Guards had lit was burning well, throwing a good heat out around it. All could see the little creamy Dragon was in trouble now, and the Guards were quiet as they lit other fires for cooking their suppers, glancing frequently at the huddle around Jeela. Gan stepped closer as the Healers moved back. He laid his hand on Jeela's foreleg, sliding it down to touch her "hand". He was shocked at how cold the soft hide was and on touching her, he was aware of how deeply the cold had penetrated her body. Brin called that he would hunt, and returned a while later with a volu. He put it beside Kija and the gold Dragon tore small pieces from the carcass, urging her daughter to eat.

It was fully dark when Jeela seemed recovered. Mim explained to Gan that they had been unable to use the Power to thaw the ice from Jeela's very bones because she had weakened so much. She had to be left to warm steadily; heating her fast would have put tremendous strain on her heart and indeed, could have killed her. The Healers had already given Gan a similar diagnosis.

'But will she go back to Gaharn, Mim?'

The brilliant blue eyes with the vertical pupils again filled with tears. 'No.'

'But she has to, after this.'

'No,' repeated Mim and turned away.

Trem was beside Gan, listening, and now he said: 'Sir, the

Dragons are having a fearful argument – can you hear?' He shook his head, still amazed that he could hear Dragon speech. He was also amazed that he had been so stupid as to believe only the People, and a few humans like himself, were "intelligent" enough to use the mind speech.

Gan concentrated on the Dragons. They all appeared at ease, reclined around the fire, all except Jeela a short distance from the heat. They seemed relaxed, quiet, but as Gan focused harder, he realised Trem was right. Kija was furious; indeed, relaxed as she still appeared, her eyes were beginning to flash sparks of reflected fire. Ashta and Farn were listening to Kija, but taking no part in the argument. Brin looked wonderfully innocent for his massive size, his head tilted back, eyes searching the sky for a few stars that had escaped the cloud cover.

'She must return to the Lady.' Kija was saying. 'She will die if she again gets as cold as she has done this day.'

Jeela, still draped in Lorak's cloak and her head over his shoulder, appeared quite unconcerned. Gan and Trem realised why as she said to her mother in perfectly reasonable tones: 'I will travel on with you all.'

Kija snorted, a rather undignified sound. 'And you, Brin, to encourage her. I cannot believe you could be so irresponsible at your age!' She looked at Fenj. 'Have you no influence over this half-wit son of yours?'

Fenj rattled his wings. 'No,' he replied shortly.

Farn was gazing at Brin with open admiration for the crimson Dragon. Brin lowered his gaze to Kija. 'Tika can give her some protection and she is such a tiny hatchling.' – Jeela flashed a glare at him – 'I can carry her with no problem.'

'Of course!' Farn let slip, wilting instantly as Kija's fury turned in her son's direction. 'Don't you dare try to copy this foolish one's ways!' Her wrath was almost visible now, but she caught herself from saying more, instead lifting rapidly from her place and soaring into the darkness.

'She is still very bossy,' Brin remarked.

'Yes,' replied his father. 'But will you truly be able to carry Jeela? We have a long way yet to go.'

'I believe it is about three more days until we near the place where the other Kin found me. I think we should call to them as we approach. If we do so, they may hear us, even below the mountains as they usually seem to be.'

Fenj sighed. 'I like this not, my son. But I pray to the stars, you remember how many lives may depend on you now.'

Chapter Twenty

Gan forced the pace over the next two days. The weather was rapidly worsening with sleet blown sideways by a vicious wind. During the second night, the wind died away and snow began to fall. Brin had carried Jeela while Tika had used the Power to help all the Dragons withstand the biting cold. She had taken strength from both Mim and Gan, but still found that the continuous concentration was deeply tiring. Ashta and Farn were beginning to weaken in the unrelenting coldness, although the adult Dragons were still strong.

Gan had discussed with his officers the strange fact that the Guards had become greatly concerned for the Dragons' well being. Although Nomis had worked with fengars most of his life, as they had never evinced responsive characteristics, he was not emotionally involved in their care. But he admitted that he too was worried for the Dragons – especially the smallest.

Drak reported that several men had asked if there was anything they could do, or give to, the little Dragon, to make her better. Trem nodded – he too had been asked the same questions. Soran commented: 'I tried to choose men who had trained together, and who had been on patrols to the west and fought together, to remain in this company. But still there are several separate groups within these fifty men. Yet they are united by their worry for these Dragons.'

'They do not see them as mascots, or lucky charms, Sir,' said Drak. 'I heard some talk of the way they used fire against the Shardi, but also of the golden Dragon's obvious concern for her two young ones. The men seem to regard them as members of the Guards – if you see what I mean Sir,' he ended in confusion.

Gan nodded. 'I do indeed Drak. And I have to admit to being worried at the outset by the presence of Dragons, and of a Kephi, and of old Lorak. The Dragons, as you say Drak, seem to unify the men. That Kephi,' he looked around warily, 'seems to cheer them with her antics, and Lorak with his jokes. 'I hope it is only jokes,' he added. 'Has anyone noticed any signs of his concoctions – around the camp?' His officers grinned, but all denied any such knowledge.

Brin began mind calling that night. He called at regular intervals, then listened, as did the other Dragons. Mim and Tika slept soundly, Khosa making herself comfortable inside Mim's shirt.

'We heard no response to Brin's calls,' Fenj told Gan the next morning. 'He will call aloud as we fly, perhaps you should warn your two legs. Jeela will continue the mind call as we travel.'

'Will the snow hinder you Fenj?'

'We cannot fly too long or too fast when the snow is so heavy,' Fenj admitted. 'We will not travel far ahead of you this day I think.'

Tika and Mim looked fit after their night's rest, although Mim was shivering already. Gan knew better than to suggest the two rode on fengar back – he had done so previously and they had adamantly refused.

'This one thinks fengars are very unsafe creatures,' Mim had said, leaving Gan rather nonplussed. They thought nothing of perching on Dragons and flying high in the air, yet the idea of riding fengar back obviously terrified them.

Gan had given a message for Emla to a Merig. Kija had bespoken to a pair as she had said she would. Gan was rather amused – he suspected Emla had not bothered to test these rather tattered looking birds. He regretted he could not see her reaction when they arrived at her House and proceeded to give a fairly full report of the company's progress.

Now, there was only a slight lightening of the sky to indicate the sun had risen far above the great billows of snow clouds. The Guards struck camp and began the day's march. They were climbing higher into the mountains now rather than skirting the foothills, but Soran reported no grumbles – as yet.

Tika was still using the Power to give some shielding to the Dragons, but suddenly she struggled through the knee-deep snow to pull Gan's cloak. 'They have been answered!' Her green eyes sparkled at him. 'Jeela says three answered – one of the Kin and two not.' As she spoke, Mim caught up with them, Sket at his side.

'Look!' he said.

Fenj's great black shape was descending through the thickly falling snow. As he landed, all the company gathered near him. His eyes whirred kaleidoscopic colours with excitement as he bespoke Gan. 'Brin spoke truly! There are Kin here, even now!' Mim spoke Fenj's words aloud so all the Guards could follow the Dragon's news. 'We must go higher still, Gan. Will your two-legs be able to manage? And these fengars?' He sounded doubtful.

Nomis told him aloud: 'We will bring the fengars as far as we can get them. They are unlikely to survive now if we release them here.'

Soran agreed. 'How far are we from these Kin of yours?'

'It will take the rest of this day for you to climb to the place they described. They will meet us there at nightfall.'

'Right.' Gan looked at his men. 'A hard climb, Fenj says, and no sign of the snow letting up. Unload most of the supplies from the fengars and distribute them through the company. A man to walk each side of a fengar. The rest of you, in twos ahead of them.' Tika murmured to Gan, and he added: 'Lorak, you and Mim continue with Fenj.' The old man protested that he was quite able to march on, but the greyness of his face belied his words. Mim also protested that he would remain with Tika.

'Ashta and Jeela have need of your support,' Gan lied blandly. Lorak and Mim both stared hard at him, but eventually they moved towards the Dragon.

Khosa's head popped above Tika's cloak. 'Is it likely you may slip over high rocks or cliffs?' she enquired.

Tika chuckled, removing the sack in which she carried Khosa, from around her neck. 'Go with Mim and Lorak, brave Kephi!'

Rhaki had been receiving conflicting reports, which displeased him immensely. One told of Emla's Guards returning to Gaharn, greatly reduced in numbers. Another said the band was still heading north, but through the high mountains. That was arrant nonsense of course: even Guards could not be so foolhardy as to try to go higher in the worsening weather. Another report told of the total defeat of the Cansharsi he had moved to the far west.

Led by the Lords of Return and Far, the humans had chased them down and slaughtered them to the last one. That at least, was what he had anticipated there. Verim was reported killed in the fighting, but Rhaki felt sure he had merely transferred his allegiance to the Lords of the west.

In the south, the Cansharsi were still harassing farms and villages, but there was something amiss: Rhaki's informers spoke of groups of Linvaks suddenly appearing, attacking the Cansharsi, and retreating again. Each time leaving a few less Cansharsi.
These informers all spoke of one or two Nagums being seen with the Linvaks. Rubbish, thought Rhaki. Utterly impossible. Nagums were timid fools who never left their precious woodlands. Why would they be in the company of Linvaks?

He had ordered Jal to go through the deep passageways, alone, to try to ascertain if the Guards really were advancing north. Jal had gone yesterday, with instructions to be as swift as he could. Rhaki had allowed him to ride on one of his new fengars. He had been experimenting with them for some time, breeding for a more docile strain. He had long thought they might be useful for general travellers, not just as fighting men's mounts.

Rhaki was most enraged with the Shardi. He had expended a great deal of Power in taking control of one of their leaders, but he had been unable to override the panic that took over once Dragonfire was used. It had taken him hours to recover his strength and he promised himself he would make the Shardi suffer exquisitely for failing him.

He had at least had the opportunity to glimpse the Dragons. Jal had borne the brunt of Rhaki's fury: 'Three huge adult Dragons, you imbecile!' Rhaki had screamed. 'You reported two young ones, and what do I find? Three monstrous creatures spitting fire everywhere!'

'Master,' Jal was on his knees, 'my spies did see only two young ones, a pale green, and a silver blue.'

'I saw no Dragons that colour through Shardi eyes, fool. The three I saw were black, crimson and gold. And very large.'

'They must have followed the others, Master.'

'Of course they must! Stars, am I served by incompetents? Leave me now, but I will summon you again this day. Wait nearby.'

Jal bowed himself backwards from Rhaki's study, closing the door gently before straightening with a sigh of relief.

'The Master is far from happy.'

Jal nearly leapt to the roof as the whisper came from beside him. Bark's tall, skeletal figure stood there, smiling. It was not an attractive smile, Jal thought. 'No,' he replied as calmly as he could while his heart was still trying to return to its rightful place and speed. 'He becomes – unhappy – far more swiftly of late, I find,' he ventured.

Bark's smile became even less attractive. 'He does, does he not?'

Rhaki had ordered Jal through the passageways. He told him how to undo the rock door near the entrance, which made it seem merely a cell-like chamber, rather than the start of a passage through the mountain. Jal had been riding for several hours, his way faintly lit by widely spaced glow lamps. He wondered who came to tend the glowers down here, they had to be fed after all, then he shivered as he tried not to imagine any of Rhaki's creations creeping about down here. And who had made these great tunnels? Shivering again, he decided it would be best not to think of such things.

Several other passages led off from the one he travelled, but they were all in deepest darkness. He rode from pale light to pale light at a steady lope. Fengars could go for great distances at this pace – the sort of speed a man could run only for short bursts. Twice before had Jal taken this route for Rhaki, and yet he realised he only now remembered the fact of those previous trips. The Guardian must make him forget when he returned, he decided.

Jal reckoned maybe four hours had passed as he rode between the unchanging walls of the passageway. He reined in the fengar and dismounting, poured water from a leather bottle into a dish for it to drink. It would not be fed now; a short halt for water and for his weight to be off its back, and it would be fit for another four hours steady run.

Jal squatted on his heels, the rein wrapped around his hand, and chewed a piece of bread and meat. Then he froze. The fengar's ears twitched back and forth, then ears and head pointed towards the blank side wall. Jal rose silently, moving to press himself against the rough rock.

There was something moving on the other side of the rock. He strained to decipher the faint noise. After a while, he relaxed again. The fengar had lost interest; whatever it was, it was gone. He swung into the saddle and rode on, wondering if it could have been Shardi, and should he mention it to the Guardian? Or perhaps – Bark?

Bark was sitting outside the Guardian's study. He sat upright, his hands loosely clasped on his lap, his face hidden beneath the cowl of his robe. Many Cycles before, he had been a student in Gaharn. He had been slow to join conversations since childhood, preferring to listen and think on what he heard. No one showed him any scorn or mistreatment, that was not the People's way, but because of his unwillingness to speak, he became a solitary child and young man.

When he entered the Asataria with others of his generation, he was surprised and flattered by Rhaki's increasing attention. The mercurial Rhaki, considered by many, especially himself, to be a brilliant mind, adored having Bark's silent company. In his self confidence, Rhaki never suspected that beneath Bark's silence ran rivers of thought, deeper by far than his own, and pondered over for Cycles rather than the brief hour Rhaki might spare on a problem.

Rhaki allowed Bark alone to hear his jealous tirades against his sister Emla, of his contempt for the Seniors who instructed them, and for the People in general. Never once, in all those Cycles, had Rhaki asked for Bark's opinion, assuming Bark saw him as he saw himself – beyond compare to all others.

Then no one, including Bark, knew of Rhaki's fascination with genetics, or of the small experiments he had already attempted. By the time Rhaki was raised to the Guardianship, many had become wary of him. They could not say specifically what made them cautious, but something was separating Rhaki from most of the People of Gaharn.

When Rhaki, Bark, and a retinue of specially selected human servants arrived at the Guardian's stronghold, Rhaki's first act was to dismiss all the previous Guardian's household. His next was the setting up of the first of a series of ambitious breeding programmes. He lectured Bark fully on his plans in that field and also his plans for gaining control of this world, especially the Realm of Gaharn.

Bark, as always, his self hidden deep in his own mind, was at last appalled at Rhaki's ideas. He had not yet decided whether the damage Rhaki had inflicted on his mind was a deliberate act to keep him subservient, or truly accidental. Rhaki had had Bark well tended, nursed back to physical health. He assumed that the blank emptiness he saw within Bark's mind, as season followed season and Cycle followed Cycle, was to be Bark's permanent state now.

But from that cataclysmic moment when Bark felt his mind disintegrate, a tiny part had remained aware. Through these long ages that part had slowly – oh so slowly – grown. And he had spoken to Jerak. Unknown to Rhaki, Jerak had sought out Bark and talked with him on four occasions before Rhaki's final outburst of arrogance.

The resulting contest of Power had stunned all in the stronghold. Indeed several deaths had resulted from the reverberations of Power shattering the very particles of air. Most had regained their senses to an eerie quietness. Bark had recovered quicker than most and gone to Rhaki's study. He opened the rock door that Rhaki foolishly believed was known only to himself. He had hurried down the passages until he found the Guardian slumped unconscious at the open door of the Chamber of the Sacred Balance.

Bark had stood looking at Rhaki for several moments, then he stepped over his body and entered the Chamber. So easy to leave him to die! So easy to help him beyond! But that was not the way of the People and the People were more than this one poor example. Bark had carried Rhaki back to his rooms and tended him for days.

Bark pondered these things as he sat, still as stone, beside Rhaki's door. The time was very near now, when Rhaki would control the Balance. Jerak had said: 'Two young ones come, Bark. They are Chosen. But if they fail, the task is yours.' Jerak had told Bark nothing of the young ones he mentioned. Bark had heard Rhaki screaming at Jal of a human and a Nagum, and of Dragons. Unmoving, Bark sat, his thoughts gathering speed and moving in the only direction he could see as rational.

All these ages mending, and the wish growing in him to be back in Gaharn, listening to the words and the thoughts of the People. All this time, spent here, listening only to Rhaki, whose finely balanced intelligence had long since toppled into insanity. But he had loved the young Rhaki. Oh indeed, yes.

Bark lifted his head. He rose, his attenuated figure casting a spidery shadow on Rhaki's door as he moved to answer the summons from within. He knew he was weakening physically; he was but in his middle years as the People reckoned age, but the damage Rhaki had done him long ago had speeded him on his life's journey. He opened the study door and entered noiselessly, already bowing submissively to the Guardian. May the stars give him strength once more, enough for him to be finally true to his People.

Chapter Twenty-One

Finally the company had reached the place where the Dragons awaited them. The last hours of the climb had seen the wind rise again, hurling snow and ice grains into their faces. Gan had been in the front, with Soran. A dozen Guards followed, then Tika between Sket and Motass. She knew she could easily take Power to help herself, but she also knew the Guardian would feel any use of Power now they were halfway between Gaharn and his stronghold. He would surely know their company was moving north and no doubt had watchers hidden somewhere on their route. Tika did not think he knew that either she or Mim were able to use the Power to the extent they in fact could.

He would know that Gan was the leader of the company, and as a Senior of the People, Gan could use the Power to some degree. The small amount Tika would need to help her resist the cold and exhaustion could pass as that which Gan might use. She chose not to risk even that; she just prayed she would soon be with Farn and, stars be kind, sheltered from this snow-filled wind.

Tika now had a better idea of how she could manipulate threads of Power but she understood that weaving shielding to block the wind, for instance, was a very different thing to what she suspected she might have to do all too soon. Part of her was still a girl child of fifteen Cycles, and wished only to be warm and safe somewhere. The other, larger, part accepted that that was not a real option any more. Using the Power she could get herself off this ghastly mountain and to a town, houses, other humans. But how could she go anywhere without Farn?

Tika was aware, too, that Mim would never let her down. Fearful he might be, but he would never willingly leave her to face any danger alone. And the Dragons. Tika was almost sure they knew more than they admitted about the Power. The more she worried at it, the more it seemed that their whole moral code was formed to contain and control access to the Power.

Her feet moved automatically, her thoughts successfully distracting her from the aching calf muscles, the ice-scratched face and the overall coldness of her whole body. Sket and Motass linked arms behind her back, trying to protect her from some of the storm. Black curls, blown across her forehead, had frozen to her skin, and her eyelashes were caked with snow.

Tika became aware they had stopped moving. She had not the energy to really wonder why. Sket moved in front of her so she was between his body and Motass. The sudden cessation of the wind made her knees buckle, but then Sket moved away again and on they went. 'A fengar over the side, Lady!' Motass yelled above the screaming gale.

The path narrowed, Sket went ahead, reaching back for Tika's hands. He pulled her along with Motass keeping close behind her. It seemed they climbed endlessly and the storm shrieked its rage at their invasion of the mountains, doing its best to dislodge them. As a gust of air wound round her legs, feeling almost like hands grabbing her ankles, Tika knew this was Rhaki's doing. She would ask Gan, but she was suddenly sure the Guardian was an adept at weather Power. While he might not yet know who they were, she was positive he had set wards even this far from the Realm of Ice, which uninvited visitors would trigger into action as they passed.

To maintain such wards over such distances signified a very strong wielder of Power. How could she, even with Mim, Gan, and the Dragons, hope to succeed against such a one, she thought in despair. She stumbled, would have fallen if not for Sket's hard grip of her hand.

She heard him shout to Motass and something was passed from him over her head to Motass. Then she was pulled up and found herself held tightly across Sket's chest, her face against his leather coat. He wrapped his cloak across her and the wind was vanquished. Motass, carrying Sket's pack now as well as his own, moved closer to hopefully prevent Sket sliding or falling on the treacherous path.

Tika had no idea how much longer Sket struggled on. She became aware that his breath was coming in gasps and she tried to wriggle herself free to walk again. He simply tightened his grip on her and went doggedly on. And then he stopped, his chest heaving under her cheek. Hands were pulling her free of Sket's locked arms and someone else held her. Another hand gently brushed at her eyes, freeing her lashes from the frozen snow. She opened her eyes at last to see Mim peering at her worriedly. Then she heard Gan in her mind and knew he was speaking to both her and to Farn: 'It is all right, we have arrived.'

Gan laid her against Farn's chest and she saw a fire was already blazing, snow hissing as it met the flames. Kija said: 'We used our fire to heat small rocks and Lorak had those little lumps that burn in his pack, which he put on the rocks.'

'Splendid creature!' murmured Fenj.

'Give my Tika some of that concoction, Lorak,' Farn ordered.

Gan watched as Lorak took a leather bottle from among the several that he had apparently neatly hung in his cloak. Lorak tilted the bottle to Tika's mouth, allowing her a small sip. Gan bit his lip as Tika swallowed, choked and sat upright in surprise. He noted the colour suddenly tinting the high olive cheeks and that her eyes were watering.

'Have you enough to spare a sip for all the men, Lorak?' he asked quietly.

The ancient gardener grinned. 'To be sure, Lord Gan. It is only a herb or two, mixed with any liquid, to give a zest.'

'Zest is to do with plants?' Fenj enquired with interest.

Gan received an evil wink from Lorak as he handed over the leather bottle. 'A sip each will be enough, Lord Gan.' Then Lorak and Fenj were deep in a conversation, which Gan really preferred not to hear.

As the men huddled round the fire, cooks thawing their hands enough to try to get some sort of food ready, Brin suddenly called his great bass note, startling everyone. Faintly, they all heard a higher note through the roaring wind. Kija called, a mellow tone harmonising with Brin as he too called again. The reply came closer. The company forgot their coldness and weariness as they watched the three adult Dragons rear erect, bracing themselves against the storm and all staring into the wall of snow.

One moment there was a flurrying white denseness, and the next two more Dragons stood before them. Both were silver with golden specks tipping each separate scale. Their prismed eyes blazed with curiosity and excitement. One was just smaller than

Farn and Ashta, the other no bigger than Jeela. They, too, raised themselves upright. The larger Dragon said: 'May the stars guide your paths. I am Meppi.'

'And I am Ulla,' added the smaller Dragon.

Emla sat frozen in mid sentence in the library where she was working with Kemti. After a glance at her face, he realised someone was bespeaking her. 'Kemti,' she whispered, indicating that he was to listen, too. He heard a gentle voice in his mind, calling Emla's name, at the same time as a raucous croaking came from the Garden below. He followed the Golden Lady to the window, even their tall graceful figures dwarfed by the immensely high embrasure. On the lawn below, two tattered, feather-ruffled black Merigs stood, staring up at them.

'Merigs?' Kemti asked aloud in some astonishment.

'Merigs,' agreed Emla. She unlatched the middle section of the window, pushing it wide, as she said, in the mind speech: 'You are welcome, dear ones.'

'Hmmmph!' a Merig replied as they both flew heavily up to land on the sill. They seemed much bigger seen so close and Kemti noted just how large and businesslike the great horny beaks were. 'Never bothered to talk to us, have you, Lady?'

'No,' Emla answered slowly. 'For which, I truly apologise.'

'Well, we are not attractive to the eyes of two-legs, we know. Although I find us the most beautiful of the races of feathered ones. We bring a message from one Gan,' he concluded.

'Wait then, if you please, until other Seniors can listen to you also. Would you prefer to stay out there or –?'

'We will come in, to see your nest,' the Merig announced, and flew over the lower part of the window, followed by his mate. Bright black eyes stared around the library as the Merig perched on the back of a chair. 'Somewhat like a large cave,' he was saying, as Iska and Yash arrived. His mate was busily examining some wall hangings and clearly had no interest in conversation at this point.

'Can I offer you any food?' Emla asked politely.

His head on one side, the Merig's beady eyes regarded her. 'I think you may not have meat several days old?'

'Erm, I fear not. Perhaps we should just hear your message

then?'

The Merig ruffled his feathers and drew himself up. 'Thus begins my message.'

Thus the Golden Lady and three Seniors learned what had befallen the company.

Iska immediately went to alert the household of the imminent return of seriously-wounded Guards. She summoned the most skilled Healers from Gaharn and warned that there would soon need to be a full Gathering of Seniors to consider recent events.

She went back to the library, aware already of the hum and bustle as the Lady's staff began converting several guest rooms into nursing accommodation. The Merigs had not chosen to leave yet, the female had pulled out several books from a top shelf half hidden by woven hangings. Kemti had rescued the books and raised an eyebrow at Emla. It was plain the female Merig had serious ideas for a future nesting site. It was with mixed feeling that they heard the male announce that they must leave.

'I have messages to carry to the Wilderness.'

'The Wilderness? I believed that to be a barren land, its soil somehow poisoned long ago?' Kemti asked in surprise. 'May I ask to whom you carry messages there?'

The Merig blinked. He dropped the formal voice for a more gossipy tone. 'Not so much a particular message, more like general news you know.' Then he blinked again and became vague. 'Many live in the Wilderness – I forgot that you did not know. I think it is time that we left.'

He rasped a croaking screech at the female. She responded vigorously and noisily, obviously preferring to remain longer to further investigate the possibilities of nesting places here. A rather deafening disagreement ensued, ending with the male flapping weightily out of the window. Another few throaty grumbles and then the female departed also. Kemti quickly shut the window behind them. 'A fortunate thing, perhaps, that it is not the egg-laying Season, Lady. I do not believe she would have left that shelf if it was!'

'They are readying rooms, Emla,' said Iska. 'I asked that one of the Healers here try to mindspeak a fellow Healer with the wounded. It will help them to prepare better, prior to the arrival of the injured. I also summoned more from the City."

'Well thought, my dear,' Emla smiled. 'And what is your opinion of our "messengers"?'

Iska grinned. 'I suggest that you keep these windows closed as the next Cycle warms – I suspect that female Merig may remember how ideal the bookshelf seemed!'

'Speaking of the new Cycle warming, it is snowing now!' Yash was standing by a window. 'It is far too soon for snow such as this, surely?'

The others joined him, looking out. Only shortly before, the two Merigs had stood on a green lawn. It was now thinly covered with snow, which fell thicker and faster as they watched.

Yash glanced at Emla. 'Rhaki always enjoyed playing with the weather, as I recall.'

She replied thoughtfully: 'He did, did he not.' She tapped a fingernail against the glass. 'Do you know of any Seniors who are now adept at such things? A student, even?'

'Not off hand Lady, but I will check for you.'

As they returned to the fireside all suddenly chilled, Kemti remarked: 'His use of Power must be great indeed to affect the weather this far from his Realm.'

'No.' Iska held her long hands out to the fire's warmth. 'I do not know enough of this myself but – clouds travel on the winds. I think it may be that he creates certain conditions quite nearby, then he causes the wind to carry the snow, or the rain, or whatever, in the direction he desires. So the Power may be used only locally to him.' She looked up at their faces from where she knelt before the fire and smiled. 'Then again, that may all be wishful thinking, but the idea of Rhaki having use of such tremendous Power, I find rather alarming.'

'There must be a full Gathering, Emla,' Yash said. 'Events are moving too rapidly. When all the People, and the humans with whom we share this Realm, learn of the numbers of Guards hurt by the Shardi, there will be much fear. Better we tell of it immediately.'

'I took the liberty, Emla, of warning that a full Gathering would be called very soon when I bespoke the Healers in Gaharn earlier.'

Emla nodded. 'Very good, Iska. What would I do without you three?'

Kemti caught the Lady's hand and raised it to his brow. 'Students in the Asataria, Juniors, and then Seniors. We have travelled long and far together Lady.'

As they began to move out to the staircase, Emla said: 'I think I at least will remain here to oversee the arrival of the Guards. I would like to speak to each, to thank them, before I come to the Gathering.'

'I too would stay,' Iska interposed quickly.

'Kemti and I, then, will go to Gaharn to ensure all attend. Shall we arrange it for two days from now Lady?'

'Three days, I think,' Emla decided. 'The wounded are being moved only as fast as the Healers deem suitable. I imagine that means very slowly, so I will join you in the Chambers of Gathering at midday in three days from now.'

Kemti and Yash wrapped themselves in several layers of robes, weatherproof cloaks on top, pulled on sturdy boots and strode off towards the City. It would take several hours for them and their two Guards to descend from the Golden Lady's House to Gaharn. The Guards were trained to move at a fast trot, to enable them to keep pace with the enormous strides the People normally travelled at.

The Lady herself enjoyed the walk into the City, although she was usually accompanied by a formal escort of Guards as well as two carts for her maids drawn by pairs of male kalfi. These were as placid as the female kalfi, which were kept for the milk they yielded in plentiful supplies.

It was midmorning on the second day after the Merigs had brought their news, that the fengar-drawn carts crawled through the Upper Pass to the Lady's House. The snow had continued unabated but Emla had men keeping the main paths clear. As the wounded men were lifted gently to be borne into the House, Emla was appalled at their injuries.

Iska began work at once, assisting the dozen Healers who had hurried from Gaharn to join the Healers already present. Emla insisted the Healers who had travelled with the wounded go immediately to rest – they were swaying on their feet with fatigue. Despite their protests, she told them not to try to use their Powers until a full day's rest had restored them.

It was late that evening before Shan managed to make Emla go to her private rooms and eat something, and it took a near tantrum to persuade her. 'A bath is ready my Lady, and I will brush out your hair for you later.' Shan was peeling the blood smeared top robe from Emla as she spoke. She tutted as she saw blood had soaked through to the Lady's under robe. 'You have many willing servants, Lady, and all those Healers. Why must you work on those poor men yourself? Just look at you!'

Emla saw tears on Shan's round cheeks. The girl adored her mistress, and was distressed that Emla had done what Shan saw as menial work in bathing the men and getting them clean. She took Shan's face between her slender hands and held her still.

'I know it upsets you dear one, but if one can do something, however small, or dirty, then one must. Think of what those men have done for the rest of that company that left here so short a time ago! Some are sorely hurt Shan. Some will never see, or walk, or have their wits, again. Compared to that, what is a soiled robe or two when, stars know, I have so many?'

As Shan was about to reply, Emla laid her long fingers across the full lips. 'Hush! I will soak in my bath – it smells wonderful! Then I shall eat a little honeybread and drink some of your splendid tea – truly, no one makes it so well as you! Now, do you promise, no more scolding?'

Shan's huge blue eyes spilled fresh tears as she nodded. Emla kissed Shan's brow and went towards the steaming bathtub.

'Lady?'

Emla slid lower until she was almost submerged, sighing in pleasure. 'Yes Shan?'

'Will that little Tika, and Mim, and the Dragons come safely home?'

Emla kept her eyes closed. 'Only the stars know the answer to that. All we can do is pray it will be so.'

Seniors of all Disciplines sat in the galleries ringing the Great Chamber of Gathering. Juniors sat on benches around the floor space and many, if not all of the students of the Asataria thronged the lesser Chambers opening off of the Great Chamber. It was the first time a full Gather had been summoned since Jerak's disappearance. There was some murmuring – no Justice had been Named to replace Jerak, and it was the Justice who was the leader of such Gathers.

The low hum of many conversations faded into silence as the Golden Lady entered alone. She halted in the middle of the Chamber, standing in the centre of a circular mosaic of crystal, gold and jet. Her simple robe of palest green, threaded with gold and silver, gave a subdued shimmer with each movement she made. Her black hair was unbound, falling straight to her waist, and her green eyes dominated her narrow face. Into the silence she spoke the formal words of welcome, which the Justice would have done. Then she began the whole telling.

When she had finished, she bowed low, turning so she paid respect to all of the Gathered. Then she waited for the questioning to begin. A Junior fetched a stool for her to sit on, and students moved among the Gathered ones, bearing trays of hot spiced tea.

The Discipline Seniors, the colours of their robes indicating their fields of study, nodded to their spokesman. He rose, leaning his tall frame lightly on the gallery railing.

'The Lady has given us a great deal to think on. We suggest that we Gather again tomorrow morning, to discuss any conclusions we may have reached. Then, perhaps, decisions can be made.'

All the Gathered People stood, their heads tilted back as they looked up to the high dome of the Chamber's roof. A mosaic circle, mirroring the one set in the floor, glinted down, a blue star pulsing in its centre. Then heads were lowered and the People quietly filed out of the great room leaving Emla, standing now, in the middle of the floor.

Iska's arm went round Emla's shoulders. 'You spoke well Emla. Now we can only wait.'

'That is all I seem to do!' Emla cried out suddenly. She clenched her fists. 'Surely – surely – there is something I can do – other than just wait?'

Chapter Twenty-Two

The appearance of the Snow Dragons had greatly heartened the company high in the mountains. 'So far, so good,' the Guards agreed. They had been aware of the doubts about the crimson Dragon's story of Dragons and a human-type race living here, but at least the Dragon part seemed to be true. Tika also had harboured doubts, mainly because Brin's adventures here had been so very long ago – she knew only too well how situations could change at great speed.

Farn was the only one who had expected the arrival of Snow Dragons. Brin was a marvel to Farn's eyes; brave, much travelled, mightily strong. When Kija overheard Farn extolling Brin's virtues to Ashta and Jeela, she had said: 'Brave and fearless can quite easily be another aspect of stupid and careless, Farn.'

Poor Farn had tried to work out whether she had been approving of Brin, or critical. He still was not entirely sure, but sadly suspected Kija did not see Brin as the heroic creature he himself did.

What the company had first assumed was snow encrusting the newly arrived Dragons' faces, hands and feet, was in fact a very fine covering of hair – obviously a useful development in this environment. The larger of the two, Meppi, had begun a rather formal speech, which promised to be somewhat prolonged, when Ulla interrupted:

'We have food for you, in our tunnels. We will have to stay here tonight, but early in the morning you will have fresh meat.'

The Dragons were relieved. They had not eaten for two days. They would waste too much energy flying back to the lower slopes to hunt, and then battling the snow and wind to return. Gan had offered them the dried meat the Guards carried, but after a taste, they had politely declined. A sip of one of Lorak's "concoctions", at Fenj's suggestion, had been a little help to them.

190

All were somewhat surprised by the fact that both Meppi and Ulla were very aged Dragons, not the hatchlings their size suggested. Brin had found Kija's apology most amusing when she realised she had addressed Meppi as if he were a child. She rewarded him with a withering glare from eyes sparking red glints, which, to Farn's worshipful astonishment, merely made Brin chuckle aloud.

The cooks had managed to make a hot broth for the men, who then curled up in what shelter there was and slept in exhaustion. With great effort four windbreaks had been wrestled into place, tents were beyond their weary muscles. Two fengars had been lost on the climb, and Tika remarked quietly to Mim that perhaps the other six would be a nice present to the Snow Dragons.

Mim grinned. 'This person too, saw the Snow Dragons look at the fengars with a certain interest! Did you see Kran and another Guard were gashed by the bad tempered creatures, just as they reached here?'

'Yes. They seem very ill-natured all the time. Stars know how they will behave if we start travelling underground. I am sure Gan only insisted on bringing them as an emergency food supply.'

'What will it be like do you think – underground? This one does not like the idea of being beneath all these great mountains.'

'At least it won't be snowing in there, or windy. If Dragons have lived here all this time, it must be safe enough Mim.'

'But does anything grow here? This one has seen nothing, not even lichen or moss. Surely there must be something?'

Tika shrugged and pushed Khosa across to Mim. 'Perhaps the race who live with these Dragons will tell you. No Khosa, I am warm, you sleep with Mim.'

Khosa hissed softly. 'It is very cold. I did not expect to spend this adventure stuck in a sack and freezing near to death.'

'Do not exaggerate. You are getting the easiest journey of all Kephi! Perhaps we should let you walk tomorrow, like the rest of us?' Khosa's eyes nearly crossed in fury, but she said nothing, simply burrowed under Mim's shirt for the night.

The Dragons were able to eat next morning – one of the fengars died in the night, its body stiffly frozen under the snow. Kija belched fire lightly over the corpse, enough to make it pliant enough to eat. If anything, the snow was even thicker.

Gan and Soran had the men roped securely together in groups of five, in the hope that they could save any from falling. Trem commented cheerfully that perhaps the heavy snowfall was an advantage – at least you couldn't see the sheer drops alongside their narrow path. Men who led fengars were ordered to release them the instant the fengars balked at the path or began to slide. Soran told them he did not wish any men to be dragged over the cliff edges by difficult fengars.

Gan had a brisk disagreement with Mim and Tika. They both announced that they would walk for what Meppi promised was but two or three more leagues to the entry to the Snow Dragons' domain.

Jeela was fascinated to meet Dragons so small. She had grown a little after she had hatched, but not a fraction since. Ulla had been equally intrigued with Jeela – so small and pale! So like a Snow Dragon in fact! Ashta and Farn were also excited by this encounter. But Tika knew that Fenj and Kija were reserving judgement, that they were both very worried as to where and how this journey would end.

Old Lorak seemed to distract Fenj, and to cheer the ancient black Dragon considerably. But Fenj had grown more slow to speak in the last days, while Kija snapped at everyone. As Tika muffled herself in her cloak, her eyes met Kija's.

'I am sorry, small one. My fear makes me angry. I would fight any visible foe for you all, but this not-knowing drives me to distraction.'

Tika waded through the snow to the great gold Dragon's side, looking up at the beautiful long face, snowflakes clinging to the long eyelashes. Kija lowered her head, her brow pressing Tika's.

'I know,' said Tika. 'And I want you to know now, I will do all in my Power' – she emphasised the word – 'to keep Farn safe.' She felt warm affection pour through her mind, then Sket was stamping his feet at her side, only his brown eyes showing over a scarf wrapped round his head and face.

'It'd take so long to unwrap ourselves if we was attacked now, we'd be dead on the spot!' he said brightly.

Mim and Motass joined them and they filed behind the first of the Guards. The wind hit them with renewed force as they left the relative shelter of their overnight stopping place. Mim gasped as the cold knife of air thrust him almost to a halt. He pulled his scarf across his face more securely, ducked his head and kept his eyes on Motass's heels as they began trudging through the snow.

The Dragons had flown on only minutes before the company began to march. All of them struggled to get aloft and then, beating hard to make headway, immediately disappeared from sight behind the wall of unceasing snow.

It was, truly, no more than three leagues to the Snow Dragons' tunnels, but it took the marchers a long morning to get there. Motass yelled something incomprehensible back to Mim, who was quite beyond trying to understand. Then suddenly the ground under their feet was grey rock, scoured by ice particles, not deep, slippery, hard-packed snow. A low cave opening was directly before them. As their eyes stopped watering, they saw Ashta and Farn waiting, and a pale light creeping out from deeper in the cave.

Ashta's eyes whirred in concern for Mim's shivering and she urged him inside with her, nudging him round a sharp-angled, narrow curve. As Tika followed with Farn, she wondered how Fenj and Brin, and even Kija, had squeezed their great selves through the tight corner.

She heard Gan behind them, checking the Guards as they all arrived. She heard the beginning of trouble with screams from the fengars, wondering briefly how they had any energy left to be so belligerent, then she was round another tight corner and stopped in disbelief.

In front of her was a large cavern, so large as to still seem spacious even with the six Dragons of the company there. One of the Snow Dragons, Tika thought it was Meppi, was speaking with Fenj. Ulla appeared from a tunnel at the far side of the cavern and Tika stared again.

Two human-like creatures were with Ulla, but unlike any other humans Tika had ever seen. They were small, as small as she herself, and one had black hair and the other tawny brown.

The Guards were pressing in behind Tika and she moved forward with Farn and Sket beside her. Ulla bespoke Tika and Mim as they drew close.

'These are our life-friends. Serim,' the male bowed low, 'and

Berri,' the female bowed also.

"I am Tika and this is Mim. The very tall one yonder is a man of the People and is called Gan."

Mim bowed as Tika introduced him. 'This person is honoured to greet you,' he said aloud in his lightly fluting tones. 'This one is Nagum, from far distant woodlands. May he ask of what race you are?'

Berri reached her hands up to Mim's face. 'Our common name is merely Delvers, our proper name you will learn in time. But you are so cold – come, warm yourselves.' She indicated they move closer to a nearby brazier and it was only then that Tika and Mim saw there were several such spaced round the cavern. Guards stood quietly round each one, thawing themselves, but still watchful of everything.

Serim walked across the cavern, bowing to left and right, and vanished around the corner leading back to the entrance cave. Another of the Delvers arrived, this one wearing a blue leather band round his brow. Berri introduced him as Falim, one of their Healers.

'We know you have Healers of your own in your company, but they may be unaccustomed to treating the hurts the cold can inflict,' Falim said. 'These men should not be warming frozen hands as they are. May I speak with your Healers?'

'I would welcome your advice as I am sure they will also.' Gan had joined them, and now led Falim to meet the company's Healers. He rejoined Mim and Tika, his height emphasised even more as he stood beside Berri.

Berri chuckled. 'You will have to sit when you speak with us, Gan, or we will all end with twisted necks!'

'The difference in our sizes is indeed somewhat great,' Gan agreed with a smile. 'We have no knowledge of your race living here though, Berri.'

'We will speak later of these things.'

There was a grating, rumbling roar, then fengar shrieks of anger. The Guards looked towards the entrance, still nearly numb hands trying to grasp their swords.

'You have sealed the entrance, I presume?' Gan asked calmly.

Berri inclined her head. 'This entrance has not been used in any of our memories. We had nearly forgotten that it existed.'

'Fortunate for us that you did not forget.'

'If you will follow us now? As I said, we have not been in these tunnels for a long, long time. We have quite a distance to go to reach the outermost edge of the areas we now use.' Serim turned towards the tunnel from which he, Berri and Falim had emerged, but he hesitated. 'Your animals, Gan? I can have food brought for them here if you wish to maintain them?' He looked searchingly up at their faces. 'We would use such creatures for food – they are not suited to our way of life.'

Gan gestured to Soran and Nomis. 'If they will contribute to your food supplies, then they are yours. We have provisions in our packs,' Soran explained. 'We do not wish to take your food and leave your supplies low.'

For the first time Serim grinned. 'Have no fear. We are well maintained. Hunger is not acceptable among us, and we have long forgotten such a hardship!'

The Guards, hearing these comments, glanced at each other. No hunger? Living under these great cold and barren mountains? Perhaps the Delvers used magic. The thought occurred simultaneously to several Guards and their faces reflected a slight apprehension. Serim observed their expressions and grinned again, but all he said was: 'Bring the fengars as far as they will willingly come.' He turned and led the way into the mountain.

Berri waited until all had left, then she doused the embers in all the braziers and trotted to catch up with the company. The tunnel was lit as by pale moonlight. Small lamps, with only a single glower within each one, were hung every fifty paces. As Berri reached the first lamp, she unhooked it and carried it with her. At the next lamp, she opened the front of it, removed the glower and popped it into the lamp she carried. When that lamp was packed full of glowers, she took the next lamp with her and began to fill that one too.

Kran glanced back from his place at the rear of the company and slowed until Berri came up with him. 'I will carry the lamps for you Lady.'

Berri laughed. 'They are certainly not too heavy,' she said, 'but it is kind in you to offer assistance.' She passed him the lamps full of glowers. 'And I am Berri, not Lady.'

'And I am Kran.'

'Are you wed?'

Kran looked startled. 'Erm, no Lady – Berri.'

'A fine man like you? Not wed? We could use a fine fellow such as you,' Berri said, her eyes sparkling with mischief if Kran had but realised it. His startled look changed to one of intense worry.

'Guards do not usually marry until they are near the end of their term of service to the Golden Lady. We are very likely to be hurt, or killed, you see. How could we leave wives and families unprotected?' He glanced at her, hoping his explanation deterred her from pursuing this unwelcome topic.

Berri handed him another lamp full of glowers. 'Ah, but here you would not be a Guard so it would be unlikely for you to be "hurt or killed you see."' Then she took pity on the poor creature and changed the subject. Stars, but he was so agitated he could easily drop the poor glowers! Wouldn't this tale make the others laugh later though, she thought, and then politely asked him to tell her something of Gaharn.

They managed to cajole and bully the fengars to within a league of their destination, according to Serim. He organised the tying of the beasts, well spaced, along a section of wall. As Berri and Kran caught up with them, Serim asked her to add extra glowers to the lamps here so that the fengars were in a well-lit area and less likely to lash out at each other.

Mim walked with Ashta, behind Fenj. The Dragons were all getting sore feet, unused as they were to walking such distances. Brin, Kija, Farn and Tika followed them. Jeela was the only one not to seem bothered by walking so far. She fairly danced along with Ulla and Falim, ahead of all the rest.

Farn stopped, looking at his feet rather sadly. 'Jeela seems to be able to walk with no trouble. Why do my feet hurt so?'

Tika hugged him quickly. 'She is so small. She has less weight to carry so she moves more lightly.'

Serim was near enough to hear this exchange and he said: 'Soon you will be able to soothe your aches, all of you. I do not know if you Dragons from Outside like to bathe or swim?'

Brin's eyes began to glow. 'I remember! You have those large warm pools with water that tastes strange! Yes,' he nodded happily, 'I remember those.'

196

As Kija, Farn and Tika looked puzzled, he showed them a mind picture of an underground lake, a strange mist lying over its surface. Then Brin surged forward to join his father and explain the pleasure ahead.

Farn wriggled his toes and sighed. 'I hope it is not much further.'

Kija turned her head to study him for a moment. She said quietly: 'Bravery is tested in many strange ways my son.'

Farn looked at her anxiously, sapphire eyes whirring. Tika met Kija's golden look and nodded, putting her arm lightly across Farn's shoulder. 'That's right Farn. Perhaps anyone can battle a raging fengar if they have to, but to walk a league with hurt feet that no one else sees or knows about is a different sort of bravery. But it is bravery just the same.'

Farn's head lifted a little higher. He took a deep breath and began to pace firmly forward. 'Well, come along. We do not want to be the last of all, do we?' he asked.

Kija's eyes shone their affectionate pale honey colour at Tika briefly, then they both hurried after Farn.

The tunnel had been sloping very gently downwards with several places curving to the right. Tika guessed the afternoon would have darkened to nightfall out in the upper world. The Guards had become more relaxed as they walked, old Lorak spinning his tales to them. Tika heard snatches of his stories, each more convoluted and unbelievable than the last. Lorak's face had lost the grey tightness it had developed over the past days and he seemed back to his usual self. Ahead of her, Mim still clutched his cloak around his thin body, obviously still thoroughly chilled.

Tika herself, had pushed her cloak over her shoulders, she felt almost warm compared to her recent coldness. Sket and Motass stumped along behind Mim, ahead of Tika. Occasionally Sket looked over his shoulder at her, clearly they took their idea of being personal bodyguards very seriously.

Suddenly silence spread back from the leading members of the company. Everyone behind hurried the last steps to see what lay before them. The enclosed tunnel widened, becoming a broad ledge open on the right side, winding down to a pool. Rocks gleamed and shone with a strange greenish light. The glow lamps

197

still lining the left wall beside them only reached a few man
lengths across the water. The company could not guess how far
the pool might extend. The mist Tika had seen in Brin's mind
was coiling lazily over the water's surface.

Peering down, they saw more Delvers with small carts and
several braziers, settled near the water's edge. The Delvers were
looking up at the arrivals, most faces showing welcoming, and
curious, smiles. A feeling of a certain relief made the company
hurry down to meet their hosts. Names flew back and forth, hot
food and drink were offered and gratefully accepted. Tika's head
spun as she tried to remember names and which faces they
belonged to.

As she joined Mim, Khosa emerged from her carrying sack
under Mim's cloak. Some of the Delvers noticed her and drew
the attention of their fellows. It was into a silence that Khosa
stalked regally to the nearest brazier. There she sat, her tail
thrashing impatiently. Lorak took a piece of meat from his dish
and held it to Khosa's nose. Her whiskers twitched, she turned
away with a look of unmistakable disgust and fixed her glare on
Berri.

'I am Khosa, a Queen of the Kephi. I eat fresh meat.' The
words rang imperiously in every head. Farn looked horrified, but
Berri picked a chunk of uncooked meat from a basket and,
kneeling, offered it to Khosa. Khosa sniffed it daintily, then
deigned to consume it rapidly.

'Aah,' crooned Berri. 'Isn't she sweet?'

Farn moaned and shut his eyes. Khosa crooned back at Berri
and climbed onto her lap. Berri stood up carefully, cradling the
orange Kephi against her shoulder. As she turned to carry this
amazing little creature to the other Delvers to admire, Khosa
looked back at Lorak, Mim and Farn. Her expression was
insufferably smug but it changed to her more usual glare as Tika
and Mim began to giggle helplessly.

As Gan came through the crowd and found Mim and Tika
convulsed with laughter, his first thought was – Lorak. His gaze
fell on the old gardener, who sat leaning against Fenj's side.
Lorak lifted his eyes to meet Gan's and gave him a horribly
innocent grin. 'Oh no, Lord Gan. It's the Kephi made them
laugh. Not me.'

Fenj looked down onto Lorak's battered hat. 'Splendid creature!' he murmured.

Gan knew he was growing to hate that phrase, but Serim appeared before he could make a comment he might regret.

'If any of you wish, the water is hot. Bathe your feet, or swim. There are substances in the water, which refresh and soothe. We have towels and blankets for you.'

Brin was already paddling they realised, his eyes rosy prisms of delight. As they watched, he waded deeper, stretching out his wings. Tika and Mim were pulling off their boots and Farn, Ashta and Jeela were heading towards Brin. As Kija rose to follow, Gan saw his Guards removing boots and cloaks. Several Delvers were walking in the shallowest water.

Fenj surged to his feet. He looked down at Lorak. 'Shall we join them all and bathe, Lorak of the Garden?'

Gan knew he would gloat for days over the look of utter horror that spread over Lorak's face at Fenj's suggestion. As Fenj waited patiently, Lorak finally managed to sputter: 'Well now. It isn't good for old human bones, Lord Fenj. Rots 'em like. I'll just wait here and watch.'

Before Gan could make the scathing comment he had ready, Serim rejoined them.

'If your company is able to keep a good pace, we will reach Amud about this time tomorrow.'

"Amud?" Gan queried.

'It is one of our main settlements. Our Wise One, Nolli, is travelling from further north to meet you there. Then perhaps, some of your questions may be answered.'

Chapter Twenty-Three

Except for Jeela, the Dragons were badly tired by the time they had travelled the tunnels and arrived at Amud. As they neared the settlement, more tunnels merged into the broad one they marched along. Delvers came from these side tunnels, most with handcarts, and apparently in family groups. The company noted the carts were laden with various kinds of produce.

Serim explained: 'They heard of the arrival of strangers from Outside and they use the excuse of bringing supplies so that they can see you.'

Soran and Trem were looking at the contents of some of the carts. As Serim moved on to speak to Tika and Mim, Soran said quietly to Gan: 'These goods, Sir, surely they cannot all be produced underground? These Delvers must have contact with someone Outside.'

Gan replied equally softly: 'I have noticed, Soran. They must indeed trade goods somehow. Go among the men and tell them to say as little as possible if they are questioned about Gaharn, or the Lady, or our Realm. And the little they do say should be as unhelpful as they can manage. Just in case.'

'The Guardian?'

Gan nodded grimly. 'I have never heard even the wildest rumour of these Delvers before, so they cannot be trading with any races that we know of.'

The settlement appeared spread below and around them. A roughly circular bowl of a cavern, with dwelling places honey-combing the sides. All was brightly lit with glow lamps, and water poured into a narrow stretch of a pool to one side. The smoke, which the company now knew to be steam, rose from this water as it had from the first pool.

The doorways and window spaces of the dwellings were screened with a roughly-woven, fibrous material, although most such door hangings were hooked open as the company arrived.

They were offered adjacent dwellings in which to spend the coming night. Mim and Tika hurriedly explored one such, finding three modest-sized rooms behind the first one. They threw their packs into a corner, Tika leaving her cloak as well although Mim still kept his around him. Then they ran down the sloping rock towards the pool where the Dragons were paddling.

Fenj was, in fact, almost totally submerged beside Brin, their eyes closed in pleasurable relief. Ulla and Meppi were with them, laughing at Farn's attempts to go underwater without drowning himself. Jeela turned as Mim and Tika arrived. 'Is it not amazing?' she asked. 'This warm water is wonderful!' Her eyes whirred all colours in her excitement. 'And to think Mother tried to stop me coming with you all!'

Ashta came dripping from the pool to Mim's side. Tika heard him say: 'No, Ashta, this one is warming now.'

If he was not still cold, what was troubling him? Before she could ask, Farn rose, snorting and showering them all as he burst up from the water. He looked as excited as Jeela, and Tika was reminded again of how very young he, his sister and Ashta were.

There was a festival atmosphere as Delvers called them to come and eat. Meppi took the Dragons off with him as Tika and Mim joined Lorak in the central area. Low tables had been set up and were covered in an amazing assortment of different foods.

'Have you learnt where these fruits grow, Lorak?' Mim asked, sitting down by the old man.

'They told me they grow some of this themselves. They did not reply when I asked to see.' He leaned closer. 'Can you feel if they have Powers, Mim?'

'They can all use the mind speech,' said Mim, his mouth full of an extraordinarily juicy, oblong fruit. 'This person feels there is shielding around some.'

Lorak nodded and muttered under his breath.

Tika was sampling some dark squares of what looked like bread but tasted of tea and nuts, when Khosa pushed her head against her arm. The Kephi lay on Tika's legs, her front paws tucked neatly beneath her and her eyes half closed. 'They have secrets.'

Tika did not pause in eating and she smiled at a Delver opposite her as she asked: 'Did you learn these secrets?'

201

Khosa's ears twitched. 'Not much. They speak with ones who live in the Wilderness.'

Tika's mind registered blankness. Khosa tutted. 'The Wilderness. The land beyond these High Land Mountains, where no one ever goes. Or if they do, they do not seem to return.'

'But I thought it was a place made up by the storytellers?'

'Oh you.' Khosa began her crooning hum. 'You thought Dragons and Nagums were monsters not so long ago!' A stretch rippled her spine and she rolled over on Tika's lap, suggesting her paler orange belly now be rubbed. 'Several are shielding their minds,' Khosa continued. 'Of course they may suspect you of being servants of the Guardian.'

'But the Shardi attacked us!'

Khosa yawned hugely. 'The Shardi attack everyone. But I advise caution now Tika.'

Sket sat down beside Tika. 'Their food is good anyways Lady. Have you tried these?' He offered a plate with tiny purple berries upon it. His free hand landed gently on Khosa's exposed throat and he rubbed down from her jaw to her chest and back upwards. Khosa moaned in delight and Tika dumped her unceremoniously onto Sket. 'Excuse me a moment Sket.'

Tika moved through the crowd, looking for Gan. Several Delvers spoke to her, to whom she replied with a smile but without stopping. She saw him sitting on a rock, slightly apart, with Kija reclining nearby. As Tika wandered casually in their direction, she was aware that they were mind speaking to each other on a very tightly directed beam of thought.

She went to Kija, reaching to stroke the golden cheeks as she asked: 'Do you have any idea how we would get out of here if these Delvers are not what they seem?'

Kija lowered her head to press against Tika's brow. 'The Delvers believe the Snow Dragons to be totally open and under their control.' There was a trace of amusement in her tone as she went on: 'Although it suits them to live closely with these Delvers, they keep much of themselves very private. As the Golden Lady thought she knew us, so the Delvers believe they know everything there is to know of the Snow Dragons. They will lead us out of here if we ask it of them.'

'I had just asked Kija the same question,' Gan said aloud,

smiling, as a Delver passed quite close by them.

'Do you know when this Wise One Serim spoke of will arrive?' Tika asked, also aloud.

Serim himself replied, having approached suddenly behind Gan. 'The Wise One is very old, oldest of all in fact, and is much fatigued by the journey. The Wise One sends greetings and regrets, but must rest now and will speak with you in the morning.' He smiled faintly as he spoke, aware that his sudden appearance had not startled them as perhaps might have been expected.

Gan stood, his great height towering over Serim, and bowed gracefully. 'Of course Serim. We look forward to speaking with your Wise One. We will all have clearer minds after a good night's rest, I am sure.'

'Without freezing, or wondering if Shardi will attack, or worse!' Tika added cheerfully.

'Do you set watchmen?' Gan asked.

Serim laughed. 'We need no watchmen here, Lord of the People.' He said no more but stood smiling gently.

Gan nodded and glanced at Tika. 'I suggest we all get that rest then.'

'I will be here,' Kija said, her words clear to all. 'Farn and Ashta will probably insist on sleeping near you.'

Tika felt affection again from the She Dragon and she smiled. 'Good night then, Kija.'

'Sleep well, small one.'

Sket and Motass had already spread out their bedrolls in the entrance room of the cave Tika and Mim had chosen. 'We'll take turns, Sir,' Motass announced as Gan and Tika entered.

'Just in case,' Sket added as he cleaned his sword.

Khosa appeared from the rear rooms. 'Lorak and Soran and Trem are playing one of those games with small stones. When I try to play, they become quite ill mannered.' Her expression was one of injured majesty.

'Where is Mim?' Tika asked, remembering she wanted to ask him several questions.

Gan looked out of the doorway. 'He is near the pool, with Ashta. Is he all right Tika? He is still wrapped in his cloak yet it is not cold here.'

'That is one of several things I mean to find out,' she replied.

Much later, Gan was still wide-awake. He went quietly through to the back rooms. Soran, Trem and Lorak all slept, snoring inharmoniously. Gan moved to the next doorway and looked in. Mim lay curled in his cloak, his head on Tika's lap. She sat leaning against the wall, seemingly asleep, her arm protectively across Mim's body. Her eyes were closed but Gan realised her face was wet. Before he could do anything, Khosa wound between his feet. 'Leave them,' she commanded.

He stood a moment longer then crept back through the rooms to the entrance. He nodded to Motass and, pushing aside the screen, slipped out of the cave, nearly treading on Ashta's nose. He held his breath but Farn and Ashta did not stir. The Kephi leaped lightly over them and walked away down the slope, her tail waving upright.

Gan looked into the central space of the cavern. A few Delvers lay asleep beside their carts but most seemed to have found accommodation in the many holes and caves lining the cavern. Fenj, Jeela, Brin and Kija looked to be asleep, against one of the rocky walls. Quietly, Gan followed the Kephi as she walked purposefully away from the Delvers towards the pool.

As Khosa sat herself on a convenient rock she said: 'If any come, I suggest you tell them you could not sleep because your feet pained you.'

Obediently, Gan sat next to her, pulled off his boots and dangled his long feet in the warm water.

'What troubles them?' he asked.

For the first time, the haughty Kephi seemed hesitant. 'It is not for me to say. Something has happened which upsets Tika more than Mim, but you must take great care with them both now.'

Gan puzzled over this gnomic statement, trying to make some sense of it. Khosa spat.

'Oh you two-legs are so stupid! And you are surprised that many of us of other races choose not to involve ourselves with you mentally?'

Gan was completely perplexed. 'Do you mean that they will marry?'

Khosa stared at him contemptuously. 'Of course not! Your

minds are very limited, are they not? No, no. I only try to warn you to be careful of them. I cannot tell you more, that must be their choosing. I think Ashta knows, and perhaps Farn, but Tika will need more help than Mim.'

The water lapped a little harder against the rock on which they sat and Khosa moved back, shaking a fastidious paw. She leaped down and stalked off, saying: 'I go to listen to dreamers.'

Gan spent the remainder of the night trying to estimate the distance north they had travelled. He was fairly sure the Delvers had led them north continuously, although the tunnel had curved gently, and perhaps deceptively, in places. He felt certain he would sense any major change of direction. He reckoned they must be nearing the White River, which bordered the Waste Land, which, in turn, bordered the Realm of Ice. He had no idea if the Snow Dragons and Delvers had tunnels leading right into the Guardian's Realm – that was a question he hoped their Wise One would answer.

The men seemed to be a cohesive group at least. He had seen that all of them had drunk sparingly of a beer the Delvers offered. He had tasted it, to be polite, finding it had a pleasant taste and promised a powerful effect. He had given no instructions to the men and he knew his officers had not either, yet the men had taken care to keep their wits about them.

And now a problem of some kind with the human girl and the Nagum boy. He had half expected Khosa would say they had become more involved with each other than with the task ahead of them. They had somehow been changed into uniquely different beings – it would not be surprising if they clung to each other for more than moral support.

Delvers were beginning to stir as Gan made his way back to the dwelling cave.

'Everything all right Sir?' Sket asked softly as Gan entered.

Gan stretched. 'I hope so Sket. Tell the men I was proud of the way they conducted themselves last evening. I am sure they must have been sorely tempted by that beer!'

Sket grinned. 'Very tasty it were, Sir. But we are all determined now Sir, after them nasty Shardi killing so many comrades.'

'Yes Sir.' Motass emerged from his blankets. 'You won't

find any letting you down Sir.'

Gan smiled. 'Thank you. And don't forget to tell the men what I said!'

Shortly after, several Delvers arrived with breakfast, which they were obviously intended to eat within the dwelling. Gan noticed that Tika looked very pale, although Mim was his usual self but for the fact he held his cloak tight around him. Before long, Serim was bowing in the doorway.

'The Wise One approaches,' he announced.

They went out onto the rock walkway and saw Delvers standing quietly down in the central space. As they stood there, a drumbeat began to echo from one of the tunnels – impossible to tell from which one. Four Snow Dragons paced steadily to the centre of the cavern where they took position facing outwards at the Delvers. Then two young Delvers appeared, pulling a cart very similar to the ones the company had observed the supplies arriving in. This one, though, was elaborately carved from a very dark wood and held an equally ornate chair on which sat the Wise One. A solitary drummer walked behind. A sigh of respect whispered through the cavern as the Wise One was carried in and placed in the midst of the four Snow Dragons. The two Delvers bowed low, both extending a hand to help the Wise One rise from the chair.

Lorak muttered, 'Stars, another female in charge!' He grunted as Tika stepped back onto his foot as heavily as she could manage.

The Wise One was looking up in their direction now and Serim said quickly: 'Come down now and be received by our Wise One.'

As they descended, Ashta and Farn moved close beside Mim and Tika, and the four other Dragons flanked the company. They halted by the first Snow Dragon, who reared erect for a moment, then sank gracefully back to a reclining position. Fenj moved forward, past the Snow Dragons, to within a man length of the Wise One. Then he too reared erect, his huge black bulk giving an impression of enormous strength. His words rang through every mind: 'I am Fenj, Eldest of the Broken Mountain Treasury. I offer greetings from all this company to you, Wise One of the Delvers.'

Close to, they saw the Wise One was indeed an incredibly old female. She leaned on a stick, the hand grasping it swollen and misshapen. But her voice was surprisingly strong and almost youthful as she said: 'Thank you Fenj. I offer welcome to you all. My name is Nolli and I would prefer you to call me that.'

Fenj lowered himself as the rest of the company sat on the rock floor and the Delvers crowded round as well. Only Gan, Tika and Mim remained on their feet. Gan introduced the three of them formally. The Wise One's wrinkled face suddenly split into an almost toothless grin. 'I fear we will all have to sit, Lord Gan. I cannot stand for long anyway, but staring up at you will make me dizzy!' She looked at Tika, her dark eyes bright and quick, and Tika knew this Wise One was able to use the Power. 'Tell me how you come to be calling for our help, and why you travel in these parts.'

One of the low tables was hastily brought from the nearest dwelling and Gan seated himself on it, Tika and Mim perching beside him. Even so, Gan's head was higher than the seated Wise One. She rested her hands on top of her stick and closed her eyes as Gan started to speak.

When he finished, the Wise One's head had sunk to her chest and he half suspected that she had fallen asleep. A silence spread like an almost visible cloud over his whole audience. He waited. The Wise One raised her head and stared at Gan. He felt a sudden burst of Power enter him and knew, even though he was a Senior of the People, he could not hope to contest the strength of this tiny old creature.

He knew immediately that she was checking the truth of what he said and he held himself still as she swept through his mind. Tika had sprung to her feet, Mim clutching her arm, the instant Power was called forth, but she restrained herself from forcing away the Wise One's attention. Ashta and Farn moved restlessly and the other Dragons half rose. Then the Power was gone and the silence disintegrated. Bodies shifted, murmurs were exchanged, and Tika and Mim resumed their seat.

The Wise One rapped her stick on the floor of her cart. 'You have all heard Lord Gan's words. I know we must help this brave company, although we are sworn to keep ourselves aloof from all the outsiders who live between us and the dying sun. Therefore, I offer whatever assistance we can give. We know more of the Guardian than these travellers' – there were cries of agreement interspersed with groans. 'We will tell them all we know and, I repeat, we will help them. If any disagree, they will come to me and speak their reasons and I will listen. You have until the mid mealtime to voice any objections. After that, I will speak with these travellers and tell them in what ways we may help them.'

The two young Delvers escorting her stood up and pulled the Wise One's cart towards one of the dwelling caves and in through its door. The screen was lowered across the entrance behind them.

'Come.' Berri was there, Khosa cradled in her arm. 'This is my dwelling and tea is ready to brew. All that talking Lord Gan – you must be as dry as a bone!'

Soran and Drak had also come up to Gan and they joined the group entering Berri's cave. Berri served them tea, similar to what they were accustomed to but fruitier, less spicy, and amused them with innocuous tales. She confessed to her continued teasing of Kran, how the poor man jumped from his skin whenever she appeared. Soran laughed. 'I had noticed he seemed a little jumpy!'

Tika and Mim listened and smiled but said nothing, until Tika eventually suggested they should return to their dwelling and get their packs readied for the next stage of their journey. Berri at first tried to persuade them to stay chatting a while longer, then, seeing they were determined to leave, she smiled them out of her door.

'You did notice she arranged that we sat with our backs to the door and the window?' Gan remarked.

'But I could see out,' Khosa said smugly.

'I know. That is why I made no attempt to move. So Khosa, who did you see enter the Wise One's cave to object to her helping us?'

'Serim was the first. There were three more, one of them female. I do not know how they are named, but I would recognise them again.'

Delvers again brought food to them all in the dwellings that had been assigned to them, and as they finished eating Serim bowed at the entrance.

'The Wise One waits your presence.'

It had been decided that only Gan, Mim and Tika would go to the Wise One and they now walked down and across to her cave. Khosa skipped playfully round their feet and Farn and Ashta pressed as close as they could. Fenj had already taken up his reclining position beside the entrance and the two young Dragons settled beside him. The Snow Dragons were also lying there, all seeming relaxed and calm.

Gan bespoke Tika and Mim as they reached the doorway. 'I suspect she may tease or test you. Keep a very tight hold on your feelings.' Although he spoke to them both, it was obvious his words were directed at Tika.

The screen was drawn back and one of the Wise One's young escorts bowed, directing them through to a room deeper in the mountain. The strangely young voice called, 'Come in, come in! Don't dither at the door! Surely you can have no fear of such a one as I?'

Chapter Twenty-Four

Gan was dismayed to find Serim was with them as they entered the Wise One's inner room. Before he could think of a polite way of asking that he should not be present, the Wise One herself said: 'Thank you Serim. You may leave now.'

'But I should remain.' Serim protested indignantly. 'As the Elder here, I insist I remain.'

'You are indeed the Elder of Amud, Serim,' the Wise One agreed. 'But I am the Wise One of Asat, and I insist that you leave us.'

With very bad grace, Serim turned and left. The young Delver escorts also retreated through the rooms to sit by the door facing the Dragons.

'You need have no fear of him, Gan. His pride is overgrown, but he has not yet succumbed to the Guardian.'

'I admit to harbouring that thought, Wise One.'

She tutted crossly. 'Nolli, not Wise One. I am only the Wise One at formal moments.' She leaned back in her carved chair. 'And you are Tika, and sad.' She studied Tika briefly, making no attempt to enter the girl's mind. 'And you, Dragon Lord, are Mim, and – sad also?'

Gan saw Tika grow paler while Mim smiled his sweet smile at Nolli. 'This person is amazed, not sad. But,' he added, 'this one will not speak of it yet please.'

The Wise One nodded. 'I will speak with you alone, should you wish. It has happened before.' Then she looked at Gan. 'Even here we knew the Balance had been disturbed in some way. And to save you asking – the Guardian does not know of our existence here.'

'I have two questions, Wise – Nolli. How far do your tunnels extend to the north, and are there races living now in the Wilderness with whom you have contact?'

Nolli laughed. 'The previous Guardian, Kovas, learned of us

but swore he would tell no one unless we allowed it.' Her expression grew sorrowful. 'He knew he was weakening and he asked that I meet him one last time.' She smiled at Gan's look of surprise. 'Oh yes, I am indeed so old! He feared that Rhaki would be Named his successor, and he warned us of him. Most of the tunnels began to be sealed from that time. We deliberately left a few tunnels open on the dying sun side of these mountains, leaving that world – we thought – for good.' Khosa chose that moment to leap lightly onto Nolli's lap. The twisted hands rested on the orange fur as Khosa began humming softly.

'Rhaki uses some tunnels for ease and swiftness of travel – he likes suddenly arriving among some of his followers as if "by magic". It saves him expending his Power. Shardi live in a few of the smaller tunnels, which makes it hazardous for the occasional messenger or spy whom Rhaki sends that way. Since Kovas's time, we have not travelled into that Realm. The tunnels are still there but in what state now I cannot tell. Also, there were traps laid near the Guardian's stronghold lest Rhaki learnt of those passageways.'

Nolli fell silent, apparently lost in distant memories. Khosa batted her arm gently with a slender paw and Nolli sighed. 'I will take you onwards, through this Domain of Asat, but I think I cannot come all the way with you – I would hinder you too much.' She waved a hand distastefully at her own body. 'This body fails me now. I was happily anticipating going beyond when I heard of your coming, and now I am angered that this body prevents me helping you as fully as I would wish.'

Again she paused. 'To your second question, I will answer only "yes". It is not for me to say more,' she said firmly. 'I suggest we begin our journey very shortly. Day and night mean little here, as you would imagine. I think Time is pressing on us now.' Tika and Mim looked at her sharply, she had seemed to emphasis the word "Time", and Time was involved in the suspension of the Balances. What did this ancient Delver know of such things?

Gan stood up. 'I will get the men ready then, Nolli. I hope the journey will not be at too great a cost for you, and that we will have some time to talk along the way.'

Nolli smiled. 'It matters not the cost now, Gan. It will take several days to pass through the Domain of Asat to the northern limits. I will be ready within the hour.'

Gan hesitated, half turned to go, then he turned back to Nolli. Bending, he gently lifted the poor swollen hand and pressed it to his brow. He met her eyes for a moment, then abruptly turned again and left.

Tika and Mim were also standing now. Mim bowed and said: 'This one will speak with you soon Nolli, if he may.'

'Certainly Mim, whenever you wish.'

As they moved away, Nolli caught Tika's sleeve between her knotted fingers. 'Wait, child. I will speak with you now.'

Mim smiled at Tika, nodding, and followed Gan out of the dwelling.

'Not so defensive child, I will not hurt you.' Tika gradually relaxed as the old fingers slid down her sleeve and tried to clasp her hand. Khosa lay between them, buzzing very softly, her eyes tightly shut.

'There is a different future for Mim, child. And he has accepted it. You must search your heart and understand that he is content. I know he is as a brother you never had, near as your soul bond, Farn. And I wish to have many talks with you on this journey – so much I would learn of the Outside Dragons, and of the People. But child, you must not darken what could be Mim's joy.'

They were ready to begin when Serim arrived with a pack on his shoulders. Nolli had just joined the line, with six young male Delvers and a not so young female.

'You will not be travelling with us, Serim.'

'I have every right to join this foolhardy journey,' he retorted.

'You have indeed, if you were not the Elder of this place. As Elder, your duty is here.'

Berri slipped between them. 'Can I not come? I have not travelled far for a great time and it would be such fun to keep Kran company!'

Nolli stared hard at her, then gave a curt nod, signalling her escorts to pull her on.

Falim was also travelling with them. He had become inseparable from the company's two Healers and walked with them now, deeply engrossed in complicated healing procedures.

Gan had no reservations over Falim's presence: Healers were everywhere respected and quite impartial – any who needed their skills, received it unquestioningly.

Farn walked close by Tika. 'That Kephi! Just look how she manages to avoid walking!'

Tika laughed, the first real laugh since they had entered this Domain. Khosa sat upright on Nolli's lap, eyes sparkling with regal authority. This was obviously Khosa's idea of how majesty should travel.

'Would you prefer to sit in a cart, hatchling?' Nolli enquired tartly.

Farn's eyes whirred in embarrassment. 'Oh no, Wise One. I can walk for leagues and leagues. Besides, I would not fit in a cart.'

Tika saw Nolli's mouth twitch and her eyes glitter. Nolli glanced at her and away again quickly. Tika slid her arm over Farn's shoulder. 'You would look very undignified in a cart, Farn. I think it best you just concentrate on walking.'

Jal had returned to the Guardian to report absolutely no sign of Guards or Dragons anywhere near the High Land Mountains. Rhaki had accused him of lying, causing Jal to prostrate himself in terror. Again and again, Jal swore there had been no indication of any incursions towards the north. He eventually mentioned the broken remains of two fengars, clearly killed by falling a great distance.

'Only now you tell me this?' Rhaki screamed. 'How would fengars come to be there, and from whence did they fall? And do get up – you speak to me, not my carpet.'

Jal cautiously pushed himself up to his knees. 'Master, perhaps they fell from Dragon claws?'

'Since when do Dragons fly in snowstorms, carrying fengars?' He paced furiously across his study and back again. 'Did you go as far as the place where the Shardi attacked them?'

'Yes, Master. Little is left,' he swallowed. 'They eat their dead and wounded as you, of course, know. A few bones, that was all I found.'

'Through Shardi eyes I saw a company of Guards, I saw Gan of the People, I saw large Dragons.' He glared at Jal. 'So where

213

are they? You would have seen signs of their retreat if they had indeed gone back to their cursed city.'

'There was no sign, of any creatures.' Jal repeated yet again.

'Arrange for the Cansharsi to move across the Middle Plain towards the Realm of Gaharn. And I need a Linvak prisoner – who is still fit enough to be questioned. And a Nagum,' he added.

'But Master…'

'But, Jal?' Rhaki's voice rose in astonished disbelief. 'You question my order?'

'Oh no, Master, indeed not. Never.' Jal bowed from his kneeling position, sweat trickling down his back.

Slightly mollified, Rhaki sat down at the table and asked: 'But?'

'It was just that I feared it might be a little soon to send Cansharsi against the Guards on their own territory, Master.'

Rhaki yawned. 'You have told me that, no matter where the company is that Gan led from Gaharn, your spies say he has not returned to the city, or to the Lady's Estate. Without Gan, the Guards will be undisciplined and easily overcome. Send messengers speedily to the Cansharsi, Jal. And I would have a Linvak here equally speedily.' He flicked his fingers in Jal's direction and Jal took it as the dismissal it was. He wriggled abjectly back to the door, pulled himself to his feet and bowed himself out.

Rhaki continued to sit, his chin resting on one hand, gazing unseeing at the parchments and books littering the table. Where had they gone? Gan's use of the Power was very limited so he could immediately discount the idea of any shielding being used. Tunnels?

As the thought occurred, Rhaki sat upright. He had discovered the tunnels by accident soon after he arrived here. A few comments, scribbled in Kovas's hand inside books obviously in use until the old Guardian's death, had set him looking. It had been a desultory search, he had placed no real value or importance on the existence of any tunnels.

And then, one afternoon, he had discovered how to open the door in the rock in this room. It had been fairly straightforward working out how to operate other doors and follow tunnels through the mountain. Could there be others, he wondered? It was quite an extensive network he had found, but was there more?

Rhaki began to rummage through the parchments heaped on the table, muttering to himself. Papers and books fell to the floor unheeded, until he found the one he sought. He banged down four ancient books on one end of the roll and held the other end down with the flat of his hand. It was a map, showing this stronghold (under his palm), and the short stretch of the Ice Mountains merging with the High Land range, right down to Gaharn (under the books).

Still muttering, he traced a line with a long forefinger where he estimated the tunnels ran. He stared at the map, placed more books on it to keep it spread open and straightened. Rhaki walked to the fireplace, then to the window, from which only swirling whiteness was visible. Then he strolled back to the table and looked down at the map. Once more, he traced a line down through the mountains, and bit his lip.

So. All the tunnels *he* knew of were on this side of the mountains. Were there tunnels on the other side, facing the rising sun? If so, were they being used? By whom? He began to crack his knuckles as thoughts chased one after the other through his mind. Was he observed even here, inside what he had believed was his impregnable stronghold? Is that why he had the sensation of being observed sometimes, in the room of the Sacred Balance for instance?

But no, Jerak would surely have made some comment about his "experiments" if he had known of them. Who else could have access to the tunnels Rhaki was now convinced must run parallel to the ones he had discovered? Kovas must have known. Rhaki looked at the wall full of books, trying to remember, after all these Cycles, which were books that had belonged to Kovas. Where had he put all the others when he himself had arrived here to replace Kovas? Ancient texts, of no use whatsoever to one dealing with genetic plans for the future.

Would Emla know any of this? Who was working closest with her now? He cudgelled his brain to recall who had been her intimates during the ages of student-ship. He could only bring the name of "Kemti" to the surface, and he knew Kemti was now a

Senior of high repute, a powerful mind devoted to learning ancient ways.

'Bark!' he roared suddenly.

The study door opened silently and Bark moved into the room. 'Master?'

'Who were Emla's friends at the Asataria? Kemti is the only one I recall.'

Bark was silent a few moments. 'There was Yash, Master. Gan and Perik.' There was another silence. 'Iska and Kera. Those seven were always together Master.'

'Hmm.'

'Was there anything more, Master?'

'Eh? Oh. No Bark. Wait!' Bark turned back from the door. 'Do you ever feel there are others within this stronghold Bark?'

Bark's face was shadowed by the hood of his robe. 'Others, Master?'

'Yes. Others than the staff and my – beasts. Others who should not be here?'

'No, Master.'

'Are you sure?'

'Oh yes, Master.'

'Very well. Leave me.'

As Bark closed the door behind him, his eyes shone deep in the shadows of his hood.

Rhaki lifted a jug of wine but replaced it in the hearth without pouring himself any of it. A clear head was essential right now. He thought of the names Bark had given him. Yash – a far seeker of considerable Power and extremely sensitive to the emotions of any near him. Gan, he did not even bother to consider. Perik. Surely Perik had been killed by Gangers on one of his mad expeditions to the far west? A foolish dreamer, as far as Rhaki could remember. That left Iska and Kera. Iska was strong in manipulative Power, in healing, but not inclined to use her manipulative talents at all. He recalled part of an argument he had overheard. Iska had been insisting that she would work only through suggestion, not force any changes in any minds. She had been arguing with one of the Discipline Seniors he thought, but he had not really been interested enough to pay much attention at the time. Kera was a Discipline Senior in the Asataria and had

rarely left the Buildings of Learning since being raised to that
position.

Iska would seem to be the only choice, but how to get her out
of Gaharn? Or was she at Emla's House? It would be easier if
she was in between the two places Rhaki thought morosely. He
stopped cracking his knuckles. If he could arrange for her to be
summoned, from one place to another, surely even his dolts of
fighters, under Jal's command, could manage to capture one
female? He began to smile.

Jal had eventually said nothing to Bark about his hearing
sounds beyond the tunnel wall, mainly because confronting
Rhaki's fury occupied his mind too greatly. But Bark had heard
noises too, over a considerable period of time. Bark spent a lot of
his days sitting still. Rhaki assumed it was merely a symptom of
Bark's broken mind that he sat, passive as stone, for so long. In
fact, the stillness of his body had encouraged his mind to heal,
and his hearing seemed to have become unnaturally sharpened.
In all this great stretch of time, he had not attempted to summon
Power to himself.

Bark had known when his mind was first devastated that
calling Power would destroy him utterly. As he strengthened, he
continued to avoid even thinking of trying to use the Power. In
the Asataria, he had been known affectionately as the "Silent
Thinker" and was gaining respect as an analyst and philosopher
when he was drawn to Rhaki as a filing to a magnet. After only a
few Cycles here in the Grey Guardian's stronghold, Bark had felt
a growing unease for Rhaki's stability and a growing horror
concerning his genetic experimentation.

Bark could even now not be sure that Rhaki had deliberately
let Bark's mind be shattered. He had described his plan to merge
his mind with Bark's. The idea was to use Bark's mind for his
solid strength, to support Rhaki's guidance of a tremendous burst
of Power. A long time later, as Bark's mind crept towards
recovery, he wondered that he had been so trusting – or so stupid.

It had not even occurred to him to enquire what Rhaki's great
burst of Power was to be used for. He remembered only the pain,
then a long, silent nothingness. Gradually, he remembered how
to speak, and stand, and move. Rhaki had checked his progress
regularly to begin with, but when he found the same reactions for

several consecutive Cycles, he told Bark that he believed the limit of his recovery had been attained.

Bark realised only now that his mind had, of its own healing volition, thrown up the shielding that all the People were taught as one of the earliest lessons in their training. Bark still could not reckon the passing of time – only in terms of long or short – could not think of the next Cycle, or the tenth to come. But Jerak had woken him further from the strange state he had dwelt in for such ages.

His mind had absorbed Jerak's information and he had pondered on it – briefly for the "Silent Thinker" – only over three Seasons rather than many full Cycles. Bark knew his mind to be fragile, but also strong enough to do what he now saw he must. He knew he would not survive another blow such as the one Rhaki had already dealt him, that he did not have a fraction of the strength needed to confront Rhaki.

But he had heard them, those others, through the walls of rock. He knew there were minds capable of using Power, minds that he must risk contacting, and very soon.

Chapter Twenty-Five

Over the long span of time that the Delvers had lived inside the mountains, they had developed a means of judging time by distance. Certain distances could be travelled within a time period and thus they usually referred to distances as so many "walks". The company gradually understood that it would be at least eight such "walks" to reach the place where tunnels had been sealed.

'Where do you go, Farn, when Ulla takes you all to feed?' Tika asked as they began their second "walk".

Farn's eyes flashed in silvery blue discomfort. 'I cannot say, Tika. They ask us not to tell anyone.'

'That's all right,' she bumped her shoulder affectionately against his folded wing. 'I do not ask you to break promises. But do you go outside – can you tell me that much?'

'Nearly,' said Farn, but he was clearly uncomfortable and Tika changed the subject to reminiscences of his accident with the stone statue at Emla's House. Farn's embarrassment over that catastrophe had long vanished in his pride at his accuracy with fire. They still thought it wiser not to mention it in Gan's presence, but it always brightened Farn's mood.

Farn had been unlike his usual self, Gan had noticed, since their time in the Delver settlement of Amud. He knew the young Dragon was reflecting Tika's mood, but after Khosa's enigmatic warning, he had felt unable to question Tika. Mim appeared cheerful enough, although he continued to be the only one of them, other than old Lorak, to wear his cloak, and Ashta seemed even more protective towards the Nagum.

Nolli was clearly very tired by the travelling she had already done in coming to meet them but she dismissed concern for her impatiently. 'This body will do as I command for a while yet. Please do not waste time thinking of it,' she had told Gan briskly.

The Delvers of Amud had given them four carts which the

Guards took turns pulling. They had also been given ample food to last the two or three 'walks' before they would reach the next settlement, Arak. When they halted for the night, Lanni, the female Delver serving Nolli, quickly organised cushions and blankets carried in the storage space beneath the Wise One's chair. Lanni made a comfortable nest and only then was Nolli helped from her chair. At the first halt, Gan had offered to lift the Wise One. Her escorts were deeply shocked at what they viewed as impertinence, and Nolli herself was irritated by what she called his "fussing".

The Guards had spread themselves along the line: six walked at the rear, four in the lead with Trem and Drak. The rest walked with the Dragons, still finding it hard to believe that these great creatures could not only speak to human minds but could hear the Guards' replies. Lorak walked beside Fenj. Gan suspected Lorak of providing the huge old Dragon with something more than conversation, but the Eldest of Broken Mountain Treasury was finding this sort of travel very wearing, so Gan said nothing.

Jeela and the Snow Dragons of Nolli's escort moved lightly just before the Wise One's cart. Tika and Mim saw Nolli's delight as she watched the small Dragons dancing ahead of her. Several Guards surrounded Brin and when the others heard snatches of Brin's extremely lofty tales, they understood why he had a fascinated audience.

The tunnels had been continuing a downward slope and with a tendency to bear to their right. Now, halfway through their third walk, Gan realised they must be approaching Arak as the number of side tunnels increased, again to their right. Delvers came and went, giving the company curious glances and the Wise One respectful greetings and deep bows.

Arak was a far more populous settlement, a small town in fact, with some of the front rooms of the cave dwellings used as shops. They were shown to higher caves where they overlooked the settlement, and were brought hot tea before they had even set down their packs. A plumply built Delver bustled up to introduce himself as Torim, Elder of Arak. 'I must make my respects to the Wise One but then I shall return. I would gladly show you our settlement.'

'I want to see some plants agrowing,' Lorak growled. Torim

looked a little startled but bowed to them all once more and trotted off to where Nolli was installed.

'A little blunt perhaps, Lorak,' Gan said mildly.

'No, no,' said Fenj. 'Lorak of the Garden misses his growing things. I wonder if there is a warm pool here. My feet are a little sore.'

'We will ask as soon as Torim comes back,' said Tika.

Jeela reappeared, having gone off with three of the Snow Dragons, the fourth reclined by Nolli's cave. 'There are three small pools not far away.' Fenj and Brin brightened visibly.

'You certainly seem to like their company,' Kija remarked. Jeela's eyes whirred embarrassment.

'I have not meant to neglect you! Did you wish me to do something for any of you?'

'Enjoy yourself while you may, hatchling,' Brin interrupted. 'But we will thank you to lead us to the pools. My honoured father Fenj admits his feet are a little sore – mine are *very* sore!'

Kija snorted annoyance but followed them without comment.

Tika stood beside Gan, watching them. Ashta and Farn were slowly following the other Dragons, with frequent glances back. Without turning, Gan said: 'Are they all right? Are you and Mim all right?' And held his breath for fear he had made an error. But Tika only sighed, didn't snap at him as he had half expected.

'It is my fault with those two. I have been trying to accept things inside my head, and in turn it unsettles and worries them. Kija is not too tired, but Fenj and Brin are really weary of this kind of travel.'

He noted she had not referred to Mim, and asked, fearing she would tense again from her apparently relaxed mood: 'And Mim? Is he still suffering from the cold?'

He thought she would not answer, she was silent so long. 'Mim is well. I think he will tell you soon.'

Tell me what, Gan wanted to yell but restrained himself admirably. Tika looked up at him and grinned her old grin suddenly, green eyes sparkling. 'As you said of Mim in the sword practising – you control yourself well Gan!'

He opened his mouth but Torim popped up at his feet, very like a large hopper Gan thought furiously.

'Shall I take you to see Arak now, Lord Gan? All your

company are welcome to join us but many of them seem busy already.'

He smiled as Gan looked towards the centre of the settlement. Most of the Guards were browsing over the goods displayed, both in the cave shops and on stalls laid out in a line through the middle of Arak. He sensed no shielding being used, a freer atmosphere than he had felt in Amud, and looking down on this small fat Delver, he smiled. 'We would appreciate a guided tour very much, Elder Torim.'

'Oh dear me no. Just Torim please. One of you wishes to see our growing things?'

'Yes. I do.' Lorak, Mim and Motass beside him, emerged from the dwelling.

Torim was the complete opposite of Serim of Amud. He scarcely stopped for breath as he trotted along beside them. Explanations poured forth as he described how the caves were extended back from the original small holes in the mountain wall. As they whisked down a sharply cornered side tunnel, a tight fit for large Dragons, as Mim commented, Torim agreed.

'We used some of the rock we excavate to narrow some of the tunnels.' He looked a little nervous. 'Discourages unwelcome visitors you know. Oh dear yes.'

Then they were round the twisting turn and stared in silent amazement at a flat stretch of ground. A large field in fact. They realised that glow lamps were helping the light, but that natural light also filled the area. All eyes lifted to the roof and mouths fell open. A clear dome roofed the whole area; at present snowflakes flattened on the panes of which the dome consisted. But even so, late afternoon, Cold Season light gleamed down into the mountain.

Torim was delighted by their obvious astonishment and began more explanations of watering systems, heating systems, and what plants seemed best suited to this unusual environment. Lorak and Mim began firing questions at the poor Delver, who very soon called over a Delver who was working nearby. Mim and Lorak wandered off with Bikram, instantly involved in gardener's talk.

Torim looked relieved. He said: 'There is a tunnel at the far end which leads Outside, so we can adjust the flow of air currents into the growing place.'

'Are there many such as this in this Domain?' Gan asked.

'Oh dear yes. All the settlements have at least two. We have five,' he added proudly.

'And how many settlements are there?'

'Why, there are thirteen settlements the size of Arak. Asat is far bigger, and then there are twenty or so small ones, such as Amud.'

Tika glanced at Gan. The Captain of Emla's Guards seemed rather stunned by this information.

'I thought there were only a few of you here,' he said finally.

'Oh dear me no!' Torim threw his head back in delight at Gan's mistake. 'There are between fifty and a hundred Delvers in the small settlements, and up to perhaps five hundred in ones like Arak. Asat has the most, but it is the centre of the Domain, you see, so most important.' He rearranged his belly over his sash more comfortably and beamed at them.

'So there are around – ten thousand Delvers living inside these mountains?'

'If you say so Lord Gan! I have no head for numbers. Oh dear no!' Torim chuckled at the very idea.

As they returned to their quarters, Farn and Ashta arrived back from the warm pools. 'Oh dear, I forgot to show you the way.' Torim looked aghast at this lapse.

'Don't worry, Torim,' said Tika. 'The Dragons will show us the way if we decide to go there.'

'Well, if you are sure? I will go and make sure the feast is as perfect as possible. It isn't everyday we have the Wise One's presence and Outsiders. Dear me, no!' And he bustled his rotund self off into the settlement.

'He's a jolly sort,' Sket said.

Gan realised that Sket still followed Tika closely, and realised too that she was aware of it.

'Go on, Sket, go and see what's for sale. Gan is here, and Farn. I have my sword. I think I am safe enough!'

'Well…'

'Go along, man. Do you think I could not protect her?' Gan raised an eyebrow in mock sternness.

Sket grinned. 'You should be able to manage all right Sir,

with that there Dragon along of you now!' And he wandered off
as Gan growled.

Nolli attended the feast, but only stayed a short time. She
thanked the Arakians for their kind welcome and begged they
excuse her, as she needed her rest. As she was helped by Lanni
the few but painful steps to the dwelling she had been given, Mim
caught her eye. She paused, then said: 'Give me your arm,
Dragon Lord,' and Mim went to offer her his arm.

Mim remained closeted with the Wise One for a long while,
but after the first minutes Gan saw Tika's shoulders relax their
tenseness, and she chatted cheerfully enough with fat Torim.

Two more walks and another settlement, Akan, the size of
Arak, with a female Elder, Monni, as thin as Torim had been fat.
She was pleasant and friendly though, as had Torim been – both
so different from Serim of Amud. At each place they found the
warm pools, some large, some small. Monni told them the
Delvers believed the water came from deep inside the ground
whence came the liquid rock sometimes, or so they had heard tell
in ancient tales.

Tika approached Nolli when they had halted again,
presumably it being night-time Outside.

'Wise One, Fenj suffers, and Brin and Kija are beginning to.
Is there any way we can help them without using the Power?'

'Nolli,' the ancient Delver corrected automatically. 'I fear not.
We are taking the most direct route northwards. You will not see
Asat, where Healers could perhaps help them without Power.'
She stretched her nearly useless hand towards Tika. 'We are
going to stop at a place, in three walks time. My people do not
know of it, it is shown only to a Wise One. It is hidden – but very
simply. The tiniest Power, and the correct touch with the correct
words, reveals the place. I believe what I will show you there and
what I can tell you only there, may give hope to your great
Dragons. Such hope may lift them from their tiredness, and urge
them on more cheerfully.'

Tika was stroking Nolli's twisted hand as she listened. 'I think
hope in their hearts will help better than salves for their poor feet.
But Fenj was preparing to go beyond when he felt he must
journey with us, and I fear sometimes he thinks of that again.'

Nolli smiled, the bright dark eyes amazingly alive in the

wrinkled face. 'I too, was planning to go beyond, but our wishes must be put aside now and we must give all we can to restore balance to the world. If it was just your Outside world,' she grinned, her bereaved gums pink in the glowers' light, 'then perhaps we Inside would not concern ourselves.' Her grin vanished. 'But all the world is affected. We have marked increasing changes throughout this Cycle. So – we must give all we can.'

Khosa leapt between them onto Nolli's lap. 'You are an odd little creature!' Nolli quickly corrected her words as Khosa began to bristle. 'I mean, of course, oddly interesting. I have not seen your like before. You say you like to hunt squeakers? Have you any friends who would live among us perhaps? We have much trouble with squeakers at times in our food stores.'

Khosa settled herself to her satisfaction and closed her eyes. 'I have many Kephlings who would come here, if I command it.'

'Would they be as superb hunters as you are?'

'All of my children are superb hunters – I train them myself.'

'Have you many children?'

'Far too many.' Khosa wriggled crossly. 'Always squabbling. I will tell them they are to come here when I return to the Lady's Estate.'

Nolli met Tika's eyes, but Khosa said complacently: 'And I will return to the Lady's Estate.'

'Why did you allow Berri to come with us?' Tika kept her voice low. 'She teases Kran, and most of the other men now, but I cannot work out why she wanted to come.'

Nolli sighed. 'Long time past, I had hopes of Berri. She gave signs that she could grow to be Wise One. But she found intrigue, teasing, and sarcasm more to her taste. She did not know that I watched her, or that I believed she might succeed me.'

'Is she strong in the Power then?' Tika asked in some surprise. 'I had not sensed it in her.'

'Wise Ones do not have to be strong in the Power, child, that is not their task. But they must care for all other Delvers at whatever cost to their own desires.' Nolli laughed, knowing Tika's unspoken question. 'I paid the price, child, and hard though it was at the time, I was soon glad to have done so.'

Lorak came to join them, a cup in his hand. 'A sip for you, Nolli?' he asked.

'I think so Lorak. Your potion eases my bones quite well.' She took the proffered cup carefully between her two hands. 'Did you realise you can heal, Tika? When you touch my hands, the pain recedes. It has nothing to do with the Power.'

Tika stared at her. 'Really? No, I was not aware of it.'

Lorak squatted on his heels beside them. 'Old one, I saw growing plants in Arak, but I see no other growing things.' Tika frowned and waited for him to go on. 'I mean little 'uns. Don't Delvers have little 'uns? But I saw Delver females with bellies growing babies, so where have you got the children hid?'

Nolli smiled. 'It has long been our custom, since way before my time, that the instant Outsiders enter our Domain, our young ones are taken to hidden places. Our old tales say a generation of children was lost to Outsiders whom we had welcomed as guests. Since then, they are hidden.'

A great shout of laughter erupted from the Guards settled around Brin – obviously one of his fantastic stories had reached its conclusion. The young Dragons and Nolli's Snow Dragons had also been listening but only Farn seemed to have believed every word. Gan strolled across to Nolli. 'I did not know Dragons had such powerful imaginations,' he remarked.

Nolli tutted. 'I feel sure there is truth in most of what he tells.' Then she grinned her toothless grin, adding: 'but he adds to the truth, I am equally sure!'

Two more walks passed uneventfully. Fenj was plainly tiring, his prismed eyes a dull slate colour most of the time. He made no complaint, replied to any who spoke to him in his usual courteous manner.

They were clearly nearing the northern borders of the Domain of Asat – no local Delvers appeared from the decreasing number of side tunnels. They had been travelling only a short while on their eighth walk since entering the mountain when Nolli called a halt. As the company gathered round her, she indicated a narrow slit of an opening, not the usual kind of tunnel at all.

'We must travel a distance from our main route now. It is not too far and those who wish, can remain here. But I must go. Tika, Gan, and the Dragon Lord must accompany me. And I beg that you do also, Great Dragons from Outside.'

In the end, everyone followed Nolli. Fenj and Brin struggled through several places where the rock walls seemed to be pressing closer together. There were no lamps set along this passage and, on Nolli's instruction, the company had unhooked lamps from the main tunnel to light their way now. Khosa sat upright on Nolli's lap, her eyes shining with excitement. Secrets! She was sure there were secrets to be found, just ahead!

At last the passage widened but as the company crowded up and more light shone about them, it seemed as if a rock fall had blocked their way.

'All of you must turn your backs!' Nolli's youthful voice suddenly commanded. 'All of you, except the Dragons. And the Dragon Lord must help me now.'

Mim moved between Ashta and Gan, squeezed past Tika and helped Nolli to her feet. They heard Nolli shuffling forward, softly murmured, indistinguishable words in her voice, and Mim's fluting tones joining with the Wise One. There was a low rumble and a gust of air swept against their backs, but none dared to risk a glance over their shoulders. Again there came the sound of Nolli's painfully shuffling feet and then her voice: 'You may see now, what the Wise Ones guard so secretly!'

The company turned. Nolli and Mim stood inside a small, round chamber, on a circular mosaic set with crystal, gold and jet. As Mim held his glow lamp high, they saw niches recessed into the wall. Each niche held a dully gleaming oval shape and Tika gasped, the first to realise what they were. Her hand fumbled at her shirt and she pulled free the pendant taken from Fenj's collection. Hundreds upon hundreds of them shone back, as hers reflected Mim's lamplight.

Chapter Twenty-Six

Emla had remained in Gaharn for three days. The Discipline
Seniors had agreed that all their individual studies must be
suspended indefinitely while they searched their archives for any
clues for dealing with these troublous events. In the Buildings of
Learning, the great Asataria, Seniors still paced with dignity
through the halls and corridors, but there was underlying sense of
urgency about them now.

Emla felt helpless; all her books, the ancient library of many
previous Golden Ladies, were two leagues away in her House.
Finally she visited the study of Discipline Senior Kera, her friend
from childhood days.

'Kera, I cannot stay here any longer. I must go to my House
and study the books there. I am also concerned for the wounded
ones I left there. Stars, Kera, some of the injuries were beyond
the worst nightmares.'

Kera put her finger on the line she had been studying when
Emla burst in. 'I think it is quite reasonable for you to leave.
You have no study here to work in, and the main libraries are, I
am told, knee deep in Juniors and Students!' She smiled. 'I must
say, it is good to know we are still the friends we were so long
ago. I did not realise until I saw you in the Chamber of Gathering
how much I have missed you.'

'You always buried yourself in work more than we did,
especially when you decided you would become the youngest
Discipline Senior ever raised!'

'But I did it,' retorted Kera. 'I will inform the others if you
want to leave immediately though.'

Emla moved to Kera's side and, stooping, put her arms around
her shoulders. 'I pray there is a solution to these troubles Kera. I
feel I am rightly judged as appallingly careless to have allowed a
Weight of Balance to be removed from my care.'

'Put that thought from your mind Emla,' said Kera firmly.

'None of us believe that, I swear it. So go on with you, and take the others with you. They can work as well at your House as they can here. I know Iska is fretting to get back to nursing those Guards at least!'

Emla kissed her friend and strode to the door as Kera remarked mildly: 'And now I have lost my place.' Her head was already bent again over the faded script she was working on and she didn't hear Emla's farewell.

Emla was glad that Yash and Kemti were quick to agree to return with her and Iska. They both had small chambers within the Asataria where they usually worked and she had thought they might prefer to remain here. But in a short while, the four were walking rapidly away from the Buildings of Learning, Guards trotting behind and before them. The snow lay thickly piled beside the cleared pathways and was still falling, but in lazy flakes rather than the blinding blizzard that had begun days before.

As they began the final climb from the Upper Pass, a tattered looking black Merig flew heavily alongside. Emla halted, looking at it a little doubtfully.

There was a laugh in their minds. 'Can't tell us apart, can you? Well, I am the one who spoke to you before.' He landed on the path in front of them.

'You have more news?' Emla asked.

'Well, not exactly. A friend told me that the company that you sent forth has entered the mountains.'

'Entered the mountains? Which mountains? Why?'

The Merig rattled his feathers. 'The High Land Mountains. Just beyond the river that you call Skar. To escape the snow storm I expect.'

'Do you mean they have taken shelter in caves or something?' asked Yash.

The Merig chuckled throatily. 'No cave would long protect a company of their size from the storms that have raged there of late.' He walked stiffly closer to the People and blinked slowly. 'Delvers took them in. They sent Snow Dragons to guide them.' His tone indicated amazement and awe, and he stepped back a little to study their reaction the better. He gave a loud harsh croak of amusement and rose into the air. 'You do not know, do you? I will be in your grounds for a while, if you wish to speak with me.'

They watched him beat slowly ahead of them as they resumed their climb.

'Delvers?' asked Kemti.

'Snow Dragons?' queried Iska.

Emla shook her head, snow scattering from her hood. 'I have no idea. I have never heard of either. I do hope those children are safe.'

They had reached the entrance to Emla's Estate and Guards saluted her as she passed through. Shan held the main door wide as the four People hurried up the steps.

'Oh Lady, I have been worried,' Shan began as she shut the great door. She helped Emla off with her cloak as Bara helped Iska. 'The snow seems to have eased a little but it feels colder than ever I've known it.'

Two male servitors brought hot tea as Shan pulled Emla's boots from the Lady's feet. 'You are freezing Lady! A bath would be best to warm you up.'

'That sounds an excellent idea,' agreed Kemti. 'Why do we not all bathe, thaw ourselves, and meet in your study after?'

Yash nodded, chaffing his long thin fingers against each other to restore some feeling in them while Iska was already halfway up the stairs.

Kemti was the last to rejoin them later. He waved a battered book at them. 'Tales for children! That's where this book was filed. "The Treasure of the Snow Dragons." It makes no mention of Delvers as such, but tells of a race of very small humans who live with these Dragons. I suppose small humans equals children to whoever stored this book.'

'I have no recollections of hearing any such tales,' said Yash.

'Nor I,' agreed Emla.

'I think we should ask the Merig what he knows.' Iska grinned at Emla as she added: 'and it might be safer to see him on the veranda, in case his wife is with him.'

Emla looked out at the snow-covered gardens. 'I see no sign of them. Perhaps we should just summon them with the mind speech, as he bespoke me.'

Before more could be said, the Merig bespoke them, almost,

they suspected, as if he had been eavesdropping. 'My wife is visiting friends nearby. I will come inside now.'

Yash opened the window where the Merig had landed, dislodging lumps of frozen snow from the sill. The Merig dropped onto the floor and walked towards the fire. He shook out his shabby feathers and hopped onto Emla's usual stool. 'You wished to question me?'

'Who are the Delvers you spoke of?' Emla asked at once.

'A race of small humans who long, long ago chose to retreat inside the High Land Mountains. They listen to news of this outside world if we happen to meet any of them, but they are not really interested.'

'But how can humans live, inside those bleak mountains? Do the Snow Dragons you named hunt meat for them?'

The Merig managed to look definitely shifty. 'I have entered their Domain only a few times. I must not speak of Inside.'

'Their Domain?' asked Emla.

'The Domain of Asat,' the Merig replied.

'Are they fighters?'

The Merig put his head on one side to look at Yash. 'Most surely not. They are led by a Wise One. The present Wise One is called Nolli and she travels with your company now although she is near ready to journey beyond.'

All four of the People looked startled at the Merig's use of that phrase. 'She leads them far to the north of her Domain.' He shivered, his feathers rattling back into place. 'I heard the words "Dragon Lord" spoken once when I was there, before the storms reached down to these lands.'

'Dragon Lord? Could that be Mim?' Emla's voice rose. 'If we only had contact with them, this not knowing is terrible! I am nearly persuaded that I must follow them myself.'

'What of these Snow Dragons?' Iska enquired, hoping to distract Emla's thoughts, if only briefly.

'They are mostly white, or very pale colours. They are small, smaller than most hatchlings of Outside Dragons. They live within the mountain but they are more accustomed to the cold and hunt for themselves and for the Delvers.'

'Hunt where?' Emla glared at the Merig. 'In the Wilderness, that's where you will tell me they hunt, won't you? If they hunted on the Upper Plain, they would have been seen and we would know of them.'

The Merig hopped from scaly foot to scaly foot, blinking rapidly.

'Don't Emla, you will upset him and he will tell us nothing more.'

The Merig gazed at Iska with deep admiration. 'A fine lady,' he said pointedly.

Emla sighed. 'I am sorry Merig, but I am so very concerned for all that company, but especially for the two young ones.'

'They all seem well, from what I heard, except the two great male Dragons suffering with their feet. The Kephi was enjoying herself at least,' he added.

'I still can't think why Tika wanted to take it.' Emla sounded distracted.

'"It" is the Queen of the Kephi here, as she keeps reminding everyone apparently.'

'Reminding everyone?' Emla gaped at him. 'You mean the Kephi also use the mind speech?'

'Naturally.' The Merig sounded smug. 'But a lot of us choose not to speak to your kind. I think I shall go and find food now. I will stay in your gardens for a few days though, in case you think of any more questions.'

As Kemti shut the window behind the departing Merig, Emla began to pace. 'Why, by the stars, was I Raised to the Ladyship? All the studying I have done, and the wisdom I proudly assumed I have accrued over these Cycles avails me nothing in this time of trial! The Wilderness seemingly inhabited, Delvers, Snow Dragons, such intelligence in Merigs – and Kephis!'

'Calm down Emla.' Yash tented his fingers and tapped them against his chin. 'At least we now know of these things. The question is, does the Guardian also know of them?'

Far to the north, the company stood gazing into the chamber on whose central mosaic were Nolli and Mim. Tika lifted her lamp and moved hesitantly forward, glancing once at Nolli to receive her nod of consent. Around the circular chamber the oval shapes glinted and shone. Tika moved closer, seeing all of them were filled with amber and contained a tiny speck of something, as did hers and Mim's.

But some were half shelled not in gold, but in precious stones somehow – crystal, bloodstone, sapphire. Spaced around were empty hooks, clearly meant for lamps. Her lamp held high in her right hand, her left rested on the hilt of the sword she now hardly remembered she wore. The first murmurs faded into silence as Tika walked slowly round the chamber, returning to stand beside Gan. Mim placed his and Nolli's lamps on the nearest hooks, freeing her hand to join the other on top of her stick.

'This is what the Wise Ones promised to guard throughout time.' Nolli's voice was clear and strong. 'We have been called "Delvers", indeed we refer to ourselves so to any others, but we are the Kraneechay – Keepers, and this is what we must keep.'

Tika had been aware of the Dragons' growing agitation. As she looked at the great adults squeezed in behind the young ones and the Snow Dragons behind her, she saw faceted eyes flashing at increasing speed. She looked back at Nolli, Mim standing at the ancient one's shoulder. Nolli now said, simply: 'You have seen. Now a Dragon Lord comes and at last the Kraneechay hand over this secret to one who will use it.'

With great difficulty but with immense dignity, Nolli turned her back to the company and, bowing low to Mim would also have knelt before him had he not held her upright.

Mim, the Nagum boy, threw back the folds of his cloak, his blue eyes blazing almost like Farn's. He pushed his shirtsleeves up, past his elbows, and thrust out his arms towards the company. Gan glanced quickly at Tika, seeing tears pour down her cheeks, but she was smiling despite the tears. A moaning came from the Dragons as they looked, with the others, at Mim.

Tiny scales rippled on Mim's arms, down over the backs of his three fingered hands; scales of gold, tipped with silver. Gan stared as hard as everybody else, seeing the glowers' light catch a glitter now at Mim's throat, now at his temples. Gan's mind raced. Clearly the Dragon patterns that Mim's body had accepted were proving stronger than Emla and the three Seniors had thought likely or possible. How far would this change go, and what did it imply? He disregarded the implications – that was for other minds to concern themselves with. For now, Gan had to concentrate on each step on this strange journey, not worry about

steps far ahead. The thought whispered in his mind – "steps we
may not reach" – but Gan quashed that thought instantly.

'It is cramped here, for so many,' Nolli said now. 'Let us all
withdraw to the main tunnel. We will travel no further today but
we will talk. At least, I will tell all I know of the appointment of
my race as the Kraneechay and maybe the Outside Dragons can
tell us even more if they so choose.'

As Lanni came to help Nolli, the company filed back through
the narrow space, leaving the Dragons still staring into the
chamber. Nolli touched each beautiful slender face as she passed,
and each bent to touch their brows to hers.

'Look!' said Mim.

Gan and Tika joined him in the centre of the mosaic. He had
tilted his head back and was gazing up at the domed roof. A
mosaic circle had somehow been set there, and in its centre a blue
star pulsed.

'But,' Gan bit his lip but Mim and Tika had already turned
their eyes to him. 'This circle below and above, and the blue star
– it is exactly so in our Great Chamber of Gathering in Gaharn.'

'As it is in the Pavilion of the Golden Balance on the Lady's
Estate,' said Mim.

'Is it? I have never entered the Pavilion, only stood at the
entrance.'

Tika nodded. 'It is the same though. I wonder if it is in the
Guardian's stronghold, wherever his Balance Weights are kept?'

'It will be.' It was Fenj. 'They were all made the same.'

Gan, Tika and Mim turned to the entrance where the Dragons
still clustered.

'You know how to unseal such doors, do you not Fenj?'

'It is the same simple seal we use to hide our collections Tika,'
Fenj agreed. 'Come Kija, all of you. Mim will hide this place
once more.'

Silently Kija and Brin eased their great bulks around to work
their way back to the main tunnel, the smaller Dragons behind
them. Fenj was able to turn more easily in the emptied space.
Khosa yawned delicately, having sat unnoticed at the entrance to
the chamber. Fenj looked at her.

'And you too will speak what you know, Khosa of the Kephi.
Those two will need whatever help we can give if they are to

hope to succeed.'

Khosa hopped over his tail and danced beneath his chest. 'You do not need to give me such orders, mighty one. I have every intention of sharing my wisdom.'

Fenj rumbled faintly as he scraped through the passage behind her.

'You remember how the Dragons did it, don't you Tika?' Mim smiled at her.

'I think so, but you do it and I'll watch – just to be sure another time.' She smiled back as Gan watched.

Mim stood quite still, his eyes blank. With a soft grating crunch, the rock closed together, leaving no hint that a chamber lay concealed beyond it. As they began to make their way back to the main tunnel, Gan asked: 'Mim? Are the scales uncomfortable?'

'Oh no. At first they itched, but that stopped once they were through the skin.'

As they emerged into the wider tunnel, they found Guards had begun heating water over one of the small braziers they carried in the carts. The usual chatter and movement was noticeably reduced and Mim received many quick and curious glances from the men of Gaharn.

He went straight to Ashta, leaning against her pale green shoulder and speaking only to her mind. Fenj reclined against the wall beside Nolli's chair with a sigh of relief as Lorak rubbed a salve from one of his numerous containers, on the soles of Fenj's large black feet.

When all were settled, Nolli began. 'So far past we do not remember how far, we lived peacefully Outside. But strangers came, bigger than we, and aggressive where we were peaceful. We spoke to all creatures with the mind speech then, including the Snow Dragons. They lived in these mountains always, even further north, to the place of Ice.' Nolli sipped her tea, then continued.

'These strangers killed many of us – we did not understand why. They trampled our gardens, they didn't take over our land so why kill us? Then the Snow Dragons invited us here to share their lives, telling us there were many more of this killing race spreading across the world, and that we would die if we remained on the Plains.

'We were always led by Wise Ones, and they told tales of Dragons from an even older age who had ruled the whole world with great wisdom and kindliness. The tales spoke of a Dragon Lord – or a Dragon Lady – one who was neither Dragon nor human yet was both – who came in times of great turmoil. When we moved into this Realm of Asat, we found the Snow Dragons had very similar stories to tell. The Eldest of the High Land Treasury told the Wise One at that time of the chamber I have just revealed to you. It was then that we took the name Kraneechay.'

Fenj had listened with his eyes closed and his chin resting on the top of Lorak's head. Now he stirred. 'Our memories tell of a time we lived here too. We remember Shardi appearing, and seeking out our nesting caves, destroying hatchlings. Most of us fled further south, although a few chose to remain. We always believed that they had all perished long ago. The eggs in this chamber – we have no memories of such things.' He pushed himself further upright. 'But there is something. When the Golden Lady showed me what we must provide for Tika from our collection, I felt something stir.' He shook his head. 'I have tried to follow the thread of this memory, but have failed.'

A voice called from among the Guards. 'Is it all to do with magic?'

'No!' Nolli and Tika spoke together, then Tika stood up to speak. She was so small, those sitting further back could not see her otherwise. 'Magic is not good or bad,' she explained. 'It is the use of a Power which is all around us, and it is "making" rather than "magic".'

She saw puzzled faces in front of her. 'Like this. Only really you don't need to do any movements, it is all inside your thoughts.' She reached a hand out as though taking a handful of air. Using both hands, she appeared to be moulding invisible clay. But then, as they watched, they saw something between her fingers, something which seemed to uncrumple and stretch and become a single bloom of a white cup flower.

Collective breath was released in a sigh as Tika held the flower towards them. Mim grinned. 'Anyone can see you know little of plants.' He went to where she stood and delicately touched the petals. Faint green veins webbed the whiteness. A tiny drop of moisture clung to the lip of the cup and Mim laughed. 'Like so!'

Gan sat watching, totally amazed at this simple yet so powerful example of using the Power – an example such as he had never seen before. As the flower was passed among the men, Jeela sprang to her feet, her eyes quite still. Kija called to Tika urgently, to see what or who was mind-calling the little Dragon. Tika went quickly to Jeela's side, her mind already burrowing along the beam Jeela held.

She spoke the words aloud, that all might hear: 'I will give what help I can, but I am weak, and time is short. Listen for me again my friends.'

Chapter Twenty-Seven

Tika spun round to face Gan, her eyes green fire. 'Who is it?' she asked furiously. 'It is a male voice, not Delver, not human. The voice of one of you People! Emla said only the Guardian came north, none of you would travel with him. He took human servants and soldiery, so who called us? Is it the Guardian himself? Does he know we are here and he thinks to play games with us?'

Before Gan could reply, a Snow Dragon, Uma, spoke. 'No Tika. It was not the Grey One. We would know his mind's voice. We hear him often – his voice is a wild, higher, sound.' Her wings quivered and her eyes shone clear crystal prisms as she fell silent again.

Tika and Mim continued to stare at Gan. He stood up, towering suddenly over them all. 'None of the People come north with Rhaki. He made it plain he wanted no one.' He spread his hands towards the whole company. 'Truly He was a magnet to many when he was first a Student – quick minded, loving fun and pranks, but it became more of an unpleasant bullying and bragging. An uncomfortableness surrounded him and after a Cycle or so as a Student, he was usually alone.'

He stopped, frowning. 'There was one – the Silent Thinker. He was called that because he was so quiet and thought so deeply on every matter. No harm in him though, I am sure.' Gan still frowned, trying to recall far off days at the Asataria. 'I wonder. I left the Asataria just before Rhaki was Raised, and I have seldom returned for more than a day or two. Iska would know. But Bark – the Silent Thinker – may just have accompanied Rhaki here.'

Gan looked at Tika helplessly. 'You know I have limited use of the Power – by my own choice. Thus I did not hear the voice you have just heard. If you permit, I would listen through your mind if this voice speaks again.'

Tika removed her hand from her sword hilt, nodding slowly.

Gan spoke truly on this matter. 'If this Thinker has chosen to spend these many Cycles with Rhaki, why would he now say he will help us?'

It was Uma who replied. 'When I was but a hatchling, there was a great pain.' Nolli's head nodded in agreement and it was she who continued.

'All of us felt it – Dragons and Delvers. There was an agony in a powerful mind. We talked of it when we recovered and we decided that the Grey One had hurt someone irreparably in his mind although the body still lived. Could that be this Thinker?'

'Bark. His name is Bark.' Gan sat down again, still head and shoulders above everyone else. 'He could have argued with Rhaki. He was known for taking so long to think over ideas, but he was also known to be true and honest. That may have been why Rhaki liked his company. Perhaps he thought the rest of us would believe some of Bark's good character would rub off on himself.' He looked at Uma then at Nolli. 'If it was not the Guardian, I believe it could only be Bark.'

'He has lived all this time with the Guardian, damaged, so Uma believes. Is it possible that he could be able to mind speak us, and should we trust him?' Tika asked.

Fenj answered: 'There have been ones of the Kin who have suffered accidental hurt to their minds. Some of them went beyond, some remained with ruined minds, and some recovered part of their abilities. It has always been the hardest thing – to judge truth from just the mind speech. We ourselves see patterns within a mind when we are able to be face to face with another. It is unwise to judge from a distant mind alone.'

Khosa jumped down from Nolli's lap and did her hind-end-up, front-end-down stretch. 'Are there really not even the smallest holes where a Kephi might creep through? If I was to find this Bark and one of you stronger mind listeners stayed near me beyond the rock, I could speak what I see to them?'

Farn's eyes whirred with excitement. Khosa turned her cool stare on him and for the first time, he stared straight back. 'That is a brave idea Khosa,' he said admiringly.

Khosa blinked slowly. 'I know,' she agreed.

Mim choked but turned it into a cough. 'This person thinks that is a reasonable idea. Are there any such crevices linking the

239

two sides of these mountains, Nolli?'

'I will have to think closely,' replied the Wise One. 'I believe so, but exactly where will take me time to recall.'

The company began to relax from the formality of the preceding discussion, and as they were staying where they were until the next day, food was set cooking.

'Uma says you may come with us, if you wish Tika.' Farn was speaking privately to her mind.

'Oh yes, I would. Should I tell Gan?'

Farn shifted slightly from foot to foot. 'Erm, no. Not yet.'

'Lead on then,' she laughed at him. She saw Mim move beside Ashta and followed them back the way they had come earlier. An unlit side tunnel dived sharply to their left, and Fenj led the way down it. The faintest light shimmered around the Dragons, enough for Tika and Mim to tread confidently along the passage. Light grew ahead and a gust of icy air whipped past them. They both shivered as they went on round a final tight curve and found themselves on a low-roofed ledge facing the open air.

Despite the coldness, both Mim and Tika gulped in the fresh air. The tunnels of the Domain of Asat were well ventilated, but this was real fresh air, the first they had breathed in nine days, they realised.

'It is too cold for us to come with you!' cried Mim. 'We will wait for you here!'

The Dragons launched themselves one after the other from the ledge, soaring quickly up and outwards. Mim shared the cloak he still wore with Tika and they huddled together, peering out from the lip of rock. Snow covered the land as far as they could see. The sun was nearly set behind the mountains at their backs, and dark shadows stretched far in front. The half moon was risen already and made snow and ice glitter in its light.

'This is the Wilderness,' whispered Mim. 'This one never dreamed he would see beyond his own woodlands, and here he sees the Wilderness!'

'I wonder why the People never travelled here – there must be volu, and other beasts – at least, the Dragons seem to find food quickly enough.'

'Tika, this one is destined to help you. If we survive,' he

240

grinned at her, squeezing her closer where they shivered beneath his cloak, 'then there are things a Dragon Lord must accomplish. But only after your task is complete.'

'I'm sorry I was so upset when you began to change Mim. I just found it so difficult to understand, or accept. I was afraid you would not be "Mim" anymore, and I have grown fond of Mim, he is the brother I would have chosen if I could, and I feared, having found you, I would now lose you. It was selfish, I know, but that's why I was angry to begin with.'

'I know,' said Mim quietly.

It took a moment for Tika to understand what he had said. She pulled free of him, ignoring the icy wind gusting onto the ledge. She smiled then, putting both hands to Mim's face where the tiny scales were starting to peep through on the high cheek bones. 'You said "I" Mim!'

'My heart tells me I must be responsibly grown now. There are decisions I have already made and more to make all too soon. So yes, I am "I" now.'

The three young Dragons arrived back at the ledge, their eyes sparkling in the cold air. Frost glittered along their backs in the darkening twilight.

'Jeela still finds the cold hard to bear,' Farn announced, and Jeela's tail whipped smartly across his shoulder.

As they moved to find their way back to the company, Tika suggested: 'A little tact would be good, Farn. Try to think before you say things.'

'I didn't mean to offend her,' he replied sadly. 'I never do. It just happens.'

Some of the Guards had been telling stories to which the Delvers, and Gan, had listened with close interest. Nolli agreed that many of the Outsiders tales bore strong similarities with the Delvers' oldest tales.

'Gan, are there any of the People left now who were not born in Gaharn?' Nolli was asking, as Mim and Tika rejoined them.

'I believe Jerak was the last of those born elsewhere,' he replied thoughtfully. 'What do you know of the People, Nolli?'

She ignored his question, replying with another of her own. 'Where was Jerak born then Gan?'

A silence grew as all awaited his answer. 'I think you know

241

already, Nolli, that Jerak was born beyond, as were all of his generation.'

Tika was aware that there was no surprise in the Dragon minds, or in Nolli's, as there certainly was in hers. Nolli looked sternly at Gan.

'Jerak and his generation poisoned the land this side of the High Lands, and they named it Wilderness. In these countless Cycles no one of the People came to try to mend this land.'

'I have never heard tell of the arrival of Jerak, Nolli. I know of their travelling but not of their arrival. We were told, as children, of their journey, then of the building of Gaharn. Nothing of the Wilderness was ever spoken.'

The Wise One nodded. 'We had guessed that the People had said nothing to their offspring. We watched Gaharn grow and saw the quiet learnèd lives you led. Your Realm is well regulated. The humans who share your lives are content and peaceful. You discovered the Weights of Balance there and then the other Weights in the north, but you guarded them wisely, so we continued only to watch. But we waited in vain for the People to make atonement for what they did in making the Wilderness.'

Gan raised an eyebrow. 'You speak of watching and waiting Nolli. That implies that you would have attempted some force against us should you have judged us unfit to care for the Balance?'

Nolli gave him her toothless smile. 'Together with the Dragons, both Inside and Outside, we would have had an effect upon you People.'

Gan looked very thoughtful as Nolli continued to smile. 'You made a grave mistake in assuming that as none challenged you, physically or mentally, you were therefore superior to all.'

Two days passed before the bodies of four Guards were discovered hidden in the Upper Pass. There was no sign of Iska and the continuing snow had obliterated any tracks that could have been followed. Baras had assumed command as the highest officer on his return to the Lady's House with the Guards wounded by the Shardi. Now, as his men reported their discovery of their fellows' bodies, he did not relish an interview with the Lady. Nevertheless, he hurried to the main House and asked urgently for the Lady and the Lords Kemti and Yash. Baras was staring into the flames of the great fire blazing in the chamber's hearth as Emla descended the stairs with Kemti beside her. Yash appeared as Emla and Kemti approached Baras. Emla stopped, alerted to bad news by the nervousness emanating from the officer.

'What is it Baras? Tell us quickly.'

'My Lady,' Baras laid his right hand above his heart on the insignia of his blue cloak. 'Four Guards are dead, in the Upper Pass.'

'Dead? How – dead?' Kemti asked sharply.

'Slain my Lord. Their throats cut. Their heads near severed.'

'Iska,' Emla whispered. 'Oh dear stars, it is for Iska they died. You did not find her?'

'No Lady, and because of the snow, no trail to follow, no way of knowing who, how many, or where they have gone.'

'Such a thing would only be planned and executed by the Guardian.' Yash sat down beside the fire. 'But why would he want to take Iska?'

Emla rubbed tears impatiently from her cheeks. 'To learn what he can of us here. He must know of Tika and Mim somehow, but not enough. Therefore he would question Iska. Iska would be the easiest of us to take – you two would no doubt put up more of a fight, and Iska is the one of us who travels most frequently between this House and Gaharn.'

'Surely she would have bespoken us?' Yash asked.

Emla shivered as Kemti answered. 'There are herbs to cause instant sleep if only inhaled lightly – as you well know. If he wanted her alive, that would be the obvious way to get her to his stronghold.'

'And what will he do with her there?' Emla shivered again. 'She is strong, but not strong enough to hold out against such a one as he.'

'Lady,' Baras spoke hesitantly.

'Yes Baras?'

'When I visited Gaharn but a few days past with your message for Discipline Senior Kera, she did not really seem aware of my presence.'

'She is always like that when she's busy, she meant no

rudeness.'

'No, no, Lady, I realise that. But she was talking to herself – I took no special notice then, but you speak of the Guardian taking the Lady Iska to the Realm of Ice. Discipline Senior Kera was muttering, over and over, "Is Bark still with Rhaki?" I have not heard the name of "Bark", though I know "Rhaki" is the name of the Guardian.'

Baras looked at the Lady and the two Seniors. All were now seated and looking at him as if they saw a ghost.

'Bark,' whispered Emla. 'I had forgotten Bark.'

'He went north with Rhaki at his Raising did he not?' Yash asked. 'I was away in the Lower Plain at that time.'

'Yes.' Kemti sighed. 'Bark, the Silent One. The few words I spoke with him led me to believe he was of a true mind. What could have made him stay, all this while, in the northern Realm? Perhaps he no longer lives.'

'Ask among the Archivists – they would know if he had gone beyond,' Emla said. 'I spoke with him a few times also, and I found him kindly and gentle. Iska spent more time with him.' Her eyes met Kemti's. 'I cannot believe Bark could fall into Rhaki's twisted ways, but then why would he remain with him?'

'Could Rhaki hold Bark so long without using the Power? But surely, he could not maintain such a holding force continuously over these ages?'

'I don't know, I don't know. But it is not Bark we must concern ourselves with now, but Iska.'

'Emla,' Kemti leaned to touch her arm. 'Perhaps a Merig would have some information?'

She stared at him, then her eyes went blank and he knew she called to the Merigs. Baras remained where he was, unsure if he should discreetly depart or await orders. A harsh screech sounded beyond the main door. Emla rose and hurried to let the Merig inside. Baras's jaw dropped as a scruffy Merig walked stiffly across to the hearth and hopped up onto a stool. His feathers rattled with a brittle noise as he shook snow from his person.

'More questions?'

'Do you know anything of the Lady Iska's capture?' Emla asked, remembering as she spoke that the Merig had seemed to admire Iska. He blinked at her and answered, clear in Baras's mind as well as the People's:

'We did not see this, but heard her call – very faint and short. It was only because we were near that we heard her. We flew at once in the direction of her cry and saw many men carrying her in their midst.'

Baras managed to close his mouth at last as he listened in astonishment to this dishevelled creature.

'Do you know who the men were, who ordered them?'

The Merig blinked again. 'The name "Commander Jal" was spoken. They travelled fast to the north. I followed them until I was sure they were aiming for the tunnels.'

'Tunnels?' Emla gasped. 'The tunnels you spoke to us of before?'

'No no.' The Merig clattered his horny beak testily. 'I spoke of the Domain of Asat.' He blinked at Baras. 'These tunnels are in this side of the mountains.' He fidgeted. 'Delvers sealed off all tunnels to their Domain, leaving only one or two for the new Guardian to discover.'

'Did the old Guardian then know of Delvers and their Domain Merig?'

'Mmm.'

Baras cleared his throat. 'Could I take a company through these tunnels my Lady, in pursuit of the Lady Iska?'

Emla looked at the Merig for his opinion. As usual, he blinked.

'I could show you where the tunnels begin, that lead to the Guardian's stronghold.' His feathers creaked as he shivered. 'Stars know what you might meet in them.' He leaned forward perilously from his perch on the stool. 'Shardi,' he explained succinctly.

'Shardi use these tunnels?' asked Baras.

'Sometimes. When the Guardian wants them to move rapidly down into this region or further. Mostly they don't actually live in the tunnels. They fear them, only use them when the Grey One orders.'

Emla was pacing, her hands knotting and unknotting at her breast. 'Baras, ready a company. We will accept the Merig's kind offer to guide us. Within the hour.'

'We?' asked Kemti.

245

Emla stopped beside the fire, her chin raised firmly. 'Yes Kemti. I at least will travel north now. I can do no less. I have been worried sick since those children left, but now Iska has been taken from us in such a fashion, I *will* go after them all.'

'Then I go too,' said Kemti.

Yash frowned. 'I would also come with you, but I feel one of us must stay in Gaharn.'

Emla hugged him gratefully. 'I agree. I know you would prefer to come with us, but one must stay, and you in fact can far speak best of the three of us. You have also worked most with Iska. Your thoughts may reach her, even from here, and I ask you to go to Kera as soon as we leave. Tell her all we know. Between the two of you, you may be able to reach us, if not Iska.'

The Merig said: 'I am a messenger, as are all my race. I will gather some of the others in the neighbourhood and we can carry news for you. This once. It is a hard flight back and forth, especially against the wind and snow.'

Emla knelt by the fireside stool. 'I thank you for your offer of help and your kindness in speaking to us. May we know your name – it seems impolite to keep calling you just "Merig"'

The Merig gazed at the Lady, their eyes level. 'Merig will do, thank you. It is not that we don't wish you to know our names, but I think you could not say them.' He gave a guttural squawk with a rasping trill in the midst – it sounded very much as if he was being done to death, agonisingly. He bent forward slightly, head to one side. 'That is my name.'

Emla sat back on her heels and gave him a faint smile. 'Perhaps "Merig" is safer,' she agreed. He hopped to the floor and walked stiffly to the door. 'I will visit others and ask who will come. Oh.' He turned back. 'The Kephi Queen wants some of her young ones sent to the Delvers.' He stared down at his scaly toes morosely. 'I don't know if you are to deliver them now, or later.'

Kemti had opened the door and the Merig plodded through. 'And how do we explain kidnapping various small Kephis? Will they allow us to mind speak them, as their "Queen" has decided to do so?'

'That is the least of our troubles Emla,' Yash said impatiently. 'You told Baras to be ready to leave within the hour. Go and

246

ready yourself. I presume Baras will use fengars for speed – will they venture inside these tunnels do you think?'

'I have no idea.' Emla was hurrying up the stairs. 'I hate sitting on them, but we do need their speed.' She disappeared along the upper gallery.

'I pray you get to Iska before Rhaki does her harm,' Yash said. 'And by the stars, ensure Emla's safety. She has named no successor yet; she is the Lady. You must bring her back to us.'

'I know, Yash. And you must call another Gather of the Discipline Seniors and stir them to some sort of action, preferably within a few days rather than a few Seasons or Cycles!'

Yash grimaced. 'I'll do what I can. I think once I can get Kera's mind focused on these events, she will be like a whirlwind. Getting her attention, that will be the worst problem.'

Kemti headed for the stairs. 'I must ready myself.' As he passed Emla's open door he saw Shan, scarlet faced and indignant. He heard: 'How dare you, my Lady, even think of travelling off, stars know where, among all these rough men, with no maid to tend you? Of course I will travel with you, don't you even think of trying to stop me my Lady!'

Kemti groaned and hurried on to his own chamber.

Chapter Twenty-Eight

Iska knew nothing. She had been deep in concentrated thought as she strode along the path from Gaharn back to Emla's House. She saw men leap at the two Guards trotting in front of her and blood fountained as those Guards fell silently to the ground. She began to turn when a moist cloth slapped across her face. She managed to register the strongly astringent smell of the herb verain mixed with other herbs and then – nothing.

She was unaware of being bumped carelessly along a narrow gully for half a league and then being thrown across the back of a fengar. Ropes secured her hands and feet beneath the animal's belly as a leading rein was held securely by Jal who rode alongside. Jal forced a hard pace, choosing speed over caution. His band rode on, the moon shivering on the snow giving enough light for a reckless rider. He knew the risk he had taken, creeping not only within the bounds of the Realm of Gaharn but advancing so close to the city where minds could sense his presence all too easily.

Despite the cold, sweat trickled down his back as he chose the place to snatch the Senior Lady Iska. Rhaki had instructed him on how to call Iska from the city. Jal could not remember just what he'd had to do – he called his Master, and emptied his mind. Afterwards, he reckoned only a short time had passed before he came to himself again. The notion was clear in his mind that the Lady Iska would walk this pathway within a few hours, but he had no idea of what Rhaki had wrought through him.

Jal called the order to halt and his men were glad to do so. Moonlit riding over ever steeper terrain was wearing on the nerves, coming at the end of a stealthy journey deep into enemy territory, a kidnapping and an excessively rapid retreat. Even the fengars were blowing hard and their heads dropped down between their knees. Iska was pulled carelessly from the fengar and left to lie where she fell.

When Jal returned to her from giving orders for a brief meal and rest to his men, he muttered under his breath. Pulling a weatherproof cape from his pack, he laid it on the snow, rolled Iska onto it and then wrapped it across her. He squatted beside her, noting she was as pale as the snow she lay on, her dark hair strewn wildly about her face. Jal thumbed back one of her eyelids, then put his fingers against the pulse in her neck. Not good. But he had only administered the herbs in the exact amounts and at the regular intervals Rhaki had explicitly commanded.

Jal had never seen one of the People unconscious or sick. He had no idea if herbs worked in the same way on them as they did on humans. He knew all the People could summon the Power, which was the main thing that set them apart. He had more experience than he wished as to how that Power could be used, since entering Rhaki's employ.

He knew only that this Lady was a Senior in the Asataria and therefore she had a talent in the Power. About half of the People chose lives connected with the Buildings of Learning. The other half lived in almost human fashion – almost. Never could they be mistaken for humans though. Apart from their tallness, thinness and dark hair, which made them such a contrast to the stockier, smaller, fair-haired humans, there was this presence of Power in each one of the People.

The People of the Asataria lived and worked surrounded by knowledge, learning, and – the Power. Those who dwelt in the city or the surrounding countryside administered the running of the day to day lives of themselves and the humans who shared the Realm of Gaharn with them. Cycles past, Jal had met some of these more 'ordinary' People, but always he had felt a tingle of apprehension, nervousness, in their company. And yet he had still taken employment with Rhaki.

As Jal sat, sleepless, through the short halt as most of the band slept, he thought of Rhaki's charm, his flattery which had seduced Jal into going to the stronghold from his birthplace beyond the Ancient Mountains. Such dreams of riches Rhaki had convinced him of! He knew the reality now, enough of it anyway to terrify him. And he had captured this Lady of the People.

He groaned quietly as he held the special cloth, carried in the bag Rhaki had provided, firmly over Iska's face as he counted slowly to eight. If she lived and woke, what might she do to him? If she died – his mind fled from the thoughts of what the Grey One would do to him in that event. Jal removed the cloth from Iska's face, replacing it quickly in its bag and fastening the latches securely. He checked the pulse at Iska's throat again – rapid still, and stars help him, fainter.

'Up!' he shouted at the sleeping men. 'We ride on!'

The sky lightened when Jal's band had ridden many leagues albeit slower the higher they climbed. As sunlight fingered weakly through the snow flurries, they reached the insignificant looking cave that was the entry to the tunnels leading, eventually, to the far north. The men were subdued. They had been shocked to discover the existence of these passageways, having always had to travel the tortuously winding mountain trails as they went about the world on the Guardian's orders. The thought of encountering Shardi kept them quiet as their fengars sped down the tunnel, although they knew their Commander Jal could control the Shardi – to a certain degree at least.

They lost track of time, Jal calling brief halts only when the fengars reached the limits of their endurance. An hour or two, slumped against the rock wall, too tired to eat the dried meat in their packs, then up and on again. At each of these halts, Jal lifted Iska's head, checking her colour, her breathing, her pulse, holding the drug-soaked cloth to her face. At the last halt before the final dash to the deep caverns below the Guardian's stronghold, not one observed a small, orange furred creature crouched by a narrow hole high in the passage wall. It watched, motionless, as Jal checked the Lady's limp body yet again, and it felt the panic within Jal's mind.

As the band remounted and hastened on, the creature wriggled round and squeezed into the hole, calling ahead as it crept through to the Domain of Asat: 'The Lady Iska is held captive. She is near death!'

Khosa popped, corklike, from the other end of the narrow tube of a crevice, dropped onto Fenj's head and ended perched on his shoulder. Her eyes were slitted, her tail thrashed. 'One holds a strong smelling thing on Iska's face. It keeps her deep asleep – so deep she has no thoughts or dreams. Bad smell.' She spat. 'The one who leads them is afraid of the Lady, but more afraid of the Grey One. He hurries to get Lady Iska to his Master before she dies.'

'How far Nolli?' Tika asked urgently. 'How far to the stronghold?'

'Not far. Another one-walk if you take a fast pace.' She looked unhappy and worried. 'I will slow you. You must go without me, but now I will follow to the end. I said I would remain in Asat, but that is not to be my fate. Gan, one has been following us.'

Gan smiled. 'I know. My men knew as soon as we left the last settlement.'

Nolli tutted. 'So you play games with me Lord Gan?'

'No. She was recognised as being a child of your line. The men had seen her visit you several times and been informed who she was. So we let her be.' Gan looked enquiringly at the Wise One as if he expected an explanation. Khosa spat again and Farn moaned, his eyes spinning sapphire.

Nolli glared at Gan. 'Privately then,' she said.

The Guards and Nolli's servants withdrew a small distance and Nolli said softly, looking at Tika: 'I still had to seek a successor. I did not know a Dragon Lord would come. The one who follows is of my line. She is very young – fourteen cycles only, yet she shows more wisdom, more promise, than I have found in all these ages of seeking. I refused to allow her request to come with us, believing she must be kept safely in our Domain lest anything happen to myself. I did not realise at first that she followed, until she called to my mind saying that she must travel with the Dragon Lord and the Lady of Light.'

Mim nudged Tika, smiling, and she closed her mouth with a snap. 'And this young Delver of yours is strong?' she asked Nolli.

'Yes child. Not as strong as you, but stronger than any other I know of.'

'Tell her to join us,' Tika demanded.

They stared at the dark passage behind them and a tiny figure came pattering into the light. Dark curls, shorter than Tika's and with a definite shine of copper in them, uptilted dark blue eyes, and a wide mouth. She was even smaller than Tika but as she walked through the smiling Guards, her eyes were calm and serious. Unlike most Delvers they had seen, she was dressed in trousers and over shirt, very like Mim's and Tika's garments, and she carried a pack over her shoulder. She bowed as she came within a few paces of Nolli and waited patiently, though she studied Tika and Mim with open interest.

Berri wandered over to join them. 'What made this infant dare follow us?' she asked Nolli.

But the new arrival answered for herself: 'It is my duty to be with this company.'

Berri laughed. 'Your duty is to be home, going about your tasks, girl.'

'Enough. She is welcome.' Tika smiled sweetly at a discomfited Berri. 'Come, meet Farn, my soul bond.'

The tiny Delver followed Tika out of earshot of the others. 'Sorry,' Tika whispered. 'I do not know your name – I did not mean to sound bossy!'

The small Delver grinned at her. 'I know. My name is Dessi. You need not fear Berri. She is arrogant but she is not wicked.'

Tika studied her for a moment then she returned Dessi's grin. 'This is Farn.'

Farn's prismed eyes flickered 'Even smaller than you, my Tika! I will have to be careful where I step!'

Dessi laughed at him. 'I will be sure to avoid your great feet Farn!'

Kija welcomed Dessi gently and Tika guessed the golden Dragon had met the Delver girl at one of their earlier halts at a settlement. Fenj and Brin greeted her gently too, lowering their long faces close to hers.

'You are small enough for me to carry,' Jeela said gleefully. 'Would you ride on my back Dessi?'

Dessi's eyes sparkled back at Jeela. 'That would be wonderful – are you sure you would permit me?'

Jeela stretched to her full height, eyes whirring many colours. Kija spoke in Tika's and Farn's minds: 'You see? This Dessi did not ask, "Are you strong enough Jeela", but only "Would you permit." Do you see Farn, how Jeela's value of herself has grown with such a simple, tactful remark?'

Farn moaned softly. 'Mother, I am trying, really I am.'

Kija's tone warmed. 'I know you are my son. And you show improvement. Especially since he spends less time with that overgrown hatchling Brin,' she added to Tika's mind alone.

Ashta, Mim and Jeela were deep in conversation with Dessi and Kija sent Farn and Tika to join them. Dessi turned as Tika came up, 'There is one in the Grey One's stronghold who will help.'

'We heard him call,' Tika frowned. 'Can we be sure of help from one who has lived so long with the Guardian?'

'I believe so, but he is much weakened, damaged somehow. But he knows where the Chamber of the Balance is, and how to reach it. We will need that information.'

Their eyes met and Tika realised that this Dessi did indeed know far more than even the ancient Nolli was aware of. She felt quick sympathy from Dessi as she thought fleetingly of how she must destroy one of the Weights of Balance.

'I will be with you,' Dessi whispered, sliding her hand into Tika's. 'Do not think of it until we are there.'

Gan watched, as Dessi seemed to be absorbed into the group of Dragons as naturally as Tika and Mim. 'Do you see the future, Old One?'

'No Gan. I see possibilities. I see no certainties and no compromises. There are two outcomes possible to this venture – only one concerns us, and towards that we must all strive.

'Gan, it will be difficult, but there must be no time wasted. No matter for whom, you cannot stop to worry, or to grieve, once you are within the Guardian's stronghold. Each of you must keep looking forward, no matter what happens to your companions.'

Gan looked deep into Nolli's dark eyes and slowly nodded. 'You are truly named Wise One. I will remember your words.'

Nolli's twisted hand caught his sleeve suddenly and Gan turned to follow her gaze. Ivory Jeela was moving slowly to the north, her neck stretched high but her head tilted to one side. Her eyes were still, almost blank. She stopped, her head now tilted back and then song washed through their minds. Ashta moved quickly to Jeela's side and her voice soared in and around Jeela's melody. The company watched and listened, frozen where they stood or sat, to the two young Dragons' song.

'To whom do they sing?' Gan whispered.

Nolli murmured back: 'To the Damaged One.'

Bark sat in the small chamber that had been his since the disruption of his mind. A bed, a straight backed chair, a table and a small window which looked out onto two arm lengths of space then a wall of ice. Light came from above, but how far above it was impossible to judge. The window was too deep set to allow anyone to crane out and look up, or down.

He remembered when he had first accompanied Rhaki here, believing it was for a visit which would maybe last a Cycle or two. He had been given a set of fine chambers, one for sleeping, one for bathing, a study and a chamber in which to sit or receive a guest. He had watched as Rhaki grew ever more wilful, listened as the Guardian talked of his right to do as he pleased. Rhaki increasingly referred to this "right" of his: he had the greatest Power, thus he could do whatever he wished and none should dare thwart him.

But then, Bark had been so ill, for so long, and had finally returned to some awareness in this small cell of a chamber, remembering nothing. His body was much weakened – Rhaki had arranged only the most basic nursing for him, to ensure he stayed alive. In Gaharn, Healers would have exercised Bark's limbs, massaged him, all through the long period of his unconsciousness. Jerak had stirred him finally, stretched his mind, letting the past seep slowly back into Bark's brain.

He could now remember telling Rhaki that doing whatever one wished was not the way of a wise civilisation, that responsibility was the keystone. Responsibility for one's own actions, and for those in one's care. Bark could recall that moment. He had been seated by the fire in Rhaki's study and he had been amazed at Rhaki's sudden venomous rage. He saw the spittle frothing at the corners of Rhaki's mouth, his raised hands and then – only the pain.

Bark sat in his small chamber, beside the meagre fire. Fires were needed at all times in this icy stronghold and Bark had felt the cold deep in his bones from his first days in this place. He remembered wondering if there were other creatures living in these mountains. He also remembered that he had thought it best

254

not to mention these suspicions to Rhaki. Over the last ten Cycles or so (Bark had lost all notion of time) he heard those different mind voices calling once more.

When Bark knew that Rhaki was engrossed in one of his experiments, as he could be for hours if not days at a time, then he focused his fragile mind and sought those voices. Eventually, he distinguished two types of voices: one was of a human type. He had no idea what being produced the other voice. The voices sang, for many Cycles, harmonising gently in his mind, until one night, instead of only musical tones he heard words.

He realised that he, Bark, was being asked if he needed help, if the music pleased him, that there was still room for kindness in the world. All Bark could reply was: 'Thank you, dear ones.' He had listened through the long Cycles of time until these last days, and when he heard the singing voices again, he had sent his offer of help in return. Now the song was closer than ever it had been, and he waited, as it seemed he had spent his lifetime waiting.

There was a noise, a noise outside his mind. Bark listened, only his eyes moving, carefully searching this small room. A piece of rock rattled down the wall and his eyes moved quickly up to where it had fallen from. Another fragment wobbled loose and fell to the floor. Bark rose silently and stared up at the wall. Just above his head a fist sized section of rock seemed splintered and, as he watched, it bulged outwards. His long fingers went up to pick the fragments free. A turquoise eye glared at him.

'Well. Don't just stand there, move these stupid stones!' ordered an imperious voice in his mind.

Bark hastily jiggled the cracked stones free and stared at an orange Kephi in disbelief.

'I am Khosa, a Kephi Queen. I have a company with me and we intend to restore the Balance of the World. Would you care to assist me down?'

Bark reached up, lifting the rumpled Kephi out of the very narrow opening. 'I have not seen a Kephi, nor even thought of them, since I left Gaharn!' he said in her mind. Khosa's claws hooked into the shoulder of his robe and she crooned at him. His bony fingers slid down her spine then up to scratch round her ears. He lowered himself carefully to sit on his bed and studied Khosa. 'Who is your company?'

255

Khosa slitted her eyes at him for a moment. 'There are humans, Delvers, Dragons, a Dragon Lord and one of you People – Gan.'

Bark's hand stilled until Khosa bumped her head against it, reminding him to continue his ministrations.

'Dragons? A Dragon Lord? Delvers?' Bark's hoarse whisper sounded loud in the room.

'They have to know how to reach the Weights of Balance,' Khosa explained.

'They must find Rhaki's study, the entrance leads from there.'

'They dare not use the Power to bespeak you lest the Grey One becomes aware too soon.'

Bark nodded. 'My strength is minimal. That is why I have not replied to the Singers before. But since Jerak spoke to me, I have been mustering what strength I can for the trial ahead.'

Khosa opened her eyes wide. 'Singers? You mean the Delvers and the Snow Dragons.' Her crooning buzzed lower. 'Rhaki has captured the Lady Iska – she will be carried here within this day I think.'

'Iska?' Bark's hand tightened over Khosa's back. She wriggled free of his grasp and sat up straight on his knee, glaring at him.

'Gan and Fenj are organising, now, while I came to attempt contact with you.' Her tail thrashed as she stared at Bark.

Bark's face hurt. Then he realised he must be smiling. After all this time, a haughty Kephi had made him smile again. 'You are indeed brave to creep alone through the mountain Kephi.'

'I told you, Khosa is my name,' she snapped.

'Well Khosa. Do you stay here, or crawl back to your company?'

'I return to the Domain of Asat, if you would help me back up there.'

Bark stood up again, lifting her majesty carefully. 'If you leave this hole open, I could use it again.' Her small form squeezed into the hole, she brandished her tail saucily, and she was gone.

Chapter Twenty-Nine

Jal rushed along the steeply winding passage to the Guardian's chambers. The weight of Lady Iska's tall body hindered him not at all – he was appalled at how light she seemed. As he rounded the last turn, the fighter he had sent ahead came back towards him.

'He awaits you Sir.' The man muttered, jerking his head over his shoulder at Rhaki's open door.

'Go back to the others. Tell them to prepare for the ones who followed us.'

Then Jal was on the threshold of Rhaki's study. The Guardian's expression changed from one of satisfaction to one of concern, and he came quickly to Jal.

'Master, I administered the herbs exactly as you said, but I fear for her.'

Rhaki leaned close, sniffed Iska's skin, then laid the back of his hand against her brow. He scowled. 'Bark! Bark!' Still staring at Iska's face, he pulled Jal along the passageway. 'In here,' he ordered, throwing open another door. He pulled back the covers from a great bed and took Iska from Jal's arms. Rhaki laid her down tenderly as Bark appeared. 'You must rouse her Bark,' Rhaki said peremptorily. 'I would question her as soon as she wakens.'

'Master.' Bark bowed and moved silently to the bedside. 'I will need certain herbs, water, heated stones.'

Before his hoarse whisper had ceased, Rhaki waved a hand dismissively. 'I will send servants. Jal, to my study.' Rhaki ordered servants to be sent to do Bark's bidding as he strode back to his study, and as Jal closed the door behind them, the Guardian leaned on the mantel shelf, smiling.

'You have done excellently, Jal. Let us just pray that the Lady lives and awakes.' He bent his head slightly as though praying in truth, but the deep-set dark eyes remained fixed on Jal. Jal ducked his head briefly while silently sending a desperately genuine plea that the stars allow Iska to wake.

'All went as simply as I had said they would?' Rhaki asked.

'Yes Master. The Lady was with four Guards who offered no resistance – we put their bodies a short way from the path. The snow covered all traces within minutes. The fighter I placed to keep watch behind us, caught us up last night. He reports a force of Guards following fast and he thinks there is at least one of the People with them.' Before Rhaki could comment on this vagueness, Jal hurried on. 'He did not wait to be sure of the number of Guards or People – I had told him only to report if any did indeed follow, Master.'

'Hmmm.'

'I ordered men to prepare to welcome those followers, Master.'

Rhaki strode to the window and stared out as Jal forced himself to remain still. Rhaki spun round, making Jal flinch despite himself.

'Prepare a dozen Cansharsi also.'

'Yes Master.'

'Well – go then! See to it. I will check the Lady's recovery and then I will come to the lowest barracks where you will assemble the men. And the Cansharsi '

Jal bowed himself out of the study, took a breath to steady his nerves – something he seemed to need to do increasingly, he noted – and hastened to obey his orders.

Rhaki stood gazing at the fire flames, rubbing his hands together with a dry, whispering sound. Emla dared order her precious Guards to his stronghold, did she? The fact that he had arranged the abduction of not only a Senior, but a close friend of Emla's, was no reason in Rhaki's view for invading his Realm. He swung his heavy wool cloak from its hook to his shoulders and went back along to the chamber where Iska lay.

Three servants were busy following Bark's instructions. A fire was already blazing in the wide hearth and several glow lamps illuminated the bed. A kettle had been swung over the fire and one servant was holding a pan containing hot embers, moving it along the length of Iska's body at Bark's direction. Rhaki stood for a moment, noting no change in Iska's colour. He tugged at his lower lip.

'I will return shortly Bark. Do all you can to rouse her. I *will* speak with her.'

'Master, rousing her too quickly from the state she is now in could cost her life.'

'Do it.'

Rhaki's cloak swirled like a dark cloud as he swept from the room. As he approached the lowest section of the stronghold, Rhaki held his cloak close about him for warmth. The clamour of voices stilled instantly as the Guardian appeared, replaced by only the creak of leather tunics as men held to attention in their ranks. As he came to a halt before them, a vigorous stench rolled through the cavern.

An iron gate clanged against rock and Jal appeared ahead of twelve Cansharsi. The fighting men glanced at the Cansharsi then quickly away, several paling noticeably. The Cansharsi were all walking upright on their triple taloned hind feet, making them half as tall again as the human fighters. An acrid smell preceded them, a musty, stale urine and rotting compost perfume which caused men's eyes to water and throats to clench.

The Cansharsi were in a state of excitement, saliva drooling from the tusked jaws, but they controlled their urge to fall upon the men before them. The Guardian's tall figure stood unmoving as the Cansharsi clattered up to him, his eyes glittering in the light of the pitch torches clustered in wall brackets. Rhaki took one of these torches and held it high as the Cansharsi neared. Lips curled back and a few squealed irritably but were hushed again with snarls from their fellows. Cansharsi still disliked fire, Rhaki noted.

'There are trespassers daring to advance to this Realm.' The men remained silent, the Cansharsi fidgeted, eyes rolling and taloned hooves clicking on the stone floor. 'You Cansharsi have more speed, but you will hold back, move only at the speed of these men. Only when Officer Jal orders you, will you go ahead.' Rhaki forced each Cansharsi to meet his eyes. 'You will obey Officer Jal as you would obey me.' He kept his gaze on them a moment longer then turned back to the fighters. 'You of course will obey Officer Jal, but if there are any of the People among these trespassers, I would have them brought to me alive. There will be silver for all of you, but there will also be gold for you for living prisoners.' Rhaki thrust the torch he held into the hand of the nearest fighter and stalked from the barracks.

As Rhaki had left the chamber where Iska lay, her eyes had opened. She looked straight at Bark, her mind fully aware in spite of the fearful lassitude of her body. Bark returned her stare steadily, letting her see into his mind, holding no shielding whatsoever against her. In moments, she knew where she was, how she had been brought there and also what dreadful damage Bark had suffered.

A servant slid into the chamber. 'The Master comes, sir,' he called softly.

Bark's hand tightened on Iska's but she closed her eyes and looked quite unconscious again. Seconds later Rhaki stood beside the bed. 'Surely you could have woken her by now Bark?'

'Master, the Lady has not responded to any of the inhalants I have used so far.' Bark kept his head down, apparently occupied with crumbling dark leaves into a dish held by another servant. 'I have sent for other herbs, Master – it may take a while to obtain them.'

'I want her awake quickly Bark. Today, not tomorrow. I must know what Gaharn is plotting.'

'Plotting, Master?'

'Yes Bark, plotting. Clearly they seek to redress the Balance since that fool Emla lost one of her Weights. They have always feared my great strength but now they realise they will soon be utterly powerless against me.' His voice had risen as he spoke but Bark did not look at him. Rather, he bent closer over Iska's still figure.

Rhaki watched as Bark sprinkled the crumbled herbs into a jug of boiling water and reached to lift Iska's head that she might breathe the rising fumes. Rhaki scowled, his brows making a black line above his eyes. Iska gave no indication of any change, and he turned away angrily.

'Use anything you can think of Bark. Just get her conscious for a few minutes. I will be in my study.'

The door thudded behind him and the servant holding the warming pan nearly dropped it as Iska's eyes opened again.

'Speak not with your mind Bark – he may be alert for any

mind speech.' Iska's voice was a mere sigh.

Bark nodded. 'But I fear he will attempt to enter your thoughts forcibly if I do not wake you.' He bent closer. 'Guards followed Rhaki's fighters. Seniors are with them but he is ready for them."

Iska closed her eyes for a moment, fighting the narcotics in her body. 'You must not let him know how much strength you have regained yet Bark. Call him in here in a little while, saying you think I am waking. As I open my eyes, I will send a call as strongly as I can to the south.'

'There are others within these mountains who say they will help.' Bark whispered. 'Rhaki will immediately sense your call. He is unstable – he could kill you.'

'Whatever happens Bark, you must play no part in this. You have another task to do in this battle – for battle it is now.'

'Stars help you then Iska.'

'And you also, Silent Thinker.

Baras had led the following party at a rapid but steady pace. The tunnels were wide enough for three fengars abreast, but neither fengars nor men had ridden in such enclosed spaces before. Some of the fengars had resisted and caused some delay before they were brought under enough control to force them into the darkness. The Merigs had led them to the entrance to the tunnels and had agreed to lead more Guards from Gaharn's main barracks.

Emla and Kemti had both exchanged their usual robes for trousers and shirts beneath heavy cloaks. Kemti rode at the head of the troop with Baras, who had insisted the Golden Lady rode, Shan at her side, within the main body of the Guards. She had argued that she would ride with Kemti, but Kemti had supported Baras's argument that she must accept the protection of the Guards rather than ride in the lead.

They had no means of judging time other than their own weariness and that of their mounts, but after what they guessed as four days riding, they had halted once more. Baras had equipped each Guard with several torches, not knowing how long they would be under the mountain or if the tunnels would have any form of illumination within them, left perhaps by Rhaki's fighters. He set men to watch a short distance ahead each time they halted, to warn of any attack, as others fed the fengars and shared rations among themselves.

'They will know we follow, Lady.' Baras squatted beside Emla and Kemti. 'They must have been led by an experienced man – they will expect us to follow. No attempt was made to disguise their direction once they had the Lady Iska.'

'So you expect a welcoming party fairly soon, Baras?'

'It is what I would do, Lord.' Baras agreed. 'But what bothers me is, who will welcome us? So far there has been no hint of Shardi. Men we can deal with, but in this confined space, with Guards who have not faced Shardi before, I fear we could suffer heavy losses.'

'What about the fengars?' Emla asked. 'There is height enough for them to rear and do battle, but would they cause more trouble to ourselves in this – as you say – confined space?'

'That is what has been occupying my mind Lady.' Baras paused for a moment. 'I think at the first sign of trouble ahead, all should dismount and let the fengars go forward riderless. Then we should light the torches as swiftly as may be to see just what we face.'

Kemti nodded and Baras left them to speak with his Guardsmen.

'You and I are not enough against Rhaki, are we Emla?'

She sighed wearily. 'I do not know. Unhappily, I suspect not. But how did all this start Kemti? Just the one Weight of Balance lost and suddenly chaos threatens.'

'I think perhaps we had become complacent. We thought we knew most things about this world – at least the things of any importance, and so let our lives drift on along their untroubled paths. Our scholars have lost themselves in matters of the mind rather than seeing the outer world in its colourful confusion.' Kemti stretched his aching back. 'Even we are not free of this guilt – look how amazed you were at finding intelligence had been deliberately concealed from you – I mean the Merigs, the Kephi – and the great Dragons.'

'We have been complacent indeed, and how much have we ignored or chosen not to notice in these last Cycles? I have felt events pressing on us since Jerak – disappeared. And now we face Rhaki, unprepared as we so foolishly are.'

'Sir! Sir!' Several voices called suddenly in alarm.

Kemti pulled Emla to her feet as Baras moved in front of her, his sword bared. They looked where Guards pointed. A section of the tunnel wall seemed to shimmer, then, with a slow soft grumble, it slid apart into two halves.

'Dear one!' Emla laughed aloud as a long silver blue face peered through the opening. Sapphire eyes whirred in delight as Farn advanced to the Lady and Kemti. Tika slipped through at his side, then Jeela and Dessi and two of the Snow Dragons. After touching brows with Farn and Jeela, and hugging Tika, Emla looked in amazement at the other three newcomers.

Tika touched the face of one Dragon saying: 'This is Uma, and this,' she touched the second, 'is Ulla. And this is Dessi. She is Kran – '

'Delver' interposed Dessi, smiling up at Emla.

'The Merigs told us of Delvers within these mountains. I am glad to be able to greet you Dessi.'

Tika interrupted these formalities. 'The larger Dragons have gone outside, Mim and Ashta with them. A Snow Dragon guides them to an upper part of the Guardian's stronghold where they believe they can force their way inside. Nolli will unseal a tunnel soon and Soran and the Guards will enter that way. We will come with you through this side of the mountains. We decided you would need some help from Dragons.'

Emla's expression conveyed some misgivings. 'You will use fire, within these tunnels?'

'Of course!' Farn's cheerful reply resounded in everyone's thoughts.

Emla's eyes met Tika's. Tika grinned at her. 'As Farn says…'

'Hmm. Well, let's discuss it with Baras, shall we?'

'There is nothing to discuss Lady,' said Farn. 'We will stand ahead of you. Our fire will not harm any of you then, only whatever comes in front!'

As the new arrivals moved further into the passage, Dessi turned to the opening in the wall. As she stared, so the two sections slid gratingly together, not the faintest scratch indicating where the opening had been. Dessi had just rejoined Jeela when a

Guard shot round the curve of the tunnel ahead.

'Something comes Sir! Stars know what it is, but the smell is worse than any midden!'

Before he had finished speaking, they were all assailed by the pungency wafting down the tunnel.

'Farn, Jeela, to that side. Uma, Ulla – this side. Stay as close to the wall as you can!' Tika drew her sword and stood at Farn's shoulder. Jeela stood between her brother and the rock, the Snow Dragons taking similar positions against the opposite wall.

Some Guards were bringing the fengars forward as others lit more torches. Tika noticed, with some concern that even the normally evil tempered fengars were dismayed by the thickening stench rolling towards them and were almost quiet. She saw that Kemti had pushed Emla and Shan behind the Snow Dragons, but she also saw that Emla had her cloak thrown back and a naked sword in her hand while Shan stood firmly beside her Lady, a wicked looking curved knife at the ready.

Tika drew a shallow breath, wanting to retch as the foetid stink filled her lungs. Then she concentrated on finding Kija's mind beyond the rock. Swiftly she warned of what was happening, and instantly felt Kija's strength and love pour back to her. 'Stars guide you, small one, and my son.' She felt warmth from the other Dragons, and from Mitu, as a clattering of hooves began to sound from beyond the curve ahead.

Dessi had squeezed in beneath Jeela's chest and she murmured aloud: 'It is the Guardian's monsters, but they have no true Power, except the power to terrify by their appearance.'

Tika glanced at her, about to reply, but Farn was stretching up, his eyes glittering blue ice. 'Fear not, I will die before you are harmed.'

Tika and Dessi both looked at the magnificent silver blue Dragon who, as Tika knew only too well, was still really only a baby. Tika's eyes filled with tears, which she dashed furiously away on her sleeve as she returned her gaze ahead.

Now a screaming sounded above the rattling of hooves, an inhuman screaming, but they gradually realised mangled human words were mixed among the screams. 'Kill' was the clearest word and every hair on Tika's body stood on end. She made herself relax her over tense grip on her sword and let her left hand rest on Farn's smooth scales.

Baras stood just in front of her, his sword raised as he watched the tunnel. For a brief second, the clattering faltered, as though whatever approached had decided on some caution before rounding a corner beyond which light showed clearly. Then the screams rose to a crescendo and the first Cansharsi crashed into view. Baras's arm dropped, Guards released the fengars who joined their battle shrieks to the Cansharsi screams as they charged to meet them.

While there was still space between the two groups, Farn and Ulla both loosed jets of flame and the first two Cansharsi's battle screams turned to howls of agony as their bodies were seared with fire which burnt deep as knives. Then others were pushing past the writhing bodies and storming on to crash into the advancing fengars, and battle was joined.

Chapter Thirty

Gan, on Fenj's back, was huddled as low as his tall form would
allow, Lorak considerably sheltered behind him. Brin flew
directly behind his father carrying Trem and Kran. They were
following the Snow Dragon, keeping close against the towering
ice cliffs on their left. Ashta and Kija brought up the rear. Kija
was alert for any sign of Ashta weakening as they fought not only
the howling north wind but the sudden gusts and eddies which
swirled up from bottomless crevices below them. The Snow
Dragon, Meppi, warned them he was about to fly sharply upwards
and they watched his manoeuvring ever more closely as the snow
thickened.

Mim, clinging to Ashta with Khosa silent deep in her
travelling sack against his chest, began to think they would reach
the very stars themselves when Brin swerved ahead of them,
angling his great crimson body down between two sheer ice
walls. Mim blinked snow from his lashes, trying to see more
clearly. He realised Brin's wingtips only barely missed touching
the sides as he flew. A concentrated jet of fire from the Snow
Dragon was reflected again and again in the ice alongside them
and then Ashta was slowing, as though preparing to land.

Mim rubbed his eyes free of the frozen snow and looked over
Ashta's head. He saw that Meppi had cleared a narrow ledge
with his fire. The Dragons stood now on a lip of rock, its wetness
from the melted snow already freezing again.

Meppi said: 'Inside this part is where dwells the Damaged
One. We have sung to him through much Time but there is no
tunnel near where we might reach him.'

'Can we call him?' Gan asked, as he slid carefully from
Fenj's back.

'No!' Meppi's answer was sharp. 'These who ride with you
must make their way in – there is an opening below this ledge.'

Gan immediately peered down and if not for Lorak grabbing

his arm, would have slipped straight over. He nodded thanks to the old man and looked at the ice behind them.

'There is nothing we can fasten a rope to, to let us lower ourselves.'

'I will hold a rope,' Brin rumbled.

Kran pulled a coil of rope from his pack and handed it to Gan.

'We will wait a brief time,' said Meppi. 'In case you have to return this way. But we must go higher and around this peak to the main entrance to the stronghold.'

'The main entrance?'

'It is sure to be the easiest place for those of our size to enter, Gan,' Fenj said, 'and we thought the more distractions the better – it will give Tika more chance to get to the place where the Balance is concealed.'

Meppi drifted out over the chasm and searched for the place he had in mind.

'It is directly below here,' he announced as his talons scrabbled for a hold on the ice-covered ledge beside Ashta.

Trem wrapped a length of rope around one of Brin's forearms, looped it once over the other, and the Dragon gripped the end in his jaws. Ashta's agitation became apparent as Mim stepped forward to grasp the rope.

'No.' Gan put his hand against Mim's chest. He glanced at Ashta. 'You go with the Dragons, Mim – one of us should be with them and surely it should be the Dragon Lord?' Gan stared at Lorak who was leaning against Fenj for shelter from the driving snow. 'You also Lorak, will go with the Dragons. You are not trained to the use of weapons – the five of us will not have time to keep watch over your safety, and we will be moving fast once we are inside.'

Lorak looked hard at Gan from beneath the snowy brim of his hat, then he nodded, climbing onto Fenj's back without a word.

Gan pointed at Trem and the officer moved to take the rope and prepared to descend over the ledge.

'Tug the rope to signal for the next of us to come down,' Gan told him.

'Sir.' Trem, the rope secured around one arm and leg, stepped backward into swirling snow-filled space.

After what seemed an interminable wait, three steady pulls

came on the rope under Gan's hands and he nodded to Kran to go next. When Sket and Motass had also vanished down the rope, Gan turned to the Dragons, Mim and Lorak.

'Stars guide you, my friends, and protect you now.'

'You also Lord Gan,' Kija replied. 'We will wait here only a short time and then we will go to the great gateway Meppi spoke of.' She moved forward, lowering her head until her golden brow touched Gan's. He stroked her beautiful face lightly with his gauntleted fingers, then turned to grasp the rope Brin held.

He gasped as the wind clawed at him, turning him to smash, like a plaything, against the glassy wall of ice. Gan fought the wind and the rope to twist himself back so that his feet could hold him clear. He lowered himself carefully, an arm length at a time, until at last he felt his ankles held.

'Keep a hold the rope Sir, there's no room to stand here.'

Gan peered down and saw only the top of Motass's head and outstretched arms gripping Gan's lower legs. As he let himself down the final distance, Motass guided his body through a small opening, a window, he realised as he squeezed his shoulders through.

Trem was standing by the door as Gan unwound the rope from his arm. The exposed skin of his face burnt and stung now that he was out of the relentless wind and snow. Sket pulled at one of his gauntlets and Gan grimaced as he flexed his fingers.

'It's a servant's room Sir, but quite isolated. Officer Trem went along the passage a short way, and he says there be other storerooms, half empty, but none where it seems anyone lives,' Kran explained quickly as he pulled Gan's other gauntlet free.

Gan stared at the small hearth with its heap of dead ashes. He looked at the single chair and the table and lastly at the long, narrow bed.

'This is where Bark has lived,' he said, almost to himself. 'All these Cycles, shut away in this cell.'

He tucked his gauntlets firmly under his belt and moved to Trem's side. He looked out into the dimly-lit passageway.

'All the rooms to the turning are empty Sir. No servants or fighters.'

'Did you look beyond the corner?'

'The passage leads downwards. There are similar doors as

along here, but no sign or sound of occupants, although I didn't venture to check Sir. I thought I should wait till we were all inside.'

Gan nodded. 'You and I lead, Trem. Sket, watch our backs.' And sliding his sword free of its scabbard, he moved silently out of the room.

A faint metallic ringing told him that all swords had been drawn behind him as he went towards the corner. The light was dim but sufficient; glow lamps holding only one glower apiece were set at regular intervals along the wall. The five men made their way quickly but cautiously round the corner and on down a passage identical to the first. Gan stopped close to the first door then silently lifted the latch. He pushed the door open fast, keeping hold of it lest it bang against the wall. Empty. As Trem said of the first rooms, this one too seemed to be a long neglected storeroom, thick with dust and ancient spinners' webs. He stepped back into the passage, closing the door gently again. With a glance at Trem, he moved on past the remaining doors to the next corner.

Ahead, the passage split, the right fork continuing a downward slope and seeming to be completely unlit. The left fork remained level and Gan guessed it was a quick route directly to the Guardian's quarters. The rest of the Gaharnian forces would be in the lowest levels and Gan decided his party's best plan would be to continue downwards. Hopefully they would at least disconcert or distract any of Rhaki's fighters who might be already engaged with Soran's group.

Gan took the right hand passage, unhooking a glow lamp as he passed. The path turned and twisted but led always down and, after perhaps thirty minutes, Gan stopped again. He looked at the floor ahead. There was a thick layer of dust over his boots and as Gan stooped, holding the lamp ahead of himself, it was clear that the dust in the passage had lain untrodden for a long time indeed.

'I judge we must be nearly to the depth we were in the Delvers' tunnels Sir,' Motass said quietly.

Gan nodded. 'Just pray this isn't a dead end,' he whispered back.

They hurried on, a sense of urgency building in all of them.

'Sir! Listen!' Trem caught Gan's sleeve.

Faint and distant cries came to them and the ring of metal, then the sounds ceased. Gan increased the pace and the five sped along the seemingly endless passage.

Soran and his Guards had watched Nolli stand before a solid wall of rock. She lifted her hands and the rock trembled into two halves, opening with only the faintest sigh. She turned to Soran.

'You must go on now. Choose only paths to your left. I will follow, slow though I may be. Stars guide you all.' She remained standing, Lanni's arm round her waist, as Soran raised his sword before his face in salute then moved past the Wise One with his men behind him.

They travelled at the loping trot they were trained to, five Guards carrying lamps to guide their feet. But this tunnel had not been used since the days of the previous Guardian Kovas, and was as thick with dust as the one Gan's group travelled. Several times the tunnel divided and each time, Soran led his men without hesitation to the left.

Soran estimated they had travelled a little more than two leagues when the way ahead was blocked by another wall of rock. The group stopped, looking to Soran. They had expected no further barriers. As they stood, Soran felt a faint buzzing vibration pass through his body and, as before, the rock opened smoothly in front of him.

Once more they settled into the steady pace of Gaharnian Guards until Soran suddenly gagged. Seconds later, the rest of his men had stopped behind him. Soran drew a more cautious breath and grimaced as the stink filled his nostrils. Drak came up beside the officer.

'It is not the stench of Shardi, Sir.'

'No, I realise that. I fear whatever smells this bad will be proportionally worse than Shardi!' He looked over his small band. 'Prepare yourselves. Try to block your minds of whatever your eyes see, as the Healers and Seniors have tried to teach you.'

No sounds accompanied the awful stink at first, and Soran led his men onward. Then they heard shuffling and clattering. Soran stopped. The Guards drew close around him and he indicated they cover three of the lamps. They strained to decipher the noises ahead.

Finally, Nomis whispered: 'It sounds like stabled beasts – kept in a group rather than individual booths, but it doesn't smell like fengars, Sir.'

They remained listening a moment longer, Soran nodding as he agreed with Nomis's interpretation of the noises.

'The Guardian has Shardi at his command. We may expect worse than fengars I fear. Come.'

They moved quickly now, swords drawn and shields transferred from backs to forearms. The passage grew narrow. Soran swiftly indicated the remaining lamps be covered as light showed where the passage walls nearly met, leaving the barest space where a man might squeeze through. Keeping close to the sides, they crept to the opening and peered through. Soran bit his lip to keep himself silent while several Guards who glanced through turned hurriedly away and lost the contents of their stomachs.

Breathing as lightly as he could, Soran counted the number of monstrous creatures beyond. Most were lying down, but several stood on their hind legs and an argument was clearly escalating between two in particular. Soran took note of the claws, the tusks, the muscular limbs, as one of them half turned and lashed out with a hind leg. As its opponent moved back to avoid the taloned hoof, it threw its upper body forward, grasping the other's head with its forelegs. Tusks scored grooves down a neck, but the first shrieked in fury and thrust its own tusks up into the chest of the second. One of the beasts lying down rose onto its hind legs faster than Soran would have believed possible and it rammed itself between its two snarling and bleeding fellows. Its head turned from one to the other and sharp guttural noises came forth. Soran realised it was using language, the human features of their faces belying the bestial grunts he was hearing. The one who had put himself between the two who argued stamped on the floor. His head swung between the two and slowly they both backed away, lowering themselves to move on four limbs rather than upright on two.

Soran moved to see around the area where these creatures stood and lay. He could see a barred gate at the far end of the cavern and as he watched, a man moved into view for a moment then disappeared. Soran stepped back a few paces and gestured

271

for his men to withdraw with him.

'It would appear to be a holding cave for these – things. But there is a guard at the door. I count eighteen of the creatures. If any of you...'

Before he could continue asking for suggestions, there were shouts from within the cave. Soran swiftly returned to the crack in the rock wall. Four men in the black leather tunics of the Guardian's fighters had entered the enclosure. All the beasts were up on their hind legs, crowding together, some silent, some squealing. The men held naked swords in one hand and three pronged lances in the other. One man came towards where Soran and his Guards were concealed, but his eyes were fixed only on the beasts. Two others took positions at the sides. The fourth man shouted for the animals to follow him and to remember they were to obey him as they would the Guardian himself.

With a certain amount of barging and glaring stares, the beasts followed him out of the cavern, the other three men flanking them. Soran held his breath as the last man out pulled the barred gate closed behind him. He let the breath out in relief as he saw the gate had not been secured on the further side. In fact, it had swung slightly ajar again as the sound of clattering feet and occasional snarls and grunts diminished.

It was a tight squeeze for all of them getting through the crack into the beasts' enclosure. Soran went first and raced across to the gateway. The rest followed as swiftly as they could.

'It's my guess those things were not being taken out for exercise. I'd say they will be used to attack Lady Tika's group. We must follow them closely now.' He looked at each of his men as they stood around him. 'At least we have seen these creatures and thus will not be taken by surprise at their monstrosity. We must pray there are none worse. Let's go.'

Ashta was struggling as the Dragons rounded the central peak of the Guardian's stronghold. Kija spoke urgently to Meppi's mind.

'Not far now, Kija. Another few wing beats and we will be sheltered.'

Brin dropped back to fly alongside Ashta, breaking the ferocious force of the ice-laden wind. Then they followed Meppi's swerve to the left and it felt as if the wind had vanished.

In truth, it still blew but to such a lesser extent it felt almost a balmy breeze. Meppi swung them up and onto a sloping ledge from where they looked down at the approach to the stronghold.

Mim saw far below, through much gentler falling snow, a thin strip joining this mountain with the main range beyond. Rubbing his eyes free of ice, he realised how only a few fighters could hold the entrance against any invading forces.

'The gateway is directly below, where that span of rock meets this side.' Meppi's crystal-prismed eyes flashed in the gloom of the mountain shadow as he spoke.

'Well Mim, what's to do?' Lorak grinned evilly as he rummaged under his cloak. 'If we be going straight in there, let's have a tiny restorative sip first, eh?'

Kija groaned as Fenj murmured: 'Splendid creature!'

Khosa's head appeared cautiously from her travelling sack. 'You do remember Tika must find the Grey One's study?' she enquired, sniffing daintily as a leather bottle arrived in Mim's hand.

'We remember,' agreed Mim, holding the bottle angled so the Kephi could lap a few drops. He laughed as she sneezed, and gulped a mouthful himself.

'Keep it with you boy. I have more.' Lorak patted his cloak.

'Tika is embattled already,' Mim said. 'We should waste no time. I will lead from here.'

'No.' Brin rustled his wings. 'I lead, and you follow me.'

Mim began to argue but was overruled by both Kija and Fenj.

'It will be as my firstborn says.' Fenj's tone brooked no further discussion. 'And if it is the time for any to journey beyond, I wish safe journey and may the stars guide your path.'

Lorak grunted and slapped the huge black Dragon's shoulder. 'No need to go talking like that, Lord Fenj. I'll wager you two hoppers that we'll have many a good talk after this is done, you see if we don't.'

'You have great faith, Lorak of the Garden.' Fenj's eyes whirred the shadows-on-snow colour. 'I accept your wager.'

Mim laughed aloud again, the hood of his cloak falling back. For a moment they studied the once-Nagum boy, then Brin gathered himself to lift from the ledge. Ashta rose directly behind him, Meppi nearly level with the pale green Dragon. Kija and

273

Fenj moved into position and the five Dragons formed a close V formation. Brin flew further out from the mountainside then pulled in his left wing and dived, roaring out his deep bass call.

Lorak shut his eyes firmly as Fenj also called, the tone trembling through his massive frame and into the old gardener's body. Mim's eyes blazed as he watched over Ashta's head Brin's first blast of fire at the gate which was suddenly in front of them. Brin pulled up to circle back as Ashta and Meppi sent streamers of fire into the gate, then they too were flying upwards in a tight sweeping curve. As they came round again on Brin's tail, Mim heard screams and yells fill the silence following Kija and Fenj's attack on the gate.

This time Brin slowed and came low enough to land as he sent another scorching blast through what was left of the great gate. The iron hasps and studs crashed from the flaming wood and the remains of several black clad bodies lay motionless as smoke rose from them. Brin folded his wings tight to his sides and lunged inside bellowing his call and belching fire. Ashta was close behind him and moved up to his shoulder as they found there was plenty of space within the entrance.

Fighters came pouring from two passages, skidding to a halt as they saw what confronted them. Mim saw one fighter, grey flashes on his shoulder presumably marking him of higher rank, tumble into the chamber, take a cool look at what was happening and then sprint for another passage which clearly led upwards. Mim slid from Ashta's back and raced after the man. Ashta roared and swung away from Brin to follow her soul bond.

Meppi followed Ashta as Brin reached the passages from which the fighters had appeared. A man emerged from an opposite passage and stood gaping at the sight of a great crimson Dragon in the entrance chamber. He was in different clothing from the black uniformed fighters and he stood, eyes popping and a faint wail issuing from his open mouth. Kija, behind Brin, studied him, her golden eyes whirring. A servant of some kind, no warrior this one, so she sent only a small jet of fire to scorch the stone in front of him. The wail rose to a shriek and he grasped handfuls of his long robe and fled back whence he'd come.

'You watch the passages on that side Kija. I will guard these.

274

Father, be sure no secret ways open near the gate lest they try to surprise us.'

'Ashta and Mim…' Kija began.

'The ways are too narrow, Kija,' Brin said gently. 'All we can do is wait for them now.'

Chapter Thirty-One

Rhaki had immediately known when the wards he had set around his stronghold were breached. He stood in his study, utterly still, as he sought with the Power where the breach had occurred and who had dared such a thing. His mind probed deep into the roots of the mountain, following the direction he had ordered his fighters and the Cansharsi to take.

Emla! Rhaki stiffened as he recognised the signature of his sister's mind. No. It wasn't possible. She would never leave the great House. There were other minds he could not recognise near hers. Rhaki clenched his fists in fury and hurried back to the chamber where Iska lay.

As he stormed in, he knocked a servant crashing to the floor, regardless of the man's grunt of pain as the hot water he'd been carrying spilled over his chest. Rhaki stood opposite Bark and stared at Iska's white face and closed eyes.

'If she is not awake, I must enter her mind anyway. Move aside Bark.'

Rhaki stooped lower, placing a hand each side of Iska's shuttered face. He took a steadying breath and a rapid stream of thought screamed through and past his mind. He knew at once that Iska's call was directed towards Emla, although he was unable to take it in. His own mind had been focusing to needle its way into Iska's and this sudden strong eruption from her mind hurt him immensely. He gasped, his hands falling away from Iska's face as he pulled his mind free of her. He regained his control almost at once and tilted his head on one side as he looked down into Iska's open eyes. He smiled and shook his head slightly.

'That was very wrong of you Iska.'

Bark's hand began to rise towards the Guardian but Rhaki had already placed the middle finger of his right hand gently on the centre of Iska's forehead. She convulsed, a light blazed momentarily in her eyes before they went blank and she lay still.

Bark's hand dropped back as he stared at Iska. 'She is dead Master!'

'And so will all be who dare cross me.' Rhaki snapped back. 'Come,' he called as a knock sounded at the door.

Jal entered, breathless from his race up from the lowest levels.

'Master, the Cansharsi are slain,' he blurted between gasps for air. 'They had Dragons in the tunnels with them. Smaller than Dragons I have seen, but well able to spew fire, Master.'

'Killed *all* my Cansharsi?' Rhaki scowled at Jal.

'Of the first group, yes Master. And there are Great Dragons at the main gate.'

'Are all the Cansharsi now deployed with fighters?'

'Yes Master.'

'Do your utmost to protect this place Jal. I will be in my study – I have much to do which does not concern you. But this stronghold will be defended to your last breath. You understand me?'

'Yes Master.' Jal glanced at Bark who still stood by the bedside where the Lady Iska lay. His eyes went to the Lady and he swallowed as he recognised only too well that it was a corpse lying there now.

'There was something else Jal?'

Jal swallowed again and bowed hastily. 'No Master. I will return to my men.'

Rhaki's gaze moved to Bark. 'You have seen death often enough before Bark. Why such sorrow for this one?'

Bark raised his head to meet the Guardian's eyes.

'Master, this was Iska. We studied in the Asataria with her. She was always kindly.' His ruined voice was barely audible.

'Always interfering, as I recall.' Rhaki turned away as he spoke. 'Stay with her if you wish. I have things of importance to attend to. I will not be disturbed Bark,' he said warningly. 'No one enters my study until I call.'

'Yes Master.'

As the door slammed behind the Guardian, Bark winced. A servant touched his sleeve.

'May we help you with the lady Sir?'

Bark looked down at the face turned sympathetically up to

him.

'That is kind Galt. I'm sure the lady would appreciate your help.' Bark leaned over Iska's body and his long fingers gently closed her eyes.

Rhaki was already in the chamber where he kept his amplifying bowl. He fought to control his breathing and his tension as he sat, the bowl before him. After long seconds, he placed his hands around it, envisaged his sister and demanded to see where she was. The deep blackness of the bowl stirred, quickly clearing to reveal Emla pulling a short sword from the chest of one of his fighters. As she raised her arm again, she faltered for a moment and then vanished from Rhaki's scrying bowl. Rhaki smiled grimly. She had been aware of the touch of his mind and had shielded herself from him. He sat back, thinking fast.

His decision made, he hurried back to his study and began taking certain books and scrolls from his shelves and worktable. Carrying as many as he could manage, he went swiftly to his secret chamber. After several such trips, he loaded a leather bag with his most precious documents, including the records of his genetic experiments. Once more he went along the dark passageway. Carefully he lifted his black bowl and placed it beyond the door.

Stepping back, he cast an eye over the jumbled contents of the chamber then pressed the stones that sealed the room. Rhaki bowed his head then raised his hands, chanting softly all the while. Picking up the bowl, he returned halfway to his study and stopped, again putting the bowl on the floor. He stood in the passage, his fingertips just touching the walls to each side, and chanted another incantation. Back in his study the bowl was carefully wrapped in cloth and placed into his bag. Rhaki smiled as he looked round his study. He would make things very difficult for those fools should they reach this room!

He sealed both the inner and outer doors, then pulled the thick carpet from the floor before the hearth. He had to heave the table aside to get the carpet free to reveal a mosaic circle, inlaid with crystal and jet. Wrapping his thick woollen cloak around himself and a weatherproof cloak on top of that, he carefully placed his leather bag at his feet as he stood in the centre of the mosaic

278

circle. The air seemed to fizz and crackle as Rhaki's voice rose steadily higher.

There came a sound like a great gulp and the room seemed to shiver and lose all its air. Then the chamber settled again and air returned. But the Guardian was gone.

Emla sat on the floor, her back against the wall. Just beyond her outstretched legs lay the grotesque form of one of the creatures they had fought. And beyond that corpse, the body of a Guard lay in the first boneless collapse of death. She drew her knees up and rested her sword across them. Her hand felt glued to the hilt and she saw it was indeed stuck – with dark thick blood.

Tika slid down beside the Lady. Emla looked at her. Despite her pallor, her eyes were glowing with the residue of the rage that seemed to have engulfed her as the fighting began. Farn's silver blue head loomed over the two.

'The few who lived, ran away, my Tika.'

'Gone for help I expect.'

Baras joined them with Kemti as Tika spoke.

'Exactly, Lady Tika. So we must hurry on, get further into the stronghold before more fighters arrive to keep us held back here.'

Emla groaned but reached up to Kemti's hand, hauling herself to her feet. She pulled Tika up with her.

'Onward it is then.'

She stiffened suddenly, her hand tightening on Tika's wrist, but all of them felt it. A blast in their minds, a warning, a plea to trust Bark, a direction, then emptiness. Farn's eyes flashed the softest blue and he moaned. Emla swayed and both Kemti and Tika held her from falling. Gently she freed herself from their hands and drew herself upright again.

'He has killed the Senior Lady, Iska, my dearest friend. For this alone, he will pay with his own life.'

Her voice was low but it rang with true conviction.

Guards were dragging corpses to the sides of the tunnel to leave a clear path; as Baras pointed out, there would be another band of Guards coming, only a day or so behind them.

Emla began to stride forward. She paused as she came level with Uma and Jeela, touching their faces lightly with her long, red stained fingers.

'You have done brave work, dear ones. There is more to do.'

Having seen his Lady use the sword, Baras was no longer inclined to insist she stay within his men's protection. All had seen the fury with which both the Golden Lady and Tika had wielded their blades. The Guards saw that neither of them flinched from giving a death blow and surprise was replaced by respect.

The Delver girl had stood quietly beside Jeela during the ferocious encounter, her arms loosely folded as she watched. Farn had become enraged as one of the Guardian's fighters had pushed Tika off balance and she had slipped in a pool of blood. Even when he saw her thrust her sword up into the fighter's belly from her half-crouched position and then move on to face another, Farn's anger would not cool. His eyes had lost the crimson blaze only when the remnants of the fighters fled.

As Tika walked beside him, she felt a sadness that at last Farn was aware that this was more than a game.

'Can you reach Trem or Gan?' she asked Kemti.

'I tried, but Gan's mind is shielded. He knows the Guardian would feel his presence should he try to contact us with mind speech. And,' he added grimly, 'Gan would have felt Iska's call as we did. The Guardian must know we are very close now. His fighters will have surely reached him by now to report on us.'

Baras halted suddenly, holding his sword aloft.

'Listen!'

As the sounds of fighting reached them, Emla moved past Baras.

'Come,' she called, 'but remember – the Guardian is mine.'

Farn surged past Tika and Emla, Jeela close to his flank. The two Snow Dragons pushed up along the opposite side as they rounded a curve into a wide well lit cavern. Ahead, they saw Soran engaged in a fierce battle with more of the foul beasts like those they themselves had just despatched. Black uniformed fighters were pouring in from the far end of the cavern, but before they could join with the Cansharsi attacking Soran, Farn roared in anger.

The fighters in the front ranks screamed as fire licked over their bodies. They fell writhing onto the stone floor as Jeela roared at the next row of fighters. But two higher ranked fighters yelled above the screams and pushed some of their men to run fast towards Soran and his Guards. The Snow Dragons waited, unable to use their fire for fear of injuring the Guards, as Baras charged forward.

Tika and Emla were close at his heels as some of the remaining Cansharsi whirled to face them. A Cansharsi towered above Tika snarling, its taloned forefeet extended and ready to disembowel. Farn bellowed and trampled towards Tika as another Cansharsi sprang from the melee. His bellow of rage turned to a howl of agony as talons ripped down his neck.

Tika's scream hurt Kemti's ears and he leapt over a fallen Cansharsi to her side. Tika's eyes were green fire as she swung her sword with both hands, lopping off a Cansharsi arm. She reversed the swing of the blade and sliced the beast open from belly to throat, forcing it staggering away from Farn. As Kemti reached them she stood braced in front of the silver blue Dragon who had slumped against the wall.

Kemti looked back over the confusion of struggling men. All the beasts were down at least and no more fighters were coming into the cavern. A Snow Dragon stood at the entrance, ready for any who attempted to join this fight.

'Look to Farn. I will be here.' Kemti touched Tika's shoulder, turning her round to the Dragon.

Tika took a step towards him, her sword slipping from her fingers. She knelt by his head, lifting it to her lap. Then she looked at the gaping wound deep along his neck.

'Mend me, my Tika.'

'I don't know how!' she wailed aloud.

'You do,' Kemti snapped from behind her. 'Your mind knows even if you say you do not. Find the place within, as Iska and I showed you. Then you will find the knowledge you need.'

Farn's blood was pooling beneath Tika's knees as she tried to calm her thoughts, but the fear and panic were too intense. Hands rested lightly on her shoulders and Dessi said softly:

'You must find the calm place Tika. Let me take your fear.'

Tika couldn't understand what the Delver meant, then she felt Dessi's mind touch hers. She forced herself to relax, her first instinct was to lash out at the intrusion, and she felt her panic draining from her. She took a breath. The fear was still there but pushed to the edges of her mind, and there was the still centre.

The world vanished as Tika became wholly mind, diving into the torn flesh of the Dragon. She saw where muscles were ripped, the ends of blood vessels needed finding and joining. She had no idea how long she worked until she was finally sealing the skin across the long wound. Some scales were gone in a long line, leaving only the soft blue hide which at last closed over the injury.

Tika slumped forward, trembling from the strain. 'He will live.'

'Yes.' Dessi's arm was round her as she too crouched beside Farn. 'He will be weak until his blood is replaced. It will take a few days so he should rest here. And it will take time for you too to regain the strength you have used in this great healing Tika.'

'No,' Tika muttered. 'I have to go on, to find the Balance. But Farn can rest here.'

'No.' Farn struggled to lift his head and Tika winced as she felt his soreness and weakness within herself. 'We are soul bonds. I go with you, my Tika.' His eyes whirred, a muted sapphire, as he gazed down at her crumpled against his side.

'You cannot,' she argued wearily.

'If we held him with our strength,' Dessi spoke softly, 'I mean the other Dragons and I, he could travel with us for a while.'

Tika moved her head as though it weighed an enormous amount too much. 'It would not harm him to move with us in that way?'

'I think not – for a short time only,' the Delver warned, 'and it will then take longer for him to recover than the few days I spoke of.'

Tika was so tired she could scarcely think. Every part of her being cried out for Farn's presence with her to do what she must when they found the Balance. A tiny whisper suggested she was selfish to make him struggle yet further, only to witness her destruction. But she needed him so. She pushed herself up and caught the long blue face between her palms.

'You will try this then Farn?'

'Of course!'

The prismed eyes whirred ever faster, and Tika burst into tears.

282

As Mim raced after the man who had fled from the entrance hall, Ashta hurried as best she could behind him. A dozen passages suddenly split off from the one they were using. As Mim stood undecided, three men emerged from one of them, carrying brooms and pails. They gaped at Mim, pails rattling to the floor. He caught the nearest one's sleeve.

'Where is the Guardian?'

'Up in his apartments, Lord. I don't know for sure. Oh please Sir, don't do us no harm, we be only workers Sir!'

The man choked as Ashta arrived at Mim's shoulder. His eyes rolled and he crashed full length at Ashta's feet.

'A strange greeting,' she remarked. She looked at the remaining two men. They fell to their knees before Mim.

'Rudd spoke true Sir! We don't go near the Master's apartments, 'tisn't allowed. 'Tis high up, along that way Sir!'

The one who spoke held a shaking arm out in the direction of one of the further passages. Mim moved quickly where the man indicated, Ashta at his heels.

The two men climbed shakily to their feet and bent to their unconscious fellow. Knife points suddenly pricked the skin at the base of their throats.

'Where is the Guardian?' A voice hissed behind them.

'Oh Sir, don't hurt us. Dill told the other one – it's that way!'

The knives moved slightly away from throats The two men gulped as they turned slowly to find four men and one of the People standing there.

'Other one?' Gan, for it was he, glared down at the servant. 'Well? What other one?'

'A strange looking one Sir. He had armour growing from his skin and,' perspiration rolled down the man's face, 'there were a Dragon following him Sir.'

'A pale green Dragon?'

'Yes Sir. They went that way Sir.'

'And that is the way to the Guardian's apartments?'

'Yes Sir.'

'Would Bark be there?'

The man shook his already trembling head. 'I know of no Bark Sir. I only work down here, never up there Sir. Truly Sir.'

283

'And do you serve the Guardian willingly and loyally?'

'Oh Sir.' Both servants collapsed to their knees again beside the faintly stirring body of their companion. 'Our fathers' fathers were brought here Sir. We are bred to work for the Master Sir. We have no choice.' They showed confusion at the very idea.

'Very well. Gather all the servants you can find and let them wait here until I return. No weapons.'

'Sir, we are forbidden weapons. Then you will spare us, good Sir?'

Gan studied them. 'For now at least. Know that there is no escape, there are Guards within this stronghold sent by the Golden Lady herself. The Dragons serve her also.' He turned on his heel and headed for the passage the servant had pointed out, his men close behind him.

Ignoring the groan from the one lying prone beside them, the two still kneeling servants stared at each other.

The one called Dill whispered: 'When he said 'Dragons, Sim, do you think he meant there be more than that one we just seed?'

'That's what I were wondering,' Sim whispered back. He clutched Dill's arm. 'Why don't we go and fetch the others together Dill?'

Leaving their pails and brooms scattered around their workmate, they hurried to obey Gan's orders.

Chapter Thirty-Two

Gan had not travelled far when he came to a halt so sharply that Sket trod on his heels. As Sket opened his mouth to apologise, he too felt the ringing call in his mind. Gan, as one of the People, absorbed Iska's cry fully. He looked at the four men and they stepped back a pace at the glittering anger in his eyes. A moment longer he stood, then he began to hurry back the way they had come.

'The Lady Iska is dead,' he said tersely. 'The Golden Lady herself has brought Guards here. Our first duty is to aid her.'

They approached Rudd, who was climbing dizzily to his feet. His eyes widened in alarm as they advanced.

'Tell me the swiftest way to the lowest levels of this place,' Gan ordered him.

'Down there Sir, to the main entrance. Any passage to the left takes you to the barracks but only fighters are allowed there.'

He quailed as Gan stared at him, and groped for the wall to help him stay upright. Gan nodded but as he moved past, Rudd said tentatively: 'I thought there was a Dragon here just now Sir?'

'There was, and there will be more.' Gan flung the reply over his shoulder as they rounded the corner. Rudd sagged and slid back down the wall, clutching his head.

They met no one else as they half ran down the gently sloping passage and turned a final curve. They found Kija towering up so that her head was level with them despite there being a considerable distance for them to reach the floor of the entrance chamber. Her eyes flickered with gold and scarlet lights and she lowered herself again as she recognised Gan and his men.

'We must find the lower levels,' said Gan. 'The Lady Emla is there with more Guards.'

Kija made a growling sound deep in her throat. 'Tika is there also, and both of my children. The ones in black clothes came from those tunnels which Brin watches.'

Gan glanced towards the smouldering remains of the great gateway and saw Lorak standing by Fenj. Lorak raised his hand.

'Lord Mim went up where you came from Lord Gan.'

Gan nodded and walked across the hall to Brin.

'I give you sympathy for your Lady Iska,' the crimson Dragon murmured.

'Thank you Brin. The Guardian will pay.'

Gan and his four men passed quickly into a passage leading downward much more steeply. In another open space a dozen fighters were huddled, apparently arguing as Gan appeared. Instantly, Gan launched himself in their midst. Two died before Sket and Trem reached the fighters, Gan's sword slashing and cutting with no wasted movements. Kran and Motass set upon four fighters who sought to flee, killing them before they had run ten paces.

As the last of the fighters fell to Trem's sword, they heard a Dragon's screaming roar, a roar of fury and pain. They stood frozen as Gan tried to focus on the meaning of the sound. The roar came again, and yet again. Gan began to run on down to the lower part of the stronghold.

'Sir,' Sket ventured, 'what was that Dragon cry for?'

'It was Kija. Farn is badly wounded and Kija cannot reach him. These tunnels are too narrow for the great Dragons. Quickly now!'

His men needed no further urging, especially Sket and Motass who regarded Tika and Mim and the two young Dragons as their special responsibility.

They met more fighters in straggling groups, some helping wounded comrades along. A few of these instantly engaged with Gan's men, but others wearily threw down their weapons and hunched by the wall. Angry as Gan was, he did not order death for those who capitulated. One fighter, his hands tightly clutching his upper leg where blood pumped through his fingers with each heart beat, looked up at Gan from where he lay propped against a comrade.

'Not many now Sir,' he answered in reply to Gan's question as to the numbers of fighters.

'Stay here then, until we return. Any of you who are uninjured, see to your fellows who are.'

He turned away and continued along the passage.

'Stars! What's that?' Kran spat as a stink filled their nostrils. He stared with the others in horror at the beast that lay sprawled before them. They moved past, noting that the creature appeared to have dragged itself some distance with mortal wounds, judging by the blood trail beyond. Then they all paused.

The next stretch of well-lit passageway was littered with many more of the monstrous bodies. Men in the Guardian's black uniforms lay among them. There were also blue uniformed Guards lying motionless. A Snow Dragon confronted them, eyes blazing white ice, but calming to a pale butter colour as she recognised Gan. Gan's sight was fixed on a group against the rock wall. Kemti stood with his arm across Emla's shoulders. Jeela's head hung low over Farn's silvery blue form, and even from where he stood, Gan could hear Tika's sobs over the groans of the wounded.

Somehow he found himself next to Emla. She turned to him smiling, despite tears gleaming on her dirty face.

'Tika healed him Gan, but he was sorely wounded.'

Gan saw the long line of naked hide curving down Farn's neck and could imagine all too well how near to death the young Dragon had come. He touched Jeela lightly.

'Your mother knew Farn was hurt. Does she know he is well again?'

'Yes.' Jeela's eyes were bright-faceted diamonds. 'She said she has never heard of such a great healing, Gan.' Her tone in his mind was filled with awe.

Farn lifted his head carefully, and sapphire eyes met Gan's dark stare. Gan nodded and stooped, lifting Tika easily from Farn's side. He carried her to a clearer space and looked down at her. She was covered in blood, most of it Farn's but he guessed quite a bit was from the bodies scattered around the passage. Sket leaned over his shoulder.

'Looks like you remembered your sword lessons, Lady!' he said softly.

'Looks like,' she agreed.

Sket nodded and turned away to help with the wounded Guards. Tika looked at Gan. 'Sorry,' she said, rubbing at her teary cheeks and making an even worse mess with her bloody fingers.

Gan grunted and used his cuff to wipe some of the worst of the grime away. She seemed quite contented, lying against his shoulder, but he was aware it was her utter exhaustion – physical and mental – that kept her there.

Mim had met no resistance, only servants who flattened themselves to the wall – or the floor – at sight of Ashta trailing a few paces behind him. Most of the servants were struck dumb, quite unable to answer Mim's question as to the Guardian's whereabouts.

He staggered back against Ashta as Iska's final cry flooded through them. Ashta moaned in distress and Mim turned to comfort her. She finally calmed.

'She was nearby when she called,' she told Mim. 'Very near.'

Mim drew his knife and proceeded along the passage. A door ahead opened and an elderly female servant came out. She was weeping and did not notice Mim and Ashta's approach.

'Where is the Lady Iska?' Mim asked quietly.

The servant sniffled her tears back and then stared in shock at the pair who stood beside her.

'We wish you no harm,' Mim said hastily. 'We seek the Guardian also.'

'And Bark,' Ashta added in his mind.

'And Bark,' Mim repeated aloud.

'Bark is inside. He weeps for the Lady.' The servant shuddered. 'The Master said he was going to his study and none must enter until he summoned them.'

This female was the first to retain some semblance of normality in the presence of Ashta and Mim. Her eyes strayed from Mim's face to Ashta's, then settled on an orange head poking from a bag hanging from Mim's neck. She bobbed a curtsey and put her hand to the door latch.

'Bark will be glad to see friends, I am sure. I've always thought he seemed so sad and lonely. Though the People are so different from us, Bark has always been kind. My old mother used to say: "You can take any troubles to Lord Bark and never hear a cross word."'

As she pushed open the door her hand fluttered toward Ashta

then hesitated. Ashta's eyes whirred and she moved her head to bump gently against the woman's hand as she passed through the doorway. The door closed and the servant stood staring at her hand.

'I touched a Dragon! Stars, but I touched a Dragon!'

In the chamber, two servants stood frozen, one stooped by the fire, the other in midstep towards the great bed. Khosa wiggled free of her travelling bag and leaped upon the bed. Bark sat beside the head of the bed leaning forward with both his hands enclosing one of Iska's and his head sunk onto his chest. Khosa walked daintily along the side of Iska's body then sat neatly, her tail wrapped across her front feet, and gazed from Iska up to Bark. She gave an odd little chirruping noise and then began her buzzing croon.

Bark raised his gaunt face and the corner of his mouth twitched a fraction.

'You visit me again, little Kephi.' As the croon paused, Bark amended: 'Your majesty.' A skeletal finger touched Khosa's head and the croon continued. 'You choose a sorrowful time to visit, Khosa. This beautiful Lady is dead and I wish it were I in her place.'

Khosa glanced at Mim and he took a step forward, Ashta keeping close. It was Ashta who spoke in the mind speech Bark had used to Khosa.

'We knew Lady Iska. We grieve for her also.'

Bark stared at Ashta, his finger still resting on Khosa. Then his sunken eyes moved to Mim. He rose from the chair, a frail ghostly giant, and went to stand before Mim. He placed his hands on Mim's shoulders and stared at the strange eyes with their vertical pupils, and at the scales now plain across Mim's cheeks and brow. Bark sank to his knees, his head level with Mim's.

'A Dragon Lord,' he whispered aloud. 'I have read of such things but I believed them only to be children's tales unfounded in truth.'

Ashta hung her head over Mim's shoulder and said proudly: 'I am Ashta, his soul bond.'

Bark studied her for a moment then he put one of his hands to the side of her face.

'So beautiful Ashta, and so young!' He stood again, extending his hand towards the bed. 'Speak your farewells to Iska and then you must tell what your arrival here means.'

Bark went to the fireside and asked the servant crouched motionless there, for a warming drink.

'Will they harm us Bark?'

'No, no, Galt. They are friends.'

As Mim lifted Khosa to his shoulder and crossed the room to join Bark, the cry came. Ashta's prismed eyes flashed wildly from pale green to dark green with red and gold sparks, and she shifted from side to side, clearly in anguish. Bark felt it too, the pain searing through his damaged mind.

'What is it Bark?' Galt caught Bark's arm tightly. 'What's wrong Bark?'

Bark opened his eyes. 'One of the Dragons is dreadfully wounded.' He looked at Mim. Mim leaned against Ashta's shoulder, his lower lids brimming with tears.

'Tika is attempting to heal Farn,' he whispered.

'Tika? Farn?' Bark asked.

'Another soul bonded pair,' Khosa said in an unusually subdued tone.

Bark shook his head. 'Another pair,' he echoed.

Ashta said: 'Emla is there. She fears that Farn will die.' She became greatly agitated, insisting that she and Mim should go to the lower levels were Farn lay so hurt. Mim held her tight, asking her to wait, to see if Tika was able to heal Farn. It seemed an endless time. Ashta grew quiet, clearly watching through Jeela's mind, what was happening to Farn.

Galt had made some hot tea, moving soundlessly by the hearth. Now he put a cup into Bark's hand and raised an eyebrow towards Mim questioningly.

'Not yet,' Bark whispered. 'But thank you for the thought.'

Suddenly Khosa did her hind-end-up, front-end-down stretch, then began to give her ears a thorough wash. Bark watched Ashta and the boy holding her. He could feel their communication with others but he was incapable of intercepting it himself. But seconds after Khosa's stretch, Bark saw relief and tears on both the boy's face, and amazingly, on the Dragon's. Khosa crooned as she continued her washing.

'Farn will live Bark,' she announced. 'I expect Mim could

drink some of that dreadful hot stuff now.'

Ashta reclined and Mim sat resting against her chest. His tears shimmered on the tiny gold scales edging his cheekbones.

'The Delvers and the Snow Dragons told us of your presence here Bark. They could not get close enough to really help you though, but they hoped their singing gave you some comfort.'

'I did not know who they were, but yes, they felt kindly to me. But why are you here now – Dragons, and a Dragon Lord – I do not understand.'

'There are Guards – '

'And the Lady Emla herself,' added Ashta.

'– in the lowest part of this place. I came with the great Dragons to the main entrance – they are too big for the last tunnels.'

Mim handed his cup back to Galt and smiled. 'Thank you,' he said. 'Will you stay with Lady Iska?' Galt nodded wordlessly. Mim stood. 'Then come, Bark. I think we should return to the entrance chamber. The Guards are coming up and will be there soon. Then we can begin the search for the Guardian.'

'He went to his study but he will have warded the door, I'm sure.'

Bark opened the door for Ashta and Mim and the three went down the curving passages until once more Kija's golden head confronted them. Bark stared in amazement then he bowed deeply.

'Greetings, beautiful one. I am Bark.'

Kija's eyes were still flashing with anger and concern for her son but after a short pause, she lowered herself and replied: 'Greetings, Bark. I am Kija.'

Bark's wondering gaze moved past Kija to the huge crimson bulk of Brin, lying relaxed, but facing the tunnels leading down to the barracks.

'That is Brin, the son of Fenj. And this is Fenj.' Mim's hand pulled at Bark's sleeve drawing him towards what was left of the entrance gate.

Fenj rose erect, his eyes grey slate with jet lights in their depths.

'Greetings to you, damaged one.' He lowered himself and added, 'This is Lorak of the Garden.'

Bark blinked at the ancient human who was bowing before him.

'Pleased to meet you Sir. You look as though a restorative would be of assistance?' Lorak suggested thoughtfully.

'Splendid creature,' Fenj murmured. 'I highly recommend you try a sip, Lord Bark.'

As Bark was offered a leather bottle, the sound of feet and of voices came from the tunnel to the left of where Brin kept watch.

Rhaki stepped out of the mosaic circle and conjured a small flame on the tip of a finger. Looking round, he found an oil filled lamp just where he had left it several Seasons before. The flame on his finger winked out and the lamp lit with a faint hiss. He was in a cave in the far southern reaches of the Ancient Mountains. In fact this cave was inside mere foothills, the mountains scoured down in the long ages since their birth.

Rhaki was drained from his expenditure of power in the setting of wards in the Realm of Ice and the much greater effort of using the circle to move himself bodily over such a vast distance. He exhaled slowly and his shoulders sagged, but he had to do one more thing before he could rest. He moved to one section of the circular cave and pressed the rock delicately, muttering as he did so. A space slid open and Rhaki lugged his leather bag unsteadily through to the newly revealed chamber. With the last of his strength, he fetched the lamp, sealed the doorway behind him and sank to the floor.

It was many hours before he awoke and he groaned as he moved. Lying on the stone floor would have been bad enough but his use of power had left him aching in every joint and muscle. He lay still, concentrating lightly on the worst hurting places – the hip on which he'd lain, his back and his head. He managed to reduce the pain to a persistent but bearable ache before he attempted to sit up.

He looked around. The few items were as he had left them, not that anyone would have found their way to these caves. There was a wooden chest with blankets neatly folded on its top. Rhaki wished ruefully that he could have managed to have reached them at least before he collapsed. He got to his feet and staggered. Stars be cursed, but he was weak! When his vision stopped its vortex swirling, he tottered to the chest, pushing aside the blankets. Lifting the lid, he peered inside. A couple of scrolls and books he had left there ages since, a metal canister, a plain goblet and a tall, narrow jug. He knew he had to wait for his strength to be renewed, he could not risk the humans here seeing him in this parlous state.

Rhaki straightened, holding the jug, and nearly toppled into the chest as dizziness swept him again. He gritted his teeth and waited for the spinning to stop. He let the outer, weatherproof cloak fall from his shoulders as, moving like a decrepit ancient, he made his way out of the chamber. He skirted the mosaic circle and found the concealed door beyond. Even directing the tiny amount of power involved in opening the door nearly sent him to his knees. He braced himself against the rock and felt his way along a narrow twisting tunnel.

One more wall to unseal and then he was in a wider passage. Soon Rhaki could hear the gentle trickle of water and he gave a relieved groan. A spring filled a shallow basin of rock a few paces on and beyond that branches tangled across the outlet to the cave. The faintest starlight prickled through and when Rhaki had filled his jug with water, he stepped closer to the overgrown entrance, trying to judge the position of the stars.

He had been unconscious at least half a day but he had no way of guessing if this was the second or even third night since he had fled his stronghold. Biting his lip to suppress a groan, Rhaki shuffled back through the passage and the mosaic chamber to his hiding place. His breath gusted out in a sigh of relief as he sealed himself in again.

Taking the canister and goblet from the chest he put them on the floor beside the jug, then heaped the blankets against the wall. He rested himself on them for a few minutes before pouring icy water from the jug to the goblet and raising it shakily to his lips. There were dried fruits in the canister but he hadn't the energy to reach for them. Pulling his woollen cloak close around himself, Rhaki lay flat. He would have to rest longer than he might have wished, but he knew he had to be back to his full strength before appearing to the local humans.

His mind drifted lightly to the Realm of Ice and his mouth curved in a smile that did not reach his eyes. He had lost that battle, but the war was by no means over, for war it was. At least those cursed followers of Emla's would not reach the Balance. He frowned. He didn't think they could – but then, he hadn't expected them to break into his stronghold.

He had plans already sketched in his mind; it would be simple to implement them. After all, he knew more than any other of those smug Seniors just what might be done when one as knowledgeable as he combined innate power with this world's own power. Oh yes. Rhaki slid into a deep, restorative sleep. No dreams or nightmares could worry such a Master as he.

Chapter Thirty-Three

Kija's eyes blazed golden fire as the Snow Dragon Uma emerged first from the barrack tunnel. Brin moved back, towards Fenj, and watched as Guards followed the Snow Dragon. Then Jeela came into the entrance hall, her head turned to watch behind her. Kija took a step forward as Farn appeared, the other Snow Dragon, Ulla, on one side and the Lady Emla on the other. Kija looked at her son as he tried to pull himself up and raise his head. He paused and Ulla and Emla moved a little away from him as he looked back at Kija. Her prismed eyes blurred to a honey colour as she said softly: 'Welcome, my son. I rejoice to see you safe. Are you and your soul bond well?'

'Of course.' Farn walked unsteadily towards Kija before crumpling to the floor.

Kija's head lowered over him as she noted the great scar down his slender neck. She settled herself around him and he sighed in content as his head and neck found support on her shoulder. Farn was asleep even as Kija looked back to the tunnel as Kemti and more Guards came up. Finally Gan appeared carrying Tika and with the tiny figure of Dessi trotting beside him. He came straight to Kija who sniffed lightly at Tika's face.

'She has done well to save my son. Take her to Fenj. He can perhaps lend her strength to speed her recovery.' She curled herself tighter around Farn as Gan moved on to Fenj.

Lorak had put a bedroll against Fenj's side and Gan knelt to lower Tika carefully onto the roll. Fenj curved himself around her and his eyes paled to the shadows-on-snow colour as Lorak squeezed in too, to wrap Tika more closely.

Gan got to his feet and found Mim beside him with Ashta.

'She needs to rest, Mim.' Gan noted the increasing change in the Nagum boy's appearance, even in this short day.

'There is Bark.' Mim indicated the gaunt figure at Fenj's side. 'We left servants to watch over Iska's body.'

Gan nodded. 'And I ordered the servants to gather – have you seen any of them?'

'There were only three men cleaning as we went to where Iska lies, and three in that chamber. I saw none as we returned here.'

Gan turned to Soran. 'Have a couple of men seek out the servants of this place and bring them here. Have we lost many Guards?'

'We lost seven to those monsters. Most of us have minor injuries but four are badly hurt, Sir. And there are several prisoners, some of whom are injured also.'

Guards began talking as they cleaned their blades and honed them on the stones they carried in their packs.

'Be there no kitchens here, where we'd find summat warm to eat and drink?'

Several voices made similar comments as a group of thirty or so servants was ushered into the entrance hall. Gan beckoned Bark to join him.

'Is there a housekeeper or chamberlain to oversee the servants and the running of this place? Perhaps it would put them more at ease if you were to speak to them Bark, and assure them that we have no intention of harming them.'

Bark went across to the group of servants, many of whom were clearly petrified by the presence of Dragons. Within a few moments the servants scattered, giving the Dragons a wide berth if their route took them in their direction. Bark returned to where Gan was checking the wounded Guards.

'I asked for food to be prepared, Gan. These servants are not here voluntarily – Rhaki imprisoned humans soon after he came here and used them to breed more. They know of no other life.'

Gan's lips tightened, as did Emla's. She had joined them and overheard Bark's words. Bark bowed to her, saying:

'I was with Iska, Lady. She chose to send to you, knowing what Rhaki would likely do.'

Emla touched his shoulder, as Bark remained bent before her.

'We owe you much Bark. Not one of us remembered that you had come here with Rhaki. Not until we heard of a damaged one living here did we think of you. I tremble to think of what you have suffered, receiving no help from Gaharn.'

Khosa wound herself round Bark's ankles and as he lifted her to his shoulder, Emla shook her head.

'That Kephi seems to get everywhere.'

Khosa's turquoise eyes slitted at the Lady.

'You forget names as easily as much else do you not?'

Emla blinked and cleared her throat. 'Apologies Khosa. There seem to be so many new and strange things happening, my memory definitely appears to be failing.'

Khosa turned her gaze very deliberately back to Bark.

'He is no longer here is he Bark?' It was more statement than question.

Bark shook his head. 'I think probably not. He disappears sometimes for several days, but I do not know where he goes nor in what manner.'

Emla touched Bark's shoulder lightly again as he showed distress.

'I could not stop him killing Iska, Lady. There was nothing I could do to help her!'

'You helped her by your presence, Bark. She understood what Rhaki was capable of perhaps better than any of us, yet still she called out to us.'

Bark looked down. Dessi, her head barely reaching his hip, looked back at him.

'I am Dessi of the ones who sing to you, damaged one.'

'Are you then,' Bark smiled shakily. 'I have appreciated your songs but I can no longer use the mind speech over any distance so I could not tell you how you comforted me.'

'We know,' Dessi smiled. 'Our Old One is on her way here. She would speak with you if you permit. She is very old and travels slowly.'

There was a commotion among the wounded being tended and Emla and Mim went to see what was amiss. Sket spoke to them quickly.

'Their officer is among the wounded Lady. Of all crazy things, he seems to be the big brother to Motass! He's hurt quite bad – his sword arm is torn to shreds. Motass recognised a funny old scar on his chest.'

Emla and Mim followed Sket to find Motass kneeling beside a half-stripped fighter. A healer knelt the other side of the unconscious man and he shook his head as Emla asked about the injury. He lifted a blood-drenched cloth, exposing an arm nearly severed at the elbow.

'I guess one of those monsters either ripped him or bit him – this is not the work of a sword.'

The healer fell silent until Motass asked: 'Can you save him, if you take it off?'

'He would have a better chance of surviving yes. But he has lost a great amount of blood, and I have no way of knowing if there is venom carried by those creatures which may already be in his system.'

'Try then healer, please. I will give a year's wages to the Guild of Healers if you save him.'

The healer sighed. 'Motass, I will do my best but I do not do so for the offer of your money.' The healer got up from the floor. 'This would be best done elsewhere – is there a chamber we can use where he can lie quietly when the arm has been removed? And we will need one of you to assist me in keeping him calm with your power while I work.'

'I can do that,' Dessi spoke confidently, although the healer looked very dubious. She was so very small but as she met the healer's stare, he nodded.

Gan went to organise Guards to remove the wounded who needed more serious treatment, while Bark arranged for chambers to be readied for use by the healers.

Several servants arrived with trays laden with bowls of broth and chunks of bread and they were greeted with cheers from the Guards.

'Tika and Farn still sleep,' said Emla, 'but we must decide our next move. Bark, show us where Iska lies. We would pay her our respects. Then perhaps somewhere we can plan?'

Nomis and Kran were detailed to go back through the barracks to meet the next group of Guards who should soon be nearing the stronghold. Gan left Sket and Trem to stay in the entrance hall as he, Kemti, Emla, Soran and Baras followed Bark to the upper levels.

'We must dispose of all the bodies in the lower levels fairly quickly,' Gan commented to Bark. 'What is the usual procedure here?'

'I don't know Gan. I'm sorry. I've never thought where

bodies are laid to rest when servants die.'

Gan sensed Bark's guilt at his ignorance in this matter.

'Could you ask one of them then, for we must remove the corpses soon.'

They had reached the chamber where Iska lay and conversation ceased. Quietly, they all went to the great bed and looked down at Iska. Emla bent and kissed the already cold, smooth brow and straightened, turning as Bark gave a grunt of pain.

The five Gaharnians crossed to the hearth where Bark slumped in a chair, his hands over his face. The servant Galt, stood helplessly beside him, his arm across Bark's shoulders. Emla looked at the servant enquiringly and after a glance down at Bark, Galt stepped towards her and bowed.

'Bark asked what was done to the bodies of the dead,' he whispered. He glanced again at Bark. 'The Master sometimes took a corpse, we know not for what purposes.' He shuddered. 'Usually, the dead were taken below – to be fed to his beasts.'

Emla swallowed the bile she felt rising in her throat.

'There is no burial chamber, or place of cairns, for the proper laying of the dead?'

'No Lady.'

'Dear stars! What has he become?'

'We could put them in one of the chambers in the lowest level and then seal them within,' Soran offered hesitantly.

Gan nodded at him. 'Make such arrangements when we return to the hall, Soran.'

'Where are Rhaki's quarters?' Emla asked.

'Further along this passage. But beware, he will have warded the door. He always does when he wishes to be sure of no interruptions.'

'Hmm.' Emla spun on her heel and headed for the door.

'Emla,' Kemti hurried after her. 'Wait Emla! I can feel the wardings already, surely you can also sense them?' He caught her elbow. 'Wait I say!'

Reluctantly she stopped a few paces from a door, which looked exactly like all the other doors they'd seen in this place. They probed the wardings, seeing wavering lines of red flickering in an inconsistent pattern all around and through it.

From behind them, Bark said: 'The Balance is beyond the study. I know how to unseal the hidden doors but Rhaki will have warded them all. My power is so limited I can only tell that wards are set, I could not begin to unravel them.'

'They are complex indeed, Bark.' Kemti wiped his forehead where concentration had caused sweat to run.

Emla agreed. 'We will have to wait for Tika, I think. And I have no idea how long that will be. But at least Rhaki is no longer in this stronghold. We can reach the Balance without interference from his presence.'

A Guard approached and saluted the Lady, hand on the insignia above his heart. 'Lady, the reinforcements are arriving.'

'Well. We had best go and meet them, and arrange quarters for everyone. There can be no planning until Tika recovers.' Emla frowned. 'I had hoped that we could deal with the wards and save her some of this work.'

'No,' said Kemti. 'It is clear. Rhaki has greatly increased his knowledge of many things over these Cycles, not least these wardings. At least we know we must be ever more wary if this is his idea of just a simple door ward.'

They joined the much larger crowd now gathered in the great entrance hall. Brin and the Snow Dragons had gone to find food. Gan wondered where that could be. On his brief excursion outside, he had seen only snow-covered peaks and crevasses. Soran went to arrange the removal of bodies and confer with the officers of the newly-arrived squad of Guards. They had been appalled at the grotesque creatures lying in the tunnels and were amazed that so few Guards appeared to have been able to slaughter them all.

Sket was sitting beside Fenj and Lorak, all three watching Tika's sleeping form. Kija had Jeela and Ashta lying beside her as she still curled protectively round Farn. Gan pointed out that Farn's scales were brighter, seemed to have lost the dull, tarnished look they'd had since his wounding. Fenj told them that Tika was stronger but she was burrowed under the blankets and all that was visible was tangled black hair.

Shan brought a tray of tea and honey rolls to the Lady. There was a difference in her, Emla thought, as she accepted the tea gratefully. There was a new awareness in the round blue eyes and

Emla realised that her flighty maid had seen things during the last few days for which she had been quite unprepared. If Guards had paled at the sight of those monsters, how much more shaken must this simple child have been? And yet there must have been a core of strength within her, which made her able to offer a tray of tea with steady hands. Emla confessed to herself that she had expected Shan to collapse in hysterics, but though the girl proved her judgement wrong yet again, Emla was proud of Shan's steadfastness.

A Guard trotted out from the barrack tunnel and craned to look over the scattered crowd.

'What now?' Kemti asked ruefully as the Guard headed purposefully in their direction.

He saluted as he stood before Emla. 'Officer Soran is escorting a party of – Delvers – to your presence Lady.' The blankness in his eyes indicated that very little else would surprise him after recent events. 'It is their leader. She is very old,' he added.

Emla was suddenly aware of what a mess she must look, but Shan was beside her holding a bowl of warm scented water and a towel over her arm.

'Thank you, dear one.' Emla scrubbed her face and hands, noticing that the water turned an unpleasantly dirty red, as did quite a lot of the towel.

'Sit, my Lady, there is time for me to brush your hair,' Shan ordered.

Kemti's eyebrows rose but Emla glared at him as she meekly sat on the floor at Shan's feet.

The buzz of conversation died gradually. The silence spread as the Guards nearest the barrack tunnel rose to their feet to stand to attention.

First to appear was a Snow Dragon, prismed eyes like sparkling crystal. He paced steadily through the Guards, halting a short distance from Emla. Two male Delvers drew Nolli's travelling chair up beside the Dragon and took one step to each side, turning to face each other. Lanni and Berri moved forward, each supporting one of the Wise One's arms. Nolli batted the helping hands aside and stood, leaning on her stick. Her sharp black eyes flicked over the four tall People, then she gave a gummy grin.

'Manners, Lord Gan! Can you not offer an arm to an ancient crone?'

Gan grinned back at her and went to her side, bowing with a rather over embellished flourish.

'At your service, Wise One.'

Leaning heavily on her stick and Gan's wrist, she crept the few paces to stand before Emla. Tilting her head far back she gazed up at the Golden Lady.

'Greetings at last, Golden One.' The naked gums shone pinkly again. 'It is most uncomfortable – talking to you People whilst standing.'

Emla seemed lost for words faced with this diminutive female of such great age, until Kemti nudged her rather sharply.

'Oh. Will you not sit in your chair Wise One? We will sit on the floor.'

The male Delvers pulled the odd little cart up behind Nolli and she sank back gratefully. Gan signalled his men to carry on as before Nolli's appearance and sat on the floor with Emla, Kemti and Bark. Even then, the People's heads were still level with the Delvers'. Khosa stalked between them and leapt to Nolli's lap. A twisted hand settled on the Kephi's back.

'So, my little queen, you keep your eye on all that passes as usual.' Nolli chuckled. Then she looked at each of the People and said in her oddly young voice: 'The Grey One has fled. But he will have to be dealt with before much more time has passed. I offer you our sympathy for your Lady Iska.' Nolli's gaze settled on Bark. 'And you are the damaged one.'

He inclined his head in silent assent.

'Long we have sung to you, knowing your pain. I tell you, it will soon cease.'

Bark nodded, his lips stretching in the unfamiliarity of a smile. Dessi stood beside Bark and Nolli stared steadily at her.

'You took life.'

'Yes, many-times-grandmother. I could not see a friend die.'

Nolli waited.

'It is not so straightforward as I had believed.'

Emla and Kemti studied the Delver child and they both slowly realised she had altered since joining them in the tunnels. Faint

302

lines were scratched at the corners of her eyes and her mouth. She had aged. Nolli stretched out a swollen hand and Dessi moved to her chair. The twisted knuckles brushed lightly over Dessi's face as Nolli said: 'This time I can help, but you know now what taking life will do, child.'

Dessi pressed a kiss on Nolli's hand and slipped back to stand near Bark, the tiny lines smoothed away from her face.

'This Lady Iska,' said Nolli suddenly. 'She was as a sister to you Emla?'

Emla's eyes shone even bigger, magnified by unshed tears. 'She, she was killed. She cannot travel beyond.'

Nolli shook her head. 'She prepared for what she did, Lady. Did you not hear her call? Her spirit went beyond, willingly and safely, before Rhaki killed her body. Even as her cry came to you.'

Emla frowned, trying to remember exactly.

Kemti remarked: 'We were a trifle occupied at the time, Wise One.'

Nolli smiled. 'Hmm. With those poor creatures I passed below?'

'Poor creatures?' Kemti repeated in disbelief.

Nolli tutted. 'You don't think they were happy do you? Twisted perversions constructed by the Grey One.'

'Happy or not, they were trying rather hard to rip us to pieces,' Kemti retorted.

Nolli laughed aloud. 'And probably they are glad of their release from torment.'

Shan offered a tray with a bowl of steaming, fragrant spice tea. Her eyes dropped to the misshapen hands and she put the tray on the floor, knelt and held the bowl questioningly near Nolli's face. Nolli's black button gaze pierced into Shan's round blue eyes, then she nodded slightly. Gently, Shan held the bowl as the old one sipped a few mouthfuls.

'Thank you child.'

Suddenly, Lorak was there, a grimy hand leaning on Gan's shoulder.

'Tika's near waking. Lord Fenj says another short while and she will be up again!' He beamed at them all and Nolli beamed toothlessly back at him, then he trotted off to spread his good news.

'He has his task to do in all this, as do we all,' said Nolli quietly. 'Obstinate he is, as are many, but he has given his love and loyalty to you and he will be obstinate in that, as in all else.'

'But he's my gardener!' Emla objected, and looked surprised when the others laughed.

Nolli leaned forward. 'I tell you quickly now, for you to ponder. Rhaki used the circles to make his escape.'

Her listeners looked blank.

'Circles such as those in your Gathering Chamber and in your Pavilion of Balance. There are many such, but alas, we have no remembrances of how they are used. Clearly the Grey One has discovered this, but I would guess that he would take the book wherein he found such wisdom with him, or he has destroyed it once he had it in his mind. The only place where knowledge of such things may still exist, is in the Wilderness, far, far towards the rising sun.'

Chapter Thirty-Four

Guards had checked through all of the lower levels, the kitchens, servants' quarters, and barracks. Apart from a few Guards on duty, most of the Gaharnian forces had moved into the fighters' barracks. Brin returned with the Snow Dragons, laden with meat for the Dragons still in the entrance hall.

Emla and Kemti had stared in amazement when Mim strolled over to them. He had discarded his cloak and rolled up the sleeves of his shirt as if he at last felt warm again. The tiny gold scales glittered cross his face as he smiled, sweetly as ever, at their astonishment. Emla's finger lightly traced along one of Mim's arms where more scales gleamed.

'It began in the Delvers' Domain, Lady.' Mim's fluting voice was the same at least. 'I am glad, for now I am truly of the Dragon Kin and I have a family once more.'

Bark approached to tell Emla that chambers had been made ready for herself and for Nolli. It was late in the evening and a good night's sleep could only benefit all of them, Tika especially. Gan bent to tell Nolli of the arrangements and a small altercation seemed to take place. Gan stood patiently, arms folded, while the Wise One muttered darkly. Finally she banged her stick on the floor and Gan, his face expressionless, lifted her easily in his arms and carried her up to the next level of rooms. Lanni and Berri trotted along behind him.

'Where is Shan?' Emla looked around the hall, now nearly empty except for the Dragons.

'She sits with Iska,' Bark replied.

Emla looked at him in surprise. 'I will join her for a few hours Bark.'

'I will take my turn watching when you retire to your chamber Emla, but I have been worrying where we should bury her.' Kemti commented.

'She cannot be sealed in this place.' Emla was firm.

Kemti sighed. 'We will decide tomorrow. I will get some rest while you sit with her Emla.'

Night quiet slipped over the stronghold. The young Dragons slept curled near Kija and Brin. Mim lay beside Ashta. Only Fenj seemed awake still as Gan softly re-entered the hall.

'She is safe,' Fenj murmured to Gan's mind.

Gan settled himself against the wall and waited, sleepless, for the night to pass.

As the stronghold stirred awake for its first day under a new rule, Kemti joined Gan in the great hall.

'I have been studying the wardings on Rhaki's door.' He shook his head. 'I see no way myself to unweave it. Tika will need to use power to release it, but how strong is she now?'

Before Gan could say anything, Kemti lowered his voice further. 'The healing she wrought in Farn – I have never seen the like, Gan. He should surely have died, yet she wrestled the wound, fought every tear. And she has never seen healing like that attempted, let alone tried any such herself before.'

Gan studied Kemti's face. The Senior had dark rings beneath his eyes and a frown above them.

'And the fighting, Gan. You said Tika and Mim were scarcely better than useless with weapons, yet her blade moved like a lightning tongue leaving death wheresoever it licked.'

'Do you think she herself was aware of power working through her, or it was doing so unaware, or was she using the skills we tried to teach her?'

'I know little of the art of swordplay Gan – merely the basics we all learnt so many Cycles past, but she looked a champion blade.'

As Kemti finished speaking Fenj stretched his neck, revealing Sket and Lorak either side of Tika's waking figure.

Groans sounded above Lorak's gravelly murmurs and then Tika hauled herself to a sitting position with the help of Lorak's shirtfront. She sat slumped against the old man for a moment, then lifted her head, squinting at the glare of snow beyond the hole where the great door had stood. Leaning heavily on Lorak's shoulder, Tika climbed to her feet, staggered, and would have fallen if not for Sket reaching quickly to hold her.

306

Gan and Kemti sat quietly watching as the small filthy figure tottered in Kija's direction. As she closed the distance between them, a silver blue head lifted waveringly over Kija's golden back and sapphire eyes whirred in welcome. Ashta nudged Mim and he rose, hugging Tika as she drew level. Then he and the younger Dragons headed for the gate and Brin.

Servants appeared from the direction of the kitchens and bore covered trays up to the higher levels. One male servant came hesitantly towards Gan and Kemti, offering hot tea and fresh bread.

'Sirs, we will bring a proper meal to you if you wish, but perhaps you will join the Lady and the others?' He looked nervously towards Fenj and Kija.

'Very well,' Kemti answered. 'We will go to her shortly.'

The servant bowed and retreated. The two Seniors got to their feet and Gan moved in Kija's direction. Farn's eyes glimmered at Gan as Gan asked: 'Will you join us all for breakfast Tika?'

She looked at him and it was an effort for Gan to keep his expression neutral as his heart tightened with pity. She was really dirty, her clothes stiff with dried blood, her hair a tangled mess and her eyes – so very tired still. She touched Farn's face gently and Kija's, then took a pace towards Gan.

'I am hungry I think, but I need to get cleaned up first.' She gestured at her clothes.

'There are chambers above for you to use, and I'm sure Shan will enjoy scrubbing you.' Gan allowed a tentative smile to touch his face. 'Let me clean your sword and I will return it to you at breakfast.'

Tika looked at her hands and shuddered at the now brown blood clogged under her nails. Carefully, Gan bent and unbuckled the sword belt and lifted it away from her as Kemti held out his hand.

'Come then Tika and submit to Lady Shan!'

Tika glanced at him as she hesitantly took his hand. 'I thought I dreamt hearing Shan ordering Emla – it wasn't a dream then?'

Kemti chuckled. 'Oh no. We seem to have a rather different Shan now!'

When Tika came into the chamber Nolli had been given, and where breakfast had been set, her hair was still damp and her skin

307

tingling from Shan's ministrations. Emla rose immediately to
enfold Tika in a close hug, deeply relieved to see her so
recovered. Nolli stretched out a twisted hand and Tika went
round the long table to kiss the wrinkled old cheek. Shan began
to serve their food from another table but Emla caught her maid's
arm.

'Sit down, dear one. You eat with us now.'

Shan's cheeks paled, then flushed scarlet. 'My lady…' she
began.

'Sit down,' Tika ordered from Emla's other side.

Conversation was slight, as they were all hungry for decent
food after the dull trail food they had eaten for days. As Tika
reached for another hot roll of black bread and a thick slice of
cheese, Gan appeared carrying her sword. He looped the belt
over the back of her chair without a word and went round the
table to sit beside Kemti.

Last to arrive were Mim and Bark together, and the difference
between the two caused what little talk there was to cease completely. Bark looked more frail and spectral than ever, having sat
with Iska all night, while Mim shone with strength and vitality.
He brought the sharp smell of frost and snow with him from his
hunting flight with the Dragons and his eyes sparkled with life.

When they had all eaten enough, it was Nolli who spoke:
'Tika, the Grey One learnt far more than we realised. The
wardings he has set on his door are beyond both the Lady and
myself. I believe Dessi will be able to help you – if only to
bolster your own strength as you work.' She struggled to her feet.
'We must make a start.'

Tika stood to buckle on her sword belt, wincing at the aches
still in her shoulders and arms, as Mim said: 'Ashta and Jeela are
outside – and so is Farn.'

Tika's gaze met Gan's and he read her terror that her soul
bond was nowhere near fit enough to have climbed the slope from
the lower floor, let alone go with her further still.

Dessi had opened the door and the two young female Dragons
stood either side of Farn, Sket behind them all. Farn's eyes
whirred as Lorak moved out of the chamber first.

'You look much better, young Farn. I must go down to Lord
Fenj – things to do, you know!' He winked as he went past the

Dragons.

Tika stepped close to the silvery blue Dragon, her hand moving just above the long line of his wound. 'Oh Farn, you should not be up here. You need much more rest. I cannot let you come any further.'

'Of course you can.' Farn sounded indignant. 'Bark said it is not much further at all now.'

Tika looked at him then turned to Mim. 'Well – let's get on with it.'

The slowness with which Farn moved the relatively short distance along to the Guardian's quarters underlined just how badly weakened he was. Emla, Kemti and Dessi drew level with Tika and Mim when they were several paces from the warded door.

'Complicated,' said Mim, then he frowned. 'But maybe not.'

Tika gave him a weak smile. 'Two different types of wardings – one laid over the other?' she suggested.

Mim nodded. The Seniors, Nolli and Dessi, watched as Tika began unravelling the weave of the warding. They could see the pulses of white, flickering erratically through the more solid red. Slowly, inch by inch, Tika snuffed out each white flash until at last only the red glimmered around and across the door. She blew out a gusty breath as tension drained from her shoulders.

Mim lifted a hand and concentrated on eliminating the red lines and as they vanished he grinned at Tika. Bark slipped past them and put his hand on the latch. The latch snicked and Bark took three paces inside before stopping abruptly.

'What is it Bark?' Emla called.

Bark moved aside so all could see the litter of books and papers, but eventually all eyes lowered to the circle inlaid in the floor.

Nolli grunted. 'I said he used the circles to escape this place.'

Khosa walked stiff legged, tail upright, through the group outside to stalk around the circle. Suddenly she jumped and landed hissing, fur on end, at the bare rock wall.

Tika managed a smile. 'Khosa, that is hardly nice language for a queen to use.'

Bark had moved towards Khosa and now said: 'This is the door Rhaki believed no one else but he knew of. But it is warded

309

anyway.' He looked back at the others. 'I have never known of the circle here.' He pointed to the carpet heaped at the end of the room. 'Always it has been covered – I had no idea.'

Tika and Mim approached the wall and studied the pattern of warding again.

'Not as complicated as the first one,' Mim said in Tika's mind.

'No, but I wager there will be more traps beyond this one.'

Steadily, they focused their attention on the unravelling of the threads of power criss-crossing a section of wall.

'It's clear,' Tika said.

Again Bark moved ahead and his bony fingers seemed to caress the rock. As he stepped back, the door slid open, revealing the dark passage behind it.

Rhaki woke again and smiled. He propped himself on an elbow and poured some of the still-cool water. He drank thirstily and refilled the goblet, taking smaller swallows this time. He opened the metal box and took a handful of dried fruits. As he chewed he reviewed his plans.

He was but a few leagues from Return. The so-called Lord, Hargon, was a smart fellow – for a human – but Rhaki had no doubts that he would be able to manipulate him with ease. He had contemplated going to the town of Far, but the Lord there was little more than a brutish simpleton. Hargon had demonstrated a certain inventiveness on past occasions and Rhaki felt he showed promise.

He got to his feet and lifted his scrying bowl from the leather bag. Unwrapping it, he placed it on top of the wooden chest and sat cross-legged on the floor. He visualised the Lord of Return clearly in his mind, put his hands to the sides of the bowl and demanded: 'Show this one to me.'

The blackness swirled and blurred then cleared to reveal a stocky, fair haired man resting on brilliantly coloured pillows as two women wearing nothing that could honestly be termed clothing, swayed around him. Rhaki snorted. That sort of amusement did not appeal to him. But at least it meant that Hargon was occupied in his manor. His men would also be nearby, which would allow Rhaki to move closer to Return unobserved. He had previously arrived in this fashion. Sentries found him sitting calmly beneath a tree at the edge of the town at dawn. It all added to his air of mystery and power.

Rhaki sorted the contents of his leather bag into two piles. Two ancient books, a small roll of blank paper and his precious record book went back into the bag, along with several small packets of certain herbs. The rest, he packed carefully inside the chest with his scrying bowl. He folded the blankets and put them on the lid again. Finally, he tied a heavy leather purse to the belt around his waist and pushed it to his right side. A slender knife was sheathed at his left side. Hooking the bag over his shoulder, he glanced around the small cave, lifted the lamp and unsealed the door. Resealing it, Rhaki skirted the mosaic circle and opened the second door.

For a moment he stood thinking, then decided to leave the door closed but unwarded, in case he needed to let himself back inside in any haste. On this trip through to the outer cave, Rhaki trod with firm steps, unlike the staggering crawl of his earlier visit. The sound of the spring splashing steadily into the basin warned him of his nearness to the exit. Extinguishing the lamp, he set it on a high ledge to his left. If any dared creep into the cave, they would not be tall enough to see the lamp, let alone reach it.

Stars glittered through the branches ahead and Rhaki studied their position and that of the moon. Halfway to dawn, he estimated. Time enough to walk to the outskirts of Return. He walked steadily, not striding out, and noted the fields cultivated with beans and corn in the faint moonlight. Hargon had a few good administrators and the sense to let them get on with their work without his interference.

The moon was low in the sky as dawn began to hint at its arrival when Rhaki reached a small grove of fruit trees. He sat himself down at the edge of the track and waited patiently. The town of Return was but half a league distant and he saw the thin threads of smoke crawling up from the earliest risers' cooking fires. The growing light slowly revealed the high mud brick wall circling the town and tiled roofs grouped around a higher central building, like chicks round a mother hen.

As the sun finally rimmed the horizon, a flock of goats came noisily from the town's main gate, followed by two young boys.

They turned away from the main track on which Rhaki waited, disappearing beyond the curving wall. Next came a squad of armed men. They split into three groups, one following the boys with their goats, another turning along the opposite curving wall. The third group came towards Rhaki.

The animals they rode were similar to the fengars of the north, but these were not carnivores as were the fengars, and were more peaceable. They had no taloned feet but solid hooves and nor were they fanged. Rhaki had studied these koninas, as the humans called them, and had tried breeding them with fengars, but the fengars had always attacked and killed the koninas at first sight.

The rising sun shone directly into the faces of the four oncoming riders and they were quite close before they saw Rhaki sitting at the side of the track. The two leading men pulled their mounts up sharply and stared at him, blades already drawn, before one recognised him. He controlled the konina with his legs as he reached a restraining hand to the blade arm of the man beside him.

'It is the Lord from the North,' he hissed.

He sheathed his blade and walked the konina nearer to Rhaki. 'It has been several Seasons, Sir Lord, since you visited Return. We will escort you to Lord Hargon if that is your wish?'

Rhaki stood, his great though slender height drawing a gasp of surprise from one of the mounted men. Obviously he had never encountered one of the People before. Rhaki inclined his head graciously.

'I would indeed be pleased to see Lord Hargon.'

The riders edged to the sides of the track as Rhaki strode between them, then turned their mounts and trotted to keep pace with him.

The townsfolk were stirring as Rhaki entered the gate, although most who were about were still too sleepy to take notice of him. The road, if it could be termed such, was just wide enough for three koninas abreast and twisted its way round the town, slowly circling inwards. The way was eventually barred by a pair of wooden gates guarded by two more of the Lord of Return's armsmen. They sprang to attention as Rhaki halted in front of them. He smiled pleasantly as the mounted man who had

312

first recognised him barked: 'The Northern Lord is here to see the Lord of the South!'

The door guards hurriedly pushed the gates open as Rhaki laughed inwardly at Hargon's temerity to title himself thus. Another arms man inside the gate saluted Rhaki and led him across an outer yard to another, open, gateway. The building beyond was stone built rather than mud brick as all the buildings so far had been. There seemed to be no doors in the lowest level of the manor, only a narrow set of stairs leading up to a wide door above. As they climbed the steps, an elderly man awaited their arrival at the door. He bowed deeply.

'It has been a while, Lord, since you honoured us with your presence. Would you like to rest, or wash, before you join Lord Hargon? The first meal will be served shortly Sir.'

Rhaki smiled. 'You may show me to a guest room, seneschal, so I may remove the grime of my travelling before I meet your Lord.'

As he followed the seneschal, he was aware that another servant would be scurrying to alert Hargon to the arrival of an unexpected guest. By the time Rhaki had washed his face and hands, and brushed the worst of the dust from his robe and boots, there was a rap at his door. He opened it to find a half-grown boy bowing to him.

'My Lord Hargon asks me to conduct you to the dining hall, Sir Lord.'

'Certainly. I will be a moment if you please.'

Rhaki closed the door and put his leather bag in the corner of the room near the bed. He closed his eyes, murmuring softly. When he opened his eyes, the bag was still plain to his view, but no one else would see it should they stare hard as they could. He nodded in satisfaction and went to follow the boy to meet his host.

Hargon stood at a window at the far end of the room, talking with another man as Rhaki entered. The arms man at the door announced: 'The Lord of the North Sir.'

'Welcome!' Hargon walked towards Rhaki, a smile on his squarish face. 'You honour us, Lord Rhaki. This is Navan, my Arms Chief – I believe you met him before.'

'Indeed I did, Hargon. I am glad at last to be able to enjoy your hospitality once again.'

'Please, be seated.' Hargon waved towards a long table set for three places. As they took their seats, serving men brought dishes of hot stew, fresh bread, vegetables and fruits. Three pitchers were placed in the middle of the table.

'There is ale in the green jug, water in the brown and spice tea in the black Lord Rhaki. If you don't mind serving yourself, we can be more private if you wish?'

'I need none to serve me,' Rhaki said jovially. 'But private matters are of no urgency. Tell me how things progress in your Domain. It seemed very peaceful and prosperous as I arrived. Don't tell me you have routed all the gangers in the region?'

Hargon laughed serving himself from the bowl of stew. 'Very nearly it seems, Sir Lord. I fear life may become rather staid with no gangers to fight!'

Rhaki sipped the tea he had poured. 'I'm sure there will be something to replace the hunting of gangers Hargon.' He smiled at both men. 'Oh yes. I am quite sure of that.'

Chapter Thirty-Five

After considerable argument, Emla, Kemti, Nolli and Jeela waited in Rhaki's study as Tika, Bark and Mim led the way into the hidden passage. Ashta helped Farn to follow behind them. Mim caught Bark's arm.

'There is a warding across the passage Bark!'

'I did not feel it,' Bark confessed.

Tika was already snipping at the lines of power.

'There is a similarity to all these wardings. Careless I would say.'

'Effective still!' Mim grinned.

The next warding Tika pointed out, Bark dismissed. 'It is a chamber where he did some – experiments. It is not where the Balance lies.'

'I'll undo it anyway,' Mim offered. 'It's better they are cleared in case anyone comes in contact with them.'

'What would happen if they did?' Ashta asked curiously.

Tika glanced back at the pale green Dragon. 'They would burst into fire,' she said bluntly.

Further they went, deeper into the heart of the rock until they reached a dead end. Tika drew a breath but Mim spoke first.

'Save your strength. Let me do this.'

As he worked on the door wards Tika bespoke Kija. 'We are at the Chamber of Balance Kija. I will do what must be done.' She faltered. 'Care for Farn, as I know you will. I love him dearly Kija.'

'I know, small one. If it is the time for your journey, may you go safely beyond. I beg the stars to spare you. Know also that as Farn is my son and I love him, so you are my beloved daughter.'

Mim stepped clear of the rock as Bark touched the contours of the wall and the entrance slid open. Bark walked inside, lighting lamps with a sparking flint round the circular chamber, till he rejoined Tika at the doorway.

Unnoticed, Dessi and Gan stood close behind Ashta and they stared with the rest at the seven golden disks hanging motionless above the mosaic circle. Mim took a pace forward but Tika's hand stopped him. She forced a smile as she looked up at him.

'No further Mim, Dragon Lord. Please. This is the task set on me alone.'

He looked at her hard for a moment then hugged her tight and as quickly released her again. She moved to Ashta, stroking her face wordlessly, then turned to Farn.

'I come with you, my Tika.'

She slid her arms round his shoulders, stroking the folded wing edge. 'No my dear soul bond. You must come no further.'

Behind the Dragons, Dessi tugged Gan's sleeve, whispering: 'He is too calm. He will try to follow her no matter what she says.'

Gan nodded and eased his way alongside Ashta, having no idea how he could prevent the silver blue Dragon doing anything at all.

Tika forced herself to release Farn and stepped firmly back, turning quickly into the Chamber of Balance. She went to the edge of the mosaic circle and gazed at the disks hanging impossibly in the centre. She was aware of Bark standing close by and she gave a near hysterical laugh

'We didn't think of that, Bark.'

He waited for her to explain.

She nodded at the disks. 'I can't reach. Can you lift me?'

He put a hand on her shoulder, turning her to face him then knelt so that their faces were nearly level.

'I believe it means you are not the one for this task. I must do it.'

'But you can't – you will be destroyed,' Tika said softly.

He smiled. 'Dear one, Rhaki destroyed me long ago. Even with the help of the healers of Gaharn, I will be forever damaged. If you let me take this task from you, I will gladly go beyond, knowing I have tried to atone for allowing Rhaki's monstrosity to reach the heights it has.'

For a long while Tika studied him, slipping into his mind and seeing the great disruptions there. She saw that she could perhaps mend some of the injuries, but not all. He was right. He could never be restored to his former state and would only live in frustration, half remembering all he once had been. She put her arms round his neck, pressing her face close to his.

'I believe you are right Bark, if it is truly what you wish to do.'

He held her away from him. 'One thing.'

She waited.

'When I take the Balance Weight, I wish you to kill me before Time can.'

As she opened her mouth Bark laid a bony finger across her lips. He shrugged and smiled sadly.

'I fear such a death Tika, but not death by your hand, or mind.'

Tika thought rapidly. She realised she could indeed use the power to destroy, and that she could do it gently. Tears rolled down her face as she slowly nodded. The bony finger caught a tear and Bark whispered:

'I do not recall anyone weeping for me. I am most honoured dear one. Now, you should tell Farn we have changed the plan, and then we will proceed.'

She threw her arms round him once more then turned to the door. She cleared her throat, clogged with tears as it was, and looked at the group waiting anxiously. Khosa had seated herself between Farn's feet and as Tika explained chokingly what Bark planned to do, the Kephi walked forward to weave herself round Bark's legs. He lifted her to his face and she crooned, bumping her head against his cheek. Bark looked at the two Dragons and Gan and Dessi and felt their respect and affection pour into his crippled mind. He stood, handing Khosa to Tika and turned to the column of golden disks.

A stillness settled over them all as Bark seemed to move in slow motion, his hand reaching up for the topmost Weight. There was a collective sigh as his fingers grasped the disk and lifted it from its place. As he took it, the six remaining Weights shivered and moved upwards, readjusting their alignment with the six Weights in Emla's Pavilion in distant Gaharn.

Bark stared at the Weight in his hand and a tremor passed through his body. He sat against the wall, the disk held to his chest.

'Quickly Tika,' he said urgently. 'You must not touch me with your hand until I am dead.'

She dropped to her knees beside him and focused her mind. Leave his poor mind, she thought, go deeper. Somehow, she saw through his flesh, beneath his ribs, to the steadily beating heart. She carefully narrowed a blood vessel, finally squeezing it closed as her awareness fled from Bark's dying body. Khosa leaned against her and Tika swept the Kephi up, burying her face in the orange fur. Eventually, she released her hold on Khosa and raised her eyes to Bark's face. His expression was peaceful but his cheeks seemed even more hollow, his half closed eyes even more sunken. But the disk had vanished, and Bark's hair was white.

Tika climbed to her feet, feeling drained and exhausted. She reached Farn and leaned heavily against him, her eyes closed. When she opened her eyes, Gan and Mim were watching her worriedly. Straightening with an effort, she said:

'Let's go back to the study and tell the others what happened.' She glanced back at Bark's body, Khosa crouched at his side. 'We will move him later and lay him with Iska.'

It was a struggle to turn Ashta and Farn in the passage but by unspoken agreement no one suggested they enter the chamber to make turning easier. As Tika stumbled at Farn's side, Gan reached out his arm to support her.

Wordlessly, they returned to Rhaki's study to find Kemti had hauled the carpet back into place, hiding the circle – no one had wanted to stand on its exposed surface. Tika looked at Emla, then at Nolli, but before anyone could speak an unearthly wailing echoed from the passage. Farn moaned and his prismed eyes darkened to midnight blue.

"What –' began Kemti.

Tears poured down Tika's face. 'Khosa – she sings the death song for Bark.'

'Bark?' Emla looked bewildered.

Mim began to explain all that had happened as Khosa's song ululated around them. She stopped as Mim's tale came to an end but almost at once, the Dragons' voices took over, their song heard by all in the stronghold.

Farn lay against the wall as Emla sat down, holding Tika close as the Dragons' harmonies flooded through them. Then again silence descended, broken by Khosa's chirruping call as she jumped onto Nolli's lap.

318

'I do not like these rooms. Could we not go down to the Dragons?' Tika asked shakily.

Nolli agreed immediately, watching sympathetically as the girl tried to control the shock and tiredness she was suffering. The Wise One made no objection, other than a scowl, when Gan lifted her and carried her from the study.

Shan chivvied servants to fetch tea for them all as they settled in the entrance hall. Kija's golden eyes shimmered as she curved herself protectively around both her son and Tika. Lorak came from where he sat with Fenj and settled near Kija, as did Sket. Nolli accepted Shan's assistance to drink some of her bowl of tea, then she rapped her stick on the floor.

'You have done well to restore the Balance, Tika. But the Grey one has fled, he has not been destroyed – as he must be.' The oddly young voice was clear. 'He has discovered how to use the circles. I fear he may well discover just how powerful they can be. I would guess he has gone to the south lands and intends to build a secure base for himself there.

'Make no mistake,' Nolli's gaze met each pair of eyes of the group to emphasise her point. 'This is only the beginning. He has allowed the idea of power to govern him totally and he will continue to disrupt the harmony of the world until he rules all. You must Name another Guardian who will protect the Balance here. Of that I will speak later. But you must seek out Rhaki as urgently as you are able.' She leaned back in her chair wearily. 'And the time is upon us when we must make contact with the ones beyond the Wilderness.'

Rhaki had spent the day pleasing Hargon. He had been shown parts of the fortified manor that had been added since his last visit and had watched the armsmen at their training exercises.

As they waited for the evening meal to be served, Rhaki said: 'I am fortunately able to spend some considerable time with you now. My Realm in the North runs smoothly even in my absence. I thought I might even build myself a dwelling in this region.'

'That would be marvellous,' Hargon agreed with an enthusiasm Rhaki found most gratifying. Then Hargon added: 'There are so few of our intelligence here, you will be precious company indeed.'

Rhaki winced at Hargon's estimate of his own acumen but kept his smile in place.

'Do I ask permission of you to build a small place beyond your town?'

'Build where you choose, Sir Lord. And use the guest rooms as if they were your own until your house is built.' Hargon waved a goblet of wine in a magnanimous gesture. 'I can help with servants or slaves later too.'

Rhaki pursed his lips. 'There is a difference here. In the North, I would say servants are slaves.'

'Not here! Servants are from poorer families usually, but they can make comfortable positions for themselves through hard work and trustworthiness. They can have their own homes and a voice at our councils. Slaves are those we take captive in raids. And they are as nothing.'

'I remember, many Cycles past, did you not show me some – "pets" did you call them?'

Hargon laughed. 'I did indeed. But then I took a female and bred three children of my own on her, so I was not amused with the pets any longer. She died,' he added.

Rhaki saw no reason to offer sympathy in the face of Hargon's evident disinterest in the death of the mother of his children.

'There was a pet who was different – a dark-haired child. That is all I recall really. A group of small children playing and just the one with such dark hair.'

Hargon frowned. 'That was Chena. She was to have become a pretty in my household but the ungrateful bitch ran away.'

'And was suitably punished when she was brought back?'

Hargon shifted in his chair. 'Never found her. My trackers said she had gone north to the Ancient Mountains, but found not a trace of her there. Eaten by beasts no doubt.'

As the seneschal arrived to announce that their meal was ready to be served, Rhaki asked: 'Is there someone you could spare to show me various places where I might build?'

Hargon thought as they walked into the dining hall. 'Mallit, I think. He would be best. I'll speak to him in the morning and tell him he is to be at your disposal.'

'You are a generous host indeed Hargon.'

Hargon beamed. 'There are still two of those taller koninas in my stable – you are welcome to use them. None of my men like them.'

Rhaki bowed. 'As I said – a most generous host.'

Next morning, Hargon introduced Mallit. He was younger than Hargon, perhaps thirty Cycles, with light sandy hair and pale blue eyes. Rhaki had already decided where he intended to build, but made no mention of that fact. He asked Mallit to show him around the area generally, to a distance of one or two leagues from the town.

Mallit frowned. 'You might prefer to be closer, Sir Lord. Gangers often raid farms too far beyond the Lord Hargon's domain.'

'I understood there is little threat from Gangers these days?'

'There are far fewer of them here Sir Lord, because of Lord Hargon's vigilance, but there are still some who find a more isolated dwelling an inviting prospect.'

Mallit nodded as a man led forward two koninas, one standing nearly an arm length taller than the other. Rhaki wore trousers and loose tunic, clothes fortunately left here from previous visits, and now he swung himself onto the taller animal. It twitched and sidestepped for a moment. Mallit rode alongside saying:

'No one has ridden him since you were last here Sir Lord.'

Two mounted armsmen followed Mallit and Rhaki. Rhaki raised a quizzical brow.

'We surely need no protection, Mallit?'

Mallit looked slightly shocked. 'No Lord rides out without escort Sir Lord.'

Rhaki shrugged and allowed Mallit to spend the day leading him around to a distance of a league outside the walls. They rode back to Hargon's manor a couple of hours before the evening mealtime. Rhaki thanked Mallit for his tour and asked to continue the next day.

Rhaki was extremely grateful that Hargon was civilised enough to have bath tubs, infrequently as he might use them himself. After soaking away the worst of the soreness and stiffness of his ride, Rhaki put on his robe and stood gazing unseeing from his window.

He would drink only water or tea until he had built his house. He needed nothing that might impair his strength. He was confident he could cut blocks of stone with the use of power. If Mallit would show him where stone was quarried, he could do it. He smiled. Let them marvel at that! But they could move the cut blocks for him. That would take too much effort on his part and he saw no need to overtax his strength too soon. But he wanted somewhere quickly, near the hidden caves, so he needs must expend power for his building.

Rhaki wasted no thought on the northern stronghold. He prided himself on casting aside experiments that failed, and he could look at the loss in the north in the same light. At the back of his mind, the idea floated that one day he would revenge himself on Emla and all the narrow-minded fools in Gaharn. But that was a distant plan, far more pressing ones occupied him now. He smiled as he waited for the boy to summon him to the dining hall.

Hargon sat at a table in the small room where he kept his gold, a few maps and his account records. Navan had just joined him and been waved to the opposite chair.

'Why is he here?' Hargon asked.

Navan shook his head. 'You know how long it takes for rumours to reach here and rumours fly faster than truth Sir. So far, not even rumours have arrived. Those monsters that appeared – they were surely his creatures, but why then does he come here himself, making no mention of them, or their destruction?'

Hargon drummed his fingers on the tabletop. 'I believe he will build a house well outside the bounds of Return – for what purpose, who knows. Mallit reported that he evinced interest in a few sites but he had the feeling Rhaki was playing with him.'

Navan agreed. 'He was always thus Sir. Pretending to admire, while unable to conceal his sneers. He seems a little different this time Sir.'

Hargon laughed but not with amusement. 'You mean his madness is more obvious Navan. But mad or not, he is of the People and we have seen him use power.' He was unable to suppress a shudder. 'For now, I play the simple southern Lord, but I want him watched carefully, Navan. Most carefully.'

A knock came at his door and an arms man put his head into the room. 'The evening meal, Sirs.'

Click to sign up for a free account.

Hargon nodded and got to his feet. 'Have ears listening for any news from the north, Navan.'

'Yes Sir.' The Arms Chief opened the door for Hargon.

'And for now, I want you present at each evening meal.'

'Yes Sir.'

As Hargon and Navan crossed the space to the dining hall, Rhaki came down the staircase.

'Ah, my Lord Rhaki! Mallit has been of help to you I trust?'

'Indeed he has. I have seen several places where it might suit me to build, but he promises further exploring tomorrow.'

Rhaki felt confident enough among these simple humans to relax during the meal. Enough that as he listened to tales of Ganger raids, he failed to notice that Hargon in fact drank little, whilst appearing to drink heavily. Hargon suddenly leaned forward.

'The monsters we recently had to fight Sir Lord! They came from nightmares. Foul things, but not too difficult to kill, once we could bear looking at them. Never seen their like!' He sat back, staring over his goblet of wine.

'The Cansharsi?' Rhaki asked.

'You have heard of them Sir Lord?' Navan queried.

Belatedly Rhaki caught himself. He smiled. 'There have been such creatures seen in the Middle Plain, I understand. They were called Cansharsi.'

Hargon shook his head. 'Next you will have us believe Shardi are real and not just tales to frighten children!'

Rhaki laughed aloud. 'They truly are, Hargon. But they are creatures of the colder lands. You need not fear their arrival here.'

He placed his long hands flat on the table and levered his tall figure upright.

'I beg your forgiveness, Hargon. I am out of practice riding your konina. I fear I must rest before tomorrow's ride with your good Mallit.'

'Certainly Sir Lord. Rest well.'

Hargon and Navan rose and bowed as Rhaki moved to the door.

They sat in silence for a few minutes after Rhaki's departure, then Hargon sighed.

'He knew of the monsters. I don't want him out of sight.'

Navan nodded and wished his Lord goodnight. Hargon remained, trying to fathom why Rhaki was here, and what ill fortune his presence might mean to his domain.

Chapter Thirty-Six

Already another day had nearly passed and Emla was concerned that nowhere had been suggested for the laying of Iska's body. Nolli had dozed in her chair for a time but now she woke.

'Lady Emla, I believe the gate to my Domain must be reopened and there is a chamber, not far, suitable for Iska and Bark's final resting place.'

She nodded to Dessi and the tiny Delver girl went to the wall beneath the sloped passage leading to the upper levels. She stood there for a considerable time, until her legs suddenly gave way and she sat down with a bump on the floor. As she did, the rock appeared to quiver, almost as though it was liquid, and then it was no longer there.

Gan and the Guards officers went to look and Soran took a few steps beneath the newly revealed archway.

'It goes a long way Sir, but there is light at the end.'

Dessi glanced up, dark marks under her eyes. 'They knew I was opening the way, so some of my people are coming to greet you.'

Baras stooped over the Delver girl, holding her as she shivered.

'It took great power to empty the arch,' Mim said quietly to Emla.

'Empty the arch?' she asked.

He nodded. 'It felt solid all the way through so if the Guardian had thought to test for tunnels, he would not have known this was here.' He joined Baras in helping Dessi to a cushioned corner beside Nolli.

Servants were still bringing pillows and blankets to the hall, somewhat confused that the upper chambers were rejected in favour of the draughty entrance hall.

Tika sat cross-legged, holding a bowl of tea in both hands, going over and over what had happened in the Chamber of

Balance. Sket tapped her shoulder lightly and she jumped. He held out a dish of dried fruits.

'Eat something Lady, you still look too pale by far.'

She dutifully took some fruit and tried to chew it. Nolli's stick rapped on the floor and heads turned in her direction.

'My people,' she said, looking to the archway.

A group of perhaps forty Delvers were emerging into the hall. Tika heard Lorak chuckle as she realised that there were not only male and female Delvers but also infants and toddlers in the group. They bowed first to black Fenj and crimson Brin, then to Tika and Emla, finally kneeling before Nolli.

'And where is Serim?' she asked sharply as Tika and Gan recognised some of the Elders they had met in their journey through the Domain of Asat.

It was the portly Torim, Elder of Arak, who replied. 'Oh dear me, Serim has left the Domain, Wise One.'

'Left? What do you mean, left?'

'He took two of the fengars our guests left behind and went from the tunnels.'

'I feared as much.' Nolli sounded sad rather than angry.

'The Merigs watched him.' Monni, Elder of Akan, spoke up. 'They said he rode to the western side of the Spine Mountains and continues south.'

'If he survives the journey, he will serve Khaki,' Nolli said, and sighed. Her voice sharpened. 'The Elders are summoned here to hear the Naming of the new Guardian.'

'The Discipline Seniors do not yet know of what has happened here,' Kemti protested. 'It will take many days to get word to them and then for them to debate the matter.'

'No. Things have changed, Lord Kemti. The next Guardian will not be of the People.'

Kemti was taken aback, but before he could argue Emla nodded thoughtfully.

'Two Guardians have been of our race and the second betrayed the trust placed in him. And, I admit it had not occurred to me before, but surely there were Guardians before we came here? So of what race were they?'

Nolli smiled, revealing pink gums. 'A long time thinking such questions Lady.' Her smile vanished. 'I will remain here to help teach the new Guardians. Yes, the Guardianship is divided now between the Dragon Lord and Dessi.'

Stunned silence greeted her announcement. 'And Berri will act as Wise One within the Domain.'

Berri gaped in disbelief then closed her mouth with an audible snap as her face paled.

'Yes Berri, you have to change parts of yourself, and you will be under my guidance, and I give fair warning I will be hard on you. But I believe, if you truly wish it, you can become Wise One after me.'

Berri slipped to her knees before Nolli and lifted one of the gnarled hands to her brow.

'I will prove worthy of your belief, Wise One.'

'I do not know what a Guardian must do,' Mim ventured. 'Surely I do not stay here all the time watching the Weights of Balance?'

Nolli grinned at him. 'Certainly not! You and Dessi will change the character of this place, dispel its evil shadows. Dessi will bring the arts of growing food here – as you see we have done in the Domain. Lorak will be a valuable help to you in that.'

'Splendid creature,' came rumbling from Fenj.

Nolli continued: 'I fear there will be other work – concerning books and such.'

Mim looked increasingly alarmed. Nolli grew serious.

'There is the necessity to search the far Wilderness, but that cannot be undertaken immediately, much as I might wish it. Did the pendant you wear harm you when Bark took the Balance Weight Mim?' she asked suddenly.

'I felt a slight heat, but the scales on my chest protected me.' He looked across at Tika.

She nodded, unbuttoning the top of her shirt. An angry red oval-shaped mark was burnt into the skin between her breasts.

'I thought it was the pain of Bark's death, but I realise it happened at the moment he moved the Weight,' she said, rebuttoning her shirt.

'They quicken,' Nolli muttered to herself, then said louder: 'When Farn is recovered you will go south, child.'

'I too,' Kija's voice was firm.

'And I,' Brin added.

327

Nolli smiled. 'Yes, and Lord Gan and Sket no doubt.'

'And I,' a regal voice announced from Khosa, sprawled languidly on Farn's back.

'And what must we do?' Emla asked.

'Return to Gaharn and rouse your People. Too long have they spent looking inward and dreaming dreams. They live in this world, let them look to it as they should have done Cycles past.'

'I said as much, if you recall,' Kemti murmured in Emla's ear.

Gan stood up, stretching his long legs.

'We will leave two full bands of Guards here, to help with the work of getting this place straight. The rest will escort the Lady back to Gaharn.'

Unnoticed, Motass stood at the back of the crowd in the dim hallway.

'Sir? Can I stay here? My brother Jal will heal but it will be a long mending. And my place is with Lord Mim also.'

Gan nodded his consent.

'Thank you Sir.'

Much later, when all were settled for sleep, Tika crept to Nolli's side.

'Must I go south Nolli?'

'Yes child. It is for you to defeat Rhaki, and you know the region where he is likely to be.'

Tika hugged her knees then winced as she rubbed the burn on her chest.

'Lorak's salve will help that,' Nolli said. 'Gan spoke with Motass's brother Jal. He said Rhaki has been to the town of Return on several occasions. Would you have seen him there?'

Tika frowned, then her eyes widened.

'I think – many Cycles past – soon after my mother died. I was one of the Lord's pets. I remember a very tall man watching us one day. Could that have been him?'

'It may well be child. Now. You have been gone from Return for a while and much has happened. You have met others – those who speak to you respectfully and listen with true interest. Can you look back at the Lord of Return and judge more fairly what kind of man he is?'

At first, all Tika could think of was the anger and fear that had spurred her to run away, but she forced herself to calm down and try to remember what she could of Lord Hargon. After a long pause, she said slowly:

'He is not an evil man I think. He acts as he has been bred to. He was considered fair in dealing with disputes and he defended the people of his town against the Gangers. But,' she finished stonily, 'he kept slaves, and he treated women and children scarcely better than his slaves. He did not consider them as human as himself. And I will never agree that such slavery is necessary or right.'

In the light of early morning, new snow had blown in the open gateway, but no snow was falling outside now. Fenj, Brin, Ashta and Ulla brought meat back for the other Dragons, and Kija urged Farn to eat as much as he could. He turned his head carefully, his neck still most tender, and found Khosa crouched on his back. She crooned at him pleasantly and his eyes flashed sapphire bright.

Tika laughed at him affectionately. 'No longer does a Kephi queen worry you then my Farn!' She stroked his beautiful face. 'It was decided last night while you slept that we must travel far south again, even beyond the Ancient Mountains. I have agreed. Is that all right?'

'Of course!' His eyes whirred with anticipation. 'When shall we go?'

A team of labourers had cleared an area not far from the hidden caves. It had not been too hard a job – the ground was solid rock covered with a dusty soil and scrubby bushes. Rhaki had paced out a circular area and marked it clearly. Hargon instructed Mallit to show Rhaki where the quarry was located. Cutting stone was a time-consuming and laborious task and thus Hargon's stone-built manor underlined his strength and importance.

Rhaki rode into the shallow gorge which Mallit had indicated was where Return's stone was obtained. Dismounting, Rhaki strolled along the rock face, studying the lines and layers of stone. Yes, he thought, it would take several days to cut the amount he needed although he was not entirely sure how much the effort would cost him.

That evening in the dining hall, Rhaki told Hargon and Navan that he would begin to cut stone the next day.

Hargon nodded. 'Using power, Sir Lord?'

'How else my dear Hargon? I would still be occupying your guest chambers two Cycles from now if we let your men hack out all the stones I need!'

Rhaki's mood since he arrived in Return had been consistently jovial and now he laughed at the wary expressions on Hargon and Navan's faces.

'I will go alone tomorrow and begin cutting the blocks. I would be grateful for the use of your carts to move them the league or so to the site I have chosen, once I have cut sufficient stone.'

'Certainly,' Hargon agreed easily.

'Will you need artisans for the actual building work Sir Lord?' asked Navan.

'No, no.' Rhaki poured himself more spice tea. 'I shall deal with that myself.'

'Furnishings,' said Hargon. 'Traff will assist you there. Bed, tables, that sort of thing – unless you wish to commission the work from the Carpenters' Guild?'

'I will need very little, I think. Once the building is done, I will find a couple of servants.' He frowned into his goblet of tea. 'I am rather particular about those who serve me.'

Navan and Hargon exchanged a quick glance.

'Perhaps slaves – those born slaves and trained in obedience from birth – would suit your needs best Sir Lord?' Hargon offered.

'Perhaps. I will think on it.'

As he tried to relax in the too-short bed, Rhaki knew he would be exhausted until the stone cutting was complete. He stared up into the darkness of his chamber. He would go to the cave tomorrow and use the scrying bowl. He needed to know if any of the Gaharnian scum knew in which direction he had gone. Rhaki could not imagine Emla ordering those pretty Guards of hers too far from Gaharn but he would like to be sure. It would take them weeks rather than days to get here, but if they were on their way, he would prefer to be within his building and strong in power once more.

His mind strayed to the books he had hidden in the cave. One of them he had discovered by chance. How long it had sat unnoticed among his many volumes he didn't know. He had taken it from the shelf in error and sat at his table. Realising his mistake, he had been about to replace it in annoyance when something about it caught his attention.

Rhaki felt the stirrings of the sense of excitement he had felt when he'd first studied it. Lying in the guest chamber of Hargon's manor, he shivered as he remembered his disbelief slowly turning to wonder as he had turned page after page. It must surely have been one of his predecessor's books, but Rhaki wasted no time wondering where Kovas might have obtained it. Enough that it was now in his own hands.

Mallit was unhappy next morning, that the Lord Rhaki should ride out unescorted. But Rhaki was adamant he would go alone. Mallit had a brief glimpse of the inflexible will under the, at present, pleasant exterior, and he froze. Bowing low, he made no further comment as Rhaki mounted the konina. Silently Mallit took the saddlebag containing food from his own mount and tied it to Rhaki's saddle. He bowed again as Rhaki crossed the yard to the inner gate, then, as he rode from view, Mallit hurried to the arms men's practice yard.

Navan came straight to him and listened closely to what the man had to say. He nodded, slapped Mallit's shoulder lightly and sent him off. Reporting to Hargon, Navan said: 'You know Mallit, Sir. His courage cannot be doubted yet he saw something in Lord Rhaki that had him pale as milk.'

'I have been trying to remember all I've ever heard of the People and their accursed power. I want to know if using the power weakens them, and if so, how much. You've seen him do tricks here before, setting things aflame across a room, making things disappear, and it bothers him not at all. But he says he is going to cut stone blocks – that surely needs a lot of this power.'

'Perhaps that's why he insists he is alone? To conceal any weakness from us?'

'Hmm. Send three of the best scouts to spy on the quarry.'

'Three Sir?'

'Yes, three. They will spread well apart, so if he sees one, at least one of the others will perhaps go unnoticed. I don't believe he will think any would dare spy on him though.'

331

'At once Sir.'

Navan left the Lord's workroom and Hargon poured himself a goblet of water. For the first time since he was a young lad facing his first fight against Gangers, he felt afraid. Then, he had feared his sword arm would tire too soon, despite the endless training sessions. Or that his stomach would turn at gruesome sights.

Now he knew he was afraid, but he did not know precisely what frightened him. Just the presence of this tall thin man, and the look in his eyes at certain moments. What havoc could this one man wreak? And how could he, Hargon, protect not only himself, but his town and his people against him? He groaned quietly and rolled the goblet across his aching forehead.

Rhaki rode at a leisurely pace along the track from Return. He looked about him, at men and women working in some of the fields, and keeping a casual watch that he was not being followed. Not that he entertained the idea of Hargon having him watched for a moment. Likeable fellow in his simple way – but simple was the most accurate word there.

Soon he dismounted, looping the reins around a boulder. Rhaki strolled towards the tangled mass of redberry bushes covering the slope ahead of him. A last look back towards Return and he was slipping through the bushes into the first cave. Before long, he was sitting before the wooden chest on which rested his scrying bowl.

'I would see my stronghold,' he demanded, laying his hands to the sides of the bowl.

As the dizzying black swirl cleared, Rhaki saw the entrance to his stronghold. The blackened timbers of what was left of the great gateway edged the empty space until that space was filled with a massive crimson Dragon. Rhaki gasped. A Great Dragon? How had Emla coerced such a one to her service? He loosed hold of the bowl then replaced his hands.

'Show me Emla.'

The bowl cleared again to reveal a cave of some kind and Emla kneeling between two biers of stone. On one lay Iska and on the other, Bark. Two small dark haired females stood beyond Emla, one each side of a figure seated in a chair. Rhaki peered at this figure. Another female, of great age, but who was she? He released his concentration and the bowl darkened to its usual black opacity.

Well, they all seemed occupied enough not to be bothering him at the moment. He would investigate more when he was safe in his stone tower, but now that was his main concern.

Back outside, Rhaki rode another league through the hills to the quarry. He sat on the ground, staring at the rock face. He estimated the height of the blocks he needed for the base of his tower. Finally, he took a deep breath and relaxed his body as he began to focus his mind.

White fire flickered up the face of the rock to a height of four man lengths. Then the fire wove sideways. Several more times the white fire sliced at the rock, then Rhaki slumped where he sat. He was drenched in sweat and trembling from the effort, but he forced himself to go and see how successful he had been. The line he'd cut was smooth and straight, the stone feeling slightly warm under his hand. He moved back and sat down again.

This time, he visualised himself deep within the rock, the white fire flaming through the darkness of the concealed stone. He shuddered as he finished and wiped his sleeve across his wet forehead. One more effort. He looked up at the sun and was not surprised to see by its position that more than half the day had passed. Once more, he focused. Eight great blocks of raw stone, smooth as if worked by master craftsmen, floated free of the rock face and settled in a line before him.

All unaware of eyes watching him, Rhaki lay where he was and slid helplessly into exhausted sleep.

Far across the Wilderness, towards the rising sun, silver chimes rang faintly in a room of pale marble. The chimes shivered and the woman who watched them pulled a shawl closer round her shoulders. As the chimes faded to silence, she turned towards the tall windows. Despite the cold, she stepped through onto a balcony and stared out.

First she looked down at the city spread below, different coloured lights glittering in the frosty air. Faint cries drifted up from the festive all-night market in the centre of the city. The woman's gaze moved on, up to the distant mountains encircling her lands. And on further, to the great velvet bowl of the winter sky, a deep blue black, studded with stars.

Soul Bonds

Never in her lifetime had she heard the chimes of discord. Until now. She shivered suddenly and turned back into the room. The chimes hung motionless, a mere ornament. She went through the marble reception hall to a smaller, cosier room, with a fire blazing in the hearth. The woman reached for a small handbell and rang it. When a manservant appeared, she asked him in a softly musical voice, to summon her council. He went to obey as she sat by the fire.

The chimes of discord had rung, which warned that the circles of power in the distant western lands had once again been used. After all this time. But by whom? She had studied the books in her years of training, books telling what steps must be taken to restore accord. Now the time was upon her, it would seem, when those steps must be taken.

The story continues in 'Vagrants' …

Books in the "Circles of Light" series

Soul Bonds

Vagrants

Drogoya

Survivors

Dark Realm

Perilous Shadows

Mage Foretold

Echoes of Dreams

Printed in Great Britain
by Amazon

31388077R00188